Repent lest the Gods forsake us.

"I heard the voice of Reorx himself," Argus Deephammer
declared to the council, raising his voice even louder, with no
hesitation or sign that his statement was out of the ordinary.
"He showed me the sins of Ironroot,
the wickedness that breeds here like rats in a sewer.
He bade me come here, to you, and deliver this message:
Repent of your evils and turn again unto your God, or this
great city of Ironroot will be utterly destroyed."

"Argus has threatened this council and the people
of Ironroot," Jon Bladehook said. "And surely he has
confederates, dwarves who are poised to provide these 'signs'
of Reorx's power should we refuse to believe their messenger.
They, too, threaten the city and her people."

"Ban the street preachers," Bradok Axeblade said abruptly,
his voice cutting through the councillors' argument.
He stood as all the eyes in the room returned to him.
"We can pass an ordinance banning proselytizing outside
the temple grounds and private homes," he explained.
"That way we get them off the str
but they can still speak their piec

"I like that plan," Much Hollowblad

TRACY HICKMAN
Presents
THE ANVIL OF TIME

TRACY HICKMAN
Presents
THE ANVIL OF TIME • VOLUME TWO

The Survivors

DAN WILLIS

THE SURVIVORS

©2008 Wizards of the Coast, Inc.

Cover art by Dan Dos Santos
First Printing: November 2008

9 8 7 6 5 4 3 2 1

ISBN: 978-0-7869-4723-2
620-21538740-001-EN

U.S., CANADA,
ASIA, PACIFIC, & LATIN AMERICA
Wizards of the Coast, Inc.
P.O. Box 707
Renton, WA 98057-0707
+1-800-324-6496

EUROPEAN HEADQUARTERS
Hasbro UK Ltd
Caswell Way
Newport, Gwent NP9 0YH
GREAT BRITAIN
Save this address for your records.

Visit our web site at www.wizards.com

To my best friend. When things got dark you were always there to hold the light. My wife, Cherstine.

CHAPTER 1

Councilman Axeblade

Bradok Axeblade rose early on the morning of his first day as a member of Ironroot's city council. If he'd known how short his tenure as a councilman would be, he wouldn't have spent so much time dressing for the occasion.

As it was, Bradok bathed and trimmed his beard. A jeweler by profession, Bradok kept his beard short so it would not interfere with his work. Some thought it un-dwarflike, but Bradok paid them no mind. His work brought him wealth, and his wealth brought him position, and that suited Bradok just fine.

He donned his best white shirt and green pants held in place by suspenders. The fabric was something made by humans that felt like silk but wore better. Bradok could afford silk, of course, but he preferred a little bit of practicality even in the most ostentatious of displays.

With the skill and precision of someone used to working with small things, he expertly fastened his shirt studs and cufflinks. Each tiny metal device had been wrought in gold with a deeply green emerald for a cap. Bradok fancied they matched his eyes.

He bound his brown hair back with a silver clip and selected a vest of a particularly vibrant red with gold trim.

1

. A grating voice cut through Bradok's thoughts. "Are you going to just stand there, preening in front of the mirror, or are you coming?"

Bradok glanced at the door to his room where an elegantly dressed woman stood. She had distinctly blue eyes and hair that had once been blonde but had grayed to platinum over the years. Her clothes were the finest Bradok's money could buy: a long lavender silk dress with a green vest and a necklace of gray pearls separated by gold links that shimmered like smoke against her neck.

Bradok felt a momentary surge of pride when he saw the necklace. The piece was one of his designs.

"Don't worry, mother," he said, the words sounding as if a heavy weight rested on them. "The session starts promptly at nine, which means that most of the councilors won't be there till ten."

"You should still be on time," his mother said, her voice softening a bit. "Others might take being late as a sign of weakness." She smiled and strode across the room. "You can't afford to appear weak on your first day as a councilman of Ironroot."

Bradok fastened his heavy gold watch to a chain that extended through the buttonhole of his vest and dropped the watch into his pocket. His mother picked up the formal long-coat from Bradok's bed and held it out for him. The coat had a dark green color to it, except where the cuffs and collar revealed a burgundy silk lining.

"There," his mother said as Bradok settled the coat over his shoulders and buttoned it. "Now you look like the leader of a city."

As he examined himself in the glass, he caught his mother's face as she brushed a stray piece of lint from the coat. The fire of greed burned in her eyes and, with a pain like a punch in the gut, Bradok realized his newly-exalted position was the cause. It could have been anyone standing in his place in the vest and long-coat, and she'd look the same—so long as that person was a new councilman, about to enter the political worlds of power and privilege. Nothing in that look spoke of a mother's love for a son.

"I'm already a respected citizen, Mother," Bradok said, irritation in his voice.

"Bah," she said, needlessly straightening his jacket. "Who are you for people to respect? You're a tradesman." She made the word sound like a curse.

"I'm one of the richest dwarves in Ironroot," he protested.

"Wealth may breed envy, Bradok," she said, "but only power can command respect. Your father—rest his soul—tried so hard to teach you that. It's a shame that only his death could get through to you."

Bradok rolled his eyes, careful not to let his mother see.

"Let's go, Mother," he said, making a show of checking his pocket watch. "We don't want to be late."

Bradok took his mother's arm, and they left the room. His work allowed him to live in one of the nicest houses in Ironroot, right off the main cavern. It had carpeted floors and paneled walls, with a dozen bedrooms and many rooms for entertaining. In the basement the builder had even tapped into a natural hot spring to make a pond for bathing.

Despite the luxury, however, Bradok rarely entertained. His friends were too common for his mother's tastes, and her own friends made him vacillate between the consideration of suicide and homicide.

They walked down the long hall, past Bradok's library and the room his mother had been using for the past month. A massive crystal chandelier hung above the grand stair-case, casting amber light onto the tiled foyer below. An immaculately-dressed servant opened the door as Bradok led his mother past, and he felt the eternally cool air of Ironroot wash over him.

3

His door led into Mattock Street, a quiet lane of rich houses and mostly old money. Neatly-laid cobbles defined the street itself, with sidewalks of broad, flat paving stones on each side. Bright sunlight flooded the street, despite its being more than a mile underground, thanks to a vein of crystal stretching upward from the roof of the cave to the surface above. Crystal lighting like that used to be common in dwarven settlements, but the trick of growing the crystals had been lost in more recent times. That left Mattock Street an oddity in Ironroot, a bright spot with gardens and flowers and green plants in front of every house.

On the sidewalk, at the base of Bradok's steps, stood a richly dressed dwarf, basking in the golden light of the morning. He stood a good two inches shorter than Bradok, and he bore the lines of years in his face. His nose was bent, and his hair and beard were gray, but he had a liveliness about him that defied the appearance of age. His clothes were similar to Bradok's, and he wore a ring on his right hand that carried a diamond the size of a marble. An enormous handlebar mustache hung, seemingly weightless, below the bent nose and it twisted upward as the mouth below it broke into a broad smile.

"Bradok, my boy," he said as Bradok descended into the light. "How are you? I see you've brought that pretty sister of yours." The elder dwarf smiled ingratiatingly at Bradok's mother and inclined his head. "Sapphire," he said.

Bradok's mother smiled and inclined her head in return.

"Much Hollowblade," Bradok said, extending his arm for the dwarf to clasp. "It's been too long."

"Not that long," Much said, turning and walking with Bradok and Sapphire. "I think I saw you last at your father's funeral. That was just a month gone."

Bradok grimaced—not at the memory of the funeral, but at the dwarf it honored. His father, Mirshawn Axeblade, had been a great barrel of a dwarf, with coal black hair and the kind of piercing eyes that could stare down anyone. More than once

Bradok had been the object of that stare, and the threat of violence that always lurked behind it—violence that Mirshawn's massive frame and bearlike hands could easily provide.

Mirshawn had started life as an enforcer for a minor criminal in the city of Ironroot, but his ambitions quickly moved him up the ladder of success. When his employer died mysteriously, Mirshawn took over his operation as naturally as if they were kin. From there, Bradok's father had gone from simple protection rackets to gaming houses and brothels. Along the way his few competitors met a series of bizarre and untimely ends, clearing the ground for Mirshawn's advance.

Finally, when he could raise his stature no more in the under-palaces of the criminal world, he made the move that few petty thugs had made so easily before him: he ran for government office. Petty thug or no, Mirshawn knew how to win elections.

He bought them.

In his first election Mirshawn deposed a dwarf who had been on the city council for fifty years. From that time until the day of his death, Bradok's father had used every scrap of influence, graft, treat, or force he had at his disposal to run the council like his own private piggy bank.

It had come as quite a shock when Bradok learned of his father's death. According to the report, Mirshawn and a dozen other dwarves had been crushed in a cave-in down in the lower tunnels. Bradok almost refused to believe the news. Everything about his experience with his father led him to believe that the old man was too wicked and cantankerous to die.

Die he did, however, leaving Bradok, his only heir, to complete his term on the city council.

"Don't worry lad," Much said, misreading the expression on Bradok's face. "You'll do fine. There isn't much on the docket today, just a trade delegation from some hill dwarf city. I think they want the council to remove the tariff on wool or wood or some such thing. I wasn't paying attention when the master of schedules brought it up last time."

Much offered Sapphire his arm, which she took, and the three of them passed out of Mattock Street and into the main cavern of the city. Main Street led straight along the long axis of Ironroot. At its upper end were the ironbound gates that led to surface world; the lower end exited out into miles of tunnels—some natural, some painstakingly carved—that made up the rest of the city.

On either side of the street, long poles reached up, almost to the roof of the massive cavern. Lanterns filled with phosphorescent stones were strung between the poles, casting the street in the glow of their slightly blue light.

Most of Ironroot's shops and business were there, with easy access to the great gates that led to the surface. Ironroot's citizens lived in the side passages and the lower tunnels of the Undercity. Smiths and other trades that required open fires were restricted to the Artisans' Cavern, a specially-constructed series of tunnels designed for maximum ventilation.

In the center of Main Street stood the central square, a gathering place and garden under the shaft of light cast by Ironroot's only other crystal vein. The central square looked more like a circle than a square and was lined with shops, taverns, and other places of business. In the center stood a great fountain with a spire in the middle culminating in a statue of Argus Gingerbeard, Ironroot's founder. Below Argus and all along the spire were figures of beasts that squirted water in all directions and served to pull some of the soot and dirt from the air. That feature alone made the fountain a popular spot for picnickers or people wishing to sit a spell.

The three walked in silence, and Bradok took the time to note his surroundings. He'd lived in Ironroot all his life and had walked that path daily for the past dozen years. On that morning, with the sunlight radiating over Argus Gingerbeard, Bradok wondered if he'd ever truly *looked* at the city.

Beyond the square, on the far wall of the cavern, the Temple of Reorx had been cut into the living stone and worked by master artisans for more than a century. As the stonework and carvings aged, they darkened from bright white to the gray of granite. That gave the temple a blotchy look, as if it had caught some disease that only time could heal. The building itself stood three stories high, its top spire nearly brushing the roof of the upper city. In its heyday, more than a dozen priests and functionaries were housed within the ornamental walls of the temple. Nowadays, however, fewer and fewer dwarves joined the priesthood, reducing the temple to five priests and an acolyte.

Sapphire's eye caught a small group of dwarves mounting the temple steps, making their way in for the Third Watch service. "Idiots," she said with a sneer, venom dripping from every syllable.

"Not now, Mother," Bradok said, trying to head off the diatribe he knew would follow that remark.

"Don't you dare shush me, boy," Sapphire said. "I'll speak my mind when I want to, and I'll call a fool a fool when I wish."

"Just because they pray in the temple doesn't make them fools, Mother," Bradok said, a sigh in his voice.

"Of course it does," Sapphire snapped. "Believing in a bunch of nebulous gods in an age of industry and enlightenment? No rational person would believe the foolish superstitions those phony priests try to push on us."

Like most of the dwarves in Ironroot, Bradok considered himself a secularist. He honored the concept of Reorx, the patron deity of the city, but he wasn't sure there ever was such a being. The secularist movement had been growing for years, ever since the dwarves began expanding beyond their homeland. Among the cities of the humans and the elves, they had seen wizards work mighty miracles just from studying moldy old books. If they had power as great as that of the priests, the secularists reasoned, then perhaps the priests used a similar kind of magic, conjuring illusions of gods to keep the people under their thumb.

Bradok wasn't sure how he felt about the whole issue of religion. His mother, however, had very definite opinions.

"The council ought to expel them from the city," she spat.

Bradok decided not to argue. Sapphire's voice had a tendency to carry loudly when she got angry.

They continued past the temple, with Sapphire muttering heatedly under her breath the whole time, and passed into the central square. Only a few people were moving among the shops and peddler carts at that hour of the morning. Wagons of trade goods bumped and clattered over the cobblestones, making their slow and steady way down toward the Artisans' Cavern. On a corner, by an alley between two buildings, a ragged dwarf stood under a glowpole, holding a sign on which a shaky hand had painted in red: *Repent lest the Gods forsake us.*

As the secularists gained power, more and more street preachers and low priests began to appear among the people of Ironroot, calling the citizenry to repentance, prophesying dire things. Mostly they were a nuisance, but occasionally one would lead a petition or rally for redress of some wrong or other that would annoy the city fathers.

A handcart bearing the unmistakable signs of hill dwarf construction stood before the Brasswork Inn, no doubt where the trade delegation lodged.

"It's still early," Much said, pulling an ornately etched brass watch from his breast pocket. "How's about a quick breakfast at the Bunch o' Grapes? I hear the ham's fresh there—not more than four days old."

Bradok hadn't eaten, but he knew that Sapphire would never approve of a tavern as folksy and comfortable as the Bunch o' Grapes.

"No thank you," he said. "Mother wants to get to her seat

8

in the gallery before the meeting starts."

Sapphire nodded stiffly next to him, though he didn't know if it came as a result of his thoughtfulness or her imminent public appearance as the mother of Ironroot's newest councilman.

"Suit yourself," Much said with a shrug and a smile. "Fasting is a young man's game, however."

He stopped and took Sapphire's hand, kissing it gently. "Enjoy the preliminaries, my dear. I'm afraid I must see to my rumbling stomach."

Sapphire smiled in return, and Much moved off to the Bunch o' Grapes. Bradok watched him go for a moment then walked his mother around the gardens of the fountain and, finally, on to City Hall.

Unlike the temple, City Hall had been built with a facade of wood, giving it the appearance of a surface-dweller's building. Brass lanterns adorned its face along with wide glass windows. Inside, the vast round audience chamber dominated the main floor. Two levels up, a ring of balconies and private boxes allowed visitors of all social standings to view the proceedings.

Bradok had arranged for a private box for his mother. Special privileges like that could be counted on to keep her happy.

The boxes lined the rear of the chamber, facing the podium. Each one had red velvet curtains—in case their occupants chose to remain anonymous—and dark cherrywood doors that separated them from the hallway beyond. Four squat, elegantly carved chairs, with padded seats upholstered in purple occupied the box, which had room for more should they be required.

Bradok ushered his mother inside the box, not really expecting her to be impressed by the richness of it. He had just held her chair so she could sit when a jovial baritone voice broke over them like a wave.

"There you are, Bradok."

The intrusion of the voice had a dramatic effect on Sapphire. Her face flushed and she quickly stood.

Bradok turned to find himself face-to-face with the mayor of Ironroot, the honorable Verdel Arbuckle. Arbuckle had been elected mayor of Ironroot a dozen years earlier and had stayed in the job, like all good politicians, through the appropriate application of schmoozing and graft.

Mayor Arbuckle wore perfectly tailored clothes over the fit frame of a dwarf just past his prime, but still well in the game. His graying hair had been pulled back into a knot, and there were silver caps on the ends of his flamboyantly curled mustache. He noticed Bradok's wary smile and nodded in the affable manner of a wolf acknowledging an equal.

The look passed in an instant, and Arbuckle stuck out a hand packed with seven jeweled rings. Bradok clasped it, and the mayor pulled the younger dwarf close enough to throw his free hand around Bradok's neck.

"Welcome, my boy," Arbuckle said with a genuine smile. "Welcome. Your father was quite a force within these walls, and though we'll miss him, I'm sure we can expect great things from you."

Sapphire beamed at the praise being ladled on him, vicariously on her, for both husband and son. Bradok managed a smile. He knew what kind of force his father had been. The man was a predator. The only thing he understood was strength and its liberal application. For the first time since he got up that morning, Bradok wondered just what the council would expect from him, the son of the iron-fisted Mirshawn Axeblade.

"Well, I'd best be going," Arbuckle said, giving Bradok an affectionate squeeze around the neck.

Bradok made to follow him, but the mayor waved him off.

"The session won't start for a while," he said. "Feel free

to take a tour of the building."

With an affable wink, Arbuckle departed. Bradok followed after him, intending to ask when the session would start, but suddenly slammed back into the door as he ran smack into someone. The scent of lavender and freshly oiled leather washed over him as he shook the stars from his eyes. When his vision cleared, he found a hill dwarf woman sprawled at his feet. She had the tan skin of a surface-dweller and hair that reminded Bradok of burnished copper. Her clothing was simple yet formal, a purple shirt and calf-hide leggings stitched with red ribbon. A look at her boots told Bradok that she walked rather than rode, and her hands were calloused as though she'd known hard work.

"I'm sorry," she said, blushing and looking up. "I didn't see you."

"Not at all," Bradok said, stretching out his hand to help her up. "I should have looked where I was going."

She took Bradok's hand, and he pulled her to her feet.

"I was just looking for the antechamber to the main hall," she said. "I'm supposed to be speaking to the council today, but I got a bit turned around."

"No problem," Bradok said, not releasing her hand. "It's one floor down near the front."

She shook Bradok's hand, and he finally let her go. Taking a step back, she looked up the hall and down before looking back at Bradok with an apologetic smile.

"Which way is the front?" she asked.

"That way," Bradok said, pointing down the hall.

As she turned to go, Bradok called after her. "Wait," he said. "What's your name?"

She whirled, sweeping her mass of copper hair over her shoulders in the process. "Rose," she said, still moving down the hall, stepping backward. "Rose Steelspar."

Bradok watched Rose go until she disappeared around the curve of the hallway; he whistled to himself.

11

"Don't be disgusting," Sapphire said, ripping Bradok back to reality.

"What?" he said, turning back to his mother. "You're always after me to get married, and she's quite the looker."

"Perish the thought," Sapphire hissed, shaking her head for emphasis. "It's bad enough that you made your money as a tradesman. Will you pollute our family with filthy hill dwarf blood too?" She gave him a look that said that all that should have been self-evident and that she detested the necessity of saying it. "Really, Bradok," she admonished. "The things you say. It's like you want to drive me to an early grave."

He resisted the urge to answer in the affirmative. Instead he said, "I think I'd better go find out what time the session will be starting."

"Before you go, Son," Sapphire said, more sweetly, rising to her feet. "I want you to remember something." She stepped close, lowering her voice as if afraid of being overheard.

"Your father made his presence felt in this hall," she said. "There will be certain expectations of you . . . and there will be dwarves waiting for you to fail."

"Mother, I—"

She waved him silent. "Whatever you do today, you must keep your wits about you. Don't speak or comment on issues you don't fully understand. Don't offer your opinion unless you are specifically asked for it."

"Above all," she hissed, holding up a warning finger. "You must not show any sign of weakness. I want you to show them that you're not weak, that you can and will take your father's place."

"I honestly don't think anyone could ever take Mirshawn's place," Bradok said. Ever since he'd left home as a youth, he'd never referred to Mirshawn as his father. He always said "Mirshawn."

A cloud crossed Sapphire's face. Then she turned and walked back to her seat. "You don't understand the game those men are playing," she said, gesturing over the rail to the council chamber below. "Their game is power, influence, and favor. If they think you are strong, they will befriend you and aid you and seek your council. If they think you are weak, however," she said, staring at him full in the face, "they will destroy you."

With that she turned her back on him and sat down.

Bradok left the box without another word but still caught his mother's trailing voice as he departed.

"Think about it," she said.

CHAPTER 2

Religion and Politics

The Ironroot city council boasted thirty members, elected from the various districts in the city. Each had a seat on a raised ring that ran around the outer edge of the circular audience chamber. Thanks to the wealth and importance of the Mattock Street district, Bradok's seat was positioned just to the left of the podium where Mayor Arbuckle presided over the council's business. The podium stood even higher than the councilors' seats and had been carved from a solid piece of granite.

Each councilman had an ornate desk with a polished top of gray marble. An inkwell and a box of paper were provided for taking notes.

The center of the chamber was a vast open area with a tiled floor, so the councilors and the gallery above could see petitioners or orators as they spoke.

Bradok entered the chamber from the back, behind the raised ring. A narrow walkway, covered with a thick, padded carpet of crimson red, allowed the councilmen to access their seats without mixing with the crowd outside. Bradok ascended the stone steps, running his hand over the polished brass railing. A fat, high-back leather chair awaited him, and Bradok sank down slowly into it, listening to the leather creak.

He didn't want to admit it, but it felt good—sitting there

in a councilman's seat. Maybe his mother was right; maybe there *was* something special about the power he was able to wield from that chair. He was a dwarf of influence.

Bradok pushed the thought away as soon as it lit on his consciousness. Looking up at the boxes above, he reasoned that if Sapphire was right about something, he probably didn't want to know about it.

His eyes found the box where his mother sat. She had pulled the curtains aside and was looking down at him with a smile of anticipation on her face.

An hour later, Mayor Arbuckle climbed to the top of the massive stone podium and struck the gavel, calling the meeting to order. The gallery and the bulk of the private boxes had filled, and the constant drone of the assembled crowd could be heard. As Mayor Arbuckle welcomed everyone, Bradok's eyes wandered over the gallery above the private boxes. There, a collection of tradesman and business owners had gathered, presumably to keep tabs on the council's deliberations and how they might affect business in the city. But as he reached the end of the gallery, Bradok beheld a strange sight. On the far left sat the raggedy dwarf from the alley, still carrying his red-painted sign.

Repent lest the Gods forsake us.

Bradok smiled at the sight. Ironroot was a city, like any other. There were good folk and bad, places of legitimate business and brothels, artisans' shops and gambling houses. Ironroot might have its share of wickedness, but Bradok reasoned that, all things considered, its people didn't have any great cause to repent.

". . . and I want you to join me in welcoming our newest member," Arbuckle's voice suddenly cut through Bradok's wandering thoughts. "One of our most skilled and prominent citizens, Bradok Axeblade."

He stood as polite applause broke out from the gallery and the other councilmen.

With the perfunctory matters dispensed with, the meeting settled down to real business. Several citizens approached with petitions of one kind or another. The council heard them and accepted or rejected them after modest debate. Bradok made his first votes—in a nervous, loud voice—much to Sapphire's delight.

When the locals had been heard, the delegates from the hill dwarf city of Everguard were ushered into the hall. Like all their brethren, they stood a bit taller than their mountain dwarf cousins. Their clothes were coarse by comparison, designed for the harsher elements of the upper world and cut to be functional without the need of decoration. As they entered, two of their number pulled the covered handcart that Bradok had seen earlier with them.

The delegation consisted of ten dwarves, representing Everguard's biggest industries. Once they had assembled in the center of the hall, their leader stepped forward and pulled back her hood.

Bradok's wandering attention was immediately riveted. The burnished copper hair was unmistakable.

"My name is Rose Steelspar," she said in a clear voice. "Daughter of Larin Steelspar, Burger of Everguard."

"That's like a mayor," Much whispered from the table to Bradok's right.

"I come to you in my father's name and in good fellowship," she went on. "As a token of that fellowship, I bring you a gift from the people of Everguard."

The dwarves pulling the handcart brought it forward and removed the tarp. Underneath were dozens of baskets stuffed with fresh fruit—something very hard to come by in Ironroot. Quickly the dwarves with the handcart passed out baskets to all the councilmen. Bradok selected a large, golden pear for himself before he sent the rest of his basket up to Sapphire.

He was tempted to just sit there and enjoy the taste of the pear and the sight of the red-haired girl, but he forced himself to sit up straight and pay attention. As a representative of Iron-root, he resolved to listen to what the delegation had to say.

Try as he might, however, his attention kept wandering to their spokesperson's pretty face, to the red hair and the dark eyes and the competent voice.

As best as he could figure out, Bradok gathered that Ever-guard would like to find ready markets for their grain, hay, cloth, and leather—things that Ironroot certainly needed. But even though Ironroot needed such goods, and even though Everguard needed ore and stone and metalwork, the council had put heavy tariffs on all those goods, which restricted their commerce. It made no sense to Bradok. Finally he leaned over and asked Much.

"We're the only source for what they need and the only ready market nearby," Much whispered. "We raise the prices of doing business here because there really isn't anywhere else for them to go. They're just a small town. They can't afford to mount big trade missions."

"So we take advantage of their misfortune to line the pockets of our tradesmen?" Bradok asked, genuinely shocked.

Much chuckled. "Of course not," he said, as if such a thing could never be. "The excess from the tariff goes to the council."

Bradok simply gaped as every petition the hill dwarf delegation brought up was rejected after a modicum of polite debate. While the farce went on, Much whispered in Bradok's ear, explaining which council members were beholden to which concerns and what their respective cut of the tariffs might be.

"But wouldn't there be more money to go around if the tariffs were reduced and the trade increased?" Bradok asked Much.

The little dwarf nodded with a helpless sort of a smile. "Of course," he said. "But if we remove the restrictions, that eliminates our rake-off, and we can't have that, now can we?"

Bradok had thought his father had been crooked, but the council was organized crookery. What he witnessed was corruption on a level Bradok could barely grasp. Mirshawn had owned brothels, drug palaces, and gambling halls, but he'd never forced anyone to frequent them. The city council, on the other hand, used the power of the law and the threat of arrest by the city guard to extort money from anyone who wanted to earn an honest living.

It made him sick.

He looked around the room at the figures behind the richly carved tables, vainly seeking a soulmate among his colleagues. Each wore fine, costly clothes with jeweled rings on their hands, gold clips on their beards, and silver buckles on their belts and boots. The dwarves of Ironroot trusted those men to rule wisely, to look out for the interests of the people and the city itself. Instead, the councilmen were busy lining their own pockets.

No wonder Mirshawn felt so comfortable here, he thought. It's nothing more than a den of thieves.

Bradok considered saying something on behalf of the hill dwarves, but he dismissed the thought almost as soon as it came. Sapphire's warning came back to him. If he took a stand, he would single himself out as an enemy of the council. Bradok had enough experience with wealth and power to know that would be distinctly unwise.

Finally, when Rose had exhausted all her arguments, she thanked the council for its time and led her dejected companions from the chamber. Bradok felt for them. He wanted to go after them and tell them that it wasn't fair, but that wouldn't change anything.

As the hill dwarves trudged away, a short, solidly built dwarf in rough leather garments entered. His hair had been combed to one side to cover a bald spot on top of his head, and his beard was braided and tied with a leather strap. Bradok recognized him but couldn't quite remember his name. He was a dowser by profession, seeking gems, crystals, and glowstones in the deep tunnels below Ironroot. Bradok had bought stones from him and knew him to be an honest tradesman.

"Argus Deephammer to petition the council," the scribe announced as the dwarf made his way to the center of the chamber.

"The council begs your pardon, Argus," Arbuckle said from the podium. "It's been a long morning, and I think we should take a short break before continuing."

Argus nodded but made no move to surrender his ground, standing in the center of the round room.

All around Bradok, the councilmen were rising, making their way along their private walkway to the back of the building.

"Come on, lad," Much said, climbing down from his bench. "The council has a fully stocked bar in our private room."

Bradok shook his head. He hadn't eaten anything but the pear all day, but after the past few hours of the session, he had a sour stomach.

"No," he said. "I'd better wait for Mother."

"Suit yourself, my boy," Much said with a grin. "I, however, am going to need a belt to get me through the rest of the session."

A few minutes later, Bradok's mother materialized.

"You did well today, son," she said with only the tiniest hint of mockery in her voice.

Bradok descended the stairs from the platform to the walkway, taking Sapphire's arm. He walked her out of the building and into the mushroom garden outside. Despate the council's being on a break, the garden was empty except for a mother on a bench by the wall, quietly nursing her baby.

"Did you see what they were doing in there?" Bradok whispered, unable to restrain himself. "Those tariffs make it harder for our own people to earn a living," he spluttered. "Not to mention our cousins from Everguard. Why, they'd be able to grow into a good-sized community in a few years if our city council just got out of their way and let them trade freely."

"And then what would happen?" Sapphire stared at him coldly. "Once Everguard got bigger, they'd start doing what they need for themselves. They wouldn't need us anymore. Then we'd be the ones paying the tariffs and they'd be the ones collecting them. You are young in the ways of the world, my son, with much to learn."

"Their spokesman was eloquent, I thought—"

"Oh, that woman you thought was so pretty?" she interrupted with a raised eyebrow. "Did you think I hadn't noticed? I didn't think you liked your women so . . . earthy."

Bradok's temper flashed.

"It's not about her, damn it," he said. "It's about what she's here representing: honor and fellowship and the brotherhood of the dwarves."

Sapphire stifled a laugh and ran her eyes over Bradok with a calculating look.

"My son, you are still a boy who must learn the ways of men. A boy who is a fool," she continued after a brief silence. "In this world you either eat or are eaten. It is the strong that rule and the weak that submit, that is the way it has always been." She stepped close and raised her lips to his ear.

"You may think it is the people who rule Ironroot," she whispered, her voice barely audible. "That is a boy's wishful idea. It is the men who sit in this room who rule. It is they who make the laws, decide the taxes and tariffs. They can let a murderer free from prison or condemn an innocent man to death."

"The people wouldn't stand for that," Bradok said simply.

"The people wouldn't lift a finger," Sapphire said smugly. "They fear lawlessness. They crave the safety of a strong government and are willing to sacrifice the occasional principle to have it."

"That's monstrous," Bradok said, teeth clenched to keep from screaming. "I don't believe things are that simple."

Sapphire laughed, loudly and with genuine mirth, as if she'd just been told an amusing story. "Yes, the world is monstrous, Bradok," she said, touching his cheek with a strange mixture of sympathy and contempt in her expression. "And we must make our place in it any way we can. I hope you see that now. This day's lesson has been a good one."

Bradok wanted to answer her, but he couldn't find the right words. Quite apart from the outrage of his offended morals, he couldn't help wondering if Sapphire was right: The strong rule.

"You'd better head back," she announced brusquely. "I imagine the council will be meeting deep into the day. I've nearly had my fill and will slip away soon. Try not to wake me with your usual ruckus if you come home late; you know how light a sleeper I am." She started to turn but stopped to regard him with an appraising glance.

"You did tolerably well this morning," she said. "If you continue like this, you might just make something of yourself." She sighed, her appraising eye turning hard. "Too much to hope for, I suppose," she said.

Bradok escorted his mother back to her booth then returned to his seat. He poured himself a glass of water from the provided pitcher, downed it, then poured another. He'd always been an honest man, a businessman who dealt fairly and gave value for value. He'd believed that the rest of the world could be that way too.

After today he didn't know what he believed.

Sapphire could do that to him. His mother had a way of twisting his insides in a way that the meanest bouncer in the lowest tavern couldn't match. He felt as if he'd gone a few rounds with that tavern bouncer and lost. He needed to sit and think if he wanted any chance to untangle Sapphire's mental knots.

Half an hour later, growing commotion in the chamber hall brought Bradok back to himself.

He hadn't noticed Argus Deephammer, still standing in the center of the chamber, stoically awaiting his turn to speak. Bradok wondered what possible business the dowser could have with the council and why his usually affable face seemed so grim and determined. Before he could give it much thought, Mayor Arbuckle banged the gavel for quiet.

"Welcome back," he said once the noise level had dropped. "We appreciate your waiting, Argus. Now what business brings you here?"

"I come before the council today on a most serious matter," Deephammer said, his voice booming off the stone walls and echoing throughout the chamber. "Two days ago I was in the deep tunnels when I heard a voice calling to me," he continued gravely. "I followed the sound of this voice, and it led me down into the bowels of the world, into caves where I had never before been. Then, in the lowest cave, I found a moonwell."

An audible gasp ran around the chamber. To the faithful, moonwells were sacred places, blessed by Reorx himself. Bradok knew them to be pools or springs where the water was so rich with dissolved minerals that it glowed a pale silvery light. In any case, moonwells were rare and their water highly prized as a curative.

"When I found the well," Argus went on, his eyes flashing around the room to make sure everyone was listening, "I could still hear the whispered voice, but I could not make out the words it spoke. I sat and drank from the fountain and, as soon as that blessed water touched my lips, the voice was made clear to me.

"I heard the voice of Reorx himself," Argus declared, raising his voice even louder, with no hesitation or sign that his statement was in any way out of the ordinary. "He showed me the sins of Ironroot, the wickedness that breeds here like rats in a sewer. He bade me come here, to you, and deliver this message: Repent of your evils and turn again unto your God, or this great city of Ironroot will be utterly destroyed."

At that last statement, a roar erupted around the room. Some were shouting that Argus was right, while others expressed outrage at such a threat. The councilmen around the ring were shouting, demanding that Argus explain himself. Mayor Arbuckle hammered on the podium for silence, which he did not receive for a full five minutes.

"What is the meaning of this?" Arbuckle demanded. "How dare you come before this august body with your childish fantasies and presume to pass judgment on us?"

As Bradok watched, Arbuckle seemed to be swelling like a toad, his face a mask of puffy red blotches.

"We are not weak-minded fools," the mayor shouted at the dowser. "We are men of the world, and we have seen the magics of the humans and the elves. What are your precious priests but a bunch of charlatans, using their magic to manufacture gods who never did exist—all so they might have power over us?

"And now you come here," Arbuckle continued. "Now you demand that we turn from our learning and our wisdom and go back to the foolish traditions of our ancestors. Repent! Repent for what?"

"Then you will be destroyed," Argus said, his voice softening but somehow carrying to the farthest corners of the room. "Next month, both the moons will be new in the sky together," he said. "I have done my part. I have warned you. You have till then."

"Says you," a councilman called from the far side of the room.

"So declares Reorx, your god," Argus Deephammer replied. Bradok was amazed at how strong, how unbowed he seemed in the face of such hostility and anger.

Furious voices rose again only to be cut off by the sound of someone clapping slowly. All eyes in the room turned to a tall, slender dwarf with a forked beard sitting a few tables to Bradok's right.

"An excellent performance, Argus," the dwarf said, rising. He walked around in front of his desk and jumped down to the floor of the audience chamber. "It's only a pity that there is no witness to your tale, no god that anyone has ever met or shook hands with named Reorx to make good on your threats."

Bradok had never met the dwarf, but his reputation had preceded him. Jon Bladehook was the closest thing the local secularists had to a leader. Bladehook had traveled extensively in his business as a merchant and had grown both cynical and rich. Bradok sat up straight, like many others in the council, suddenly focused on the showdown between the believer and the secularist.

"You say that we will be destroyed in a little over a month if we don't do as you say?" Bladehook asked.

"I have no commands to give," Argus said simply. "If you wish to know what Reorx requires of you, go to his priests."

"But if we don't, we'll be destroyed," Bladehook pressed.

"So says Reorx," Argus reiterated. "Not I."

Bladehook nodded sagely then turned to his fellow councilmen. "I wonder, brothers," he said. "What will happen if Ironroot does not heed the warnings of this mad dwarf?" He indicated Argus. "Surely a being as wrathful and powerful as Reorx would give the dwarves of Ironroot signs of his power before the deadline passes: a small disaster or poison air or a sickness perhaps? Have we detected any sign yet . . . other than this ugly warning?"

Murmurs of assent rippled around the chamber.

"Then I say we arrest this dwarf," Bladehook shouted suddenly, fiercely pointing his finger at the surprised Argus.

"On what charge?" someone called from the gallery.

"He has threatened this council and the people of Ironroot," Bladehook said. "And surely he has confederates, dwarves who are poised to provide these 'signs' of Reorx's power should we refuse to believe their messenger. They, too, threaten the city and her people."

"By thunder, he's right," Arbuckle yelled, pounding the lectern with his gavel. "Guards, arrest him."

Two soldiers rushed forward and took hold of Argus Deephammer's arms. For his part, Argus made no attempt to resist them.

Shouts of approval and a few scattered cheers erupted in the chamber. Bradok didn't hear any of it. He felt sick. The actions of the council were wrong. They had been wrong all day. He knew Argus, knew the man was good and honest. Perhaps he had fallen asleep and merely dreamed the voice of Reorx in the deep tunnels, where he found the moonwell. But Argus himself posed no real danger to the town.

He wanted to object, to stand and speak on Argus's behalf, but one look at the sputtering, angry faces around the hall told him what kind of response that would receive. And glancing up, he remembered his mother's warning: don't speak against the consensus and never unless called upon. He could well see that all his fellow councilmen were in agreement with Arbuckle.

"And what of his confederates?" Bladehook asked, climbing back up to his seat. "Who are they? Let us ferret them out."

"Good idea, Jon," Mayor Arbuckle said before turning to the guardsmen who had arrested Argus.

"Take him to prison," the mayor declared, "then go to his house and arrest his family, his close friends too. We'll cut out this zealotry before it has a chance to cause chaos and rebellion in our city."

Suddenly, without thinking, Bradok found himself rising to his feet. He stood so quickly and so forcefully, he knocked his chair over backward. The chair rolled down the steps of the platform and into the outer walkway, clattering loudly as it went. All eyes in the hall turned to stare in surprise at the new councilman. Truth be told, he was as shocked as they to find himself on his feet, and didn't have the slightest idea of what he was about to say.

A deafening silence followed, broken only by the nervous cough from someone on the far side of the hall. Bradok opened his mouth to speak, but at first nothing came out. He knew he mustn't say the words his conscience screamed out in the dark recesses of his mind. He ought to be diplomatic. Yet he could think of nothing diplomatic or anything else to say. His mind was a blank.

"Ahem. Yes. All right, the chair recognizes Councilman Axeblade," Arbuckle said, his genial, affable voice back.

"Brothers, councilmen," Bradok began haltingly, his mind frantically scrambling. "Before we allow ourselves to, uh, get carried away, perhaps we should slow down and think. Arresting Argus might seem prudent as a temporary measure, but what will people think if we arrest his family?"

He paused to let that question sink in before stumbling on. "They'll wonder if their council are a bunch of weaklings, fearing women and children."

Several people in the gallery laughed nervously and the councilmen exchanged looks.

"And what will those people do if they see us as weak?" Bradok said, remembering his mother's own words from that morning. "You and I both know that if they see us as weak, they might decide they don't need us making their decisions for them."

The silence that followed his words stretched out for a long time.

"Thank you, Bradok," Mayor Arbuckle finally replied in a small voice. "Your words speak prudence and a wisdom beyond your years." He cast his eyes around the chamber at the other councilmen. "Surely there must be some other way to find this dwarf's confederates, ways that won't rile the populace."

"You can silence me," Argus interjected, his voice still

loud and confident, "but others will come in my stead until it is too late."

"Enough of this," Mayor Arbuckle said, waving at the guards. "Take him away."

Argus Deephammer went without a struggle. Bradok watched him go, keeping his emotions under tight control. He couldn't save Argus, but at least Bradok had spared his family from rotting in prison with him.

Two pages had picked up Bradok's chair and returned it to the platform. As Bradok returned to his seat, he cast a sideways glance at Jon Bladehook. To his surprise, the secularist leader was glaring back at him with undisguised animosity. Bladehook had clearly intended Argus's arrest to be the first, but not the last among the believers. That plan had been thwarted by some upstart newcomer.

Bradok felt certain he'd made a powerful and dangerous enemy.

CHAPTER 3

Deals in the Dark

No more petitioners today," Mayor Arbuckle said once Argus had been escorted out. "Clear the gallery and seal the chamber."

As the audience above filed out, the mayor flopped back in his high chair, throwing the gavel down on the lectern in disgust.

"We have to do something," someone said from the far side of the chamber.

"Clearly," Jon Bladehook said, standing again. "Is it just me, or do these street preachers and religious zealots seem more common and aggressive than they used to be?"

An angry murmur ran around the chamber.

"Why, one can hardly walk from city hall to the Artisans' Cavern without some lunatic shouting at you that you must repent, that the end is nigh, or some such nonsense."

All around the chamber, councilmen were frowning and nodding and muttering. Bradok remembered the man with the painted sign and glanced involuntarily up at the gallery that had been so recently emptied.

"It's a public nuisance," Bladehook went on. "Not to mention the fact that any of these zealots might be in on whatever plot Argus Deephammer is hatching to stir up the people."

"Arrest them all," someone yelled. Others joined in until pandemonium filled the chamber.

Only Bradok noticed the oily, self-satisfied smile flirting around the corners of Jon Bladehook's mouth. That was the solution he hadn't wanted to propose himself.

Bradok felt the cold knot return to his stomach.

"Enough of this," Mayor Arbuckle shouted, pounding on the lectern.

The room fell silent, and Bladehook's face returned to an emotionless mask.

"As our new brother, Bradok, has shrewdly pointed out, any move by this council that is considered extreme will weaken our position."

"Well, what do we do then?" old Tal Boreshank asked irritably. "If we don't act, sooner or later it'll look like we endorse all this religious rhetoric. I, for one, have had my fill."

Angry arguments broke out all over the hall. Some of the council favored sweeping measures, while others urged caution. Bradok just sat there, thinking. He was no believer, that much was certain. Still, something about how the council had treated Argus Deephammer and his solemn warning seemed, well—undwarflike.

He looked down the row to where Jon Bladehook stood, leaning against the front of his desk. He seemed to be basking in the glow of the controversy. As a secularist, he clearly disapproved of the believers, but Bradok thought the intensity of Bladehook's emotion suggested something more beneath the surface. It seemed as though the notion that others believed in something he considered foolish was a personal affront to him.

In that moment, Bradok felt certain that Bladehook would not stop until he'd put all the Ironroot believers in jail—or worse.

"Ban them," Bradok said abruptly, his voice cutting through the arguing. He stood as all the eyes in the room returned to him. "We can pass an ordinance banning proselytizing out-side the temple grounds and private homes," he explained. "That way we get them off the street but they can still speak their piece."

A long pause followed during which no one spoke. Bradok started to worry that he'd gone too far. Then Much cleared his throat.

"I like that plan," Much said, standing formally. "It solves the immediate problem, and the citizenry will see it as a rea-sonable measure to prevent interference with daily lives."

Around the chamber, bearded heads were nodding in agreement.

Mayor Arbuckle stroked his beard, a shrewd look on his face. Finally he smiled and nodded at the scribe who sat at a low table across the hall.

"Write it up," he declared. "Make sure it's posted in the square, at the temple, and in every tavern in Ironroot."

As the scribe began scribbling diligently, Mayor Arbuckle rose from his chair and heaved a deep sigh. He tossed his gavel down on the lectern with a bang. "Well, that's quite enough business for one day," he said, donning his top-coat. "Unless anyone else has something to add, I'm going home."

It was as if a magic spell had been broken. The tension dissi-pated. Everyone rose, talking among themselves and gathering their things. Within seconds the chamber began to empty.

"You did good, lad," Much said, clapping him on the shoul-der as Bradok descended to the outer walkway. "That was excellent thinking."

"Seemed like the right thing to do," Bradok said.

Much's grip steered him in the direction of the door. "About that," Much continued in a more conspiratorial voice. "You might want to be careful not to try to do right too much of the time," he said. "Since you're new, a lot of the older councilmen will expect you to mind your place for a while.

They might feel threatened if Mayor Arbuckle takes too big a shine to you."

Mayor Arbuckle taking a shine to him? Bradok didn't know whether to laugh or cry. What he really wanted to do was tell Much that he'd fully intended to keep his mouth shut during his first day on the council. After Sapphire's lecture that morning and the warning Much had just given him, however, he reasoned that it might be better to keep his private thoughts just that—private.

"One more thing," Much said, his voice dropping even lower. "Be careful about Jon Bladehook; he's not entirely a bad one. Make him your friend, if that's still possible. He's not one to cross."

"I gathered that," Bradok said. "Don't worry. I have no intention of getting in Bladehook's way."

Much smiled and thumped Bradok on the chest. "Good lad," he said. "I knew you had your wits about you."

As they passed out of city hall and into the cool air of Ironroot, Bradok caught a flash of red out of the corner of his eye. There, at the foot of the stairs, stood the ragged dwarf with his painted sign.

Repent lest the Gods forsake us.

"Now, my boy," Much went on, oblivious to the dwarf with the sign. "We have to do something to mark your first successful day as a councilman of Ironroot."

"Much," Bradok protested, "I really don't—"

"None of that, now," Much said, taking a firmer hold on Bradok's shoulder as if he half expected the younger dwarf to make a break for it. "I told the people at the Bunch o' Grapes to cook up a goose for us with all the trimmings and set aside a freshly tapped keg."

Bradok dearly wanted to go home, to go to his workshop and lose himself in the workings of his craft—anything to take his mind off the troubling events of the day.

Much, however, was not to be resisted.

Thus it was well after midnight when Bradok made his way wearily up the stairs to his front door. The evening had passed swiftly with good company, good food, and plenty of beer. Bradok hadn't spent such a pleasant evening in a long time. There was a tense moment when Bradok caught sight of Jon Bladehook drinking with the captain of the city guard, who, Much informed Bradok, was Bladehook's brother-in-law. The awkwardness passed, however, when Bladehook caught sight of Bradok and sent him over a bottle of wine to welcome him to the council.

All in all, Bradok had had a most pleasant time. He had all but forgotten the new law he'd proposed.

Five hours later, however, the new law banning street preachers forcefully returned to his thoughts. An incessant pounding awakened him from a sound sleep.

Moments later Bradok pulled open his heavy door to find two city guardsmen on his stoop.

"To what do I owe the pleasure of this late visit by the constabulary?" Bradok asked, wiping the sleep from his eyes.

The two blue-liveried dwarves looked at each other in confusion.

"What do you want?" Bradok stated more plainly.

The taller of the two dwarves stepped forward. "Begging your pardon, Councilman," he said in a slightly jittery voice. "We've been sent to summon you to the council chamber."

"At this hour?" Bradok demanded before he realized he had no idea just what hour it was.

"Yes, sir," the second dwarf said. "The mayor has called an emergency session on account of the, uh, riot."

Bradok's head snapped up, and the fog left his weary brain. "What riot?" he wondered.

"There's a riot going on outside the temple," the first guard said. "We've been sent to ensure your safety, Councilman. Please hurry."

"Can I dress first?" Bradok asked.

The guard nodded and Bradok stepped back so they could enter his foyer.

"What's the meaning of this," Sapphire's voice floated down from the balcony above. "Why are there armed dwarves in our home in the middle of the night?"

"Go back to bed, Mother," Bradok said, climbing the stairs two at a time. "It's council business. I'm needed."

His mother protested as he passed by, but he was too dazed to pay her any mind. He threw on whatever clothes were handy, and five minutes later he was back in the foyer.

"All right," he said. "Let's go."

The guardsmen went first, walking shoulder to shoulder, with Bradok in their wake. He had checked his watch when he dressed; the hour was four. Normally at that hour of the morning the streets of Ironroot would be deserted save for the night watch and the occasional tradesman trying to get a jump on the day.

That night, however, the city was awash in activity.

Even before Bradok reached the main cavern, he could hear the hum of a crowd. The acrid smell of smoke reached his nostrils as they emerged into the main cavern. A large, angry crowd had gathered in front of the temple.

Skirting the crowd, the guardsmen led Bradok along the far edge of the cavern to the steps of city hall. A large number of armed guards ringed the building, watching the crowd near the temple with nervous glances. All of them had their hands on their weapons.

"We'll leave you here," his escort said. "They're expecting you inside."

Bradok watched the guardsmen as they turned and headed back into the city, presumably to fetch another council member.

If the outside of city hall was in chaos, the inside was pure frenzy. It looked to Bradok as if the majority of the councilmen were already there, most yelling, while some were pounding on their desks. On the high seat, Mayor Arbuckle sat, his chin resting on his hands, clearly having lost control of the proceedings.

"There he is," someone yelled, and the chamber went suddenly, frighteningly quiet.

All eyes turned to Bradok and for a long moment a pregnant pause hung in the air.

"There," a voice hissed.

"Traitor," came another.

"Silence!" Arbuckle's voice cut through the room like thunder.

"What is going on here?" Bradok demanded. He was still fuzzy-headed but felt certain something was terribly wrong.

"You brought this trouble upon us," Councilman Auger yelled.

"The riot?" Bradok asked, trying to keep his voice even. "I know nothing about that. I have just woken up and arrived here."

"It was you who thought up that law," Auger yelled. "The law that has sparked the riot. You probably plotted this whole mess with your oh-so-reasonable solution to our problem."

"It did seem reasonable, didn't it?" Jon Bladehook cut in. "Only an unreasonable person would object to it." Bladehook walked out into the center of the floor, drawing full attention to himself. "But no, we shouldn't fault our new comrade for being reasonable," he said, his voice smooth as butter. "It is the believers who are being unreasonable. I warned you they were dangerous."

"I beg to disagree. They are *not* dangerous or unreasonable," a new voice said.

All eyes turned to the entrance, where the high priest of the temple stood.

"Sarru," Mayor Arbuckle said, a note of forced joviality in his voice. "Welcome."

Sarru Firebrand had the thick, muscular kind of build

one usually associated with a bouncer in a seedy tavern, and the polished wooden staff he carried did nothing to soften his image. He had red-gold hair that he braided in two thick cords on either side of his head, and his beard was held in place with three descending gold clips. His robes were crimson with gold trim and an amulet of Reorx, wrought in steel, hung about his neck.

"I seriously doubt that I am welcome here," the priest said, his eyes sweeping over the room accusingly. "What do you mean by restricting the religious freedom of the good dwarves of Ironroot?"

"We did nothing of the sort," Bladehook said, his voice sounding suddenly less confident than it had been a moment before.

"He's right, Sarru," Mayor Arbuckle said defensively. "The law simply requires that preaching be done in the temple, where it belongs."

"That's right," Bladehook said, trying to regain his superior footing. "It keeps the preaching off the street. I should think you'd relish the idea of us eliminating the competition for you."

At that a scowl crossed the priest's face.

"I do not know why Reorx chooses to send these messengers here," the priest said after a long moment's pause. "I wonder if perhaps he is displeased with me. Regardless of the reason, however, I will not hinder his will, and neither will you."

"That sounds like a threat," Bladehook said complainingly. He opened his mouth to continue, but Arbuckle cut him off.

"Nobody's trying to prevent these people from being heard," the mayor said with all the dignity he could muster.

"Really?" Sarru answered him. "Did you know that since you passed that ordinance, over forty dwarves have been arrested? Are you aware that the Goldspanner family is in the city jail right now for praying over their food in a tavern? One dwarf was taken right off the street for saying 'Reorx bless you!' when someone sneezed!"

Mayor Arbuckle looked shocked; then his face reddened slightly. "Uh," he said, clearly trying to form a coherent response to Sarru's assertions. "Well, uh, it seems our city guard has, uh, misinterpreted the spirit of our ordinance," he muttered.

Bradok noticed the mayor cast Jon Bladehook a dirty look. Then he remembered seeing Bladehook drinking with the captain of the city guard that very afternoon.

"Misinterpretation or not, the people won't stand for it," Sarru declared haughtily. "There are several hundred dwarves over at the temple who I've convinced not to burn city hall to the ground. Right now they're willing to listen to me, but I don't know how much longer that will last, with their friends and families in jail."

"Of course, of course," Arbuckle said, taking out a piece of paper and scribbling on it. When he finished, he dribbled wax onto the paper and stamped it with the seal of Ironroot.

"Here," he said, waving a guardsman over. "Give this to the captain of the guard"—he glanced irritably at Bladehook—"and tell him, in no uncertain terms, that he is to release all the prisoners arrested in violation of the no-preaching ordinance."

The guard reached out to take the paper, but Arbuckle pulled it away before he could grab it.

"And tell that fat-headed buffoon," the mayor added, loud enough for his words to carry throughout the chamber, "that if he messes this up, he'll be a street sweeper before lunch." Arbuckle handed over the paper, and the guard departed.

"It will take more than that, I'm afraid," Sarru said tersely.

Arbuckle ground his teeth but smiled pleasantly before reaching for his gavel. "All in favor of rescinding the ordinance barring street preaching, say 'aye.' "

The room thundered with assent.

"Any opposed?"

There were none, not even Bladehook, who dared dissent.

"Then I declare the ordinance against street preaching rescinded." He nodded toward Sarru. "I'll leave it to you to deliver the news to the faithful."

Sarru harrumphed then turned and left, his staff rapping sharply on the floor.

"Everyone go home and get some sleep," Arbuckle roared once Sarru had vanished. "Jon, Bradok, not so fast, you two," he went on. "I'd like to see you in my chambers for a moment."

Bradok looked warily at Jon Bladehook, but Bladehook simply looked annoyed. As it turned out, Arbuckle met with them separately. Bladehook went in first, staying almost an hour while Bradok waited in an overstuffed chair outside Arbuckle's heavy office door. Toward the end, Bradok became aware of raised voices inside.

"You move too soon!" Arbuckle was saying.

"And you do nothing but bide your time," Bladehook replied vehemently. "We passed an ordinance, correct? All I did was tell my brother-in-law to enforce that ordinance to the letter."

"But you didn't give the people time even to learn about the law, Jon. You have incited them and called our motives into question."

"What do we do now?" Bladehook asked, clearly piqued.

"We wait, Jon," Arbuckle said. "We bide our time."

A moment later the door burst open and Bladehook stormed out. He marched past Bradok and down the hall without a backward glance.

"Sorry about that, Bradok," Arbuckle said, standing in the doorway to his office. "Jon can be a little high-strung at times. Come in."

Bradok rose and followed Arbuckle into his office. The round room had been cut from the wall of the cavern. Cabinets of dark, polished wood curved along the back wall. They had glass fronts so Bradok could see that they were full of thick leather-bound books. Arbuckle's oval-shaped desk stood in the middle of the room with two comfortable-looking chairs before it. Papers, books, and blotters littered the top of his desk.

"Sit down," the mayor said, waving his hand in the direction of the chairs.

"If this is about that ordinance," Bradok said, sinking down into the seat, "I just—"

"I know you had nothing to do with what happened," Arbuckle said, some of his easy manner evaporating. "I brought you here tonight because you seem to have a level head and a keen mind."

"Uh, thank you," Bradok said uncertainly.

"Your ordinance was a good one," Arbuckle said. "A sound idea." He got up and began to pace back and forth behind his desk. "But it seems we have quite a few citizens who took it the wrong way."

"Starting with our captain of the guard," Bradok ventured.

Arbuckle cleared his throat nervously and went on. "I don't want something like this to happen again," the mayor said in a pained tone. "Things could have gotten out of hand tonight. People could have gotten hurt."

"What do you want me to do?" Bradok asked.

"Ah, that's what I like about you, Bradok," Arbuckle said with a beaming smile. "You get right to the point."

He sat back down at his desk and leaned forward on his arms, giving Bradok an intense look.

"We need to find out what the people really want," he said. "I want to know what they *think* of the street preachers."

"I think they made that clear tonight," Bradok said hesitantly.

"No," Arbuckle said with a sly smile. "Tonight they showed that they don't want to lose their religious freedoms. That's a long way from whether or not we let wandering preachers annoy them in the public square. The problem of those preachers is still with us, and I think most of the town would like a solution."

"I see," said Bradok, nodding. "So you want to know what they want done about the preachers. Ideas for a better solution."

"Precisely," Bradok said. "Let's say you make up a survey that we can hand out to the people of Ironroot, something innocuous and nonthreatening. We'll use the pages here at city hall and ask them to take your survey and canvass the city."

Arbuckle's eyes sparkled, and Bradok couldn't help but notice that the mayor was sweating. Something about the unnatural gleam in his eye made Bradok uncomfortable with his plan.

"So," Arbuckle said. "Can I count on you?"

Bradok thought about it. The task seemed simple enough, just find out what the people wanted done with the street preachers. Yet something about Arbuckle's overeagerness was unsettling.

"I'll do it," he said at last.

Arbuckle's smile widened, seeming more genuine. He rose and extended his arm to Bradok.

"I knew I could count on you, Bradok," he said as Bradok clasped his forearm. "Take a week to prepare and conduct your survey; then let me know the results. I'm sure this will be helpful."

Bradok agreed, thanked the mayor for his confidence, and left the office.

A few minutes later, he had exited the building and was making his way through the cool air of Ironroot. The street was dark and empty. Everything had returned to normal, and that meant the streets were dark and deserted in the predawn.

Bradok should have been happy. No blood had been spilt. Those falsely imprisoned were going to be turned free, yet he couldn't shake the feeling that it was merely the calm before the storm.

He resolved not think about it.

It was a resolution he wouldn't keep.

CHAPTER 4

Tavern Tales

Over the next few days, an endless parade of city guardsmen came and went from Bradok's house, carrying copies of his carefully worded survey. As per Mayor Arbuckle's instructions, the guards moved through the city, interviewing every citizen, getting their thoughts on the problem of the street preachers.

Bradok had divided the city into small districts in order to disperse guards throughout the city efficiently. After the near-riot caused by his ordinance, he wanted to make sure the citizenry wouldn't be alarmed by large groups of guardsmen going door to door. Every couple of hours, one of his teams would return and present Bradok with a written record of their findings.

After sweeping two-thirds of the city, Bradok found that the mayor was right: Well more than half the populace considered the preachers a nuisance. Most of them, however, were not in favor of laws restricting freedom of speech as a solution to the problem.

"It's about time," Sapphire remarked as Bradok sat at his desk, preparing one of the daily reports he sent to Arbuckle.

"About time for what, Mother?" Bradok asked idly, without

looking up. In the time since his father had died, Sapphire often would seek out her son at odd hours, desiring to speak with him at length about things that Bradok couldn't care less about.

"It's about time Arbuckle and those fools on the council learned who their enemies are."

Bradok sighed. One of Sapphire's favorite topics of conversation revolved around her hatred of the believers.

"This is just a public survey, Mother," Bradok said in a strained voice. "It has nothing to do with enemies or fools."

Sapphire chuckled. Her laugh had a derisive note in it, as if she were directing it at a willfully ignorant child.

"That's what you think," she said. "Once they have that list, Arbuckle and Bladehook will know who sides with them and who is against them. Then it will be just as I say: fools versus enemies."

Bradok looked up from his desk to find his mother filling the doorway. Her face was flushed, and her eyes shone with malice.

"Mark my words," she said. "We'll soon be rid of those cursed priests. And the council will have you to thank."

A cold knot dropped into Bradok's stomach. He'd worried that Arbuckle had some nefarious purpose in the task he'd given Bradok, and as he thought about it, he realized that Sapphire was right. Those who didn't object to the presence of the street preachers were likely to be believers or people at least sympathetic to the believers. He was compiling a list of all the believers for Mayor Arbuckle, Jon Bladehook, and all those who lined up with them.

His eyes dropped back down to the daily report he'd been preparing. That very page contained the names of every member of several families who didn't object to the preachers, where they lived, and how many were in their households.

In the wrong hands, Bradok's lists could cost lives. The thought made him sick.

"What's the matter, boy?" Sapphire said, still preening in the doorway. "You look a little green."

"It's nothing, Mother," he said, straightening his papers and making a show of going back to work.

"You didn't know," Sapphire guessed. She barked out a raucous laugh. "I should have known you didn't have the stones for this. Well, I think they will reward you, just the same."

"That will be quite enough, Mother," Bradok said, rising.

He blotted the fresh ink on the paper then folded it carefully and put it in the breast pocket of his coat. "I'm going out," he announced.

"Going to warn your new friends at the temple?" she asked, still smiling like a wolf.

"Of course not," Bradok said, brushing her out of his way. "I am going to do my duty and deliver the daily report to Mayor Arbuckle."

Bradok turned down the hallway and passed out into his grand foyer. Behind him his mother's laughter echoed down the hall, mocking him.

But Bradok did not intend to go to Mayor Arbuckle's house, as he said. Instead he wandered through Ironroot, down past the Artisans' Cavern and into the Undercity.

Down one of the many side tunnels stood a decrepit facade built of wood that covered a great hole carved in the rock. A warped, wooden sign outside read *The Butcher's Block* in faded green paint. The wooden facade hadn't been repaired in generations. It leaned away from the edge of the cavern, making it possible for Bradok to see into the tavern's interior. As seedy as the place was, the Butcher's Block had the best ale in the city, and Bradok needed something stronger than his usual beer just then.

An hour later he had nursed his third ale down to the bottom of the mug, and he still had no answers. He wanted to believe that Arbuckle's motives were innocent, but at the same time he knew he had been duped. The council was plotting against its own citizens.

Bradok turned on his stool, surveying the tavern, as if answers could be found in the hardened faces of the dwarves around him. The bar stood against the back wall of the room and was stained black and pitted with years of hard use. Oft-repaired stools stood in front of the bar in a ragged row, occupied by a bunch of patrons. In the middle of the great room sat a stone hearth over which a metal shroud and flue hung. A fire crackled cheerily, spreading a dry warmth through the cool, humid air and filling the room with the scent of burning pine.

Bradok had taken the stool at the far end, by the kitchen. A barmaid with a face as haggard as the bar leaned on her arms, attempting to draw the men's eyes away from her face by exposing ample amounts of cleavage. All of the dwarves at the bar were drinking with abandon, so none of them noticed anyway.

Bradok finished his cup and pounded on the bar. The pitted-faced barmaid brought him another drink efficiently enough, but with a disinterest bordering on disdain. Bradok took a swig, but he had drunk his fill; the liquid soured in his mouth. He pushed the cup aside and stared at the fire.

Next to Bradok sat a mountain of a dwarf. Seated on his stool, the red-bearded dwarf was easily a head taller than Bradok. He'd been pounding back ale and muttering darkly to himself since before Bradok arrived, and still he showed no sign of slowing. The dwarf wore a thick leather apron of the kind smiths wore, but his clothes and boots were far too fine for such a profession. As soon as he noticed Bradok had paused in his drinking, the big dwarf slammed his mug down, sending its contents launching out of the mug and splashing on the bar.

"What's the matter with you?" he demanded testily. "You look like a dwarf, but you sure don't drink like one."

Bradok sat up as if he'd been struck by lightning. Glaring at the red-bearded dwarf, he raised his tankard and drained it in one gulp.

"No one ever accused me of being a teetotaler," he said with a growl, slamming his mug down on the bar. "Now leave me alone."

He turned back to the bar, but the red-bearded dwarf would not be dismissed so easily. With a roar of laughter, he pounded Bradok on the back so hard that the stool beneath him cracked ominously.

"I like you!" the fellow said. "You're different than most of the rest. You're not afraid to say it like it is."

"Yes, I am," Bradok said in a low voice he intended only for himself.

"So you didn't tell off those crooks on the city council," the dwarf said matter-of-factly. "That's all right by me. Being prudent with your tongue doesn't make you a coward."

"How did you know that?" Bradok demanded, seizing the big dwarf by the arm.

"That's nothing." Red-beard shrugged. "You're that new councilman from the upper city. It stands to reason you wouldn't want to say more than is prudent on your first day."

Bradok narrowed his eyes suspiciously. "That's not what you said. You said something about . . . me disagreeing with the council," he finished. He scratched his head. What *had* the red-bearded dwarf said? He wasn't sure. His head was clouded with drink.

The big dwarf grinned sympathetically at him. "You've got an honest face," he said. "It's the kind of face you only get from hard work and fair value. I can respect a face like that."

Bradok couldn't hold the penetrating gaze of the red-bearded dwarf's crystal blue eyes. The dwarf's eyes seemed to look into the very depths of his soul, and Bradok turned away before they found the thing that all the ale in the bar couldn't drown.

"I'm not worthy of anyone's respect," Bradok mumbled, motioning to the barmaid for a fresh mug.

"Why is that?"

Bradok frowned. Why, indeed? Because what he suspected about Arbuckle and Bladehook made Bradok shudder just to think of it. He no longer doubted that the lists he had been innocently drawing up for the council were intended for some kind of drastic action against the believers. Bradok himself didn't care a whit for the believers, but it just wasn't, well—dwarflike.

"Are you a believer?" Bradok suddenly asked the big dwarf, daring to look into those probing eyes for a moment.

The big dwarf laughed. "My name is Erus," he said, raising his mug to Bradok. "And you might say I'm the ultimate believer."

"Then I suggest you leave Ironroot while you can," Bradok said glumly, staring into his mug. "Take anyone you love and get out."

If Bradok's warning fazed the big dwarf, he gave no sign.

"So you think that anti-preaching law was just the beginning?" the red-bearded dwarf said in a conspiratorial tone. "That there's more to come?"

"Something like that," Bradok said.

"What about you? Are you a believer?" Erus asked.

The question almost made Bradok laugh. Then, all of a sudden, he felt like weeping, which was all the more surprising.

"I don't know what I am," he said finally. "I'm not sure what I believe."

"That's gutless," Erus declared, taking another drink.

Bradok looked up at the dwarf sharply, intending to protest, even to challenge him to a fight, but the dwarf's accusing gaze froze the words in his throat. The dwarf's eyes appraised him for a long time, their depths hard and flat. Bradok wanted to glance away, to look anywhere else, but those eyes held him fast, as surely as a vice. Then Erus blinked and looked away, accepting the fresh tankard the barmaid had mechanically brought him.

"Let me tell you something, Bradok," he said, taking the fresh drink and tackling it with gusto. "There comes a time in everyone's life when they have to make a choice. When that happens, you can't stay on the sidelines; you have to enter the fray."

"There! You've done it again. How do you know so much about me? How do you know my name?" Bradok asked.

"It doesn't matter," Erus said, setting his cup on the bar and leaning closer to Bradok. "When the time comes that you are forced to choose which side you're going to be on, I think it would be a good idea if you found out just what you did believe." Erus reached into the front pocket of his apron and pulled out a steel coin, which he spun on the bar. "Because it's much easier to make the right choice when you know what your beliefs really are."

"Easy for you to say," Bradok said, genuinely confused.

Erus smiled. It was a warm, sincere, friendly look, full of compassion. "Right you are," he said, taking a small cloth-wrapped bundle from his apron. "Here," he said, holding it out to Bradok.

Bradok took the bundle hesitantly. From its size and shape, it might have been a pocket watch.

"Take this to the Artisans' Cavern," Erus said solemnly with the hint of a wink. "There you will find the shop of Silas, the cooper. You might also find some of the answers you seek."

He got up off his stool and slung an enormous warhammer over his shoulder. "Be warned, though," he added. "The time to choose sides is almost upon you. Don't take too long to make up your mind."

With that Erus turned and strode to the door, exiting into the dimly lit tunnels without so much as a backward glance.

Bradok scrambled to dig a few silver pieces from his coin purse before he raced to the door and out into the street. The narrow tunnel ran straight to either side for several hundred yards, but Erus was nowhere to be seen. Despate the dwarf's formidable size, he seemed to have completely vanished.

Bradok opened his hand, looking at the wrapped bundle. A soft linen cloth covered the object, held in place by a length of twine that had been tied on top. He took hold of the loose end of the twine and hesitated. A strange sense of foreboding swept over him, causing a chill to run up his spine. He couldn't help feeling that he had been handed a piece of some great and terrible destiny, and he wondered if he dared accept his fate.

After a moment, however, his natural curiosity got the better of him, and he tugged on the twine, pulling the knot free. Carefully, he removed the cloth, revealing an exquisite brass device. It looked like an oversized pocket watch with fine etching covering its every surface. Bradok had never seen etching so fine; it seemed impossibly small yet perfectly straight, as if done by the most unwavering of hands. The pattern looked basic at first glance, but as he examined it closely, Bradok saw that it wound over and around itself, like a ball of knotted string.

In the exact center of the top, a purple gem had been set. It was cut to be flat on top, with flat sides around it and, although Bradok had years of experience with every kind of gem known to dwarf, it was a stone he'd never encountered before.

As he turned the device over in his hand, Bradok spotted a small hinge, indicating that the top of the object was covered by a door of some kind. Opposite the hinge, he found a small, hidden clasp. When he pressed it, however, the lid didn't move. He tried prying at it with his fingernails, but it didn't budge.

Then something suddenly caught his eye. The purple stone gave off a soft glow. Fascinated, he held it up to his eye. The light from the stone seemed to reflect on certain parts of the etched surface of the top, causing some of the lines to glow.

To Bradok's great astonishment, they formed words across the object's face, tiny yet readable words.

"A person's destination depends more on his choices than his direction," Bradok read. Still puzzling over the strange saying, he slipped the device into his pocket.

He didn't know why, but for some reason the brass device suddenly seemed more urgent than anything Arbuckle might be plotting. "I guess I'd better find this Silas fellow," he said to himself.

******

Undercity, as its name implied, had been built below Ironroot proper. To keep from undermining the stability of the upper caverns, Undercity had been built down and away, gradually curving into a descending spiral. To reach the Artisans' Cavern, Bradok had to wind his way back up, almost to Ironroot cavern, then along a side passage for almost a mile.

The connecting tunnel consisted of two parts. Along the left side ran a raised walkway, set aside solely for foot traffic. The rest of the wide tunnel contained a divided street set with rails. Metal carts pulled by donkeys moved goods in and out between a loading dock on the Ironroot side and the artisans' shops below. The carts had been put in as a security measure to control what actually passed into the Artisans' Cavern. Most of Ironroot's artisans worked with steel in one form or another, making the cavern a tempting target for thieves.

Bradok watched, fascinated as a donkey pulled a row of three cars up toward the loading dock. The cars were filled with wrapped bundles, and they jumped and jostled each other as they made their way along the tunnel. A train of five cars passed, going the other way, rattling and clanking like armor dropped down a stone stairway. Since the Artisans' Cavern had been built slightly lower than Ironroot proper, the carts could return under the power of gravity, meaning they moved faster and in greater numbers.

Unlike Ironroot cavern, the Artisans' Cavern was not natural; it had been painstakingly carved out and provided with multiple ventilation shafts that connected to the surface.

Because of the smoke that perpetually hung over the cavern, the tunnels didn't have long strings of lanterns for light as Ironroot proper did. The ceiling of the cavern had been built like an enormous chimney, designed to funnel the smoke of the many fires up and out. By law, all chimneys had to be higher than the top of the Ironroot tunnel, lest any smoke get passed to the city above. That left a layer of cleaner air, close to the ground where glow lanterns on short poles were hung. Because of the carts and the system of rails, elevated walkways continued out from the tunnel, keeping pedestrians above the clattering carts. Each of the walkways was brightly lit with glow lanterns every few feet, giving the impression of ghostly lanes hovering above the dark floor.

Bradok exited the tunnel and went left at the first fork he came to. He didn't know exactly where Silas the cooper might be found, but he knew that most woodworkers would be clustered together down one of the left-hand passages.

A few inquires directed him to a freestanding wooden structure in the corner of one of the deeper side passages. He would have known it even if he hadn't asked, as it had an enormous barrel for a doorway and a crowd of people milling around it.

Bradok hesitated for a moment. He was a public figure, and it probably wouldn't be good to get mixed up in whatever had drawn the crowd to Silas's shop. Still, the memory of Erus's words, telling him that Silas might have the answers he sought, rang in Bradok's mind.

The cool, smoky air of the cavern swirled around Bradok as he struggled with indecision. Finally, taking a deep breath, which he blew out with a growl, he set off toward the crowd. When he reached them, he saw that they weren't doing anything in particular; they were just standing idly on the walkway, trying to get a look at the simple wooden building.

"What's all this," Bradok asked a scruffy, soot-covered dwarf.

"When you find out, you tell me." The fellow chuckled. "Some say the cooper has gone mad; others say he's had a vision," he said. "Either way, it's the darndest thing you ever saw."

"What is?" Bradok asked, craning his neck to look over the crowd.

"That," the scruffy dwarf said.

As Bradok followed the dwarf's pointing finger, his jaw dropped open. He hadn't noticed before because he'd been focused on the crowd, but one side of the building had been completely torn down. Thrusting out from the space where the wall should have been was a huge framework of wood that looked for all the world like the skeleton of some enormous creature. The entire apparatus ended in a long wooden spar that stuck straight out into the cavern.

Bradok had never seen an ocean, but he knew about large bodies of water. Likewise he knew what that was without ever having actually seen one. There, more than a mile beneath the surface, in the heart of a mountain, Silas the cooper was building a boat.

CHAPTER 5
The Cooper and the Council

Bradok had to push his way bodily through the crowd until, at last, he found himself in front of the curved shop door. A sign to one side read *Silas & Son, Coopers*.

Not really knowing what else to do, Bradok put out his hand and rapped smartly on the door.

A moment later it opened.

In the opening beyond stood someone who could not be Silas or his son. Instead a human appeared, tall, like all members of his race, and pudgy, wearing a smock. Dust and wood shavings covered his clothes, hair, and apron, making it impossible for Bradok to determine the man's age or appearance. Humans were not terribly unusual in Ironroot, but to see one so obviously apprenticed to a dwarf craftsman was additional cause for curiosity.

"May I help you," the human said in a mild voice.

"I'm looking for Silas," Bradok said.

The human's face turned sour. "Master Silas is far too busy to entertain visitors," he said grumpily. "If you just want to gawk, you can stay out here with this lot." He nodded in the direction of the milling crowd.

He began to close the door, but Bradok shoved his foot into the jamb to keep it from closing.

"It's really rather important," he said.

The human appraised Bradok for a moment, looking him up and down with his dust-colored eyes, then stepped back from the doorway. "Then you'd better come in, Mister . . ."

"Axeblade, Bradok Axeblade."

The human nodded, shutting the door behind Bradok. "I am Perin," he said, indicating himself, though Bradok didn't know if that was his family name or his given. "I am the first assistant to Master Silas. If you will follow me, please."

Perin turned and opened a door just off the entryway. Steam and the smell of washed wood and fire billowed through the opening as the two passed into the workshop. A small forge had been built on one side, and two young dwarves were pumping the bellows while a smith heated a long, curved iron band for pounding on a nearby anvil. Along the opposite wall were workbenches where a burly dwarf shaped and planed wooden slats smooth. Next to the forge stood the steaming box where the slats would be cooked to make them flexible enough to bend.

Bradok took it all in with a single glance. Like most dwarven shops, the cooper's operation was neat and well ordered.

The only unusual thing was the giant boat. Its curved wooden ribs ran all the way up to the ceiling, and Bradok could see why the side wall of the shop had been torn out: The boat took up the entire length of the shop and then some.

"What in the undermountain is this about?" Bradok squawked once he'd gotten over his astonishment.

"I assumed that is why you were here, Mister Axeblade," Perin said in an even voice.

Just then a squat, solid-looking dwarf in a clean apron came around the back end of the boat. He had bristly brown hair and a beard that had been braided and thrust under his apron for safekeeping. His eyes were blue, and he had a long, beaklike nose.

"Who have we here?" he said to Perin.

Bradok stuck out his arm before the human could answer. "Bradok Axeblade," he said. "I assume you are Silas?"

"Silas Weatherstone," the dwarf said, clasping his arm firmly. "Welcome to my shop." He gestured around at the work stations that weren't obscured by the half-completed ship. "Are you here from the council in some official capacity?"

That last bit caught Bradok unawares. As far as he knew, he'd never met Silas nor done any business with him. How did he recognize him as a council member?

"Gossip gets around quickly in the Artisans' Cavern," Silas said with a smile. "Everyone's heard of Ironroot's new councilman."

"Harrumph," Bradok replied, not very sensibly. "No, I'm not here on behalf of the council." He reached into his pocket and pulled out the brass device. "Someone told me you might know what this is?"

Silas took the engraved device, turning it over in his hands. He pressed the hidden catch, but the lid of the device refused to open for him as well. "I've never seen anything like it," he said, bending close to examine the engraving. "It's exquisite, though."

Looking up, Silas handed the device back to Bradok. "I'm sorry," he said. "It might be a watch with a stuck lid or one of a hundred other things. I just don't know. Who told you I would know anything about it?"

"Who? Oh, that doesn't matter." Somewhat disappointed, Bradok took the device and returned it to his pocket.

"I noticed the inscription," Silas said. "There's something very familiar about it. I've heard something like that before." A strange look passed over the cooper's face, and he smiled. "I think, whatever it is, it might be very important, Bradok," he said. "Be sure to keep it safe until you figure it out."

"Thank you anyway," Bradok said, frustrated. "So tell me," he went on, waving at the partially completed ship, "what is this all about?"

Silas smiled and led Bradok over to the side of the land-locked vessel. "Isn't she beautiful?" he said, gesturing grandly. "There isn't anything like her anywhere."

"What is it, uh, she?" Bradok corrected himself.

"It's a ship, of course," Silas replied, as if building a ship in the middle of a mountain were the most natural thing in the world.

"I can see that," Bradok said. "But why are you building it here?"

"I believe they call it senility," a sarcastic voice cut in.

Bradok turned to find a young, well-dressed dwarf coming up behind them. He had a short beard, like Bradok's, only light blond, and he had golden eyes. His clothes were of the finest cut and the latest fashion, and the dwarf wore them well. He had a handsome face, and though his smile bore mockery, there was just enough mischief in it to beg forgiveness.

"This is my son, Chisul," Silas said, his eyes twinkling. "He believes me to be mad."

"Why is that?" Bradok asked with a smile.

"You mean you haven't heard the story?" Chisul interjected, a note of awe in his voice. He looked at his father, shaking his head, as if the cooper had committed some personal offense.

"Sit down, then, stranger," Chisul said. "And I'll tell you the most fanciful tale you ever heard. It all started one day when my father was down in the deep caves looking for good polishing stones—"

"Give it a rest, Chisul," Silas said in a weary, admonishing tone.

"Aw, Dad," Chisul said with mock sincerity. "If there's someone in the city who hasn't heard your tale of magic and mystery, then I am duty-bound to tell them."

At that, Silas seemed to resign himself, and Chisul launched into the story.

"You see, when my dad was down in the deep tunnels

looking for polishing stones, he thinks he hears this voice telling him to go lower. So he does, going down and down, deeper than he's ever been. And when he gets to the very bottom, the voice tells him that he's been called to perform a great work. And what do you suppose that is?"

Chisul winked conspiratorially at Bradok then swept his arm upward, indicating the ship. "Why to build this whopper of a vessel, of course! He comes back up from the deep tunnels covered in rubble and dirt, carrying a flat stone with the design of this boat carved on it. Says that it just appeared in the wall, right in front of him."

"So . . . the voice told your dad to perform a great work and the design showed him to build this boat," Bradok said, in his best unamused voice. He decided that he rather disliked Silas's son.

"The voice told him he had to build this boat," Chisul said cheerfully, "or everyone he cared about would die."

Bradok suddenly remembered another dwarf who had encountered a godly voice: Argus Deephammer. Then there was the dwarf with the red-painted sign warning of repentance and doom. And the strange red-bearded one who called himself Erus who had given him the mysterious engraved device, warning him to choose sides.

He scratched his head, thinking. So many dwarves seemed to be saying the same thing, that some great disaster was coming and the people of Ironroot had to choose the path of salvation.

"So why are you here?" Chisul asked, breaking into Bradok's thoughts. "Reorx send you here too?"

"What are you talking about?" Bradok demanded.

Chisul barked a short, derisive laugh. "Ever since Dad started building this thing, they've been coming around. Religious nuts who claim they've heard voices, like Dad, or seen visions, or been sent here by mysterious strangers that always turn out to be Reorx in disguise."

Bradok felt the hairs on his neck stand up. He hadn't given much thought to Erus's resemblance to Reorx, but since Chisul brought it up, Erus did uncannily evoke the god of the dwarves.

"So what happens when you finish it, uh, her . . . the boat? What are you supposed to do then?" Bradok asked, turning to Silas.

Silas smiled and shrugged sheepishly. "Reorx didn't say." He put his hand on one of the naked ribs and stroked it reverently. "My job is to finish her. What happens after that is out of my hands."

Bradok opened his mouth to ask another question, but a sudden disturbance erupted outside. He could hear raised voices and the sounds of a scuffle. With unexpected suddenness, the front door to the shop broke inward, smashed with some heavy object. A moment later five armed members of the city guard were standing in Silas's workshop.

"What is the meaning of this?" Bradok demanded.

The leader of the guards recognized him after a moment, a surprised look passing over his countenance.

"I'm sorry, Councilman, but I have my orders." He turned to Silas. "Silas Weatherstone, I'm directed by the city council to place you under arrest. Please come with me."

Bradok's mind raced. How could Mayor Arbuckle have heard about Silas so quickly?

"Sapphire," he whispered.

She must have gone to Arbuckle when Bradok didn't return home and warned him that her son might expose his plans. Arbuckle hadn't taken any chances; he must have had Bradok followed and ordered the arrest of Silas.

"Of course I will come with you, Guardsman," Silas said, putting a restraining hand on Chisul. He took off his apron and handed it to his son then turned to the lone human. "If anyone comes to help with the boat while I'm gone, Perin, please let them in and continue with the work," he said.

Perin nodded forlornly but said nothing.

Silas bade Chisul good-bye. The guardsmen had formed up around Silas, as if they expected him to attempt to make a run for it. But Silas walked easily behind the guard captain, with his head held high, trying neither to outpace him nor fall behind.

Bradok followed to the door and watched as the soldiers marched out of sight. He wanted to do something to help, but if Arbuckle were behind Silas's arrest, there wasn't much he could do at the moment. He put his hand in his pocket and felt the etched metal of Erus's strange device. Silas hadn't been any help in determining what it was. On impulse, Bradok pulled it out of his pocket. The tiny words that appeared from the intricate etching were still plainly visible in the soft glow given off by the purple gem.

A person's destination depends more on his choices than his direction.

Bradok looked off, up the passage where the soldiers had taken Silas. The whole council might be against him, but he resolved to follow after Silas and speak on the cooper's behalf; that, at least, was a choice he could make.

He slipped the device back into his pocket and started off through the milling crowd. As he made his way along the tunnel that led back to the main cavern, Bradok tried to come up with a plan, but he had no idea what he would say to the council. Arbuckle's course seemed set, and Bradok doubted he had any power to change it. Still, maybe he could bribe Arbuckle or some of the councilors to obtain Silas's freedom. Fortunately he had plenty of money and other goods to bribe the council with.

When Bradok emerged from the side tunnel into Iron-root proper, he could tell something was sorely amiss. An eerie stillness hung over the cavern. Nobody was strolling among the grass and flowers of the central square, and the sidewalks were conspicuously empty. At each street corner, however, a city guardsman stood with hammer and shield at the ready.

"Halt," the nearest one called, catching sight of Bradok.

"What's this all about?" Bradok demanded as the guard approached him.

"The council has enacted a curfew," the guard said. "No one is permitted on the streets in the upper city after ten."

"I'm Bradok Axeblade and I'm a member of the city council," Bradok countered. "I wasn't informed of this. When did the council meet to decide this new curfew?"

"It is my understanding that they are meeting now, Councilman," the guard said. "They sent word to all they could find. I'm sure they'll be glad to see you."

Bradok wasn't so sure. "Thank you," he said as the guard turned to resume his post.

Bradok turned toward the upper end of the cavern. The guards seemed to be posted at the entrances to the side tunnels, so he wasn't challenged again, though several of the guards looked at him uncertainly as he passed by.

The main cavern of Ironroot followed a natural curve, making it impossible for Bradok to see city hall until he reached the central square. Before he reached the square, he heard a low, rumbling noise. When he came around the facade of the dry goods store, he immediately knew why—city hall had been besieged.

The building itself stood at the top of a raised platform of stone with a brick courtyard in front. All around the base of the stairs gathered a mob of some twenty or thirty dwarves. Among the crowd, Bradok occasionally caught the glimpse of a weapon. At that sight, Bradok understood the curfew; it was intended to keep the mob from growing and the protest from spreading.

A dozen armed guardsmen stood atop the steps leading up to the main entrance, shoulder to shoulder, with their hands on their weapons. Even from more than a block away, Bradok could feel the tension in the air. All it would take would be one spark, one ill-chosen word or deed, and violence would erupt.

Bradok took a deep breath and pressed on. To reach the council building, he would have to pass through the angry crowd. No one seemed to notice when at first he began pressing his way to the front. He had almost broken free of the mob when a big, burly dwarf with squinty eyes and a bulbous round nose stepped squarely in front of him. He wore the leathers of a blacksmith and carried a broad, heavy warhammer as if he'd held it all his life.

"You're that new councilman, Braden something-or-other?" he said in a voice reminiscent of a stone being dragged over a sand-strewn floor.

"Uh," Bradok said, not sure he should answer that.

"Why is the council arresting people all of a sudden?" the dwarf demanded in an uncomfortably loud voice. "Did they say 'Reorx bless you' when someone sneezed? Or maybe they've got the symbol of Paladine embroidered on their underwear?"

"I don't know," Bradok said, conscious of the eyes of many nearby dwarves turning to him. "I just got here."

"It's that new councilman," someone in the crowd yelled.

"He's the one behind that street-preacher law," someone else called.

Bradok heard the stone before he saw it. Over the rumble of the mob came the whistling noise of air moving against an uneven surface. Before he could move, a stone struck him on the cheek. Bradok stifled a curse and clasped his hand to his bleeding face.

From behind him, Bradok heard the guards on the stairs come clattering down. Time seemed to freeze in that moment. But Bradok knew with exquisite clarity what was about to happen.

"Stop!" Bradok shouted commandingly, putting out a blocking hand to the oncoming guards. "If I need your help, I'll call," he said. "Till then, stay at your posts."

The words seemed to hang in the air a long time, like smoke in an unvented room. Finally, all citizens and guardsmen seemed to take a breath at once. The soldiers loosened their grips on their weapons and backed up the stairs, never taking their eyes off the crowd.

Bradok looked back at the burly smith. "I don't know what has happened here or why anyone has been arrested," he said through clenched teeth. "But I intend to find out."

"What good does that do us?" the smith asked.

Bradok put his hand on the man's shoulder and looked him in the eye.

"I give you my word," he said earnestly, "that I will find out and I will come back out here and tell you everything. Is that good enough?"

The tension still lingered in the air as Bradok's words died away. Finally the smith spoke. "I'll tell you what's happened here," he said in his gravelly voice. "The council's arresting citizens whose only crime is trying to remind us of our values, of the old ways."

A murmur of assent came from the crowd.

"Now I don't know you, mister new councilman," the smith said, "but I know that we won't stand for this persecution." The smith hefted his hammer off his shoulder and pointed it at city hall. "Now you go in there, and you tell them cowards that they can't go around arresting people at their own will and pleasure. You tell them we won't stand for it." His coal black eyes narrowed as he leaned in so Bradok would have no trouble hearing his next words. "You tell them there'll be blood if they keep this up."

The smith reached out one burly hand and shoved Bradok hard. Bradok had seen it coming, but the force of the smith's arm was not to be resisted and he staggered back.

"You tell them that, from me," he said, pounding his chest, "Kellik Felhammer."

Bradok recognized the name. Though he'd never met the dwarf, he bought all the brass he used for jewelry from the Felhammer Smithy.

"I'll tell them," he promised then turned and grimly climbed the steps up to the gates of city hall. The guards on the steps parted as he passed then closed ranks behind him.

Inside the building, scribes and clerks were running everywhere, carrying sheaves of paper and rolls of parchment. Discarded notes and what appeared to be pages torn from books littered the hallways. At every intersection, two city guardsmen stood with javelins in hand, their eyes watching for any menace.

At the corner of the main hall, Bradok turned to the back hallway reserved for councilmen.

"There you are, lad." Much's voice slammed into him with a near physical force. Rough hands grabbed him and pulled him along the corridor. "When I couldn't find you at the tavern, I feared for you, boy, and that's a fact."

Much paused, straightening Bradok's coat and brushing bits of dust from the rich fabric.

"Things have gone a bit 'round the bend here," he said with a nervous laugh. "How about that Arbuckle? He used that list of believers you made to round up what he's calling 'religious troublemakers.' "

"How dare he!" Bradok responded, though he was hardly shocked to have his suspicions confirmed.

"Oh, he dares, he dares," said Much, all too lightly for Bradok's taste.

"How does he think he'll get away with it?" Bradok demanded.

"Well, that's why he's doing it all at once, tonight," Much explained. "If they're all in jail by morning, he can tell the people it's all over. Only a few will protest at that point."

Bradok thought of the mob out front. "There's more than a few gathering outside already," he said.

"You don't understand the kind of power he wields," Much said, looking around to make sure they weren't overheard. "Most of the council is with him—"

"Are you with him?" Bradok said, seizing Much's arm in a vicelike grip.

"Don't be getting ideas," Much said, a deadly serious note in his voice. "The peace of Ironroot stands on a blade's edge, and anything could set it off. Just keep your head down in there. You can try to rein in some of the more enthusiastic members of the council, but don't make a target out of yourself. If they think you're against them, they'll turn on you like a pack of wild dogs."

Bradok wanted to protest, but something in his gut told him Much had the right of it. He'd have to just bide his time until he could figure out how to tamp it down and help Silas. Much led him around the outer walkway to where their tables stood side by side.

The council chamber was in an uproar. All around the room, councilmen were yelling to be heard while Mayor Arbuckle pounded his gavel on the lectern for order. In the galleries above, a few citizens who had political pull and others who had eluded the curfew filled the seats. They shouted to one another and to the councilmen below, some of them leaning precariously over the carved railings in an effort to have their opinions heard. In the center of the chamber, a lone dwarf stood, silent and unbent against the cacophony.

With a shock, Bradok recognized him. It was Argus Deephammer.

"Silence, I say!" Arbuckle shouted several times before, finally, the voices in the chamber died away. "You've been charged with disturbing the peace," he addressed Argus Deephammer. "Your fearmongering and slander against this council are directly responsible for rioting in the streets. Do you deny it?"

"I do," the dwarf said with stubborn fierceness. "Don't you see what's going on around you? You're losing control of everything. Reorx has abandoned you and left you to your own devices. Now you see that you cannot stand without the aid of your god. You must repent for your godless ways, or we are all lost."

"I'll not tolerate such rock-headed idiocy," Arbuckle roared, slamming the gavel down for emphasis. "The gullible people of this city have been whipped up into a religious mania by you and others like you. You are an agitator and a public menace, and I'll not have anyone running around loose in the streets inciting violence." He pounded the gavel down again.

"It is the order of this council that you be bound in Darklock Prison until such time that you come to your senses and deny your contentious religious fantasies. I don't care if you stay there till the mountains fall."

"Then I won't be there long," Argus spat. "You have only a little time left to you, Arbuckle; then you and all those who deny the gods will suffer their wrath."

"Don't tout your adolescent fantasies here," Bladehook piped up. "We have taken your confederates. Soon there won't be anyone making trouble in Ironroot so you can blame it on nonexistent gods."

"I have no confederates," Argus shot back.

"Don't deny it," Bladehook said, his face contorting into a mask of hate. "We know about your minions running around the streets with signs and folks like your friend the cooper, who's building a crazy boat in the Artisans' Cavern."

At this a rumble of laughter ran throughout the chamber. Bradok was watching Argus's face, and he could have sworn he saw a smile flit across the dwarf's face.

"Ah, at least someone is listening," Argus said softly. "The cooper is wiser than I."

"Don't praise him too much," Bladehook said with a sneer. "As soon as we've dealt with you, I'm ordering that abomination burned."

A murmur of agreement ran around the council chamber, and two guardsmen came forward and led the dwarf out.

CHAPTER 6

Civil Unrest

After Argus had been escorted out, Arbuckle ordered the gallery cleared and the doors shut.

"We have before us a desperate situation," he proclaimed to the assembled council. "These religious zealots are driving a wedge through our community. They refuse to see that their fathers and grandfathers were fooled, taken in by the so-called priests. They stubbornly cling to the old ways, ways that were put in place to keep us under the thumb of the church."

Angry mutters rose from the council.

"Brothers," Arbuckle said, standing up behind the lectern and striking what he clearly thought was a majestic pose. "We are at a crossroads. We must decide, here, now, tonight, what the fate of Ironroot will be."

"What do you mean, Arbuckle?" a dwarf with a bushy beard asked with a puzzled expression. "I thought you have always said to be patient, to wait for the old beliefs to simply die out."

"There is not time for that anymore," Jon Bladehook scoffed, standing up at his table. "These zealots, these street preachers, they're all in league. Isn't it interesting how they all have the same message, how they all say the same words?

I tell you, they've long been conspiring against us, against Ironroot itself!"

Several dwarves cheered.

"Friends," Bladehook yelled, holding up his hand for quiet. "Councilmen, I have learned the very day when the believers plan to move against us. It is in one week's time. According to my source, the street preachers say that exactly one week from today, the gods will pour out their wrath on Ironroot. That will be the day of big trouble for us or them. It's our choice."

Choice, thought Bradok.

"Preposterous," someone called.

"Of course, you and I both know that no such thing can happen," Bladehook said. "There are no gods to anger in the first place."

"Then why don't we just wait?" the scruffy-bearded dwarf asked. "When nothing happens in a week, we can show these fakers for what they are. That'll be the end of the believers."

"That would just show our weakness," Arbuckle said. "That's just what these priests and zealots want, for us to cower and wait."

Bradok couldn't believe what he was hearing. He knew both Argus and Silas, and neither of them seemed to be part of any grand scheme to overthrow Ironroot. Both had impressed him as honest and sincere men. He wondered for the first time how they could believe so fervently in a god when all reason seemed to deny it?

What did they know that he didn't?

He reached into his pocket and pulled out the polished brass device Erus had given him. He couldn't read the inscription without holding it close, but he didn't have to read it. He knew what it said.

A person's destination depends more on his choices than his direction.

"It's clear that Argus and his fellow agitators are all in league," Mayor Arbuckle said, interrupting Bradok's thoughts.

"We don't know what they're planning, we don't know what will happen one week from today, but they won't be able to carry out their treachery if they are in prison."

"What if the day comes and goes and nothing happens but the believers still believe?" Bradok asked.

"That's a good question," the bushy-bearded dwarf said. "What are you going to do then?"

"Well," Bladehook said, a look of sheer delight on his face. "If they are that crazy, that they refuse to acknowledge their folly, I suggest we execute a few of them. That should bring the others in line. Enough of this religious mania. Enough of the believers!"

"That's a monstrous suggestion," someone called from off to Bradok's right.

"We can't kill our own people," Bushy-beard said.

"What's the alternative?" Bladehook said. "Let the priests continue to stir up the people and gain power? Allow these lunatic believers to continue to live among us and spread their fearmongering and poison to our children?" He looked around the circle slowly, as if daring anyone to challenge him.

"Isn't our children's future, indeed the future of our race, worth shedding blood for? And who will care in the long run that some fools had to die to make our society better? Are their pitiful lives worth sacrificing our future?"

A long silence followed Bladehook's grim statement, and his last words seemed to hang in the air.

"You see that I am right," Bladehook said coaxingly at last. "I take no joy in this," he went on. "But I say we give the believers until the day after the supposed destruction of Ironroot to recant their foolish behavior and rejoin the ranks of civilization."

Another long silence hung in the air, with many staring at their shoes, others nodding solemnly.

"So be it," Arbuckle said at last. "Until one week from today. After that, any that refuse to see reason will be put to death." The mayor looked around the room, the gold caps on his mustache twitching, then rapped on the lectern with the gavel. "All in favor?" he said.

"Stop," someone yelled, shattering the silence of the room. With amazement, Bradok realized it was, once again, his voice. Nobody else dared oppose the measure. "Stop this!"

All eyes in the chamber turned to look at him.

"Can't you see Argus is a good, honest man? He is speaking the truth, at least from his own point of view," he said, walking out from behind his table. "I've only been in this chamber one week, and I've already seen everything he's accused us of: greed, graft, and outright theft. Aye, there is truth in what he says."

At that there were cries of astonishment and calls for Bradok to cease speaking.

"No, I must say this: I've seen dwarves care more about making money they don't need than they do about helping those who are in need. I've seen business conducted without honor, where every contracted word was twisted for the maker's advantage." Bradok swept his eyes around the chamber, half accusatory and half hopeful. His eyes lit on Much, who quickly glanced away. "And now it's come to this," he continued. "Now we're standing here, blaming an innocent dwarf for the crime of recognizing our sins, and preparing to kill those many others whose only crime is believing him? Have we really sunk so low?

"And is it possible, I have to ask myself," he added in a soft voice, "that he and the other believers are right, and that something is about to happen, something ominous, and that Reorx has done a few of us the favor of warning us of impending doom?"

"Enough!" Bladehook said, pointing furiously at him. "You've gone too far, Axeblade. You're siding with the believers now—"

"No, I'm not, if you'll just—"

"I call the vote!" Mayor Arbuckle interrupted, slamming down his gavel. "The council needs to rule on my proposed measure."

More than two-thirds of the hands went up. Bradok, looking around, took solace in the fact that neither Much nor the bushy-bearded dwarf voted aye. But neither spoke up to defend him either.

"Let the scribes write up the decree," Arbuckle said once he had gaveled the measure passed. "I don't want any of the believers to be caught unawares. Fair warning to all is fair."

"If there's no other business," Bladehook said, turning away wearily. "It's late and I'm going home to my bed."

"I have something to say," Bradok said, standing rooted to the spot. "You have all heard my views. I cannot condone this chamber's decision. While I'm not a believer myself, I have always felt that if other dwarves wish to believe in Reorx or not, that was none of my business. We supposedly live in a free society, one of laws and justice. Well, how can it be truly free if dwarves aren't free to believe anything they wish?"

"I'm sorry, son," Mayor Arbuckle said, coming up behind him and putting a hand on his shoulder, speaking in a tone that showed genuine feeling. "You're just too young to understand what's at stake here. We have to protect Ironroot for the greater good."

Bradok stared at him then pointedly removed the mayor's hand from his shoulder. "I understand that you see things that way," he said. "That's why I can no longer serve on this council."

An astonished gasp issued from the councilmen. It was a great privilege to serve on the council, and more than two hundred years had passed since any dwarf had renounced his seat.

"I wish you well," Bradok said wearily; he turned, descended the stairs behind his seat, and left the chamber.

The mob was still outside when Bradok pushed open the heavy doors of city hall. The number of guardsmen had more than doubled.

Taking a deep breath, he walked slowly down the steps and pushed his way right into the center of the mob. A rough hand descended on Bradok's shoulder, and he was jerked around to stare into the bulb-nosed face of the impassioned Kellik Felhammer.

"I take it," he said in his gravelly voice, his eyes taking in Bradok's sad face, "that things didn't go well in there?"

Bradok gripped the burly smith's arm, holding him fast even though the other tried to break free, not knowing what to say.

"They've gone mad," he managed at gasp at last. "Arbuckle and Bladehook have got them convinced that Argus and Silas and the street preachers are mixed up in some kind of plot to overthrow Ironroot and bring it under the religious rule of the priests."

"That's ridiculous!" Kellik said, his face at first disbelieving, then darkening into a scowl.

"It gets worse," Bradok said as others close by leaned in to hear. "According to some believers, Ironroot has a week to repent before Reorx will destroy the place. When . . . if that doesn't happen," he corrected himself, "the council has declared that all believers must give up their faith or be executed as enemies of the city."

Kellik swore as Bradok let him go and an angry muttering spread through the crowd. Bradok's message was passed along.

"We'll fight them," Kellik said, turning to face the crowd and raising his voice to be heard by all. "We won't let those self-important peacocks rule us by their whims. They're our representatives, they answer to us, and we're going to remind them of that fact." He thrust his hammer into the air for emphasis.

"Wait," Bradok said, lowering his voice lest he draw the attention of the guard on the city hall steps. "There are too many guardsmen here, and there are more inside. Don't act recklessly. You'll just get yourselves killed for no reason."

Kellik fixed his eyes on Bradok, his look both disappointed and challenging. "If we let them get away with this now," he said, "there'll be no stopping them. They'll rule this city with an iron fist. We have to strike now while we have the chance of surprise."

Bradok opened his mouth to argue, but he stopped when he heard his name called out by someone in the throng.

"There you are," Much said. A moment later the dwarf pushed himself through the mob. His face shone with sweat and his beard had begun to come unbraided, but he wore a look of supreme relief.

"I'm worried for you, lad, I surely am," he said, clasping Bradok by the shoulders. "What you did in there was brave . . . stupid, but brave. Now you're in a pickle, I bet."

"What did he do?" Kellik asked, clearly unimpressed by Much's praise.

"Oh, not much," Much said. "He just stood up to them, the whole entire city council. Told them what he thought of their plan and it was a damn eloquent speech too. Then he resigned."

The smith gave Bradok an appraising look then smiled. "You got stones, boy. I never would have guessed. You're the perfect person to lead us against the council."

"No," Bradok said. "A war here and now will only give the council an excuse to carry out its sentence one week early." He looked the big smith in the eyes. "Tell me, are you a believer?"

Kellik nodded.

"Trust me," Bradok said to Kellik as Much listened. "If you have loved ones, get them quickly and meet me at the shop of Silas the cooper in the Artisans' Cavern. Pass the word to any other believers," Bradok said. "But do it quickly, we may not have much time."

With that Bradok turned and pressed through the crowd to the open space beyond. Much shook Kellik's hand solemnly and hurried to follow.

Bradok's pace was measured, neither rushed nor leisurely, but purposeful. The cavern below city hall stood mostly empty, save for a few nervous dwarves, just getting the courage to emerge from their homes and shops since the guardsmen were gone.

Bradok's determined stride brought him to his home in less than five minutes. Much grabbed his arm before he entered.

"What are you planning, lad?" Much demanded.

"I'm going to the cooper's shop to finish what he started," Bradok said.

"Finish that cockamamie ship?" Much said, his handlebar mustache bending down as he frowned. "Don't tell me that now you believe he heard some god telling him to build it?"

Bradok sighed and looked back down the cavern toward city hall.

"I don't know what I believe," he said. "But I know this: If Arbuckle and Bladehook are right, then I prefer to be wrong."

"I hear you there," Much said, nodding.

"This is something I have decided to do, Much," Bradok said. "You're welcome to come with me, but I'll understand if you don't."

Much released Bradok's arm and stepped back onto the walk. He looked Bradok up and down and put out his arm. Bradok clasped it firmly.

"If this is good-bye, lad, I have to say it's been a pleasure knowing you."

"Likewise, old man," Bradok said. Then he turned and vaulted up the steps to the front door.

Moments later he threw an old suit of traveling clothes

and a heavy cloak into a worn leather pack with battered silver buckles. In his younger days, Bradok had traveled to faraway cities to complete his training as a master jeweler, and he still had his old travel kit. He unrolled the kit and laid the cloth out, quickly filling its many pockets with things he would need: a straight razor, folding knife, small stick of wax, and other sundries. When he finished, he rolled the kit up and tied it closed.

Satisfied that he had everything he needed, he changed out of his dress boots into a more comfortable and well-worn pair. His next stop was his study, where he grabbed a pen and a bottle of expensive black ink. His journal and a book on the finer points of the jeweler's craft went into his pack next.

Finally, Bradok headed down to his workshop on the ground floor. He had just stepped off the last stair and into the foyer when he heard a grating voice behind him.

"Just where do you think you are going?"

Sapphire.

"I'm leaving, Mother," he said with a sigh, looking back up to the balcony where she stood, watching him. "I think for good."

"Nonsense," she said. "Why would you do that?"

"The council plans to kill the believers in one week if they do not renounce their faith," he said. "I rather doubt many of them will, so I've renounced my council seat and I'm leaving this town. I'll not be a party to the murder of good, honest dwarves."

"What murder?" Sapphire demanded, her voice rising to a screech. "Those believers have gotten out of hand. They are everywhere now, preaching doom and gloom. They have brought this on themselves. It's about time the council did something about them."

"You wouldn't understand, Mother," Bradok said. "They're not monsters; they're people, dwarves like you and me."

"They're religious fools who don't deserve the indulgence we have granted their foolishness," Sapphire screamed.

Bradok paid his mother no heed. He turned his back and passed down the narrow hallway that separated the house from his workshop. After unbolting the door, he lit an oil lamp and hung it on a hook that dropped down on a chain from the ceiling. The light revealed a small, neat room with workbenches, rows of tools on hooks, bins of metal rod stock, and a large iron safe with an elaborate lock in its center.

He crossed the room to one of the workbenches and picked up the rolled leather kit that held his jeweler's tools, slipping them into his pack. From his belt, he withdrew a ring of keys and, selecting a small, rather plain-looking one, stepped to the safe. Ignoring the enormous lock, Bradok moved the brass plate with the name of the safe maker to one side, revealing a small keyhole. He quickly unlocked the safe and pulled open the heavy door.

The ornate lock was a trap, of course, designed to foil unwary thieves.

Inside the safe were stacks of velvet-lined cases holding his best work. Bins of raw jewels filled a shelf, along with several thick folios that detailed Bradok's business holdings.

Bradok selected a few of the velvet cases and moved them to a nearby workbench; then he withdrew the safe's only other item: a gilded sword. Leaving the safe standing open, he clipped the sword to his belt, enjoying the sudden weight of the weapon. With a deft move, he pulled it from its scabbard and held it up in the lantern light. The sword shone brilliantly. The blade was broad and beveled, with a concave rill running along its center. The crosspiece had been shaped to resemble dwarven hammers and was etched with elaborate knots, each etching done over in gold. Black leather, stained by years of sweat and oil, covered the hilt, giving it a sure grip. On the pommel sat a ruby the size of a quail's egg.

His father had given him the sword on his twentieth

birthday and Bradok had treasured it ever since. With a practiced flourish, Bradok slipped the blade back into the scabbard and slid it home with a click. His father had told him the sword was magical, made by some elf wizard-smith, but Bradok had never found any proof of that. The magic in the blade had always been the feeling of the father who had given it to him. It was one of the rare times he'd enjoyed being with his father, one of the few times he'd ever even thought of Mirshawn as a father.

Bradok pushed the bitter memories aside and returned to the task at hand. From a cabinet above a workbench, he pulled out a small sack and a long strip of soft cloth. He opened the velvet boxes and laid out the jewelry pieces they contained. Each one was a masterpiece, the pinnacle of his art and even though he doubted he'd need them wherever he was going, neither could he bear to leave them behind. He carefully laid each piece out on the soft cloth and folded it into a flat, walletlike pack that he stowed in the little bag, which then went in his pack.

With a last look at his orderly workshop, the place that had been the center of his life for more than twenty years, Bradok cinched his pack closed, slung it over his shoulders, and walked out, shutting the door behind himself.

When he reached the foyer again, he found Sapphire there, waiting for him. At the sight of the sword on his belt, her face fell. Some of her haughtiness melted away.

"It's true, then," she sniffed. "You're really planning to leave."

"Yes, Mother," he said. "There's a cooper in the Artisans' Cavern who had a vision. He's building a boat, or he was until they arrested him. It's partly my fault that he was arrested. I want to make amends. I'm going to his shop to finish the boat."

"Madness!" Sapphire scoffed. "You've always been a sensible boy, Bradok. You know there's no such thing as visions."

"No, I don't really know that, Mother," he said, turning to look her square in the face. "I'm beginning to doubt everything I thought I knew. Perhaps I don't know anything much at all."

"Well, I can agree with you on that," she returned. "But what makes you think this cooper has any answers? What makes you think helping him will make one bit of difference?"

"It's just a feeling I have in my gut," Bradok said, opening his front door. "I guess it's something you'd have to take on faith."

He left Sapphire standing in the hall with her mouth agape as he turned and strode briskly down the steps to the street. In his haste, he didn't even shut the door.

CHAPTER 7
The Day of Destruction

We should have grabbed him when we had the chance," Jon Bladehook said one week later, pacing around the front of Mayor Arbuckle's office. "We had a nice, easy plan until he came along."

"I agree," the mayor said easily, leaning back in the hard, wooden chair behind his desk. "But it's too late for that now. We just have to let things play out. Bradok and the rest of those fools can't stay barricaded in the Artisans' Cavern forever."

"They don't have to," Bladehook fumed. "Today is the deadline, and anyone who doesn't renounce their beliefs needs to be dealt with. If Bradok Axeblade can defy us, even for a single day, it will sow the seeds of rebellion among the people. They'll see us as weak."

"How will they see us if we lose twenty or thirty guardsmen in an assault on that barricade?" Arbuckle demanded. "The whole guard is only one hundred or so dwarves. How will we be seen by our enemies if a third of our soldiers are killed?"

Bladehook scowled but made no answer. He doubted Bradok and his little band of boat-builders could or would kill thirty guardsmen, but he had to agree with Arbuckle: it wasn't worth the risk.

"So we're just going to leave them down there?" he asked.

Arbuckle nodded. "They'll get hungry sooner or later," he said, smiling broadly. "Besides, every day that passes without any 'wrath' from their god only makes them look more and more foolish. I predict it won't be very long before their followers start deserting them."

Jon sighed. "I wish this day were over," he said, flopping down on a padded couch that sat against the back wall. "This day of doom! The sooner it passes, the sooner we can get back to reality."

"Patience, Jon," Arbuckle said, consulting the tall clock that stood in the corner. "In six hours it will be midnight and we will have won. The government will be all ours, without interference from those busybodies in the temple."

Jon grinned at that.

Arbuckle rose and crossed to the cupboards behind his desk. He took out a crystal decanter and two short glasses, and poured some amber liquid into each glass. "You and I, Jon," Arbuckle said, handing him a glass. "We'll rule this city like kings. Just like we always talked about."

He held up his glass, and Jon clinked his against it.

"To the kings of Ironroot!" Bladehook said with a chuckle before he pitched the drink back, downing it in one gulp.

"Care for another?" Arbuckle asked, holding up the decanter.

"Why not?" Jon said, holding out his glass.

At that moment, the door to Arbuckle's office burst open, admitting the captain of the city guard, disheveled and out of breath. Arbuckle and Bladehook were startled by the sudden appearance of the captain and spirits sloshed down Jon's front.

"What's the meaning of this?" Jon demanded, hurriedly brushing the liquor from his expensive shirt.

"The . . . prisoners," the captain gasped. "They're . . . uh, gone."

Jon exchanged a worried look with Arbuckle.

"What do you mean, 'gone'?" he asked.

"They disappeared," the captain explained, finally catching his breath. "Right out of their cells. Every one of them."

"You mean the street preachers?" Arbuckle demanded.

The captain nodded.

"Damn it, man," the mayor said. "Call out the guard. Seal off the city. I want them found. And I want to know who's to blame!"

"I know," the captain said. "I've already ordered those steps taken. But there's more. You see, I thought they might have taken refuge in the temple, so I had my men search the building."

"And?" Bladehook asked.

"And the priests are g-gone too!" the captain stammered. "All their belongings are there: the candles and fires are lit, there's even a meal on the table, but the priests have vanished."

Arbuckle swore in a long streak of barely-related expletives. For his part, Bladehook felt like he'd been punched in the gut.

"We can't let them get away!" the latter said quickly. "If they all escape, the believers will claim it was some kind of miracle, and then we'll be back where we started."

"Or worse," Arbuckle agreed.

"I've got men stationed at the upper gates and on all the side tunnels from the main cavern," the captain said. "We're stretched pretty thin, though. If only we knew where they were headed."

"They must be trying to reach Bradok," Jon said. "They're the only support left for believers in the city."

"Then we have to stop them," Arbuckle said. "Captain, assemble as many men as you can and meet us in the Artisans' Cavern."

With that, the three dwarves charged out of the room, leaving the liquor bottle standing open on the desk.

******

Bradok blew the dust and shavings from the hole he'd just finished drilling in the front end of the ship's keel. He slipped a long brass bolt into the hole and hung a small lantern on it, bolting it in place. The lantern held a glowstone, a rock that had been blessed by a priest so that it gave off a bright purplish light.

He straightened up, leaning back to crack his spine, then strode proudly to the ramp that led down from the completed ship. When Bradok arrived the week before, work on the ship had all but ceased. News of Silas's arrest had dispirited those who believed him. Since then, Bradok had rallied Silas's friends and family, convincing them that he would finish what Silas had started.

The job was finally finished.

They'd had to tear down the shop and some of the nearby walkways to find all the necessary wood, and they'd had to virtually barricade themselves inside there, away from the increasing encroachment of the city guard, but they'd done it.

"How much food do we have left?" he called to Perin.

The human looked up from where he'd been stacking their meager supplies. "Not more than three or four days, I'm afraid," he said ruefully.

"Better hurry up; get it all loaded," Bradok said. "At the risk of repeating myself, this is the day. I'm afraid we'd better get ready. Things are liable to get ugly before too long."

As if on cue, the burly smith Kellik came scurrying around the stone chimney of the forge. "Bradok," he called ahead. "There's some trouble at the barricade. You'd better get down there."

Bradok glanced back at Perin as he descended the narrow ramp. "Go ahead, get the women and children on board," he ordered.

The barricade had been erected a little ways from the shop, in a narrow part of the cavern. Almost from the day Bradok arrived to help with the shipbuilding, Kellik had joined in and made the defense of the barricade his main responsibility.

As Bradok approached, he saw a knot of ragged, armed dwarves, each gripping his weapon. On the far side of the tangle of metal and wood, he could make out a small group of dwarves milling about.

"Much!" Bradok said when he got close enough to make out faces.

"There you are, lad," the old dwarf said from the far side of the barricade. "Am I glad to see you!"

"What are you doing here?" Bradok asked.

"I . . . well, if it isn't too late, we've come to join you," Much said abashedly.

Behind Much, Bradok recognized the delegation of hill dwarves who had petitioned the council on his first day. The tall, red-haired woman who he had noticed then, and still vividly remembered, stepped up beside Much and addressed Bradok.

"We are believers," she said simply, lowering her eyes humbly. "We ask that you grant us sanctuary."

"It isn't much of a sanctuary," Bradok replied honestly. "This barricade won't hold long if the city guard attacks."

"We know all about you and prefer to take our chances with you," she said, raising her eyes to meet his. "If you'll have us."

A hand dropped on Bradok's arm, and he turned to see Silas's son, Chisul.

"We're already low on food," Chisul whispered to Bradok.

"I don't think a few more will matter much after today," Bradok whispered back gruffly. To Kellik he said, "Let them in."

"Thank you," the woman said. "My name is Rose, Rose Steelspar. We met before."

"I remember," Bradok said.

Rose put her arm around a solid-looking dwarf with a handsome face and Bradok's heart sank. "This is Tal," she said. "Our village is too poor to have a priest, so Tal trained as a doctor. He's well-versed in the healing arts."

"Welcome," Bradok said as Rose, Tal, and a considerable number of other dwarves close behind them squeezed through the barricade.

As they passed, Bradok turned back questioningly to Much.

"I'm no believer," Much declared, staring at his feet. "But I have thought about it long and hard. I can't be a part of what the council is doing. Will you have me stand with you?"

Bradok smiled and slapped the dwarf on the shoulder. "Of course, you old badger," Bradok said. "I can't think of anyone I'd rather have at my side."

"You'd better be quick about letting him in, then," Chisul said, gesturing up the passage.

Bradok turned to see, in the distance, a large group of dwarves moving toward them. Even with that gap, Bradok could clearly make out the blue tabards of the city guard.

"Close up the barricade," Bradok yelled, pulling Much through.

"Every dwarf to their station," Kellik yelled, shouldering his massive warhammer.

"Where should we deploy?" Rose asked, swiftly pulling a short sword from beneath her cloak. The other hill dwarves were also producing a variety of weapons from belts and packs.

Kellik gestured toward the dwarves lining the barricade. "Just find a hole and fill in," he said.

As the newcomers scrambled to do that, Bradok studied the oncoming force. At least half the city guard seemed to be among the contingent, as well as several members of the council. He spotted Mayor Arbuckle and Jon Bladehook in the lead.

"Bradok," Mayor Arbuckle called when he'd drawn near enough to see beyond the barricade, but outside of any hand-thrown missile range.

"Right here, Mayor," Bradok said, coming forward and gesturing so Arbuckle could see him clearly.

"What's going on over there, Bradok? We're trying to capture some escaped believers and priests. They came this way."

"No believers over here," Bradok said good-naturedly, provoking a ripple of laughter from the dwarves surrounding him.

"C'mon, you don't belong over there, Bradok," Arbuckle said, trying to sound conciliatory. "You have your father's legacy to uphold. You're no believer; you're one of us. Lay down your weapons and come back," the mayor coaxed. "Come back and all will be forgotten."

"I can't do that," Bradok said evenly. "I know what you're planning. I can't let you murder or even arrest these people. We don't want a fight, but we're ready for one, if that's your pleasure."

"Who's talking of murder?" Arbuckle said uncomfortably. He held his hands up, cautioning Bladehook and the city guard to hold their positions without advancing. "The day is gone, the priests have fled the temple in fear now that their fraud has been exposed. The believers have been proved wrong. We can let bygones be bygones. There is no reason to fear, nor any reason to fight."

"Listen to him, son," Sapphire's voice rang out as she pushed her way through the guardsmen. "I've talked to the mayor. He's even agreed to restore your council seat. Everything will return to normal. You just have to come out. Now stop this nonsense. There are no gods, and there never were."

Bradok made a show of examining his watch. "I count five more hours till this day is done," he said. "I'm busy right now. If you want to come back later—"

"There won't be a later, Axeblade," Bladehook shouted, no longer able to contain himself, as he stepped up next to the mayor. "This charade ends here and now . . .one way or another."

"We are determined to live as free dwarves," Bradok spat, his temper flaring. "And if necessary we will die as free dwarves."

"You will die for nothing!" Bladehook screamed, spraying spattle into his beard. "There are no gods! There is no Reorx! There—"

Bradok never knew if Bladehook finished his sentence. At that very moment, a shudder shook the ground so violently that he was hurled from his feet. He tried to rise again, but the ground bucked heavily a second time, throwing him onto his back. A rumbling roar swept the tunnel, followed by the tortured grinding of rocks being torn from the beds of centuries.

Kellik's rough hands grabbed Bradok and hauled him to his feet.

"Look out!" someone yelled.

Bradok didn't have to be warned. Up the tunnel, behind Arbuckle and the guards, he could see what was happening in the central cavern of Ironroot. The shaft of sunlight from the overhead crystal shone down on the statue of Argus Gingerbeard; then the light abruptly vanished and a chunk of crystal and rock the size of a building fell on Argus, crushing the statue.

The sight shook Bradok more than anything else he had experienced up to that time. To him Ironroot had seemed eternal, like the mountain itself. However, as he watched, a rain of rocks and debris poured down, obliterating everything beneath it.

"This is it!" Bradok yelled as a gout of dust whirled down the tunnel and washed over him. "Hurry! Get to the boat!"

"Wait!" a voice shrieked through the noise.

Bradok turned to see his mother, struggling to rise from where she had fallen. The ground was shaking and cracking. He didn't see Mayor Arbuckle and Bladehook; they had vanished amid the dust and landslide.

"Son!" she called as their eyes met. "Please! Take me with you."

Bradok hesitated. It lasted only a second, but that was enough. A rock the size of a cart shook loose from the ceiling and landed on top of Sapphire, flattening her.

"Good-bye, Mother," he said softly, before he turned and ran.

The hill dwarves and the believers raced ahead of him. Rose Steelspar's blazing hair flew like a banner for him to follow. In the distance, he could see Perin busily helping a crowded file of dwarves up the narrow ramp and into the boat.

He glanced back as he ran. There was Mayor Arbuckle and the guardsmen, not far behind, charging over the barricade with crazed eyes as the upper tunnel began to collapse behind them.

"Look out, Bradok!" Kellik yelled.

Bradok's head snapped around just in time for him to avoid running headlong into a chunk of rock that had fallen from the ceiling.

Kellik and Perin stood at the top of the ramp, helping Much into the boat.

"Hurry up," Kellik called over the roar of the trembling earth.

A chunk of ceiling slammed down just to Bradok's left, and he felt stinging pain as pieces of rock pierced his exposed face and arm. Blood ran into his eyes, and he could taste it in his mouth.

He staggered, trying to wipe the blood from his eyes, but raced on. His boots hit the ramp, and he surged upward. The most violent tremor yet shook the entire cavern, and the ramp shook free of the boat, bouncing Bradok back to the floor of the cavern.

"Throw him a rope!" Rose's voice cried out as Bradok struggled to regain his feet and his breath.

He looked over his shoulder as the ceiling over the barricade crumbled, crushing the barricade with the full weight of the mountain. Arbuckle, Bladehook, and the guardsmen were dodging and dashing about in a frenzy. Whether they were trying to escape the destruction or were still trying to reach him and the boat, he didn't know.

There was no time.

Perin and Kellik had lost control of the ramp. Bradok looked around at what remained of the cooper's shop. The forge and its chimney were the only remnants of the once-sturdy building left standing.

Without thinking about it, Bradok rushed toward the forge. He stepped onto the lip of fire pit and jumped up onto the chimney. His fingers closed around the brickwork, and he scrambled up as fast as he could. When he'd reached the top, he was even with the top of the ship but still too far away to jump.

Pain shot through Bradok's foot as he kicked the chimney as hard as he could. Undaunted, he kicked again and again. He could hear the ruckus below as the first guardsmen reached the ship and started pounding on its side, begging to be let on board. Someone had seen Bradok and was following him up the chimney.

He kicked again. That blow pushed a brick inward, leaving a hole where it had been. Bradok kicked again and felt the chimney shudder. He kicked again and scrambled around to the other side as the chimney began to topple.

Weakened by the loss of bricks, it fell like a chopped tree. Bradok rode it down as it fell, and just as it came even with the side of the boat, he jumped forward, slamming into the upper edge of the vessel with such force that it knocked the wind out of him.

"No you don't, lad," Much said, grabbing Bradok's shirt as he began to slide over the side.

More hands came to Much's aid, and Bradok was pulled into the boat. About fifty dwarves were cowering in front of him as the ground continued to heave and those stuck outside pounded on its side. The boat itself had no cabins, nor any real deck; there was just a large open space. Bradok hoped it would be enough.

"Bradok!" Bladehook's fearful voice called from somewhere beyond the ship. "Bradok, you were right! We admit it! Let us in!"

"Quickly!" Mayor Arbuckle was yelling to guardsmen Bradok couldn't see. "Find some wood to use as a ramp!"

"Get ready to repel boarders!" Perin called to the dwarves on the boat.

What are you waiting for? Bradok thought. I don't know if I believe in you, Reorx, he prayed silently. But if you are real, and if this is your plan, now is the time to reveal yourself.

It was the first time he'd prayed since he was a child.

Almost instantly, he felt something shake his leg. He reached into his pocket and pulled out the brass device Erus had given him. The purple stone on its lid was shining with a brilliant light, and the whole thing was vibrating so energetically Bradok could barely hold onto it.

Not knowing how he knew what he was doing, Bradok touched the hidden catch, certain it would work. Indeed, the device's lid snapped open, the purple light exploding from inside.

When Bradok's eyes cleared, he spied the figure of a dwarf, of Erus himself, standing there before him, suspended in the purple light of the device. Erus stared at Bradok then winked before picking up his enormous hammer. The image began to swell.

Screams and cries of alarm rang out as the figure continued to grow and grow, looming above and larger even than the boat.

"It's Reorx!" Jon Bladehook screamed, his voice filled with terror.

The purplish image of Reorx glanced down at Bladehook, as though amused, then turned to the back wall of the cavern. He hefted his massive hammer and swung it, slamming its metal head into the stone wall. A spiral fracture appeared where the hammer had struck, but before it could grow, Reorx swung again.

A crack ran up the wall and across the ceiling. Bradok stared as the crack grew and grew and split in two, allowing the first huge chunk of ceiling to dislodge. It was as if the whole thing were happening in slow motion, Bradok thought. The chunk of ceiling ripped loose and plunged down, narrowly missing the boat but landing square on Jon Bladehook.

A third blow from the hammer shattered the back wall, revealing a wide passage with a floor that sloped down and away from the Artisans' Cavern. With that, the image of Reorx shouldered his hammer and turned to look straight at Bradok.

"The rest is up to you," the image of Reorx said. Then the light flared so brightly Bradok had to cover his eyes.

When he could see again, the image was gone.

CHAPTER 8

Silas's Legacy

What now?" Much yelled over the rumbling and roiling earth. "What are we supposed to do? Push this thing down there?"

"I don't know," Bradok yelled back.

"You don't know?" Much said, an astonished look on his face. "We're in a ship, in a tunnel that's falling down all over, surrounded by a bunch of armed and angry dwarves trying to join or kill us, and you don't know? What was your plan?"

"I mean I don't know yet," Bradok called. "But everything has been planned out pretty well up to now. I'm sure there will be some sign—"

"Some sign!" Much muttered, rolling his eyes. "Well, unless you know how to levitate a boat, I don't see how we're going to go anywhere very fast," Much continued. "It's impossible."

A thunderous crack echoed through the tunnel, drawing all eyes toward the upper end. With a crash and a roar, the ceiling fell in. Somewhere above the Artisans' Cavern, there must have been a mountain lake; when the ceiling came down, it brought with it a torrential flood of water.

Channeled by the narrow cavern, the water rushed over

the remains of the cooper's shop and slammed into the ship. Bradok held on to the side as the ship pitched, turned, and, finding its balance, began to float. All around him he could hear the screams of the guardsmen as they were swept away by the rush of water.

From below came a grinding noise as the ship's bottom scraped over the huge rocks that littered the uneven floor. A moment later, however, the water had risen sharply and they floated free.

"Hang on," Rose's voice came from the front of the boat, a note of horror in it.

That was when Bradok remembered the steep-sloping passage. A second later, the ship lurched and pitched downward, picking up velocity. Inside the boat, people were screaming and grabbing for handholds. Bradok had just succeeded in passing Much an anchor line when the passage curved sharply and the boat slammed into the wall, throwing him forward several yards. Freezing spray washed over him as the boat twisted, whipped around, and banked downward in the narrow passage.

Bradok had only just managed to push himself to his feet when another sharp turn sent him lurching into nearby dwarves. Pushing himself up, he found he'd landed on top of the hill dwarf Rose.

"Uh-oh," he said. "I'm sorry."

She pushed him off her and passed him an anchor line. "Tie off," she said with a shy smile.

Bradok tied the line around his waist and leaned back against the side.

"Now lock arms and hang on," Rose said.

Bradok locked elbows with Rose on his right and Tal on his left. A moment later his stomach dropped and he knew the boat had reached the end of the tunnel. Screams erupted in the semidarkness as the ship shot out, unsupported, into the empty depths.

They were falling.

"Hold on!" he heard himself shout as much to himself as to anyone else.

The eerie sensation of weightlessness seemed to go on forever. Bradok knew the suspense couldn't have lasted more than a couple of seconds, but it seemed to be an eternity. Just when Bradok decided they would never stop falling, the ship slammed into water. The impact smashed him down into the bottom of the boat.

Purple spots swam before Bradok's eyes, and it seemed like a long time before his senses worked again. When he finally tried to move, he found himself in a tangle of arms and legs. He levered himself up, only to find he'd somehow landed on Rose again.

Tal grabbed Bradok's shoulder and hauled him to his feet then bent to help Rose. "Really, Bradok," he said good-humoredly once Rose was back on her feet. "If you're going to keep doing that, I'm going to have to ask what your intentions are regarding my sister."

"I, uh," Bradok stammered, blushing to the roots of his beard.

"If he does that again, he'd better send flowers first," Rose said with a sarcastic grin.

Both she and Tal laughed while Bradok tried to find his tongue.

"Too bad, sis," Tal said, his grin widening. "This one doesn't seem to have a sense of humor."

"Bradok!" Chisul's voice rang out. "Stop dillydallying. We need some help over here."

Bradok turned, surveying the ship in the bluish light of the lamps on either end. He could see the pregnant Lyra holding on to her daughter, Jade, who clung in desperate terror to her mother but seemed to be otherwise unharmed. Kellik's younger son, however, was leaning against his father, his face a mask of pain. Even from such a distance, Bradok could see that the lad's arm was bent at a funny angle where it should have been straight.

"Did you say you have some healing skills?" Bradok asked Tal, pointing at Kellik's son.

Tal nodded, already pulling a small brown kit from his pack.

The ship seemed to be slowing, and Bradok was able to stand with ease. Tal brushed past him, walking with a smooth grace that bespoke time spent at sea.

"Who has bad injuries?" Bradok called out, picking his way along the long edge of the ship toward Kellik.

"I'm bleeding," an older dwarf with a long, white beard replied as he passed. "But 'tain't nothing."

There was a long, bloody scratch on the old-timer's arm, clearly left by the nails of the dwarf girl who sat on his left. Without a word, a matronly dwarf on his right ripped a strip of cloth from the hem of her dress and bandaged the wound.

When Bradok reached Kellik, the burly smith cradled his son in his lap. "It's broken," he said glumly in answer to Bradok's unasked question.

"Then we'll need to set it," said Tal, who had followed Bradok closely.

The boy's pale face went absolutely white. Tal put his hand on the lad's shoulder and looked into his brown eyes.

He unslung his heavy pack and dropped it at Bradok's feet, pulling it open almost before it hit the boards of the barrel's bottom. His hand emerged a moment later with a small, round case, painted blue with tarnished brass hardware. Tal opened the case, revealing a rare white glowstone that was held before a reflector in the device's lid. The resulting light shone out in a bright beam and illuminated the contents of the backpack.

"Now then," he said easily, pulling out a bottle of red glass. "What's your name, son?"

"Hemmish," the boy said.

"My youngest," Kellik said, still cradling the boy. "But he's a brave one and strong as they come too."

"I'm sure he is," Tal said with a genuine, reassuring smile. "Now you just rest easy, Hemmish, and we'll get you taken care of." He unstoppered the red bottle and pressed it to the boy's lips. "Take a swig of this," he said.

As Hemmish drank, Tal turned to Bradok. "See if you can find me a splint. Any piece of wood will do, so long as it's small and stout."

Bradok turned and retrieved a scrap piece of dowel, about an inch in diameter, which they had used to make pegs when building the ship.

"Anyone got a hand axe?" he asked the group. Several hands went up, and a grizzled dwarf with an unkempt beard and a glass eye passed Bradok a short axe from his amply laden belt.

Bradok stood the dowel on its end, and after a few taps, the metal blade bit into the dowel. Then he raised axe and dowel together and brought them down on the planks of the bottom of the boat. The axe bit right through the dowel, splitting it into two thin strips of wood about the length of Hemmish's arm. Bradok passed both the strips to Tal.

"Those will do fine," he said, giving them a quick once-over.

Hemmish had drunk from the red bottle, and the boy's cheeks were rosy and his eyes were moving unsteadily in his head.

"Papa," he said in a dreamy voice. "Where's Mama? Why isn't she here with us?"

A look of pain crossed Kellik's face. It looked so out of place on the strong man that if Bradok hadn't been looking right at the bulbous-nosed mountain of a dwarf, he'd have sworn an oath that such an expression never had darkened Kellik's face before.

"She's gone, lad," he said in a gentle voice. "Gone to a

better place, I reckon. We'll be with her again one day, but not for a long time."

"That's too bad," Hemmish said drowsily. "I miss her."

"Me too," Kellik said in a voice too soft for Hemmish to hear.

While Hemmish had been rambling, Tal laid out several strips of cloth and the splints Bradok had cut.

"We're going to set the bone. I'll tie it up good and tight," he said. "Hold him."

Kellik tightened his grip on Hemmish as Bradok grabbed the boy's feet. Tal took hold of Hemmish's arm and, after carefully aligning it, jerked it into place. Hemmish cried out in pain, but his face quickly resumed its happy, oblivious look. Tal swiftly and expertly tied up the arm and splinted it. Within minutes, the doctor had slipped the broken arm into a sling made from two handkerchiefs tied together.

"That should do just fine," he said, smiling at Kellik. "We'll check it in a few days."

"That's assuming we're still alive in a few days," Chisul's voice sounded behind them, echoing through the semidarkness. Silas's son stood, leaning against the rounded side of the ship.

"Why wouldn't we be alive?" Rose said from the far side with deliberate loud cheerfulness. "Reorx didn't inspire your father to build this magnificent craft to be our coffin," she added, rubbing her hand reverently along the wooden side of the ship.

"You still don't get it." Chisul laughed. "Reorx had nothing to do with the design of this boat." He waved his arm around. "This is a barrel without one side," he said. "One-half of a barrel, just like hundreds of others that he made during his life. It's just bigger. The biggest barrel that he ever made."

Bradok frowned.

"You don't think it's just a tiny bit convenient that we're here in this ship, being swept away from Ironroot at the very moment it was destroyed?" returned Rose. "If that wasn't Reorx who opened the passage in front of us, then who was it?"

A murmur of assent ran through the barrel's passengers.

"I don't know how we ended up here," Chisul retorted. "And neither do you. What I do know is that we're lost, cut off from civilization with precious few supplies, and with no idea where we're going. Don't you see," he added. "This giant half-barrel boat isn't saving us; it's taking us further away from help every minute."

"What do you propose we do about that?" a squat, dull-faced dwarf in the front asked.

"Yes," Lyra said sulkily. "It's not like we can get out and walk."

"That's exactly what we should do," Chisul said, moving to the side. "We need to beach this craft and get our bearings."

They all stared out over the water. The boat was floating along easily in some kind of current. Across the water on either side they couldn't see much—misty shapes maybe, more water definitely.

"That's insane," a barrel-chested hill dwarf who was peering over the side said. "We don't know if there's any land out there."

"Besides," Rose pointed out, "how are we supposed to steer this boat?"

Bradok might have got around to adding a rudder to Silas's design, but there hadn't been time. He suspected he knew why Silas had left off the rudder. He had trusted in Reorx. Without a rudder, there would be no way to take control of the ship. And it would have to go wherever it floated or drifted.

"She's got a point," Much said, narrowing his eyes at Bradok as though it were all his fault.

"Uh, guys," Lyra said, pointing. "You might want to see this."

Bradok edged to the front of the ship, where the railings were short enough to look over the side. Chisul, Rose, and

Kellik all clambered up next to him to see. Bradok jumped up, catching hold of the side rail and pulling himself up to where he could swing his leg over the rail and perch there. In the dim glow of the lantern, he could spy black water about six feet below him, which disappeared in the darkness beyond the light.

"I don't see—" Bradok began; then he gasped. Something had moved in the inky water. It was long and thick and seemed to have tentacles that trailed along after it. Bradok could see it clearly because its body gave off a bright yellow light.

The creature rolled over, a black eye gazing up at Bradok, before it dived and vanished.

"What was that?" he whispered, resisting the urge to flee to the back of the boat.

"You mean what are *they?*" Chisul echoed, awe in his voice.

Bradok turned and spotted dozens of the yellow creatures swimming up in front of them. They seemed to rise and dive in manic bursts of energy, flashing their lights as they went.

"Over there too," Rose said.

Bradok craned his neck around and saw more of them swimming around off in the distance.

"This must be some kind of underground lake or ocean," Rose offered. "It's huge."

"What do you think they eat?" Much asked.

Bradok wondered the same thing.

"Does anyone have a spear?" Chisul asked. "These things might be edible."

Everyone nodded and scurried for suitable weapons.

Bradok stared over the side. The creature that had first swum close to appraise him seemed to have returned. Its body pulsed, slowly getting brighter then dimmer. In the changing light, Bradok could see paddlelike flippers attached to the front end of its body that waved up and down as it moved.

Then something else caught his eye.

From deep below he could see an answering glow that pulsed in time with the creature on the surface. As he watched the glow with widening eyes, it grew brighter and brighter and larger and larger until the pulsing thing was longer than the ship.

"Much," he hissed. "Kellik."

Suddenly the little creature went dark and plunged beneath the water. Bradok strained his eyes to follow it, but the dark water hid it as effectively as a slab of rock. As he stared, a burst of yellow light flashed up from the water. Bradok covered his eyes for a second, startled by the brightness. When he could see better, the light from below revealed a creature similar to the others only impossibly large. One of the monster's fore-flippers broke the surface and swamped Bradok with its spray.

Like the small snakelike creature, the gargantuan version rolled over until Bradok was staring into its black, soulless eye. The unblinking eye was easily as big around as a pony keg.

"What is that . . . the mother of all these babies?" Kellik asked, clearly shaken.

"Or the daddy," Much said, trying for humor.

A moment later, the eye disappeared and the massive creature vanished below the water. Bradok watched its body flash briefly as it streamed into the depths; then it was gone.

"New rule," Rose said in a fearful voice. "No swimming."

"Did you see the size of that thing?" Chisul asked. "This lake must be very huge indeed."

"Aye," Much said. "And deep."

Bradok swung his leg over the side and dropped back into the bottom of the boat.

"We might as well get comfortable," he said, sliding down into a sitting position. "This may be a long journey."

* * * * * *

After that first encounter with the huge yellow beast, there was only calm and stillness, punctuated by intermittent visits by the glowing creatures. By the third day on the lake, the tension combined with the strange tedium had taken its own toll on the group. An unnatural pall hovered over the survivors. No one spoke or sang or laughed.

"Something better happen soon, or I'm going to go mad," Kellik whispered to Bradok as the two of them sat in the front, keeping watch.

"Well, at least we're going the right way," Rose said from nearby.

"How do you know that?" Bradok asked.

"Well, I'm an optimist. What choice do we have really?" Rose shrugged. "We might as well assume we're headed in the right direction."

Bradok chuckled, the sound seeming to echo unnaturally through the stillness.

"We could just as well be drifting in circles," Chisul scoffed. "Sooner or later we're going to have to try something other than just sitting here and rotting."

"Like what?" Rose asked. "We can't get off this boat, there's nothing on board to paddle with, and even if there was, we have no idea which direction is best."

"I don't know if you've noticed," Chisul said sarcastically, lowering his voice, "but the food's running out, even with rationing. I guess we've got three or four more days' worth, and then we're going to start starving. I, for one, do not care to watch the children starve."

Silence greeted his comment.

Bradok was worried about the food supply too, though he wasn't going to admit it. They had about a dozen children with them. At some point they were going to have to try catching one of the glowing creatures and hope word didn't get back to daddy.

"He's right, you know. I think I hear your stomach rumbling from here," Rose said, looking over at Bradok.

"That's not me," Bradok said, suddenly aware that he,

too, heard something different than the eerie silence. As he strained to listen, he figured out what it was: a roaring noise, like rushing water.

Much grabbed his shoulder and pointed off into the darkness. At the very edge of visibility, a wall of rock emerged into view. In the center, right where the boat was headed, gaped an opening like an immense black maw.

"Everyone hold on to something!" Bradok cried out as he and Much leaped down to the bottom of the boat.

All the dwarves burst into action—some grabbing their possessions, others their loved ones—and clutching for something solid to hold on to.

Bradok had barely managed to grab onto one of the ship's ribs and link arms with Rose when the ship pitched wildly, entering what seemed to be a dark tunnel. Suddenly they were being swept down and away from the lake at a tremendous speed.

A thunderous crash shook the boat, and they spun around. The dwarves on board were tossed about like rag dolls as the vessel pitched and rolled and rocked out of control.

Rose clung to Bradok's arm, pressing her feet against one of the ribs of the ship to brace herself. Even as they careened through the black unknown, even as he wondered if he would live through that latest calamity, Bradok found himself distracted by the sweet smell of Rose's hair.

The ship shuddered again, slamming into something and grinding up and over the obstacle.

Bradok noticed Kellik. The massive dwarf had pulled Hemmish into his chest and was leaning over the boy, forming a living barrier to protect him. That was dangerous; he wasn't bracing himself enough. Bradok was about to call out to him when he felt himself suddenly tossed into the air, with the ship falling away beneath him. The sensation of falling lasted only a second before he was slammed into the wooden side of the ship. He could hear wood splintering and water roaring as he was thoroughly doused.

A gash had been torn in the side of their ship, and water poured in. Before anyone could make a move, however, they struck solid ground with a thud and screeched to a halt. The torn side of the boat was propped up in the air, the water no longer rushing in.

"We've stopped," Chisul said from somewhere in the tangled mass of bodies back in the center of the boat.

Bradok pulled Rose to her feet and asked if she'd been hurt. When she shook her head, he left her and moved to examine the boat and the gash in its side. Bradok could see that something had torn a ragged hole across four of the planks that made up the wall of wood. Had they been back in Silas's shop, it would have been an easy fix. Out in the middle of nowhere, however, it was a fatal wound.

"She's served her purpose, lad," Much said sympathetically, seeing what Bradok saw. He put a hand on his friend's shoulder.

"Looks like you're going to get your wish after all, Chisul," Rose said with a smile. Chisul, looking bedraggled as he stood up, snorted.

But Bradok nodded appreciatively. "This is the end of the line," he announced, moving to the opposite side of the boat, where the rail was just above the water line. "Like it or not, we all walk from here."

CHAPTER 9

The Survivors

The side of the beached ship tilted out just above the wet sand at the edge of the underground river. The smell of mineral water permeated the cool air, giving it a decidedly metallic tang.

"Grab the lamps," Bradok said, peering out over the black water.

Rose unhooked the lamp at one end of the ship and brought it forward. As she climbed up next to Bradok, the light spilled over the side, illuminating a small beach of white sand a few feet away.

Bradok took the lamp and held it high, looking back over the ship. Beyond, on the far side, he could see the mist kicked up by a waterfall in the distance that he could hear but not see. Black water extended out from the little inlet where the ship had come to rest. A rushing river hurried on past into the impenetrable darkness.

"Well," Much asked. "What do you see?"

"It's a miracle we're not all drowned," Chisul said, wringing the water from his shirt.

"The good news is there's a beach here that looks nice and dry," Bradok said. "Let's get everyone out."

Chisul shot him a sour look then stomped to the rail. "Who

elected you leader?" he grumbled.

"If you have a better suggestion," Bradok said, "let's hear it."

Chisul didn't answer, just jumped over the rail into calf-deep water and slogged his way up to the sand. One by one the survivors of Ironroot made their way out of the waterlogged ship and onto the cool, dry beach.

"We need to get everyone out of their wet garments and into dry clothes," Tal said as he made his way onto dry land.

"There are a few cuts and bruises that will need your attention too, Doctor," Much said as he limped away from the boat. Dark blood smeared the arm Much held cradled at his side.

When everyone was out and accounted for, Bradok flopped down on the soft sand. It felt good to stretch out flat again.

"We made it," he said quietly. "We're alive."

There was a moment of silence all around. Everyone was thinking of Ironroot, what happened back there, whether anyone could still be alive after all the wholesale destruction.

Chisul thought of his father, wondering what had become of Silas. Kellik thought of his dead wife. Bradok was thinking of Sapphire, that last pleading look on his mother's face before her life was extinguished.

The cool air of the cavern moved and swirled in response to the waterfall and the river. Bradok shivered as it riffled his wet shirt. Tal had been right; they'd all catch their deaths of cold if they didn't get out of their soaked clothes and into something dry.

"We need to make a fire," he said, forcing himself to stand. "Anyone with an axe, head back to the ship and cut some of it up for firewood. Start with the driest wood first."

A groan rose up from the dwarves, but several of the stalwarts stood and made their way back to the ship.

"Everyone else, we need to get everyone into dry clothes.

Men, make sure the women and children are taken care of first."

He half expected another complaint from Chisul, but Silas's son was one of the first to stand and begin stripping off his wet clothes. Beside him, two rough-looking dwarves named Vulnar and Jenner were also changing into the driest clothes they had as rapidly as they could. Bradok realized those two stuck pretty close to Chisul, and he wondered absently if they were all three friends. He hoped not; Chisul was already proving a troublemaker.

He pushed such thoughts from his mind and pulled off his wet clothes, leaving just his pants. Only some of the dwarves had gotten wet when the ship was breached, and it seemed there were enough dry garments to be shared and passed around.

The sound of axes on wood filled the air, and within ten minutes a modest fire was crackling and popping on the sand.

Bradok hung his wet items on a makeshift clothesline that the grandmotherly Isirah Anvil had strung between two stalagmites. Then he changed into other clothes from his pack. The fire had warmed the air nicely, and he started to feel like himself again. The trip through the bowels of Krynn in a boat was something he'd never forget, but dwarves as a rule are not fond of seafaring. It felt good to have dry land under his feet again.

"So where do we go from here?" Much's voice rose from the far side of the fire.

"He's right," Kellik said, looking around. "We can't stay here for very long. We're almost out of food."

"There might be some fish in the river," the rough-looking Halum Ironband said helpfully.

"I think it's clear what we have to do," Chisul stated firmly. "We need to find our way out of here and get back to our people."

"That could be the most dangerous thing to do," the grizzled, one-eyed dwarf said.

"Dangerous if we succeed and dangerous if we don't," Isirah chimed in, clutching the youngest of her grandchildren to her side. "We weren't made to feel very welcome back in Ironroot, and who knows how much of the place has survived? We could get lost and starve to death."

"That isn't going to happen," Rose said. "Reorx didn't lead us down here just to starve. He'll guide us to safety; I feel it in my bones."

"And how is he going to do that?" Chisul asked sarcastically. "Did he leave marks for us to follow or something?"

"How should I know?" Rose replied with a dazzling smile that was wasted on Chisul. "That's why it's called faith."

Chisul rolled his eyes, but many of the other dwarves were nodding. Something Rose said tickled Bradok's memory, though. He put his hand in his pocket and pulled out the strange brass device that had released the image of Reorx. Since then, Bradok hadn't opened it; indeed, he had almost forgotten he possessed it. He wondered if it would even open again. But Rose had said that Reorx would provide for them, and she had given him the idea to try it again.

He put his hand on the hidden catch and pressed. The purple stone on top flared, and the lid swung open. The inside of the device was hollow except for a purple mist that swirled inside it like a miniature cloud.

Suddenly the mist began to pulse with light. Bradok threw his hands over his eyes but not before his vision swam with purple dots. When it cleared, all the eyes in the cavern were on him. From the top of the open device, another illusion sprang forth.

It was a tall, slender woman that might be the image of a human, but Bradok couldn't really tell. She wore a fitted breastplate and an ornate helmet with a plume. The rest of her body was obscured by a long cloak. The cloak and the woman's inky black hair moved and flowed in a wind that Bradok could not feel. In her right hand, she carried a short spear, and a white bandage covered her eyes.

"It's a seer," Isirah whispered in her wizened voice.

"A what?" Much asked with trepidation.

"A seer," Isirah said louder. "They're from the old stories, blind guides blessed with the gift of second sight."

As if on cue, the seer raised her spear and pointed off into the darkness.

"I think Rose is right," Bradok said, finding his voice at last. "We have more than just marks to follow; now we have a guide."

"Hear, hear," Rose said, sticking her tongue out at Chisul. "I guess I wasn't so wrong after all."

Chisul stared daggers at her but said nothing.

"Enough of this small talk," Much said, standing up and rubbing his arm while staring worriedly at the female spirit-image that was slowly dissipating. "We've got a direction now, so let's get the supplies unloaded and be about our business."

Bradok, Much, Chisul, and the other men who weren't cutting up the ship for firewood all formed a line and quickly emptied the ship of her cache of supplies. Silas had thought of everything but a rudder, it seemed. There were spare cloaks and water bags, wrapped oilcloth bundles of rations, two long poles with mountings for the glowlamps, a keg of long knives, and a keg of assorted tools.

By the time they were through hauling everything out, Rose and Tal had already begun handing out the gear. Kellik made sure each dwarf was armed with a knife. Perin was busy showing Hemmish and his brother Rijul how a glowlamp on a pole would attract fish when held over the river.

Several hours and a dozen fish later, Bradok lay on the sand, feeling better about his prospects than he had in days. The survivors of Ironroot were no longer a ragamuffin band of strangers; they had pulled together, and their hopes and spirits were high. He still wasn't a believer, but it looked as though Reorx was looking out for them. Between the gear Silas left them and the strange compass, they should be able to make their way to safety.

The weariness of the past few hours coupled with his full belly pushed Bradok toward sleep. He lay on the sand, rolled in his thick cloak. Sleep should have come easily, but it kept eluding him. With a moment to reflect on everything that had transpired, the reality of his situation began to sink in.

Ironroot was truly gone.

His life as a jeweler and councilman was gone. His father and mother were both dead. The future lay before him like a vast, unmarked plain. It seemed like a whole world of opportunities stood before him, just waiting for him to decide which path to take. Just choose the right path . . . *choose* . . . the word kept echoing in his mind as he finally drifted off to sleep.

******

When Bradok awoke, the cheery orange light of the fire had died, leaving only the pale blue light of the lamps illuminating the cavern. In their unwavering glow, the cavern seemed somehow sinister, like an evil version of itself. He pushed such thoughts from his mind and rose carefully, so as not to wake anyone.

A few embers glowed among the coals of the fire, inviting him to feed them with fresh wood, which he did. In a few moments, he had a cheery little blaze going.

"That's much better," Rose said, materializing out of the semidarkness on the far side of the fire. "The glowlamps may burn for years without fuel, but their light has always made me feel as if a shadow was hanging over me."

Bradok chuckled quietly. "I was thinking the same thing," he admitted.

"Still," she added, turning to look at one of the lamps hanging on the end of a pole that had been thrust into the sand, "I suppose we'd better get used to them. I suspect we have a long walk ahead of us."

"I hope it isn't too long," he said, poking the fire with a stick. "We've only got food for a few days."

"Then we'd better get moving soon," Rose said.

He nodded, looking around at the still, sleeping forms. Many of the dwarves who had escaped Ironroot by boat were old, well past their prime, and there were close to a dozen children.

"And then there's Lyra," Bradok whispered to himself more than to Rose.

But Rose heard and, turning to look at the figure of the sleeping pregnant woman, nodded.

"She's tougher than she looks," she said. "She won't hold us back."

Bradok shrugged. Some of the others were beginning to wake. "But what do we do if she has her baby?" he asked quietly.

"Let Tal worry about that," Rose said, nodding at her still-sleeping brother with a smile. "He's good under pressure."

"You both have the same surname . . . ?" Bradok said, changing the subject, but letting the sentence hang more like a question.

When Rose smiled, as she did at that moment, it struck Bradok how attractive she was. She didn't have the flawless lines and elegant features of some city girls Bradok had courted, but rather a more natural, earthy beauty, like deep mountain jade.

"I'm not married," she said, lowering her voice too, the firelight burnishing a line across the hair that fell into her eyes. "Not to Tal or his brother . . . or anyone."

If Bradok had just been told that the Mountain King wanted him to design his crown, he wouldn't have been more pleased. The knowledge that Rose had a brother and not a husband made him feel like a schoolboy in love—giddy and light-headed.

If Rose noticed anything amiss, she gave no sign. Instead she pointed past the lamplight, where the image of the seer had pointed.

"Shouldn't we get going?" she asked.

Bradok took out the compass and, holding it firmly, nodded.

"Then, for Reorx's sake, let's go," Kellik said impatiently, striding into the firelight. He'd clearly overheard much of their conversation, and was shaking his head disapprovingly. "All the fish got et last night, so all we got are cold rations," he added. "We ought to put a few miles under our feet before breakfast."

Bradok would have rather eaten first, but Kellik was probably right. He had already passed by, leading his sons down to the river's edge to fill their waterskins. Rose glanced over at Bradok and smiled, amused by the smith. Bradok shrugged.

"All right, walk first," he said with a sigh. "Eat later. Everyone, wake up! Let's go!"

Before the echo of his words had faded away, however, Chisul stood up and called out the same orders in a louder voice.

"All right everyone, we need to get moving," Chisul said. "We don't know how far we have to go, so we'd better get started. Pack up your gear and don't forget to fill your waterskins."

Bradok looked sheepishly at Rose, who was even more amused.

A flurry of activity followed, during which all the rest of the dwarves got up, stretched, and prepared for the journey ahead.

"He's full of good ideas," Bradok said in a low voice, sidling closer to Rose.

Rose grinned before her face turned serious. "I don't much care for him, to be honest," she said in a low voice. "He seems to need to be right all the time."

Bradok frowned. The same thought had occurred to him. "He's probably harmless," he said.

"Probably," she agreed, sounding unconvinced.

"Well, I better go make sure nobody needs any help," he said, moving off reluctantly.

"You go," Rose said, walking toward the water. "I'm ready. But there's something I'd really like to do first."

Wondering what she meant, Bradok made his way back to where he slept and packed up his gear. As he shouldered his worn traveling pack, he opened a small oilcloth with the remnants of the previous night's fish inside. He took the fish and popped the remaining piece in his mouth. Bradok had never been much of a fish-eater, but not knowing what he'd be eating in the days ahead made the unseasoned bit of overcooked meat taste better than the finest steak.

As everyone began gathering around the lanterns, Bradok took his waterskin and strode to the river to fill it. To his surprise, he found Rose there, painting on the side of Silas's barrel-boat in large, red letters.

REORX'S HAND.

"What's that?" he asked.

"I just figured she needed a name. She deserves to be remembered," Rose said, patting the side of the ship. She stoppered her vial of paint and rinsed the brush in the river.

Bradok watched her as she climbed up the bank to join the others. Whatever dangers they encountered, he thought, he wouldn't have passed up the journey for the world.

* * * * * *

"I've never been this bored in all my born days," Much grumbled three days later.

The seer compass had pointed them toward a fissure at the

edge of the river, but for three straight days there had been no need to consult it further. The passage ran more or less straight and level with no forks or side passages or caverns along the way—just the same rough-walled passage. They'd kept up their march, by Much's watch, ten hours out of every day. Bradok guessed they must have covered forty or fifty miles, but the unending hallway of rock made it seem like they were winding in circles.

The only bright spots were the frequent streams and pools that appeared along the way. They would issue out of cracks in the walls or the ceiling and run across their path, vanishing into similar fissures a few feet from where they appeared. The water tasted terrible; it was full of dissolved minerals and metals that left a sour taste in their mouths hours after drinking. Still, while their food supply diminished steadily, they had no trouble refilling their waterskins.

But they had finally run out of solid food, and the next day would be the first without. The adults exchanged worried glances as the children complained about their empty bellies. Bradok consulted the compass every few hours, but it offered no fresh hope.

On the second day without food, the adults began to grumble and the little children wept intermittently. Kellik and Bradok took turns carrying the exhausted Hemmish until their arms ached. Still, no one thought they should stop. Everyone, even the children, knew that food must lie ahead and that to stop meant death.

On the third day, the cavern lay silent except for the shuffle of weary boots on stone and the sounds of ragged breathing. No one spoke much, preferring to save their energy for the task at hand. The children could barely walk, keeping their progress slow. Some of the adults carried the younger ones, and Rose had her arm around the pregnant Lyra, helping to steady her faltering steps. When, gasping in pain, she finally collapsed, everyone sank to the floor of the fissure with a collective groan.

"Lyra can't go any further," Rose said after a moment.

"I'm about all done in, myself," Much said wearily, leaning his head back against the rocky side of the passage.

"We shouldn't rest here for long," Chisul said, his voice raspy.

"I don't think many of us have the strength to go on," Perin said, his chubby face soaked with sweat. "I'm on my last legs."

"Us too," the grizzled Marl Anvil said. He sat with his wife slumped against him and his three grandchildren huddled close.

The pain in Bradok's stomach seemed to disappear as he imagined what the old dwarf must be feeling, the fear that he might be forced to watch his precious ones starve to death. Without thinking about it, Bradok performed the act he'd done so many times over the past few days. He slipped his hand into his pocket and drew out the little compass. As before, there was not any change or alteration in its appearance; the blind seer still hovered there, pointing, unwavering, up the same passage.

"No," he croaked, using his voice for the first time in hours. He gripped the compass tightly in his hand and stared intently at it. "We need food," he commanded, "or we perish."

Nothing happened. After a moment Chisul laughed, the sound echoing through the cavern.

"Maybe she thinks we're not hungry enough yet," he said.

"Maybe she means that there's food up ahead, just a little farther," Rose said hopefully.

"Let's send those of us who can still walk up ahead a bit," Chisul said. "If they find food, they can bring it back to the others. I'm willing to go."

The survivors of Ironroot exchanged glances with one another, and several of them nodded in agreement.

"No, we should stick together," Kellik said. "Deep caves like these can be dangerous places."

More nods than before ran through the survivors.

"We need food," Bradok said, "soon."

"Ask her again," Rose said, indicating the compass. "She's a woman; maybe she's changed her mind."

Bradok looked down at the purple stone on top of the compass. "Please," he said softly. "We can't go on. We have to have some food. Please show us the way."

He took a breath and pressed the little catch. The lid sprang open, and multicolored light bubbled up out of the little well inside, like liquid. After a moment the light flared brightly, jumping up into the air above the compass and resolving itself into a new image: that of Reorx's warhammer.

The hammer hung in the air above the compass, rotating slowly as if spinning on the pommel of the handle. The image was at least two feet high, making it easy for everyone to see it. After a moment, it began to move, dropping down to hover on its side. The hammer spun lazily for a moment; then it snapped around, its handle pointing back down the passage like a compass needle.

"That's the way we just came!" Chisul exclaimed. "We know there's nothing back *there*. What's the matter with that thing?"

Bradok ignored Chisul. Adrenaline flooded through his body, washing away the weariness and the aches of travel. He leaped to his feet excitedly, not taking his eyes off the pointing shaft of the warhammer's handle.

"This way," he said, launching himself back down the passage, back in the direction they had just traveled.

"There's nothing that way," Chisul called after him. "We know; we've already been there."

"He's right, lad," Much said.

"No," Bradok yelled back. "We must have missed something."

113

Not looking to see if anyone followed him, Bradok ran with the image of the hammer leading him. His legs carried him as easily as if he'd just enjoyed days of rest and food. The sound of people gradually picking up and following him reached his ears, and he slowed a bit to allow them to catch up.

As he reached the little trickle of water where they'd last refilled their waterskins, the hammer jumped. Bradok skidded to a halt on the wet floor.

The handle was pointing straight at the side of the passage. He ran his free hand over the stone but could detect no fissures or openings, just the tiny crack at the base where the trickle of water disappeared.

"This is it?" Rose said, panting. She was the first to reach the spot after Bradok, with the others staggering behind her.

Bradok checked the compass, but the hammer's handle hadn't moved. He closed the lid, and the image of the hammer disappeared.

"Give me a hammer," he said, stowing the compass back in his pocket.

"What for?" Vulnar said.

Bradok turned and grabbed the ragged dwarf by the front his shirt. "Just do it," he said.

"Here ya go," Kellik said, passing up a short warhammer from his place in the crowd.

Bradok took the weapon, gripping it so tightly that his knuckles turned white. He swung it back over his shoulder then smashed its narrow steel head forward against the wall. A thunderous boom resounded through the passage and a spiderweb of cracks spread out from the point where the hammer struck the wall.

"It's hollow!" Rose said, a radiant smile splitting her face. "There's something back there."

"I doubt it's someone's larder," Chisul said, drawing his short sword. "We should be prepared for anything."

"Yes, anything. It could be a way out!" said the ever-optimistic Rose.

Bradok ignored them all and swung the hammer again and again. On the third strike, the head of the hammer disappeared into the wall and a large chunk of rock fell away into the darkness beyond.

CHAPTER 10

Scarce Resources

A blast of sweet air burst over Bradok as he wrenched the hammer free from the hole in the wall. He hadn't realized how stale the air in the fissure had become. The air issuing from the black hole bore a vaguely spicy smell, reminding him of the spice rack Sapphire always had in the kitchen when he was growing up.

"I know that smell," Halum Ironband said.

Halum reminded Bradok of the kind of dwarf one might find in the seediest tavern in the lowest hall in Ironroot. His clothes were all dark and well worn, and his face bore the markings of many scrapes and brawls. When he smiled, Halum showed at least three gold teeth and the stained gums of a blackroot user.

The rough dwarf leaned toward the hole and sniffed the air like a chef savoring a fine wine. "Peppertops," he concluded after a moment.

"Is that food?" little Graylin Anvil asked his grandfather.

Marl Anvil grinned his gap-toothed smile and nodded.

Bradok hefted the hammer and struck the wall as hard as he could. That time a large slab of rock exploded inward, leaving a passage almost wide enough for him to squeeze through. Two more hard hits doubled the size of the opening.

"Bring up the lantern," Bradok called, squinting in an attempt to make out anything in the blackness beyond the opening.

One of the blue lanterns materialized, being passed down the passage on the end of its pole. When Bradok got it, he stuck it into the hole as far as the pole would reach.

A large chamber lay beyond, full of stalactites and stalagmites and joined columns of rock. The air felt drier and fresher than the air in the long, rough passage they'd been using. All along the bases of the stalagmites and around every column, Bradok could see that mushrooms were growing. Tall, speckled peppertops rose on thick, meaty stalks, while short, broad-topped honey mushrooms clustered beneath them. Bradok had never favored mushrooms as most others of his race sometimes did, but as hungry as he was, they looked every bit as delicious as a banquet.

"Well," someone demanded. "What do you see?"

Bradok's face split into a wide grin, and he felt a relief he hadn't known in almost a week. "Mushrooms," he said. "Enough for us all and then some."

Everyone rushed for the hole at once, as if they had all been launched from a siege engine. Bradok barely had time to throw himself through the gap before a crush of bodies clogged it.

"Easy, easy," he shouted, pushing himself to his feet. "There's plenty here and a few minutes' more wait won't kill anyone."

Kellik and Vulnar had their heads half poked through the hole. From beyond, Bradok heard the sound of a whistle being blown and Chisul's muffled voice giving orders. Soon the bodies blocking the hole withdrew and a more ordered stream of dwarves began to enter.

The first ones through went straight for the nearest mushrooms, eagerly tearing off their tops in chunks and stuffing them in their mouths. Little Jade Bronzecap, Lyra's daughter stuffed a piece of peppertop in her mouth and stood, fanning her tongue after swallowing. Bradok laughed, and her mother passed her a bit of honey mushroom to blunt the spicy taste.

"Don't eat too much or too fast," Tal advised, stepping through the hole. "You're too hungry. You'll make yourselves sick."

The part of the cave visible in the lantern light filled rapidly with eating dwarves, so Bradok held the light up and began to edge back into the cavern. The place didn't appear too large, but he still could barely see the far side in the blue light. As Perin brought the second light through the hole, Bradok moved back, swinging his light around in an effort to better inspect the back wall. There appeared to be a recess in the back, but he couldn't tell if it was just a side chamber or some kind of exit.

His stomach rumbled and Bradok remembered how hungry he was too. He stooped down to pick the top off a honey mushroom. As the saucer-sized top came free with a tiny snap, Bradok's eyes focused on a strangely discolored rock behind the mushroom patch. He stared, trying to see better. A moment later his heart jumped up into his throat and he leaped backward with a strangled cry.

Sounds of confusion erupted behind him as Bradok tried to hold the lantern pole steady with one hand and jerk his sword from its scabbard with his right.

"What is it?" Halum said. The dwarf rushed out of the darkness, wielding a particularly wicked-looking curved fighting knife.

Behind Halum rushed Kellik with his warhammer, and Chisul and Vulnar, each toting a short sword.

"Over there," Bradok said, pointing with his sword into the darkness beyond the mushroom patch. He raised the lantern pole, and the azure light washed over something straight out of dwarf nightmares.

The assembled dwarves gasped and readied their weapons. It took a long minute for them to realize they were gazing upon the echo of an ancient horror.

A skull.

It was a skull as broad across as Kellik's burly shoulders, with empty eye sockets the size of saucers and fangs like daggers. The skull had rolled free of a crumbled spine and rib cage, the skeletal body huge—almost the size of Silas's boat. Six skeletal legs radiated out from the ruin, ending in spearlike points with barbed, bony hooks.

"A giant cave spider," Much gasped, coming up to stand beside the armed party. "Lucky for us it's long dead."

Strictly speaking, cave spiders weren't spiders at all, but monster insects. Bradok shuddered involuntarily at the thought of what might have happened if that one hadn't succumbed to the ravages of time. He'd always known that the dwarves weren't the only creatures who lived far below the surface of Krynn, but the sight of the skeletal, once-deadly monster reminded him that unfamiliar caves could be very dangerous places.

"Check the roof," Vulnar said, his voice a fatigued croak. "I heard some of the deep miners say that they lay their eggs up high, where their young can drop on unsuspecting passersby."

Bradok held up the light, and all eyes swept the roof. A little ways to the left of the skeleton, they noticed three orbs that appeared to be attached to the roof of the cavern by some kind of paste or glue. They were all cracked and empty, but the sight gave the dwarves chills.

"Spread out," Chisul commanded, holding his sword above his head. "Make sure there aren't any more like that."

Bradok and Kellik moved off toward the far end of the cave, and the others made their way back to where everyone waited. An inspection of the ceiling yielded no more eggs, empty or otherwise. When they reached the back of the cavern,

Bradok's light illuminated a dark crack in the wall. Closer scrutiny revealed a passage leading away from the chamber into darkness.

"Should we follow this way?" Kellik asked. "See where it goes?"

Bradok reckoned that it would be a tight squeeze for him to get through the crack, and that the broad Kellik might not fit at all.

"No," he said, his stomach rumbling. "Not yet anyway. The way's too narrow as it is, and nothing too menacing will be able to get through to bother us here."

Kellik nodded and the pair returned to join the others. Rose and Tal met him with worried looks. They'd gathered a modest pile of mushrooms in their cloaks and bade Bradok and Kellik to sit and eat.

Ignoring Tal 's advice to eat modestly, Bradok stuffed himself. Between the spicy peppertops and the sweet honey mushrooms, he felt as if he'd just dined in some luxurious tavern. After he had eaten his fill and more, Bradok leaned back against a column of rock and closed his eyes.

"We should gather up as much as we can carry," he heard Chisul say just as he was about to doze off. "There's no telling when we'll get out of these tunnels."

Everyone murmured agreement and the dwarves began moving again, cutting mushrooms and wrapping them in whatever they had handy.

"You shouldn't let him do that," Tal whispered as Bradok opened his eyes to watch the activity.

"Do what?"

Tal pointed to Chisul. "If you allow him to lead, the others will begin to look to him as our leader," he said.

Bradok shrugged. "What do I care?" he said. "It makes him happy and keeps him from complaining. I don't feel like much of a leader, anyway."

"He's a spoiled kid," Tal said, fixing Bradok with a serious stare. "That kind of leader makes impulsive decisions, and impulsive decisions get people killed."

"He's right, you know," Rose chimed in, sidling closer. She was still nibbling on a mushroom.

"We have to think ahead," Tal continued. "Sooner or later we're going to get out of these caverns. Have you thought about what happens then?"

Bradok admitted he hadn't.

"What caused the destruction of Ironroot?" Tal asked. "Who knows what other destruction it caused?"

"What are you driving at?" Bradok answered, tired of Tal's know-it-all air.

"What if we make it to the surface and there's no one there anymore?" Tal said, an earnest look on his face.

"Don't be absurd," Bradok said. "The surface world is positively lousy with humans and elves and all sorts of things. What makes you think the destruction spread beyond Ironroot?"

"What makes you think it didn't?" Rose asked, exchanging looks with her brother. "What if it was a disaster that wiped out much of Krynn? What if there are few dwarves left alive anywhere? Then what?"

Bradok frowned, thinking it over. They were back to being believers. But something very bad had happened to Krynn. What had happened, why had it happened, and how far had it spread? He had to admit, he hadn't thought deeply enough about the possibilities.

"I guess we'd have to start our own town," he said finally. "Rebuild."

Rose and Tal nodded.

"Exactly," Tal said. "And who do you think will be the leader of that town? Who will they come to for advice and laws and justice? Who will wield power then?"

"Well, I guess it'll be who leads us to safety," he said, uncomfortably.

"Do you want Chisul to become our leader when all this

is over?" Tal said. "He's a good enough person, but he's also selfish and spoiled. Such a dwarf would lead us to ruin."

Bradok nodded slowly. He hated those kind of political problems, but Tal had a very valid point. Chisul was the kind of dwarf who would crown himself king if he got the chance. If only his father, Silas, were there; he might knock some sense into his son.

"So what do you propose?" he asked Tal.

The doctor's handsome face twisted into a winning grin, only barely disguised by his short, red beard. "You're already a better leader than Chisul and he knows it," he said. "You possess the enchanted compass. You found the food. All you have to do is take charge more decisively, and they'll follow you instead of him. I'm sure of that."

Bradok glanced at Rose, who was nodding encouragingly.

Bradok wasn't sure he wanted the responsibilities they were pushing on him, but Tal had been right about one thing. Chisul was a well-intentioned dwarf who would be a terrible leader. It didn't take much imagination to see in him another Mayor Arbuckle, down the line. Bradok had to step up and take command—for the sake of everyone.

"I'll gather more mushrooms," Rose said, rising. "You two talk it over and figure out which direction we should head in next."

Bradok smiled as she placed his pack next to hers to fill. He stood up, walked back to the opening he'd hammered in the wall, then moved to stand beneath one of the lanterns. Dallon Ramshorn, the wheelwright from Everguard, had pushed the end of the pole into the soft ground, leaving the lantern suspended above. Bradok took out the compass with a flourish, ensuring anyone in the vicinity would notice him. He felt completely foolish but swallowed his pride and played up checking the compass.

The moment he looked into it, however, all guile vanished. The image of the Seer was back, and she kept jabbing her spear urgently, pointing back the way they came. At first Bradok could not fathom why, but then something dawned on him.

"Everyone," he said, raising his voice. "I think it's time to leave."

Chisul looked up. "Maybe having just eaten," he said, his voice a confident drawl, "we should take some time to rest and digest."

"Normally, I'd agree with you," Bradok said; then he held up the compass for emphasis. "I think something's wrong, though."

"What's she doing now?" Much asked, standing up to look over Bradok's shoulder.

"Let me see that," Chisul said, reaching for the compass.

For a moment, Bradok considered not giving it to Chisul, thinking he didn't want to appear weak. Then he remembered how often that had been Arbuckle and Bladehook's rationale for their behavior.

Bradok dropped the compass in Chisul's hand. The moment the other dwarf held the compass, however, the Seer stopped her pointing and crossed her arms over her chest in a gesture of defiance.

"Huh! Do you always have this effect on women?" Rose asked teasingly, elbowing Chisul in the ribs.

Chisul growled and passed the compass back to Bradok whereupon the Seer immediately resumed her frantic pointing.

"What's she doing?" Chisul demanded.

"Well, she's probably just impatient to be gone from here," Kellik said. "Most magic things have a mind of their own."

"I hate to be contrary," Marl Anvil said, "but I agree with Chisul. The children are tired. Everyone's tired. We need to rest."

"We could do with a bit of a rest," Much agreed. The old dwarf lay stretched out with his head against the base of column of rock.

Bradok opened his mouth to argue, but shut it again immediately. A strange, powerful odor suddenly pervaded the cavern—the stench of rot and decay. It seemed to invade his senses, even leaving an aftertaste in his mouth. Poor Lyra felt it come upon her, too, all of a sudden; she collapsed and retched all over the floor. Everywhere dwarves began covering their noses with hands and handkerchiefs in a vain effort to ward off the stench.

Chisul stared hard at Bradok. "I think you're right after all," he said. "Everyone get to the hole!" Chisul shouted. "Get the women and children out first!"

"Look!" Halum shouted, pointing.

Bradok turned toward the back of the cavern. A quick glance revealed a pale light glowing from inside the crack at the very back of the area. Someone or something had found them.

As Bradok watched, pale white hands appeared and broke off the edges of the crack, widening the hole. Next emerged five dwarves, or at least five beings who might have been dwarves once. Each had the pale skin, white-blond hair, and reddish eyes of a Daergar, but there the similarities to living Daergar ended. They had strange gray patches on their skin, and each of them seemed to have sprouted glowing mushrooms from various parts of their bodies. Glowing roots spread out under their skin like veins from the errant fungi.

The moment the five strange dwarves entered the chamber, the stench that had preceded their arrival became nearly unbearable.

"Get those children out of here," Bradok said, breaking the spell that had gripped everyone, their eyes riveted upon the eerie newcomers. Everyone burst back into action.

The abrupt activity seemed to rouse the attention of the mushroom-covered dwarves, as if they had overlooked them at first.

"Look," one of them said in a peculiar, far-away voice. "Who are they?"

A tallish female leaned forward, squinting through her greasy, grime-covered hair. "Outsiders," she wailed. "Unclean."

Bradok absently wondered who the five dwarves thought they were to call *him* unclean. Whoever the strange dwarves were, he decided, they seemed a threat. Without even thinking about the possible consequences, he drew his sword and stepped forward, between the escaping women and children and the strange, glowing dwarves.

"They have f-f-food," a squat, mushroomed dwarf stammered.

"They've taken mushrooms from this cavern," the tall woman said in a voice of outrage.

"We must have the f-f-food," the squat one said.

With that, they shambled forward in a curious, undulating gait, as if their legs weren't working properly.

"Hold them off!" Bradok said, standing forward with his sword raised.

Dallon and Halum appeared on Bradok's right, while Kellik, Rose, Vulnar, and Chisul flanked him on his left. Each carried a weapon, but the weapons didn't seem to interest the Daergar in the slightest. As they came closer, the stench of their bodies became almost suffocating. Bradok could see the strange fungi growing on their extremities in horrifyingly exquisite detail. The squat dwarf in the center of the bunch even had a tiny mushroom growing from the front of his left eye. It shifted and danced as he looked about.

Bradok's fascination with the putrid dwarves almost cost him his life. The squat dwarf suddenly struck out at him with his arm, using his limb like one might use a club. Out of instinct more than anything else, Bradok parried with his sword. The enchanted blade sliced through the gray flesh as easily as one might carve warm butter. The severed limb spun back over the dwarf's head and away into the darkness.

If the dwarf felt anything for the loss of his arm, he didn't show it. There was scarcely any change in the weird expression on his face. But a dark liquid that resembled sap more than blood oozed from the wound, and the dwarf staggered back under the force of Bradok's blow.

Beside him Dallon had smashed in the eyes of the thin dwarf with his hammer, but the body didn't seem to notice the injury and was determined to attack anyway. The sightless dwarf's arms spun wildly, attempting to grapple an enemy it could no longer see.

Bradok stepped sideways and helped Dallon by deftly slicing through his foe's thigh. With only one leg holding it up, the strange mushroom-ridden Daergar fell helpless to the ground, its arms still flailing in a vain attempt to continue his attack.

Rose and Chisul were fighting the tall woman. The tall Daergar had lashed out with her clawlike nails, leaving bloody gashes on Rose's arm and Chisul's cheek. As Chisul chopped an arm from her body, Rose hacked at her legs. Rose wielded only a long knife, but she struck true, sending the shrieking hag over backward with a shattered knee.

Bradok turned again, just in time to see Halum and Kellik bashing and slicing their foe into pieces with brutal efficiency.

"Look out!" Dallon called just in the nick of time.

The squat dwarf was back, carrying his severed arm and swinging it like a club. The wounded end of the arm hit Bradok in the shoulder, leaving behind a smear of foul-smelling blood.

Bradok didn't hesitate. He chopped away the dwarf's good hand, then smote off his head in a single stroke. The headless body stumbled forward to continue the attack, but Dallon bashed its hip with a sideways blow of his hammer, sending it into a writhing pile on the cavern floor.

Chisul and Rose had backed away from their victim, who lay undulating on the floor, her remaining hand pressed to her abdomen. She screamed as the flesh beneath her hand began to expand in some bizarre mimicry of pregnancy.

"What's happening to her?" Rose gasped, disgust in her voice.

"I don't think we should wait to find out," Chisul said, horrified, edging back.

"Good idea," Bradok said. "Everybody out!"

They all turned and raced for the hole. During their fight most of the others had escaped, and the rest scrambled to get away.

Chisul dived through the opening, headfirst, followed by Rose. As Dallon, then Vulnar, retreated, Bradok glanced back.

The writhing woman's abdomen had distended beyond the size of mountain boulder and seemed ready to burst.

"Hurry up," he told Kellik as the big smith forced his burly body through the opening. Then Bradok plunged through the gap.

"Get up the tunnel," he yelled at the loitering dwarves. "Now!"

No one saw fit to argue. They turned and ran, chasing after the light ahead that marked the flight of the others. Dallon carried their second lantern. They had gone only a few steps up the tunnel when there came a tremendous bang and the sound of wet, pulpy material exploding against the walls of the cavern.

As they whirled in horror, they saw a golden mist flowing out of the hole. Little flecks of something were suspended in it, undulating and moving as it spread.

"Quick! That mist has to be poisonous," Rose warned before turning to run.

"Move!" Bradok echoed, and the remaining survivors sprinted away as fast as they could after their fleeing companions.

CHAPTER 11
Eyes in the Dark

Fire burned in Bradok's lungs as he ran headlong up the passage of rock. Ragged breathing filled the space around him as his companions raced with him away from the golden mist. His foot struck some unseen protrusion in the floor of the passage and he stumbled. A strong arm shot out of the darkness and grabbed his elbow, steadying him then shoving him forward, urging him on.

"What were those things?" Halum said, his voice shaky and uncertain.

"Who cares?" Vulnar cried, his voice huffing through his ragged breaths.

"That mist cloud looked like spores," Dallon gasped, his voice close behind.

"What in the world could it be?" Chisul asked.

"I don't want to find out," Rose said.

"Talk about it later," Bradok wheezed.

He could already see the blue light that marked the place where the rest of the group waited for them.

"Are you all right?" Tal asked as the panting, sweating dwarves joined them, collapsing into heaps on the floor.

"Rose and Chisul," Bradok said, leaning on his knees to catch his breath.

"It's just a scratch," Rose said, waving Tal off as he tried to examine her arm. Turning to Bradok, she said, "That mist—do you think it might follow us?"

A cold chill ran down Bradok's spine. He knew that it was more than possible. They couldn't tarry there long.

"Let's see what we can find out," he said, reaching for the compass. To his utter horror, his hand found only an empty pocket.

"It's gone," he gasped.

"What's gone?" Rose asked in a low voice, looking around to make sure the other dwarves hadn't heard and been alarmed.

"The compass," he said, frantically patting his other pockets. "I must have dropped it during the fight, or maybe when we ran up the passage."

He sprang to his feet, feeling his heart beat fast. "I've got to go back," he said.

Even before he could take a step back down the passage, Rose and Chisul had grabbed his arms.

"Are you insane?" Chisul said. "That mist could be churning up the passage right now."

"But I've got to get the compass," Bradok said, struggling against them. "We need it to tell us how to survive down here."

"Survive?" Chisul said. "I'd say we get as far away from that mist as possible, and our chances for survival will go way up."

"He's right," Rose said. "Maybe the compass has served its purpose, like the ship."

Bradok stopped struggling, and they released him. "I must have dropped it," he said ashamedly to Rose.

She put a reassuring hand on his shoulder and looked into his eyes. "Then we'll just have to go by faith, won't we?" she said gently. "Now let's get these people moving. We want to put as much distance as possible between us and that mist."

Erus, or Reorx, or whoever it was had given that compass to him for a reason, and he felt sure that reason still existed. But he had let everyone down by losing or dropping it. Some leader he was.

Bradok turned to the survivors. Anxious faces looked up at him. They had heard some of the discussion and were apprehensive about the loss of the compass. He tried to adopt a strong, stoic mask.

"All right, everyone," he called out. "The danger is behind us, but we should probably make as much distance as we can today, so let's get going."

"Very diplomatic," Tal whispered, falling in beside Bradok as the group began to move. "Just like a true leader."

Bradok shook his head. "They know the compass is gone," he said. "They'll have to hear the truth sooner or later."

The fight had taken a lot out of him. Bradok felt age and pain as they walked. He listened to the conversations around him. A young couple, whose names Bradok couldn't remember, were taking turns carrying their toddler daughter, telling her all about the wonderful things they would do when they got to where they were going. Where was *that?* Bradok wondered silently. Where would they all end up? Had Reorx intended some destination for them? What if Tal was right and the whole world was gone? What then?

Seerten Rockhide, an armorer from Everguard, was exchanging forging tips with Kellik. Much was walking alongside the pregnant Lyra and fussing over her and her daughter, Jade. She must bring out the grandfather in his old friend, Bradok thought.

Everywhere around him, the survivors were walking and talking and letting some of the tension slip away. After two days of desperate hunger, it felt good to hear their voices again.

Several hours later, they emerged into a small, round cavern. With the exception of the hole Bradok had made in the wall, it was the only change in the long fissure since they had left the beach almost a week before. Much consulted his watch and pronounced it a good time to stop and camp and review their plans in the morning.

The chamber had a smooth, featureless roof and rounded sides, like a bubble of air in a sea of stone. Two passages exited the little cave, both appearing to continue on for some distance.

Everyone had eaten so much that no one felt particularly hungry. Instead, Chisul told everyone about the gory fight with the mushroom people. He had a rapt audience. Although Silas's son embroidered his own bravery, he also gave credit to everyone else in the battle. Bradok found as he sat listening, cross-legged on the rocky floor of the cave, that he quite enjoyed Chisul's version of the fight; it made them all seem heroic.

During the story, Rose and Tal sat next to Bradok.

"Was it really like that?" Tal whispered at one point.

"Pretty much," Rose said, rubbing her arm where Tal had bandaged it.

"Don't do that," he said. "Let it heal."

Everyone agreed that those who fought to protect them should be allowed to get an uninterrupted night's sleep. Bradok had taken first watch every night since they started on their adventure, so he didn't mind a little break. As the others continued to talk about the exciting events of the day, he quietly rolled himself in his cloak and almost instantly went to sleep, snoring softly.

By the time he awoke the next morning, Rose and Chisul were already up and arguing about which of the two passages that exited the little chamber offered the best prospects. Tal glanced meaningfully at the arguing pair as Bradok took a swig from his waterskin to wash the taste of sleep from his mouth.

"I think they need a leader," Tal whispered.

Bradok stood and shook the dirt out of his cloak before wrapping it around his shoulders and hitching the metal clasp across his chest. Some of the dwarves had dug a small privy down the tunnel, just beyond the range of the light. Taking a deep breath, Bradok headed down the tunnel to relieve himself.

It took Bradok's eyes almost a full minute to shrug off the darkness and find the privy in the empty tunnel. It had been dug far enough back along the tunnel that the argument still going on behind him had faded into incomprehensible echoes.

As he stood there doing his business, trying not to think about the decisions that lay ahead, he heard a strange sound. His senses tried to grab hold of it, identify it.

It sounded like a giggle.

Thinking that perhaps one of the children had followed him, Bradok turned his head back up the passage. Finding it as empty as he'd left it, he spun forward again. His eyes swept the black depths and, for a moment, he thought he spied something. Out on the edge of his vision, he could have sworn something shifted, melting back into the darkness as his eyes passed over it.

He stared, fixedly, at the spot, but it remained unchanged, just a blank face of rock that made up one side of the fissure. Still, Bradok couldn't shake the feeling that he had seen something move there, something that had retreated when he noticed it.

The memory of the cave spider skeleton lurched into his mind, and he shuddered, turning to go back. Bradok cursed and heard the sound again—a short, truncated giggle. Whatever he didn't know about cave spiders, he knew they didn't giggle.

"Is someone there?" he called nervously.

Only silence greeted him from the depths.

"I won't hurt you," he called.

Still, nothing responded.

His hand slipped around the hilt of his sword, and he twisted it loose in its scabbard. Straining his ears, he could make out only the continuing dull drone of the argument between Rose and Chisul. He took a few tentative steps down the passageway but saw nothing out of the ordinary. The more rational part of his brain warned him not to go too far, for if something did rush him from the darkness, he would be too far away to call for help.

At length, he shrugged. It had been a long and stressful week, and he was hearing things. With a sigh he turned back to camp.

The argument he'd been avoiding was still raging as he entered the little cave. It had escalated to shouting, and had everyone's attention. The survivors looked at Bradok expectantly as he marched up to Chisul and Rose.

"And I'm telling you that way is the right way; it slopes *up*," Rose was shouting, mere inches from Chisul's face. "You remember *up*, don't you, the direction of the surface?"

Chisul pointed at the opposite opening. "As far as I can tell, they all go up, and then later they go down. Up and down. Round and round. Back and forth. That's where we've gone so far."

"There you are finally," Rose said, noting Bradok's appearance. "Will you please tell this buffoon that I'm right, and—"

Chisul looked scornfully at Bradok.

Bradok held up his hand for peace, and amazingly, both Rose and Chisul stopped arguing. He walked to the tunnel that Rose had suggested. It did slope slightly upward and looked promising.

Undecided, Bradok walked across the cave to the other opening. All eyes in the chamber followed him as he went. That passage resembled the one they'd been following for the past week, ragged and straight. As Bradok stood there, he could feel the push of air against his face. There was good air in that passage.

"Chisul's right," he said, turning back to the group. "We should take this one."

Rose looked taken aback and strangely hurt.

"I told you," Chisul said, puffing up his chest. "I told her," he said, addressing all the dwarves.

Bradok pointed up the passage. "There's air moving down this passage," he explained. "That means that somewhere up ahead, there's a way out. I think it's our best choice."

The crowd of survivors nodded their approval.

"Now let's get some breakfast," Bradok said. "We'll want to put some good distance under our feet today."

At the mention of the word *breakfast,* the gathered dwarves emitted an audible sigh of anticipation. Three days' hard marching with no food once had seemed like an eternity. At that moment it was like a bad dream to be forgotten. Everyone sat, clustered together in groups of kin or friends and brought out chunks of mushroom to share.

Rose pointedly moved to sit among the other hill dwarves, though she cast a glance back at Bradok. He sat next to Much and was joined by the human, Perin, and Kellik and his sons.

Kellik was in a buoyant mood, showing his crooked teeth in a big smile and pointing to the biggest of his two boys, a burly lad whose beard had just begun coming in. "That's my Rijul," he informed Much; then, indicating the boy with his arm in a sling, he added, "I think you already know my youngest son, Hemmish."

Hemmish smiled, a chunk of honey mushroom sliding around between his teeth, and Much grinned back.

"What happened to their mother?" Much asked quietly once the boys were engrossed in their breakfast.

A shadow passed over Kellik's face for a moment; then he sighed. "She died last year," he said in a subdued tone.

"I'm sorry," Bradok said, although partly he was sorry that Much had asked such an indelicate question.

"It's all right," Kellik said wistfully. "It's just that some-times a year doesn't really seem like all that much time."

Anxious to change the subject, Bradok turned to Perin,

"Tell us about you, Perin," he said. "What brought you to Ironroot?"

The tall human smiled and shrugged. "The man who first taught me the cooper's art died," he said. "I still had much to learn. I heard that Silas was the best cooper for two hundred miles in any direction, so I traveled to Ironroot and had to practically beg him to take me on as an apprentice. Silas was a good soul."

Everyone was silent for a moment, thinking of Silas. Bradok glanced over at Chisul, who wasn't paying any attention to them.

"No offense, but most dwarves wouldn't take on a human apprentice," Much said.

If he felt offended by such frankness, Perin didn't show it. He just smiled in an easy, knowing manner. "Silas wasn't like most dwarves," he said respectfully. "Besides, I think he wanted me around to kind of challenge Chisul to work harder, do better."

"Did it work?" Kellik asked.

Perin shook his head, chuckling. "Quite the opposite," he explained. "With me there, Chisul figured his father had someone to run the business once he retired. That left Chisul free to pursue his two favorite pastimes: beer and women."

At the mention of beer, Bradok's stomach growled angrily. "I wish you hadn't said 'beer,' " he said with a grimace. "It reminds me that I'm thirsty for something other than water."

Much and Kellik laughed and agreed.

"Wherever we finally stop, we'd better have access to some ore deposits," Kellik said as they began packing up.

"Why?" Bradok asked.

"Because I'll need some copper and iron to make a decent still," he said with a grin.

"That's not all you'll need," a feminine voice said.

Standing over them was Urlish Hearthhome, a squat hill dwarf with a plain face and clever eyes. "You'll need barley."

Kellik stood and shouldered his pack, nodding sagely. "You're right," he said. "The barley will be harder to find down here than copper and iron. A still's no good without something to put in it."

It turned out Urlish was a farm girl from a long line of farm girls. There didn't seem to be anything about planting or growing that she didn't know. They fell into step together. Kellik spent the better part of the morning locked in conversation with her about the best way to set up a large-scale brewery one day.

Kellik and Urlish weren't the only ones suddenly in good spirits. The children laughed and sang as they marched along, and Dallon, the wheelwright from Everguard, had clearly taken a shine to Starlight Anvil, the eldest of the Anvil grandchildren.

The most cheerful one, however, seemed to be the usually stoic Much. He wove through the crowd of marching dwarves, checking on Lyra, telling jokes, entertaining the children. At one point he passed Bradok, carrying Teal, the dark-haired toddler of the young couple who didn't talk very much. Bradok told himself he really should learn their names, and the names of all the children too, but he had never been good with names.

Unlike their previous travels, they encountered several open chambers and side passages, though all of those were too narrow for the group to pass through. Finally they reached a chamber with two exits. One looked just like the fissure they'd been following; the other angled up from the top of the chamber.

"We'll have to climb to reach that one," Rose said to no one in particular.

"How do we know we should take that one?" Vulnar said.

"I wish you hadn't lost that compass," Halum said to Bradok.

He didn't mean for it to be a rebuke, but it felt that way to Bradok.

"It's getting late and everyone's tired," Much said, consulting his watch to break the tension. "Let's stop here for the night. That'll give us a chance to check both passages."

Hours later, a thorough inspection of the two possible passages yielded nothing to recommend either of them over the other. Finally after much arguing and debate, the dwarves gave it up and resolved to explore afresh in the morning.

Somewhere around midnight, Tal nudged Bradok with his foot. "Get up," he whispered, waking Bradok for his watch. Once Bradok had sat up, rubbing his eyes, he made his way to where his cloak lay, waiting for him.

Bradok stretched, allowing his eyes to adjust to the dimness. They had covered the glowlamps with a piece of cheesecloth, dimming the light significantly, during the night. He strapped on his sword and made his way to the mouth of the tunnel they'd come through. He still remembered the strange noise he'd heard the previous morning, and had asked that someone watch the path behind them. To his delight, he found Rose there, waiting for him. She smiled when he arrived, her teeth flashing in the low light.

"I see you drew the short straw," she joked.

He nodded, leaning against the passage wall. "You too," he said.

Rose shook her head. "I volunteered," she said. "I like to sit and think when it's quiet. I don't get much chance to do that during the day."

Bradok wanted to ask her about her life in Everguard but thought better of it. There was a very real chance that the village and everyone Rose had known were dead—all her friends, family, if she had family. He thought of a dozen ways of starting a conversation and rejected each in turn as awkward or inane.

An uncomfortable silence stretched out between them. Bradok cursed himself; he hadn't had so much trouble talking to a girl since he was a lad. Finally he decided on an old standby. He pulled out his waterskin, took a long drink, then held it out to Rose.

"Buy you a drink?" he said with what he hoped was his most charming smile.

Rose chuckled; then her eyes went wide as a bright green light washed over both of them. Bradok dropped the waterskin and turned, jerking his sword from its scabbard.

A sight like he'd never imagined greeted him.

A glowing ball of light hovered over the floor, drifting back and forth as if caught in a current. It looked completely insubstantial, as though it were the stuff of mere light without form or body. As Bradok watched, a green patch appeared on the ground, and a second one oozed up out of the floor of the cave.

"What are they?" he whispered, amazed at the sight of the balls of light.

Rose shook her head. "I don't know but they're beautiful," she said.

The second glowing ball hovered for a moment, like the first, then it shot upward without a sound, zooming around the ceiling of the cavern. The first light reacted instantly, giving chase.

Bradok and Rose watched in awe as the pair darted soundlessly around the chamber. If the strange, ethereal creatures were aware of the dwarves sleeping below them, they gave no sign.

Every time the two lights got close enough to touch, a spark of electricity crackled between them. Finally they circled each other, the sparks jumping regularly between them.

"What—" Rose began, but at that very moment the two lights disengaged and came darting straight for the passage entrance.

Bradok didn't think; he leaped in front of Rose, knocking her down. Both of the light creatures slammed into his chest, passing right through his body and into the wall behind him.

A shock like lightning ran through him at their passing and Bradok collapsed.

His senses cleared a moment later, and he found himself lying on top of Rose.

"Hey, I thought I told you next time to bring flowers," she joked.

Bradok tried to smile but every muscle in his body seemed to be quivering weakly in the wake of the attack of the odd light-creatures. Was it an attack he had suffered? He did manage to get one arm under him, but he had no strength to push himself up.

Rose pushed up on his shoulders, trying to roll him off. She grunted with the effort, making gradual progress.

Just then Bradok heard a sound that was ominous—the click of a rock hitting the stone of the floor. Both he and Rose stopped dead, listening. Somewhere down the passage, someone had kicked or dropped or dislodged a rock.

Their eyes met and Rose nodded, understanding immediately. She rolled Bradok off and quickly crouched, drawing her long knife. Shakily, Bradok joined her as his muscles began to obey him.

Without making a sound, the pair of them advanced down the black passageway. They moved slowly, giving their eyes time to adjust to the total darkness. After a few dozen yards, they stopped. From somewhere below them, the sounds of whispered voices came drifting up. They were able to catch most of the words.

". . . you sure?" someone asked.

"Hmm, yes," a dreamy-sounding voice answered. "He's rolling around on the floor with some woman. Once they get going, we should be able to slip by."

"Ah, the good old days," a third, mild voice said.

"Enough," the first voice quieted them. "We need to be ready. As soon as we hear them, we take off."

"Go," a new voice said.

Sounds of someone moving echoed up the passage.

"No," the first voice hissed. "Omer, get back here."

Bradok gripped the handle of his sword, holding it up in front of him just as a figure rounded a bend in the tunnel not ten feet ahead of him. As his hand tightened around the hilt, he did something he had never done before: he made a wish, wishing he'd brought a light. Suddenly the enchanted blade burst into a pale, orange glow.

In the light, Bradok could see three dwarves with white-blond hair and white skin. The tallest had a braided and forked beard that decorated a shrewd-looking face. Behind him came a woman, with glassy blue eyes and long, disheveled hair. They both seemed to be reaching for the dwarf in front. He was younger, with his beard barely in, and he had an innocent, childlike expression on his face.

Bradok saw all that in the moment it took for the pale dwarves to react to the light. The big man and the woman shielded their eyes as if in horrific pain, but the younger dwarf simply stared at the glowing sword, his face contorted into a mask of rage and hatred.

"Magic!" he shrieked, his voice like an explosion in the silence of the tunnel.

What happened next was almost too fast for Bradok to follow. The young dwarf leaped as if he'd been shot from a catapult, slamming into Bradok and knocking him to the floor. The attacker's hands were around Bradok's throat, squeezing with a force unlike any Bradok had ever known. Purple dots erupted across his vision and the world went dark.

CHAPTER 12
The Outsiders

Bradok's fingers tore at the hand, clamped like an iron band over his throat. He could hear Rose cursing and other voices, too, unfamiliar voices, echoing as if from far away.

"Omer," one shouted. "Let go, boy."

"No," the young dwarf roared, not letting go for a moment. "Magic!"

"He's not a Theiwar, boy. Look at him," the first voice said. "It's just a magic sword. The sword is magic, not him. It's 'found' magic."

The vice on Bradok's throat loosened a bit, and Bradok gulped a lungful of air.

"Found magic," the young dwarf repeated, his voice changing back to a tone less threatening, the childlike innocence. "Like me?"

"Yes, like you," the fork-bearded dwarf said.

When the hand released Bradok, he scurried back, gasping. The pale youth could barely grow a beard, yet he'd manhandled Bradok like a rag doll.

The fork-bearded dwarf raised his hands, showing them he was weaponless and meant no harm. "Don't be afraid," he said. "Just tell him you didn't make that magic sword."

"I didn't," Bradok gasped. "I've never even witnessed its

magic before. My father won it off an elf in a dice game, long, long ago."

The young dwarf made a soft cooing sound, like a bird, then picked up Bradok's sword and held it out to him.

"Then please accept my apologies," he said in a slow voice.

Bradok reached out hesitantly and took the sword.

"It's all right," he said with a reassurance he didn't feel. He got to his feet, holding the sword down but still in front of him.

"Don't mind him," the dwarf said matter-of-factly. "He just hates wizards. A Theiwar wizard kidnapped him when he was a baby."

The young dwarf shuddered and squatted down at the older one's feet, putting his arms around his waist and pressing his head against the fork-bearded dwarf's abdomen.

"The wizard experimented on poor Omer, here," he said, stroking the young dwarf's hair with a gentle hand. "Unfortunately he hasn't been right in the head since he escaped."

The passageway filled with the sound of running feet, and many of Bradok's companions turned up, wielding their weapons.

"What goes on here?" Much demanded threateningly.

The fork-bearded dwarf raised his hands again. "Easy friends," he said. "We don't mean anyone any harm."

"Like we'd believe you," Jenner said, clutching an evil-looking war axe. "We wouldn't take the word of a Daergar."

The Daergar had long ago separated their clan from normal dwarf society in favor of living in the deep places of Krynn. Bradok knew the stories told about them: that they were evil, untrustworthy, and hated their higher-dwelling cousins.

"It's true we are Daergar," the dwarf said, indicating his small party. "My name is Corinthar Darklight; you can call me Corin. My friends and I were just passing through here. We mean you no jeopardy; I give you my word on that."

"Friends?" Chisul said.

"There was a woman with him," Bradok said, noticing her absence for the first time, "and I heard at least one other voice too."

"There are six of us," Corin said; then he turned and yelled back down the passage. "Come on out, everyone."

Shuffling out of the darkness came four more Daergar. The woman he'd seen before came first, followed by a short, rotund dwarf with a beard cascading nearly down to the ground. Behind him came a tall dwarf with an exquisite face and a close-cropped beard. The last man was stocky and broad, and from what Bradok could see of him, his body bore many scars that crisscrossed his flesh.

All of them squinted against the light. They were dressed in rags and wore no shoes on their feet.

"You say you're just passing through here?" Rose asked.

"Just so, friend," Corin said, an easy, unconcerned smile on his face.

"So you know these caves?" she said. "Do you know a way to the surface?"

Corin hesitated; then his shoulders fell. "I'm afraid not, miss," he said. "We're just as lost as you."

At that the woman giggled, and Bradok recognized her. That was the sound he'd heard two mornings earlier when he was using the privy at the other camp. He blushed as he realized she'd been watching him.

"Did you somehow escape?" Chisul asked.

The woman giggled again. "Oh, we escaped all right, hand-some," she replied, her amused expression transformed into an open leer.

"Easy, Jeni," Corin said.

"What does she mean?" Rose asked, suspicion clouding her face. "Where did you escape from?"

Corin sighed and cast a vaguely disparaging look at Jeni, who appeared not to notice or care. "We were prisoners in the Burning Rock Penal Caves," he said. "That doesn't mean anything to you, of course, but it's the kind of place they send you when they don't want you coming back."

"You're convicts?" Chisul asked, aghast.

Corin smiled and shrugged absently. "Call it what you like. We're ex-convicts now."

"How did you escape?" Bradok asked.

"A little over a week ago, there was some kind of a massive earthquake," Corin explained. "Most of the caves exploded or collapsed, forcing a river of magma into the few areas left intact. Just when we thought we were goners, a fissure opened in the back wall, exposing an underground river beyond.

"We had no choice," he went on. "We jumped into the river just a step ahead of the deadly magma. Twenty of us went into the river. By the time we washed up on the beach, we were all that survived."

"You probably washed up on the same beach we did," Bradok guessed.

"Yes," said Corin.

Jeni nodded and smiled manically. "We found your ship," she said.

"Very clever," the round dwarf said.

"We've been trying to follow you ever since," Corin said.

"How could you?" Rose asked. "We almost starved; we went the wrong way and doubled back; we encountered many dangers."

The scarred dwarf laughed, a hollow, mirthless sound. "One of the things they did to us in prison was to starve us," he said evenly. "They'd eventually start feeding us again, after the weak died off, so we're used to doing without food. Following you without getting noticed, that was harder."

"Are you hungry now?" Bradok asked.

Corin laughed and nodded. "Once the spores subsided, we harvested mushrooms from the same cavern you did," he said. "We'd never have found that feast if you hadn't led us there. Thanks for that."

Bradok wanted to ask more about what happened to the spores and the mushroom-covered dwarves, but Chisul cut him off.

"Well, since you've got food and you don't need our help, I suggest you be on your way," Silas's son said brusquely.

"Where would we go?" Corin said, rubbing his chin. "We weren't intending to join up with you; we were simply following. But we can't go back to where we escaped from; they kill fugitive prisoners on sight. Assuming we knew how to get back . . . or that anyone there is left alive to kill us."

"I don't care where you go," Chisul said, "as long as you leave us alone and be on your way."

Mutterings of approval filled the tunnel where the survivors of Ironroot had packed in to hear what was being said.

"You wouldn't want to go with us anyway," Bradok said in a conciliatory fashion. "We are trying to make for the surface."

Several of the Daergar paled to an almost transparent hue.

"I know that," Corin said. "We've talked it over and I want to go anyway."

"The way the ground shook," the tall, good-looking dwarf explained in a melodious voice. "It went on for three days. It probably destroyed everything down here. Nothing left for us down here."

"He's right," Corin said. "We may be the only dwarves left in this part of the world. We may not have always gotten along, cousins, but if we care about the future of the dwarf race, we should put our differences aside. Otherwise, our chances of survival will go down."

"You don't have anything we want, Daergar," Jenner said tersely.

"We aren't going to take convicts into our midst," Chisul echoed.

"I thought you might feel that way," Corin said, "so I'll make you a deal. If I can prove we're useful enough to bring along on your little expedition to nowhere, will you accept us?"

"What do you mean?" Rose said, narrowing her eyes suspiciously.

"We might just be able to help you find your way out of these passages," Corin said.

"I thought you said you didn't know your way around here," Much pointed.

"Well, I don't," Corin said. "So it's no trick. But if we can help you, is it a deal?"

"No," Chisul said stubbornly. "It's some kind of cheat."

"He doesn't seem like a bad sort," Bradok said softly. He looked over at Tal, who shrugged, and Much, who kicked stones at his feet. That left Rose, who smiled at him reassuringly.

Bradok turned back to Corin, who stood easily with his thumbs tucked into his belt. "Can you prove your worth?"

Corin nodded. "Without question. But only if you agree to take us with you."

"Your people are convicts," Bradok said. "If we take you with us, you would have to guarantee their proper behavior."

"Oh, they're all right," Corin said with a wry grin. "They were once a rough lot, of course. After all, none of us went to prison for biting our nails. But some are quite harmless now. Or, you might say, rehabilitated."

A dark chuckle ran through the Daergar.

"Never you fear; they'll mind their manners," he finished. "When a man gets a reprieve from a lifetime in the Abyss, he'd be a fool to waste the chance."

Bradok nodded slowly. He studied Corin, looking for some trace of falsehood or deception. As far as he could tell, the dwarf had been open and honest with them.

"Why did they send *you* to prison?" he asked Corin directly.

Corin smiled but the scarred dwarf spoke before he could answer. "Corin there is an admirable case. He swindled a corrupt politician out of a million steel," the scarred dwarf said. "It was revenge for the politician bankrupting his father."

Corin's face clouded for a moment; then his easy, affable smile returned.

"The funny part is why they sent me to prison," Corin said. "They didn't care about their friend whom I had ruined; they just wanted me to tell them where the money disappeared to."

"What about the rest of you?" Much said, still uneasy.

"Fair enough," Corin said. He turned and pointed at the scarred dwarf, who grinned, showing teeth that had been filed to points.

"That talkative one's Thurl Surepath," Corin said. "He was the house assassin for a wealthy family. When they fell on hard times, they sold him out to save their own skins."

Thurl bowed with a sweeping motion, his unnerving grin never wavering.

"That's Hurlic Sweetwater," Corin continued, indicating the short, rotund dwarf. "He killed his wife when he caught her having an affair. Well, that happens, don't it?

"Of course you didn't stop there, did you, Hurlic?" Corin added with dramatic flair. "He killed her entire family."

A gasp ran through the crowd, and Hurlic looked a bit sick.

"I'm sure he's very sorry, and it was all a long time ago. This," Corin said, pulling the tall, good-looking dwarf forward, "is Xurces Firebrand, the most notorious sex fiend in the history of Darkhold City. It's said he has fathered over one hundred children."

The collective gasp centered on mothers clutching their children and husbands stepping in front of their wives.

"Please," Xurces said sweetly, trying to calm the crowd.

"That's all behind me."

Corin patted the younger dwarf on the back. "That's right, all behind him," Corin continued. "The guards at the penal caverns took care of that. They castrated him."

A palpable silence followed. Then Xurces spoke. "No, it's all right, really," he said. "It sure did cure me. I'm no longer the person I was, and that's actually a good thing."

"Next we have Omer," Corin said, throwing an affectionate arm around the youngest dwarf. "After he was tortured by a mad Theiwar wizard, he killed twelve armed dwarves in a tavern brawl with just his bare hands. Ten or twelve, it depends on who's telling the tale."

"Twelve," murmured Omer, beaming.

Bradok could believe that. He'd never seen anyone move so fast or possess such strength.

"But his mind nowadays is that of a child," Corin said. "Just treat him nice and kindly, and he's docile as a lamb."

Omer leaned his head forward so Corin could tousle his hair.

"That just leaves dear Jeni," Corin said, gesturing toward the sole female. "Put your hands over your ears, dear," he said.

As strange as the request sounded, Jeni complied, putting her hands over her ears and humming loudly.

"She can't bear to hear her crimes recited," Corin explained. "Her husband beat her and tortured her mercilessly, you see. And in the end, poor dear, she went mad and killed her children."

"That's monstrous," Rose said, her voice choked with emotion.

Corin nodded sagely. "Monstrous it was," he said. "She's much better now, away from her husband. She thinks the murders were just a dream and as long as no one tells her otherwise, she's fine and dandy. You just have to treat her with kindness and she'll be all right too."

"That's quite a collection of misfits you've got," Chisul said skeptically. "You don't make a very attractive addition to our plight."

"Let me assure you, oh dubious one, that I personally will guarantee the conduct of my people," Corin said. "You have all stuck together. We are sticking together. I help them. They listen to me. None of them will give you any trouble."

"The word of a con man," Jenner scoffed.

"You can have my word," the scarred Thurl said. "If any of us revert to our old ways, I'll kill them myself."

"Kill them yourself! That's not very reassuring," Jenner said.

Thurl snorted angrily, adopting a frightening expression of rage on his face. Jenner edged back.

Corin spoke up. "You wouldn't know this, of course, but a professional assassin can only make a living if he's as good as his word," he said. "For Thurl to tell you that he would kill someone on your behalf is a vow of honor that would be worth plenty of steel to others."

"I was a very well-paid assassin," Thurl said, cooling his anger. "My word is as good as cash in the vault."

"Enough of this," Bradok said. He didn't like the idea of bringing the dark dwarves into their group, and he didn't like all their talk of killing and assassinating for pay. Corin seemed a likable enough dwarf, but not only were they Daergar, the ancient enemies of the mountain dwarves, but they were the scum of their society. "As much as I hate to admit it, Chisul may be right. We should have some evidence, first, of your value to us."

Corin reached into his ragged cloak and searched around, pulling out something smallish and round from an inside pocket. When he turned it over, Bradok immediately recognized the device.

"My compass!"

"Is it yours? Well, I picked it up for you," Corin said, polishing the purple stone on his dirty shirt. "And I'll be happy to return it to you," he added. "Provided you take us with you."

"That's ours to begin with," Jenner said angrily.

"Give it back," Chisul said in a voice edged with threat. "Or we'll take it ourselves. Don't forget, we outnumber you."

"Hang on a minute," Bradok said, stepping in front of Chisul.

The stocky son of the cooper showed white knuckles gripping his sword, and the sweat shone on his face. Bradok didn't doubt Chisul was ready to try and make good on his threat. But again, Bradok felt as though Corin was being honest and fair, in his way.

"I think we need to talk," he said in a low voice, leaning close to Chisul and signaling the others. "In private."

"That's a good idea," Much said. "Why don't we temporarily adjourn back to the cavern to discuss this matter?"

"You do that," Corin said easily. "We'll wait here."

"What if they disappear while we're gone?" Chisul said.

Corin laughed and looked around. "Now where, exactly, would we disappear to?" he said. "Besides, we don't want to go, we want to stay and join up with you. That's my offer, fair enough."

"He's right," Bradok said, eyeing Corin. "He's made us an offer. Let's talk it over and decide."

The survivors of Ironroot filed back up the passage, into the main cavern. Some of the older dwarves and the women and children huddled together, while Bradok gathered Chisul, Much, Tal, and others in a circle.

"I don't like Daergar," Jenner muttered darkly. "I don't like the idea of them joining."

Bradok turned to face him. Jenner had close-cropped black hair and a short beard over a shirt marred by burns; his large, bare forearms were also burned from working with metal. He had the kind of face that made Bradok want to hold on to his coin purse.

"If we turn them down," Bradok said with exaggerated

patience, "they can still follow us at will from a distance. They have already proven they have that ability. The Daergar have talent at tracking in the deep and dark."

"He's got a point," Rose said.

"It's on top of his head!" Chisul said exasperatedly. "We can't trust these Daergar, and we can't let them straggle along behind us." He held up his sword for emphasis. "That only leaves us one option. We can pretend to go back peacefully then attack 'em by surprise."

Much spat in disgust. "It's true they're not the most trustworthy bunch," Much said. "But you don't sound very trustworthy yourself, pretending and attacking. They've got as much at stake in terms of survival as we do. If they don't get out of here or find help, sooner or later they're goners."

"Just like us," Kellik added.

"Besides," Much went on. "They're familiar with this deep underground. They know things that are strange and foreign to us."

"That's right," Rose agreed. "They clearly knew something about those mushroom people."

"This is madness!" Chisul exclaimed. "These are Daergar we're talking about. Their people kill ours on principle, and this lot is so bad that the other Daergar threw them in prison!" He looked around at the group of dwarves, taking care to stare hard into each person's face. "We can't let a bunch of murderers travel along with our women and our children. They'd be a constant threat to us. They're a threat now. A threat we have to eliminate."

"So you propose to deal with murderers by becoming one yourself?" Much asked.

An abashed look crossed Chisul's face, and no one spoke for a long minute.

"Much is right," Bradok said at last. "If we kill them because we fear them, does that make us any better than the dark dwarves?"

"No, but it would make us smart and alive," Chisul said stubbornly. "As long as they live, I say, they're a danger to us."

"No, they aren't," Rose said. "They've got no weapons. They can't go back to their own people, and they wouldn't know how to survive on the surface without us. They need us, and they know it. They aren't going to do anything to jeopardize our help."

"She's right," Much said.

"She's crazy," Chisul said.

"This is too important. It involves all of us," Bradok interjected. "I say we put it to a vote."

He looked around and found most of the dwarves nodding. Chisul looked stone-faced but said nothing, while Jenner scowled in obvious resentment.

"All right," Bradok said. "All in favor of letting Corin and his companions come with us?"

Most of the dwarves raised their hands. Noticeably refusing to do so were Chisul, Jenner, and Vulnar. Surprisingly Tal, Dallon, and Lyra also kept their hands down.

"Clearly the ayes have it," Bradok said after a moment.

"This is a mistake," Chisul said.

Bradok nodded. "It might be," he said. "Time will tell. I'll owe you an apology if you're right. But right now, I think you're wrong."

Bradok and the others turned and moved back toward the tunnel where Corin and the others waited. Bradok felt strangely calm. Chisul had a point; Daergar were a cunning, ruthless clan and Corin and his companions were so bad, the Daergar had jailed them. Still, something told him the choice had to be taken on faith. Bradok realized that he'd started taking things on faith more and more ever since he met Silas. So far, faith hadn't served him so badly.

"What's the verdict?" Corin asked, rising from his seated position on the ground as they approached.

"You can come," Bradok said.

"Just like that?" he asked. "No conditions? No chaining us up at night?"

"Well, we don't have any chains," Bradok said with a slow grin. "So, yeah, just like that. No chains."

Corin seemed genuinely surprised for a moment. Then he held up the compass, eyeing it covetously, before tossing it to Bradok.

"You didn't have to give in so easy," Hurlic said, but Corin just shrugged.

"A deal's a deal," he barked to Hurlic. "I don't know about you, but I want to live a long, free life and this is our best chance."

He threw his cloak over his shoulders so everyone could see that he possessed no weapons. In fact he carried nothing—no pack, no gear; all he had were the clothes on his back.

"Come on, Omer," he said to the young dwarf. He pulled back Omer's cloak, revealing that the daft dwarf wore only a tattered shirt that reached to his knees. Then he put his arm around Omer and led him up the passage through the knot of survivors.

"I have a spare cloak and some clothing I'm not using at the moment," Bradok said amicably as they passed by.

"Thank you," Corin replied, nodding appreciatively.

One by one, the other Daergar displayed their similar lack of weapons and equipment and moved up the passage. The assassin, Thurl, came last. He opened his cloak, and from a hidden pocket in his shirt, he removed a flat piece of obsidian that had been polished as sharp as any dagger. That he handed to Bradok.

"Is that it?" Chisul asked.

Thurl cast the squat cooper a sour look then stepped nose to nose with him. "I told you, I'm an assassin. I don't need a weapon," he said. "And if a situation comes up where I do, I'll find one in a hurry."

Thurl stepped back then and held up Chisul's dagger, lifted neatly from its scabbard on his belt. With a sinister smile, Thurl flipped the weapon over in his hand and presented it, hilt first, to the stunned Chisul.

Snarling, Chisul grabbed his weapon, and Thurl moved off, after his companions. Bradok examined the makeshift obsidian dagger in his hands. It was as sharp as any knife and relatively well balanced.

"We're going to have to watch that one," Rose said in a low voice.

"I'm telling you, we'll have to watch them all," Chisul growled. "I want it remembered that I warned this was a bad idea."

"So noted," Bradok said. Then, with a sigh of relief, he reached into his pocket, pulled out the compass, and opened it. The Seer smiled when she appeared, as though glad to be back in the hands of the rightful owner of the compass. She extended her arm, her spear pointing up the cavern toward the camp.

"At least we're still heading the right way," he muttered.

He looked up to find everyone heading back except Rose, who had been watching him and overheard. She looked at him intently.

"Having second thoughts?" she asked.

Bradok nodded.

"Don't," she said. "Reorx gave you that compass to see us through this ordeal, and now he's used it to send us more help."

Bradok stared at the compass, wondering if she was right. "Maybe so," he said finally, slipping the device back into his pocket. Then he walked back to camp with Rose at his side.

CHAPTER 13

The Garden of the Gods

Eleven days after being joined by the Daergar, Bradok barely noticed the colorful limestone of the tunnel wall as he trudged forward. The compass had led them unerringly onward, pointing out sources of food from time to time but leading them in a seemingly endless trek. The rocky fissures had given way to old magma tubes of crumbly black rock that had, in turn, become a long chain of open caverns, and finally, the limestone passages they were in.

Bradok's mind was fatigued from the sheer monotony and boredom of the journey. He wasn't the only one suffering from nerves; everyone seemed snappish and on edge. The only ones that seemed unaffected were the children, Much, and Omer. Much and Omer took turns carrying any of the children who got tired. Their favorite by far, however, was Teal, the little toddler with the dark, curly hair. The sight of Much tromping by with Teal, usually giggling wildly from her perch atop his shoulders, forced half a smile from Bradok.

"This is getting bad," Tal said, his voice interrupting Bradok's thoughts.

He didn't even glance over his shoulder. In the past weeks, he'd seen and heard more than enough of his companions, especially Tal, who was always preaching to him about leadership.

"At least we're getting somewhere," Bradok muttered.

"Chisul and Vulnar are talking up a rebellion back there," Tal said. "They're starting to wonder if the compass is leading us in circles, that maybe we should try heading some other way."

"He's welcome to try," Bradok returned. "So long as he doesn't expect the rest of us to go off and get lost with him."

"He reckons we're already lost," Rose said, stepping up beside her brother. "And he's not alone in that idea; too many of the others are also starting to lose hope."

"They're getting desperate, I know. It's these damn dark caves," he said, waving absently at the brightly-colored limestone. "The dreariness of it all is driving everyone batty."

"I'm just warning you," Tal said, lowering his voice. "The next place we stop, there could be real trouble."

"Chisul's no real trouble," Bradok replied, irritation thick in his voice. "Just get out of his way and let him make an ass of himself; folks will stop listening to him again."

"This is different," Rose insisted. "Everyone's as raw as meat in a butcher's window. They want to believe in something other than which way the compass is pointing. They need a positive sign of some sort. It's been too long without any sign of hope."

Bradok couldn't disagree. He trudged along silently.

"Vulnar is saying our convict friends must have tampered with the compass," Rose said.

"Isn't that just the sort of thing Vulnar would say?" Bradok said disgustedly. "After all, he wanted us to kill them on the spot."

Bradok held out his hands in a pleading gesture to the roof of the cave overhead. "Why is anyone listening to him?" he said. "Corin and his friends haven't caused any trouble. And why would they tamper with the same compass they'd end up following?"

"You're thinking with your head," Rose said, putting a gentle hand on his shoulder. "These people are tired and worn out. Their heads are worn out too. They aren't thinking straight."

"That's right," Tal said. "They'll gladly grab at anything that offers hope—even if it's a bad idea coming from Chisul and Vulnar."

Bradok had finally reached a breaking point. He whirled on Tal, grabbing his shoulder and forcing him to a stop. "What do you want me to do about it?" he demanded through clenched teeth.

Tal's eyes widened in surprise at Bradok's unexpected and uncharacteristic action. If it angered him, he didn't show it. Tal simply reached up and removed Bradok's hand from his shoulder. "I don't know what you should do, and I don't know what I want you to do," he said. "I was only trying to warn you."

With that, Tal strode past him, leaving Bradok standing with his head hanging down in the middle of the passageway, the others streaming up and around him.

Rose lingered to talk to him. "You know," she said with as much cheer as she could muster. "You've been a pretty good leader up to now. It would be a shame for you to let a little boredom and aggravation change all that."

She was right, Bradok knew. Yet he couldn't seem to shake off his black mood. It felt as if his head were stuffed with angry bees who kept buzzing and buzzing, all the louder.

He put his right hand out and let his fingers glide along the wall. Taking a deep breath, he closed his eyes, using the touch of the wall to guide him forward. He let the breath out and took in another, trying to cleanse his mind. The bees just buzzed louder.

Cursing the infernal tunnels, he tried again, closing off his senses to everything but the rough, damp surface of the wall. He felt the coolness of the air as he breathed it in, focused on his lungs filling up, then on blowing the air back out his mouth.

Somewhere, from what seemed like a long way off, Bradok became aware of unfamiliar noises. They were not unfamiliar, really, but sounds and noises he hadn't heard in a long time.

He opened his eyes, and the world returned to him. From up the tunnel ahead of him, people were shouting and calling out excitedly. The joy in those voices instantly lifted a weight off Bradok's shoulders. He felt suddenly as though he could fly. Exhilaration flooded his body. He had no idea what had happened to cause such a stir, but he rushed up the tunnel.

Everyone he passed was wearing the same, hungry-for-excitement look. As he expectantly rounded a sharp curve in the rock, he thought his eyes must have been playing tricks on him. From somewhere up ahead, a pale, white light shone brightly. He held up his hands, shielding his eyes against the glow, and suddenly, a blast of cool air and the smell of water hit him.

His foot crunched on sand as he stepped out of the tunnel into an immense cavern. Everywhere he looked, different kinds of mushrooms grew: big ones, small ones, familiar ones, strange ones he'd never dreamed of. They grew clustered around columns of rock, along shelves in the rock, and even on the ceiling. Bradok could see peppertops, honey mushrooms, blackroot, and sagetube. There were tall, fat, red mushrooms and strange orange fungi that seemed to grow upside down from the ceiling. Mixed into the cornucopia were clusters of pale, glowing mushrooms Bradok recognized as the variety his clan called Reorx's torch. The Reorx's torch mushrooms were everywhere, filling the space with light.

Off to the left, Bradok could hear the sound of water lapping against an invisible shore. The air bore the pungent smell of water as well, and Bradok breathed in the water gratefully.

"This is more like it," he said to no one in particular. The bright, colorful cavern reminded him momentarily of Ironroot, and he felt a pang of loss for the home he would never see again.

The smell of water drew him, and he turned toward the sound of the lapping waves. The floor of the cavern sloped down, and Bradok could see a vast, dark lake off to his left. Even as bright as the cavern was, no light shone on the far side of the lake, giving one the impression that it simply fell away into nothingness. The cavern's floor sloped back down to a round opening with a short stretch of beach where gentle waves rolled in and out with a quiet *whoosh*. Already some of the children had their shoes off and were wading and splashing in the icy water.

"What do you think?" Much said, striding up beside Bradok with his watch in hand. "There's still half a day left to march."

"I don't care what *he* thinks," Chisul said, walking by toward the water. "This place is a dream. We should stay here for a while."

"I agree with Chisul," Bradok said easily. "We can gather food, wash out our clothes—"

"Bathe," Rose said, pausing beside him and sniffing pointedly.

"That too," he said, rolling his eyes.

They bathed in shifts with the women and children washing first, while the men stayed on the opposite side of the sloping floor gathering food. Corin and Xurces showed Bradok, Kellik, and Tal how to gather wall root, a fibrous fungus that grew out of the walls like scraggly hair. It didn't taste particularly good, but its fibrous nature made it laborious to chew, so it was long-lasting nourishment. According to Xurces, a dwarf could survive on it without any other food, if need be. Everyone hoped that would not be necessary.

There were many mushrooms that no one recognized, and they decided to leave those be since the only way to tell if they were edible or poisonous was to eat them. Still, there were plenty of mushrooms they knew to be safe. Bradok quickly filled the cloak he'd tied off as a sack and went looking for others to help. Kellik's eldest son, Rijul, seemed to have lost momentum, so Bradok went over to help him.

When he reached the lad, he discovered what had diverted Rijul from the important task of gathering food. Where he stood behind a pillar of rock, the floor dipped down, giving a perfect view of the beach. The lad's eyes were the size of saucers. As Bradok came up behind him, he, too, could see the beach and the bathing female dwarves. His eyes unconsciously sought out a form, taller than the others, topped with wet red hair. For a moment, he, too, was mesmerized like young Rijul; then he realized what he saw—who he saw—and he turned away, blushing furiously.

"That's enough, lad," he said, taking the dazed Rijul by the collar and pulling him away. "Plenty of time for that when you're older."

Once the men had gathered enough food, Bradok opened his pack and began laying out his clothes to wash and sort. Beside him, Corin sat and watched. The only clothes he owned were the ones he wore under the spare cloak Bradok had given him.

"You must have been an important dwarf above ground," Corin said, observing the quality of Bradok's gear. "Chisul keeps calling you, 'councilman.' Is that some kind of leader?"

Bradok nodded. "I was a councilman of the city of Ironroot," he said, adding, "a representative who voted for laws and public policies."

Corin seemed impressed but didn't say more.

As Bradok pulled out one of his two spare shirts, a wrapped bundle dropped from his pack and hit the sandy floor with a thud. The impact freed a delicate strand of gold that clutched a smoky gray pearl.

Corin whistled and picked up the pearl, pulling a necklace free from the bundle. It boasted gold chain-work with pearls, white diamonds, and a single teardrop-shaped ruby that, when worn, would dangle just below the throat. Bradok wanted to snatch the necklace away, but it was too late to keep it a secret from Corin.

"I'll say you were a big man indeed," he said, cradling the necklace and inspecting it with an expert's eye. "Did you convert your wealth to jewels so you could bring it all with you?"

"I was a jeweler by trade," Bradok said reluctantly. "That necklace is one of my own designs."

"It's exquisite," Corin said, clearly impressed. "What a pair we could have made," he said in a wistful voice. "In my time I could have sold this for four times its value," he said. Then with a little shrug, he handed it back to Bradok. "Not much use to any of us now, I'm afraid," he said.

"No," Bradok said with a wistful smile. Taking the necklace, Bradok carefully tucked it into the bundle again and stowed it in his pack. After a second's thought, he reached back in and moved the smaller bundle to the bottom of the pack, tucking it under a pile.

"You don't need to worry about those valuables," Corin said, a chuckle in his voice. "Down here they aren't worth much. You can't trade them to anyone, and you sure can't eat them."

Bradok smiled at the joke. It was too true. "Force of habit," he said apologetically.

The sound of tearing cloth attracted both dwarves' attention. Much had torn strips off his cloak and one of his shirts, and he was tying the strips together.

"What are you doing?" Corin asked, looking at the strange concoction taking shape in Much's hands.

"I'm making a doll if it's any of your business," Much said gruffly. He held up the mass of knotted cloth and it did, indeed, resemble a child's doll. Corin and Bradok nodded approvingly.

"It's for Teal," he said more easily with a smile that couldn't have been prouder if little Teal had been his own grandchild.

Bradok laughed and reached for his pack. He pulled out his pen and inkwell and motioned for Much to hand him the doll. With a few quick strokes of the pen, he drew eyes, a mouth, and freckles on the doll's blank face then handed it back.

"Perfect," Much said, appraising Bradok's handiwork.

"Yes, perfect," agreed Corin.

About an hour later, the women came tromping over the rise from the water. Their faces and arms were red from the scrubbing they'd given themselves, and they all seemed in great spirits.

"All right, you smelly lot," Rose announced in a loud voice. "Your turn. And don't even think of asking any of us to wash out your socks."

Bradok smiled and picked up his cloak. He'd tied his clothes into a bundle along with his grooming kit, which contained a cake of lye soap so strong the very smell of it made his eyes water.

At the beach, he disrobed and spent the next ten minutes in the freezing water, scouring his skin and hair thoroughly. He'd never been as fastidious as some dwarves, but he'd also never felt so dusty and dirt-ridden in his entire life. With the others performing similar ablutions around him, the water soon developed a filmy layer of dirt with soap bubbles floating on it.

When he finished, he combed out his hair and beard then started in on his clothes. As he splashed the water to clean out the dirt, he spotted Chisul, still scrubbing his arms, waist deep in the water. The dwarf had broad shoulders and a muscular back from all the work he'd done in his father's shop. The only blemish on him seemed to be a small gray birthmark on his upper back.

Rose's warning about Chisul returned briefly to Bradok's thoughts, but he was in too good a mood and went back to his cleaning. An hour later he flung his damp clothes over a clothesline that Tal had strung between two stalagmites and sat down heavily in the sand. Chisul and the other dwarves had changed back into their damp clothes, knowing their body heat would dry them fast enough. The human, Perin, however, kept his cloak dry and shivered under it in the perpetual cool of underground.

Bradok watched the children playing in the wet sand of the beach. Little Teal, clutching her new rag doll, ran down to the water, dipped her toes in, then retreated, squealing as the next wave came in. Omer ran with her, dancing and laughing.

Grinning as he watched, Bradok pulled the compass from his pocket and checked it almost absently. The image of the Seer pointed unwaveringly on. Normally when they reached a good spot to stop, she would lower her spear and give them a rest.

He knew without even checking that no one would want to leave the beautiful mushroom garden and sleep in the dreary tunnels again.

Still, he had to tell everybody what the compass indicated. Maybe they should move on. The last time they'd ignored the magical compass, they'd been attacked by the strange mushroom men.

He put on his clothes and turned to go and find Rose and Tal, only to spot them bearing down him.

"I've been looking for you," she said quickly. "I think there's a problem—"

"I know," Bradok said, cutting her off. "Look at this." He held out the compass.

"I warned you about that happening," Tal said.

"I'm talking about a different problem," Rose said.

Rose opened her hand. She held one of the glowstones from their lanterns. It glowed dimly in the bright light, illuminating the cavern. Bradok looked at Rose, not understanding.

"Its light is fading," she said. "I thought I noticed it yesterday, and I've been watching the lights more closely today. The stones are dimmer here now than they were when we started."

"I thought these things were good for years and years," Bradok said, searching his memory in vain to recall the last time he'd had to replace the glowstones in his house.

"They are supposed to be," Rose said, "and Chisul told me these are new."

"What is happening, then?" Bradok asked, holding up the stone.

"They must be blessed by a priest," Tal said. "Remember how that fellow from the city council told us that all the priests had disappeared?"

"Jon Bladehook," Bradok said, wincing at his name.

"What if Reorx took all the priests away for some reason?" Tal said. "What if priestly magic is beginning to vanish?"

The memory stabbed at Bradok: the grizzled dwarf with the red painted sign. *Repent lest the Gods forsake us.*

Was it true, then? Had the gods forsaken them? The prospect sent chills up Bradok's spine.

"Wait a minute," he said, pulling out the compass. "What about this? If divine magic is fading, why does this still work?"

"But how long it will keep working?" Tal asked, exchanging a worried look with Rose.

"I think we need to get going as soon as possible," Rose said.

"You've got to be kidding," Chisul said when Rose related the crisis to the rest of the dwarves—the survivors and the Daergar. "The glowstones are dimming, so you want us to panic?"

"It might be safer to sleep in the tunnels," suggested Bradok.

"Nothing can sneak up on us here," Chisul countered. "We should rest in this place as long as we can. I propose we put three guards on the beach tonight, just in case."

He turned to the rest of the group. "What say you, my friends?" Chisul asked. "Do we follow the councilman and sleep in the tunnels tonight, or do we fortify ourselves here?"

"Here!" the crowd shouted as one.

"You see, Councilman. The people have spoken," Chisul said with a smug smile.

The people cheered, and the beaming Chisul nodded at them as if he'd just been proclaimed their emperor.

"That young man is full of himself," Corin said from behind Bradok.

"Yeah," Rose said, agreeing with the Daergar.

"Full of hot air is more like it," Bradok said lightly but without a trace of humor. "I'm worried about staying here in the open."

"You think it's dangerous?" Corin asked.

"I'm sure of it," Bradok said.

"Then some of us should go into the tunnels," Rose insisted.

"That isn't a good idea," Corin said. "We'd be abandoning our friends. And if something bad did happen, they'd be right to blame us for deserting them when they needed us the most."

"Corin's right. We shouldn't go," Bradok said finally.

"What do we do, then?" asked Rose.

Bradok took out his hunting knife and passed it to Corin. "We stay armed and alert for trouble," he said. "It's all we can do." He turned to Corin. "Warn Much, Kellik, Tal, Dallon, and some of the others. Tell them to have their knives ready. Make sure at least one of them we can trust is on guard duty all the time."

Corin nodded and left.

Bradok turned to Rose. "Keep your people close tonight and be ready for anything."

"All right," Rose said after a long hesitation. "Tonight I'll do as you ask, but tomorrow you're going to do me a favor. There's something I want to discuss with you." With that she turned brusquely and walked away.

Bradok wondered only fleetingly what she wanted to talk about. Right then "tomorrow" seemed like a long time away.

He sighed and walked over to where he had spread out his cloak for a bed. There were still several hours before it was time to go to sleep, but he felt so weary, he just had to lie down.

CHAPTER 14

Silent Death

Bradok hadn't meant to fall asleep. He knew he had, though, because he was dreaming. He found himself walking through the deserted and silent streets of Ironroot. He tried to force himself to wake up, but the dream only worsened. Apart from the confusion of being in a place he knew no longer existed, he couldn't seem to remember why he wanted to wake up. It nagged at him, like the pain of a molar that needed removing.

As he walked around the statue of Argus Gingerbeard, he realized that he had developed a limp. He didn't remember hurting his leg and, in fact, his leg didn't seem to be in any pain; it just didn't work as it should. Figuring it might have fallen asleep, he tried shaking and rubbing it to no avail.

When he looked up from his exertions, he discovered the cooper, Silas, standing at the base of the statue, regarding him.

"Silas," Bradok stammered.

"It's going to get worse before it gets better," Silas told him sadly. "You need to be strong. Others will need your strength."

"I'll do what I can," Bradok said.

Silas shook his head. "You must do better than that," he

warned. "Trust yourself and have faith."

The light overhead flared, and Bradok had to shield his eyes. When it subsided, Silas was gone. Only the last words of his message, "have faith, have faith . . ." seemed to echo on in the distance.

While he stood there pondering Silas's appearance, a blood-curdling scream erupted out of nowhere.

Bradok whirled, trying desperately to locate the source of the cry. The city seemed to bend and waver as if it were melting; then it dissolved around him. Have faith, faith, faith . . .

He woke up, lying on the sand where he'd fallen asleep. Sitting up, he became aware of a long pink ropelike appendage hanging down from the ceiling, slowly wrapping itself around his leg. With a cry of disgust, he jerked his sword free of its scabbard and sliced the thing in two. Milky white liquid spurted from the wound and spattered Bradok's leg and chest. He tried to wipe it off, but it burned his hand. Cursing, he rubbed his hand in the sand to get the acidic goo off.

The pink tentacle withdrew back up to the ceiling but Bradok could see the strange orange fungi above were trailing long tentacles down among the sleeping dwarves. Already they had wrapped around some and were pulling them into the air, toward open maws. Bradok could see the orange fungi peeled back, like bananas, with tiny tentacles waving inside. They would bleed their victims dry once the pink tongues sucked them in. Bradok shouted a warning to the others, but he had his own troubles.

He tried to kick his leg, to dislodge the tentacle end that was still wrapped around his leg, but his leg spasmed. Where the tentacle touched him, it had secreted a clear substance that had soaked through his trouser leg, turning his leg numb. Using the tip of his sword, Bradok peeled the pink appendage away from his leg.

Rolling over, he pushed himself to his knees and stood, or rather, tried to stand. The moment he put weight on his numb leg, it collapsed beneath him, sending him sprawling in the sand.

A second tentacle dropped from above and struck Bradok on the shoulder. Before it could latch onto him, he chopped it away, sending the bleeding stump retreating back to the ceiling.

Off to his left, a tentacle had wrapped around one of the hill dwarves and was pulling her upward. Bradok lurched forward, putting his weight on his good leg, and chopped away the tentacle, sending the unconscious dwarf falling into the sand with a thud.

Screams and cries and the sounds of battle filled the cavern as most of the dwarves woke up to discover themselves in the grip of the nightmarish attack. Bradok hobbled over to where Kellik grappled with a tentacle that had Hemmish in its grip. Each time Kellik's hammer struck the tentacle, it would contract; the net effect was that it pulled the boy higher and higher away from his father.

"Use your knife," Bradok cried as he slashed wildly at the appendage, cutting it part of the way through and sending it spinning. Kellik swung at it with his knife but missed, leaving Bradok to chop Hemmish free when the tentacle spun back his way.

"Help me unravel him," Kellik said to Rijul as he pulled the limp end of the tentacle off his younger son.

"Hemmish," Kellik yelled, shaking the boy. "Hemmish, wake up!" Kellik thumped him on the chest, hard, and Hemmish gasped, coughed, and started breathing weakly.

"Help me!" came a terrified shriek to their left.

"Stay with him," Bradok told Kellik as he lurched to the rescue.

A few yards away, Starlight, Marl Anvil's eldest granddaughter, was struggling to free Marl from a tentacle lifting him off the ground. Marl's hip was bleeding profusely. Nearby the two younger grandchildren held each other and cried.

As thin and delicate as the tentacles seemed, the creatures were strong. By the time Bradok got there, they had lifted Marl almost out of reach. Bradok hacked away at the tentacle, trying not to hit Marl. Finally he struck a good blow. The tentacle spurted white fluid that mixed with Marl's blood, and it unwound quickly, sending the old man spinning into a heap.

Bradok grabbed Marl's cloak, still lying on the sand and pressed a corner to his bleeding hip.

"Hold this down tight on his wound," he told Starlight. "If any more of them come down, chop at them with your knives." Bradok motioned the other two children over to their big sister's side. Then he realized that one member of the family was absent.

"Where's your grandmother?" he asked. "Where's Isirah?"

With a trembling hand, the boy, Graylin, pointed up to the ceiling. Bradok looked up just in time to see her unconscious form being sucked into one of the orange fungi. It closed its maw around her hungrily, and Isirah vanished from sight.

"Damn it!" Bradok shouted just as someone grabbed his shoulder.

"Help us," Jeni, one of the Daergar, said desperately. Her hair was disheveled and smeared with the slime from the tentacles. The sticky liquid covered her left cheek, causing it to remain frozen when she talked, forcing her to slur her words.

"Where?" Bradok asked, forcing himself to rejoin the fight. Jeni ran ahead, pointing, and Bradok limped after her. On the far side of the cavern, Corin was battling for his life. He'd been almost completely wrapped in a tentacle, and his arms moved weakly as he tried to saw his way free. Xurces lay unconscious on the ground, and Omer, confused by the attack, was wailing and covering his head. The assassin, Thurl, hung in the air, trussed like a holiday duck, and of the rotund Hurlic there was no sign.

Bradok chopped away at the tentacle holding Corin then cut down Thurl, who dropped to the ground like a stone.

"Untie him," Corin gasped, pulling the ropy flesh away from Thurl's body. "The tentacles are poisoned; the longer they make contact with your skin, the more you absorb, until you're dead."

Bradok pulled away the tentacles from the semiconscious assassin. Even as he did so, he could feel his hands growing numb where the sticky substance coating the tentacles spilled on him.

"Thank you," Thurl whispered. His eyes locked feverishly on Bradok and seemed to bore into him. "I owe you my life," the assassin said weakly. "I am your man . . . till I die."

"Easy there," Bradok said. "Just rest for a minute." He turned to Corin. "You seem to know something about these strange creatures. How come you didn't warn us?" he demanded.

"I've only heard about them from stories told by old ones," Corin said, his voice raspy and strained. "Do you think I've actually seen one before? They're called cave fishers."

Bradok opened his mouth to tell Corin that he didn't give two figs what the tentacles were called when he heard a single word rise above all the chaos of sound filling the cavern.

"Rose!"

He whirled and saw Tal hanging on to his sister as a relentless tentacle pulled her upward. Tal's left arm hung limply at his side, it was clear he wouldn't be able to hang on much longer.

"Rose!" Tal shouted again.

Bradok ran toward them, forcing his benumbed leg to work by shear dint of will. As he ran, he tore off his cloak and swung it around over his head. He reached them just as Tal's grip faltered. Swinging his cloak round, he launched it up, wrapping it around Rose as she hung upside down. He caught the loose end and pulled, using the cloak as a kind of sling. The cave fisher pulled back, trying to lift them both off the ground.

"Don't let go," Tal pleaded, powerless to rise from the ground.

"It's poisoning her every second it touches her," Bradok said. "We've got to get her down or she'll die soon enough."

Tal rolled over, face-first in the sand, and forced himself to stand.

"Use my sword," Bradok said, indicating, as he twisted and turned, the handle protruding from the scabbard on his hip.

Tal flung his limp arm against Bradok, and his fingers caught the hilt. He could grip the weapon, but lacked the strength to pull it out of its sheath. Finally he simply stepped back, and the weapon slid from its scabbard and hung as loosely as his arm.

"Cut at it," Bradok gasped.

"Where?" Tal asked, swinging his body around so that the sword flailed out and smacked the tentacle with the flat of the blade.

"Anywhere," Bradok said. "Try again."

Tal swung again with similar ineffectual results.

"Again," Bradok said, his voice a near scream. "Hold on, Rose!"

Then he heard the sound of steel whirring through the air, and suddenly Rose fell free. He fell with her, quickly rolling off and tearing the tentacles away. The top of the tentacle had been cleanly severed. Bradok turned and saw Thurl, his body forced into a sitting position, nodding before he slumped over.

Rose coughed, gasped, and began breathing. Tal cradled her head in his lap as best he could, and Bradok retrieved his sword.

"Go help the others," Tal said. "We're all right now."

Bradok stood and faced the chamber. Everywhere dwarves were attacking the tentacles with knives and swords. Several bodies hung in the air, in the process of being pulled up to the ceiling, some already too high up to save. Bradok willed his eyes to avoid their faces. There would be time for a reckoning later.

A scream broke upon his ear as he chopped at a fresh tentacle that had dropped down too close to him. The sound was horrible, somehow visceral in its anguish. It took Bradok a minute to recognize the voice as Much's.

He looked over to spot his old friend racing madly from group to group, chopping at tentacles with his short sword. But he kept moving and appeared to be looking for something, or someone.

"Teal!" Much screamed, vaulting over a cowering dwarf and racing on.

Bradok remembered the curly-haired toddler and looked around. With a gasp he realized he didn't see the little girl. Fear gripped him and pulled his eyes inexorably upward. There, far above him on the ceiling, he saw a flash of color—the rag doll Much had made. The little girl Teal lay, still cradled in the arms of her unconscious mother, both wrapped by a tentacle.

"There!" Bradok yelled before he realized there was nothing that could be done. Already the mouth began to close around mother and child, and he had to turn away at the grisly slight.

Much screamed something, but his voice faded to insignificance as an animal roar erupted from behind Bradok. Turning, he saw Omer staring up at the horror. Omer's hands were clenched into fists. Even from that distance, Bradok could see veins popping in the boy's neck. An unearthly orange glow shone out from his eyes, as if his very brain were on fire. Then he screamed.

"TEAL, NO!"

The sound was so overpowering, it shook the ground, taking Bradok so much by surprise that he fell over backward from the force of the scream. Then, as Bradok lay on the ground, watching agape, the young dwarf with the mind of a child took three steps that brought him close to Bradok and launched himself into the air.

Remarkably, Omer's leap took him all the way up to the roof of the cavern. He caught hold of the cave fisher that had grabbed his precious girl and, holding it around the middle, swung his legs up so his feet were planted on the ceiling. Then he pulled.

From his vantage point below, Bradok could see the veins in Omer's arms and legs bulging and the look of naked rage on his face.

With a wet, tearing sound, the cave fisher began to pull free of the ceiling. Bradok could see its wiggling, thrashing roots flailing about. With a groan and a thunderous crack, the ceiling broke away, and Omer and the cave fisher both dropped to the ground.

The cave fisher burst open like an overripe melon, and Teal's mother slid out. Her arm flopped down, sending little Teal rolling free from her grasp. Teal ended up in a heap on the sand, still clutching her rag doll but showing no signs of life.

Bradok started forward, but Omer beat him to Teal. He leaped beside the little girl and stood there, as if guarding her. The orange glow died from behind his eyes as he reached out one of his oversized hands and nudged Teal. The girl didn't respond.

She had been too long in the grips of the tentacle, and she was so very small. The poison had taken Teal long before she'd reached the ceiling. Her tiny form lay in the sand as if asleep, but Bradok knew it was a sleep from which she'd never wake.

Omer pushed her again. "Teal," he said, his voice childlike and pleading. "Please get up. Teal?" Finally, Omer understood. He reached out with trembling hands and lifted Teal to his bosom. In his hands, she seemed like a doll.

Omer's shoulders shook as he sobbed, then he threw back his head and howled like a wounded dog. The mad howl echoed off the walls of the chamber, a howl of pain, love, and loss.

Much had come up beside Omer. He leaned down and picked up the rag doll that had slipped from Teal's hand. As the young dwarf vented his grief, Much held the doll gently, as one would a living child. Tears streamed down the old dwarf's face and wet his beard. Dwarves rarely cry in public, especially revered elders such as Much. But it took all of Much's self-control not to drop to his knees and howl along with Omer.

Gradually Omer's howls turned to hoarse sobs. Bradok looked around. Omer wasn't the only one mourning. Marl Anvil held his grandchildren as they wept for the loss of their grandmother. Urlish Hearthhome and Seerten Rockhide held each other, and both seemed to be in shock. Others sat, stunned, miserable.

The tentacles had retreated to the ceiling, but Bradok knew they'd badly hurt the survivors. Behind him Omer howled again.

"Will someone shut him up?" Chisul said, emerging from behind a column of rock. He had a long smear of the sticky tentacle fluid on his right side and cradled his right arm against his body.

Bradok was enraged. With a howl to match Omer's, he leaped at Chisul, brandishing his sword. He grabbed Silas's son by the shirtfront and pressed his sword against the dwarf's throat.

"I'd shut my mouth if I were you," Bradok yelled, tasting bile in his mouth. "That little girl is dead because of you!"

Chisul struggled in vain to throw Bradok off with his one good arm.

"I had nothing to do with that," he protested.

"You had to be the big dwarf," Bradok spat. "You had to convince everyone to stay here. The compass warned us to move on!"

He shoved Chisul away so hard, the dwarf stumbled and fell in a heap. Bradok threw his sword down in the sand and stormed off. He wanted to be mad at Chisul, but he was really mad at himself. He couldn't help thinking that he should have done more to convince everyone to follow the compass. In his dream, Silas had told him to be strong. In the future he would have to be stronger, strong enough to face down Chisul or Corin or anyone or everyone. If he weren't strong in the future, more lives would be lost.

Bradok walked back to where Much stood clutching the little rag doll to his chest.

"This didn't have to happen," Bradok hissed. "We should have done what the compass said. It's my fault. You should blame me."

"You didn't make us stay here," Much said ruefully. "We voted for that. Remember?"

Bradok held Much's eyes for a long moment. Then he turned and went back to retrieve his sword. He picked it up, slid it into its sheath, then turned to address the huddled dwarves.

"All right, listen up," he called out in a hoarse voice. "Everyone get your gear together and get down to the beach. Stay alert for any more tentacles. You have five minutes, go."

After exchanging glances, everyone scurried into action. Bradok turned to find Thurl standing quietly behind him.

"You want I should kill him?" Thurl asked, nodding toward Chisul. The assassin looked almost fully recovered. The way he asked the question was like asking someone to pass the salt at the supper table. "I can make it look like an accident," he added.

Bradok shook his head. "It's not really his fault," he said. "Besides, we may need him."

"What do you wish of me now?" Thurl asked.

Bradok stared at him. "What do you mean?" he asked.

"I am your man now," Thurl said. "You saved my life; I am forever in your debt."

"That isn't necessary," Bradok said, a little embarrassed. "I did what anyone would have done. You don't owe me anything."

Thurl shook his head and smiled, showing his pointed teeth. "I doubt anyone but you would have saved me." He nodded toward Rose. "Maybe her," he said, "but she was busy at the time."

"Still," Bradok said, "I don't need a servant or an assassin."

"The debt stands," Thurl said firmly. "But since you don't need me now, well, I'll go help the others pack up."

Bradok watched Thurl walk away, wondering what he would do about his new, unwanted friend. Whatever he decided, it would have to wait. He turned and walked down to the beach, stopping only long enough to use his sword to cut the top off of one of the fat, red mushrooms. Had the mushroom been more solid, the top could have been used as a shield. As it was, it would serve its purpose.

Much had led Omer down to the beach, away from the scene of death. He still held the body of Teal against his chest and refused to release her. Bradok came up to the small group and set the mushroom top down next to Omer, kneeling down.

"Give me the doll," he said, reaching out to Much. Reluctantly the old dwarf passed it over.

"Omer," Bradok said gently. "We need you to let go of Teal."

"No," Omer whispered. "Love Teal." Tears streamed down his face.

"I know, Omer," Bradok said. "We all loved her. But Teal's gone. We have to let her go."

"No!" Omer said. "Not let Teal go."

Bradok put his hand on Omer's shoulder. "She's already gone, but she left something behind—for you."

Bradok held out the doll and, after a long moment, Omer took it, handing over the toddler's body. Reverently, Bradok lifted the little girl and laid her on the flat underside of the mushroom top. She was still the most beautiful child, with rosy cheeks and delicate curly hair. Her tiny lips were curled in a relaxed smile, and she looked for all the world as if she were just playing peek-a-boo, waiting for someone to laugh before jumping up and surprising them all. The sight of her dead little body made Bradok ache.

"Get me some of the glowsacs from a Reorx's torch mushroom," he told Much.

Carefully, Bradok arranged Teal's arms at her sides and brushed her curls out of her tranquil face.

"Here," Much said, handing Bradok four glowing hunks of mushroom.

Bradok arranged the glowing bits around the edge of the mushroom top. He picked it up, surprised by how little it weighed, and waded into the gentle surf of the black lake. He placed the makeshift funeral boat on the water and pushed it out. It spun and bobbed until a current caught it and swept it out into the lake, a lone beacon of light against the vast darkness.

From behind him, someone began playing an ocarina, blowing a sad song whose words spoke of lost love. Bradok didn't turn around, keeping his eyes on the death boat as it receded from his view.

"Good-bye, Teal," Omer said in a small voice. "Never forget you." He held the rag doll to his chest in a fierce grip. "Always love Teal," he whispered. "Never forget."

They stood there in the gentle surf, Bradok, Much, and Omer, for a long, long time, until the boat was just a pinpoint of light impossibly far away. Finally Bradok turned back.

"It's time to go," he said and marched up the slope, away from the beach.

When he reached the exit passage, he found everyone else had gathered there, waiting for him and the others. Rose and Kellik were putting sand in a shallow grave with the privy shovel.

"We buried her mother," Rose said.

"I never knew her name," Bradok confessed.

"Lonaway," Kellik supplied. "Her husband's name was Lodan. He's one of the missing. Not much hope that he or any of them will be found alive."

"How many did we lose?" Bradok asked, not sure he wanted to know the answer.

"Fourteen," Rose said.

Bradok wanted to curse or scream or weep, but he was too weary to do anything except listen as Kellik recited a list of names.

Bradok recognized Isirah Anvil and Hurlic the Daergar. Most of the names were of dwarves he'd scarcely known, but he felt a sharp pain when Kellik read the name Dallon Ramshorn. Dallon was the wheelwright from Everguard who had fought the mushroom men beside him. Fought bravely, Dallon had. It seemed impossible that the big, easygoing dwarf could be gone, just like that.

"All right," Bradok said once Kellik had finished listing the dead and Much and Omer had rejoined them. He raised his voice for the others to hear. "We've all lost friends and loved ones here tonight. We'll mourn our dead as is proper, but for now we must go. It isn't safe here, and we must find a place to rest and regroup."

He checked the compass and found the Seer pointing onward as she had always done before. However, her face seemed sorrowful, as if she wept beneath the white bandage across her eyes.

"From now on I want four armed dwarves in the lead and two in the back," Bradok said, snapping the compass lid closed.

Kellik, Vulnar, Tal, and Corin volunteered to take the lead, and Bradok said he'd bring up the rear with Thurl. With that, the dwarves began filing up the passageway in silence. He spotted Rose. She was cradling her right arm and seemed to be limping, but she flashed him a warm smile as she moved in step with the others.

Bradok sighed and fell to walking beside Thurl. Just before the passage curved and the cavern disappeared behind them, he stopped and glanced back. He would have sworn he heard a toddler giggling.

The sound pained his heart.

He wondered if he'd ever forget that beautiful little girl and her giggle.

CHAPTER 15

Aftermath

Feeling too restless to sleep, they marched through the remaining night and well into the next day. As they went, Rose's fears became manifest. The glowlamps seemed to give off less and less light with every passing hour. When they finally stopped in a small, bare cavern with a sandy bottom, everyone noticed the difference.

"The children are scared," Much said once the ceiling of the cave had been meticulously inspected for evidence of the insidious cave fishers. "Some of the adults too, I have to admit."

"What's the big deal?" Corin said with a shrug. "We can all see in the dark. If the lamps go out, we can go on without 'em."

"That might be well and good for you," Rose said with a shiver, "but most of us aren't used to living our lives in total darkness."

"Not to mention the fact that I can't see in the dark at all," Perin said feebly. Everyone looked at him sympathetically. Perin was so quiet and helpful all the time that most of the dwarves had forgotten, almost, that he was a human.

"So you pretend to be blind until we find some more glowing mushrooms," Corin told the tall human. "We'll lead you along just fine."

Perin looked distressed but said nothing else. Bradok had the distinct impression the human was afraid of the dark.

"I'm more worried about safety," Much said. "We can't see nearly as far in the dark as we can in the light. How will we keep a lookout for cave fishers and other dangers when the glowstones fail?"

The thought of bedding down under a nest of unseen cave fishers gave everyone the chills. Even Corin had no reply.

"We'll use the stones as long as they last," Bradok said. "In the meantime, we'll harvest every glowing mushroom we find."

"Chisul and I already collected the ones we passed," Much said. "He's cutting off the glowsacs and passing them out right now."

"That won't last long enough," Corin said. "Once you pick those glowing ones, they only glow for about two days."

"So we'll keep harvesting," Bradok said. "For now, that's the only plan we have. I think we'd better get some rest."

They all looked disappointed in his leadership, Bradok thought. "I can't bless stones and make them glow," he told himself.

If the Seer in the compass had any ideas, she kept them to herself, simply standing erect and resolute each time Bradok checked. The one bright spot was that her glowing image gave off a fair amount of light and could serve as a small lamp in a pinch.

As everyone bedded down, Bradok volunteered to stand watch with Thurl. An uneventful few hours later, Perin, Xurces, and Rose arrived for the next rotation. Bradok stretched sleepily then turned to go. But Rose grabbed his arm and pulled him aside.

"I told you yesterday, I need to speak to you," she said urgently. "I've been waiting all day to get you alone. Now is the time."

"Can't it wait?" Bradok asked, weariness tugging his eyelids down.

"It's already waited too long," Rose said in a deadly serious voice.

Bradok sighed. "All right," he said.

Instead of releasing his arm, she pulled him back away from the others and toward the tunnel.

"Where—?" Bradok began, but Rose hushed him.

When they were far enough down the tunnel that they could no longer make out the dimming light of the glowlamps, Rose stopped. Bradok had no idea what she might be up to, but suddenly he felt nervous in the dark with her. The image of her, standing naked in shallow water, came unbidden to his mind and, after letting it linger a moment longer than he should have, he pushed it away.

Bradok's eyes hadn't yet adjusted to the total darkness, so he was surprised when a small light flared up between them. In her hand, Rose held a glowsac harvested from a Reorx's torch mushroom.

"Hold this," she said, passing the glowing fungus to him.

Then, astonishing him, Rose took off her cloak and dropped it to the floor of the passage. Abruptly Bradok found himself more wide awake than he'd felt in hours.

Not noticing the awkward look on his face, Rose took hold of her shirt cuff and pulled it up to her elbow, exposing her right forearm.

"Look at this," she said, holding her arm out so Bradok could examine it.

He held the bit of glowing mushroom up to get a better look. Not discerning anything out of place, he took hold of her proffered arm. Touching her arm made him shiver curiously, though her skin seemed fine, a shade darker than he was used to, perhaps, but surface dwarves got more color than their underground cousins.

"What's this?" he asked, noticing a gray blotch that looked a bit like a birthmark.

"That's the problem," she said. "That's what I wanted

to talk to you about. It appeared there a few days ago. I first noticed it when I bathed."

Bradok touched the spot and found the blotch strangely spongy. "What is it, do you think?"

"I sure don't know," Rose said, "but whatever it is, it's spreading."

"Spreading!" Bradok asked anxiously, looking from the gray patch to Rose's wide eyes, which reflected his own concern.

"It's getting bigger," she said. "And that's not the worst of it."

"What else?"

She tugged her sleeve down, covering the blotch. "This is the arm that the spore woman scratched."

A chill ran up Bradok's spine, though he tried to keep his rising fear out of his masked expression.

"I don't think we can make any connections yet," Bradok said hesitantly. "She scratched Chisul on the face, and he's—"

All of a sudden another memory came flooding back to him. When they bathed, he'd noticed a strange gray blotch on Chisul's back.

"What?" Rose asked, her voice insistent, verging on panic.

"Nothing," he lied. "Right now we need to stay calm."

She took a deep breath and closed her eyes for moment. "All right," she said at last. "What should we do?"

"We should talk to Corin," Bradok said. "He knew more than we do about those creatures, and he might be able to tell us what is happening to your arm. Yes, that's what we should do. Talk to Corin."

"Let's go, then," Rose said, taking a step back up the tunnel.

"Wait," Bradok said, catching her shoulder. He nodded up the passage. "Most everyone's asleep, but if those that are awake notice a lot of unusual activity, they're going to know something's up. I don't want everyone to panic. Besides, this may be nothing."

"Or maybe not," she said, wringing her hands.

"In any case," Bradok continued reassuringly, "let me go get Corin quietly and I'll get him to meet with us back here."

"All right," Rose said. "I'll wait here. Just don't be long."

"I'll be as quick as I can," Bradok promised, handing Rose the glowing mushroom sac.

He hurried back up the tunnel, remembering to slow down and act normally only when he passed Perin and Xurces. The Daergar gave Bradok a smile and a nod that seemed out of character, but Bradok barely noticed. His eyes swept the room and finally located Corin, rolled in his cloak on the far side of the cavern. Bradok nudged the sleeping dwarf with his boot, and he sprang awake instantly.

"What?" he said before he was even fully alert.

"We've got to talk," Bradok said.

Corin sat up wearily and motioned for Bradok to sit.

"Not here."

"Is something wrong?" Corin asked, rising.

Bradok didn't answer. He led Corin through the mass of sleeping dwarves, past the guards, and down the tunnel to where the tiny light still glowing indicated Rose's position.

"What's all this mystery about?" he asked when they reached Rose.

"What took you so long?" Rose asked at the same time.

Bradok gestured for Rose's silence and turned to Corin. "You know something about those mushroom people," he began. It was more of a statement than a question.

"Surely you've heard of the Rhizos?" Corin said grumpily.

When Rose and Bradok didn't answer, he went on. "It's caused by a fungal disease called the Zhome," he explained. "You've really never heard of it or seen anything like those afflicted people?"

Bradok and Rose both shook their heads.

Corin leaned back against the cavern wall, his mouth open in astonishment.

"I never would have believed it," he said. "It must only occur in the deep caves."

"What is it, for Reorx's sake?" Rose demanded, her voice almost shrill.

Corin shrugged. "It's a disease my people get sometimes," he said. "It's rare in most cases, but there have been big outbreaks."

"And the infected people become those things we fought?" Rose said nervously. "Rhizos?"

"No," Corin said. "People infected with the disease get gray patches on their skin; eventually, mushrooms begin to sprout from their skin. What you fought were Rhizomorphs, dwarves who have been completely taken over by the fungus. They can still walk and even talk, but they have only two desires: to eat and to infect others with their spores."

"So what about the Rhizos?" Bradok asked. "Are they curable?"

"There are many dwarves who live with the disease," Corin said. "Eventually it will take them over, but it can take years, sometimes decades."

"What's the cure?" Bradok repeated.

"Sad to say, there isn't one," Corin answered, shaking his head. "Anyone infected down here is usually sent to a Zhome colony, often in a deep cave accessible only by an elevator."

Rose gasped.

"What happens when they change into Rhizomorphs?" Bradok asked, his concern growing.

"The Rhizos usually don't let it go that far," Corin said. "Once one of their number starts showing the signs, they take him to a magma flow and throw him in." A sick look flitted over Corin's face, but it passed quickly. "Well, it has to be done, doesn't it? That prevents the spores from spreading."

Rose's eyes were flashing with fear. "You seem to know a lot about this disease," Rose said. "And you don't sound very sympathetic."

Corin nodded sadly. "Oh, I'm sympathetic. Maybe I'm just hardened by all my years of experience. My elder brother contracted the Zhome when I was just a boy," he added. "My mother went to the visitors' rock every week to see him and cheer him up."

"How did he contract the disease?" Bradok asked. "I thought you said that all the spores were contained."

"He didn't get it from inhaling spores," Corin said. "If you get the Zhome that way, you'd become a full blown Rhizomorph in a matter of hours."

"How, then?" Rose demanded.

Corin shook his head. "No one knows. There were always a few cases a year, but none of them ever had any factors in common. The Zhome just seemed to strike without rhyme or reason."

"What happened to your brother in the end?" Rose asked, her voice small.

"One week, my mother went to see him, but he wasn't there. One of the others told her that he'd crossed over." He sighed and slumped his shoulders, as if the memories carried a heavy weight with them. "My mother couldn't handle the tragedy," he said. "She went mad with grief. Father and I tried to keep her calm with various medicines, but finally she killed herself."

Bradok put a comforting hand on Corin's shoulder, but he shrugged it off. "I don't think you'd better do that," he said, taking a small step back. "At least until I know which of you isn't feeling so well."

Bradok cast a worried look at Rose, who involuntarily covered her bandaged arm.

"All right," Corin said, stepping back into the light. "Let's see."

Rose hesitantly unwrapped her arm, and Corin took another step back. He looked at Bradok and nodded.

"It's the Zhome all right," he said with feeling.

"What can we do?" Bradok asked.

"Call Thurl," Corin said with no trace of humor.

"What?" Rose and Bradok asked together.

"He knows ways to make death quick and painless," Corin said. He pointed at Rose's arm. "Death by the Zhome is neither, and to be honest, her Zhome might pose a danger to the rest of us."

"So it's contagious?" Rose gasped, looking at Bradok with terrified eyes.

"That's just it," Corin said. "I keep telling you. No one knows how the Zhome is spread." He nodded at the bandage in Rose's left hand. "By exposing it to us here, you might have doomed us as well."

"I didn't know," Rose said, sounding defeated. "I only discovered this, uh, sore, when I was bathing recently."

"With the women!" Corin gasped. "All the women could be infected."

"Stop!" Bradok said. "This is pointless. You're just scaring her. We don't know how many women are infected or how dangerous this disease is, really." He addressed Rose directly, feeling he had to say something to comfort her. "Much of what Corin has said is hearsay."

Corin snorted, though he looked at Rose sympathetically.

"Wrap that back up for now," Bradok said to Rose.

"We can't let her back with the rest," Corin said in a low voice.

"She voted to let you come with us," Bradok retorted. "Besides, we have to. If the rest get a whiff of what you suspect, we'll have a genuine panic on our hands. Even more people will die. Whoever has the disease now, has it."

He looked from Corin to Rose until they both nodded.

"I propose we let Tal take a look at it," Bradok continued.

"There may be a reason why our people don't normally get this disease. Maybe we carry a special immunity sometimes, or maybe Tal has some medicine that will treat it."

Corin shrugged and Rose looked hopeful.

"It's worth a shot," Bradok said at last.

Ten minutes later Tal was peering through a bit of magnifying glass at the strange, gray patch on Rose's arm.

"I've never seen anything like it," he declared, looking up from the glass. "I've never even heard of anything like it."

"Believe me, Doctor," Corin said. "I know what it is, and it's all too real."

Tal took out a small needle and poked the gray skin.

"Did you feel that?" Tal asked.

Her face pale, Rose shook her head.

"I wonder," her brother said, digging around in his pack for a moment. He emerged with a small, short bladed knife.

"What are you going to do with that?" Rose asked.

"Trust me, Sister," he said then slid the sharp edge of the knife over the top of the infected area. He reached down with a curved metal prong and pulled open the skin, revealing a shallow cut. The flesh seemed rubbery, like a stiff pudding, with strange yellow veins running through it. Tal poked and prodded the exposed flesh with the point of the knife.

"You can't feel any of that?" he said.

"No," Rose answered dispiritedly.

Tal ran his knife along the cut again, slicing deeper.

"Ow," Rose said, flinching as blood blossomed and began to seep up through the wound.

Tal released Rose's arm and leaned back against the passage wall for a moment, his face screwed up in thought.

"It looks like the disease is transforming her skin," he said. "Taking it over. 'Occupying' is what doctors sometimes say."

Corin nodded. "What'd I tell you? Eventually she'll start growing mushrooms. That'll be the beginning of the end."

Tal shot the Daergar a dark look. "Well," Tal said, scratching his chin thoughtfully. "The affected area's not too big or too deep. Why can't I just try to cut it out?"

"Does that work?" Bradok asked Corin, who just shrugged.

"I don't know about cutting. My people believe the Zhome is an infallible death sentence. I'm sure they tried all sorts of things in the beginning, cutting, purifying, even praying. Nowadays they just send infected people to the colony."

Rose stuck out her arm. "Cut it," she commanded.

"There's likely to be a fair amount of pain and blood," Tal said, hesitating. "Not to mention scarring. If what Corin says is true, I'll have to cut as deep as possible, past the affected tissue."

"So get started," she said again, sounding as though she had been injected with hope.

Tal exchanged looks with Bradok, who pursed his lips, frowning. "It's worth trying," Bradok said finally.

Tal dug into his bag and pulled out a silver flask. He gently pulled out the cork. Bradok could smell the potent dwarf spirits from where he stood. The smell caught Corin's attention too. Neither had known that Tal was carrying any liquor.

"Take a swig of this," Tal said, passing it to Rose. "Only one swallow, mind you. I don't want you acting like a schoolgirl all of a sudden and running naked through the cave later."

Rose blushed redder than her hair.

"That only happened once," she said, half to her brother, half to Bradok, before her face cleared and she pushed the flask away. "I don't need anything to bolster my courage."

"You're going to need something for the pain," Tal insisted.

Rose shook her head. "If I cry out, even once, it'll bring everyone in the cavern running," she said. "Better that I keep my wits about me."

Tal's face clouded. "I tell you, this is not going to be pleasant," he warned.

"We've been down here so long," Rose said with the hint of a wink, "that I don't even remember what 'pleasant' is."

"I need more light," Tal said to Bradok and Corin. "Get one of the lanterns from the cave without alarming the others."

"I'll fetch it," Corin said. "Xurces won't ask any questions."

"You'll have to hold her," Tal said to Bradok. "It'll be a shock, no matter how tough she is, and she must keep still while I work."

Bradok nodded. He hated to admit it, but the idea of putting his arms around Rose, of holding her closely while she underwent her ordeal, was the only good thing about the whole mess.

"Sit there," Tal said, indicating a smooth part of the cave wall.

Bradok did as he was told, sitting on the ground with his legs apart. Rose sat right in front of him and leaned back against his chest, her right arm extended, resting on Tal's bag.

"Put your arm around her," Tal said. "Hold her tight."

Bradok put his right arm over Rose's shoulder, draping it down so she could grip it with her left hand. His left arm he slipped around her waist. Her hair still smelled vaguely of sweet soap, and Bradok felt acutely aware of the bottoms of her breasts brushing against his arm as it encircled her waist.

A light came bobbing along the passage as, a moment later, Corin returned with a lantern.

"Here," he said, holding out a stick wrapped in leather to Rose. "It's to bite on. Might help you a little."

Rose nodded then opened her mouth and accepted the stick.

"You'll have to hold the light over here so I can see," Tal told Corin. "I hope the sight of blood doesn't bother you."

"Only when it's mine," Corin said with a hint of a smile.

"All right," Tal said as he pulled out a disconcerting number of knives and tools and laid them down in an organized row. "I'm going to do this as fast as I can. If it gets to be too much, Rose, just spit out the stick and that'll be my cue. I'll stop."

"Yust oo id," she said around the stick in her mouth.

As Tal picked up a sharp, thin-bladed knife, Bradok felt Rose's hand clamp down on his forearm. He tightened his grip on her arm and her waist as Tal began to saw away at the strange blotch.

The first cuts were shallow, allowing Tal to scoop out some of the gray skin. He quickly cleared the area, leaving only a few spots where his knife had plunged deep enough to draw blood. The next cut, however, caused Rose to grunt with effort, and Bradok felt her nails digging hard into his arm.

Tal chopped away a chunk of bloody flesh, throwing it down on the sand. Corin looked away, edging back, but Tal waved him forward again because of the light. Tal used a towel to dab the blood away before cutting again. Rose bucked hard, straining against Bradok, and chomped down on the stick, which muffled her cries of pain. But her arm stayed in place. Bradok could see the muscles in her arm tightening and jerking as she forced herself to hold her arm steady under her brother's cutting, probing knife.

"All right," Tal said after what seemed to Bradok like an hour of butchery, though it was only ten or twenty minutes. "I think I got it all. One root went very deep, but I got that out."

He laid aside his tools and began packing the wound with cheesecloth, finishing by wrapping it tightly several times.

Rose had long since stopped straining and jerking. She was panting and drenched with sweat. She spat out the stick but couldn't talk at first. She gazed up into Bradok's eyes. He thought he detected something in the look she gave him then. More than simple gratitude for help well rendered, he imagined her look said that she'd have risked such pain only if he were the one to hold her. In another moment, though, she had fallen asleep, slumping down to the cave floor in exhaustion.

"What should we do with this?" Corin said, indicating the bloody pile of flesh with disgust.

"Bury it," Tal said, "or it will stink and attract predators. Needless to say, have as little contact with it as possible."

Tal shook Rose gently. "Can you stand?" he asked.

Dazed and wobbly, Rose stood up. Tal helped her steady herself.

"You two clean this up," Tal said to Bradok and Corin, wiping off his knives and putting them away. "I'll take Rose back to the cavern and give her a medicine to help her sleep comfortably."

With that, Tal shouldered his bag, took Rose by the hand, and slowly led her away.

Corin went to get the privy shovel while Bradok got to his feet and dusted himself off. His shirtfront was soaked with Rose's sweat, and her scent was all over his body.

It didn't take long to dispose of the bloody flesh once Corin returned with the shovel. They didn't talk much as they worked, for both were anxious to get past the unpleasant job.

"I've been wondering something," Bradok said as they finished up, piling sand on top of the hole they'd made.

"What's that?"

"If your people kept all the Rhizos in a sealed cave, then where did our four playmates come from?" Bradok asked.

"What playmates?" Corin asked.

"The four Rhizomorphs we fought," Bradok said. "Where did they come from?"

Corin stopped, his shovel frozen in mid action.

"By the Abyss," he said finally, swearing in a low voice. "The caves," he stammered. "The Zhome colony must have been broken open by the earthquake, just like the prison."

"That's what I've been thinking," Bradok said grimly.

"It means that, if those four Rhizomorphs were down here, running around looking for hapless victims, so are all the rest of 'em."

Corin gasped. "There's no way of knowing how many of them survived the earthquake," he said, "nor any way to stop them from tracking us. We're in Reorx's hands, for sure, this time."

"Reorx!" Bradok muttered angrily, adding quickly, more respectfully, just in case the god was listening. "Reorx."

CHAPTER 16

The Well of the Moon

The slap of boot leather on stone echoed through the stone passage. It had been six days since the cave fisher attack and one since Rose's disease had been operated on by her brother, and the survivors of Ironroot made little other noise as they marched. No one spoke much; no children were laughing anymore. Everyone kept their loved ones in sight and their hands on their weapons. To Bradok it seemed as though a gloomy fog had descended on them all.

The glowlamps that had so brightly lit their way had slowly dwindled to feeble points of light. Bradok, holding his compass open in the palm of his hand, walked in front of the group, using its small but clear light as a beacon, but that only seemed to emphasize the desperate nature of their situation. He couldn't be sure, but he thought its light, too, was beginning to fade.

In the evenings people spoke only in whispers, and no one had gotten a good night's sleep for several days. Without any light for protection, they avoided the caves at night. But sleeping in the tunnels was cramped and difficult, making everyone cranky.

That day the light in the tunnel was not so bad, and that gave Bradok an opportunity to step to the rear. Three other dwarves walked wearily along with him, their hands never far from their weapons: Corin, Much, and Rose. He had asked for those three stalwarts to join him. Bradok was tired of so many of the others, who whined and complained at every juncture.

"We have to do something about this infernal darkness," Much said as they shuffled along, their darkvision adequate enough to show them a grainy, black-and-white view of the path ahead.

"True, the darkness is depressing. But what do you suggest?" Rose asked, a hopeless note in her voice. "We've wracked our brains."

"Everyone is on edge. People need a break," Corin said.

"They need to rest," Bradok agreed. "Everyone's been sleeping with one eye open, and it's wearing them down. If this keeps up, we won't be able to make a full day's march soon."

"We need to find a place that's secure," Rose said. "If everyone felt safer, they might be able to sleep better."

"We aren't likely to find any place guaranteed to be safe," Corin said.

"Maybe if we could just close off the passage behind us," Much said. "Then we'd only have to guard our camp from one direction."

"That's a good idea," Bradok admitted. "It might work. But we'd have to find a weak part of the passage to pull down, and we don't have the proper tools. Someone would have to take risks."

"It's too dangerous," Corin said. "Trying to collapse the ceiling."

"It'd be suicide for whoever volunteered," Rose said.

"We still ought to consider it," Bradok said without much enthusiasm.

"There you are," Chisul's voice reached Bradok before Chisul himself did. Bradok's stomach turned sour. He was back there in the rear precisely to avoid trouble-making dwarves such as Silas's son. "I've been looking for you. You're pretty far behind the group."

"Imagine that," Corin said with mockery in his voice, "the rear guard actually bringing up the rear."

"Well, get your rears moving," Chisul said, "if that isn't too much to ask. The people want a word with their great leader, Bradok."

Bradok ground his teeth in frustration. Every time anyone had a hangnail, they brought the problem to him. He made a mental note to find an appropriate way to thank Rose and her busybody brother for foisting upon him the leadership of the survivors.

He glanced guiltily at Rose. She seemed better, though now and then she stroked her bandaged arm. They had told the others that she had had a bad stumble and Tal had fixed her up.

"What do they want this time?" Bradok asked wearily as Chisul fell in line beside them.

"Oh, I imagine it's the same as before," Chisul said with a shrug. "They want you to do something about the darkness."

"What do they think I am?" Bradok yelled, causing Rose to start. "I'm not a wizard or a priest. I can't wave a magic wand or anything." Bradok's voice echoed down the passage, so the others could hear, but he didn't care any longer. He poked Chisul in the chest, causing the younger dwarf to stagger back. "I can't just say let there be light and have it spring up out of no—"

Just then a burst of brightness washed over Bradok. It couldn't really have been very bright but, with his eyes accustomed to total darkness, the sudden intensity of it burned like fire. When Bradok tried to open his eyes, he had to shield them with his hands against the ball of orange energy that had materialized in the passage ahead of them, hovering just a few feet away.

"Your friend's back," Rose said, shielding her eyes as well.

It did look like the orb of light they'd seen before.

"You've seen that one before?" Corin asked, awe in his voice. He eyed Bradok with an intense look, his forked beard quivering.

"Yes," Bradok said. "A couple of 'em appeared and one flew right through me one night while I was on guard duty. But they were green then. Why?"

"My people call these things 'dark lights,' " Corin said in a hushed voice. "To see one is considered a good omen. There are stories of them leading travelers out of trouble." The Daergar shrugged; then his face lengthened. "Of course there are also stories of them leading the unwary to violent deaths."

"Great," Chisul said. "So now we have a light guiding us that can think for itself, and we can't trust its motives."

"That's about it," Bradok agreed wryly.

"Still," Corin said, a thoughtful note in his voice. "It touched you once and now it's back. That has to mean something. Maybe it's a good omen, after all." He laughed suddenly. "If there were any members of the Magma Tube Clan around, they'd find it absolutely fascinating that you actually touched a cave light."

"You mean they'd revere him?" Rose said.

Corin nodded. "Right before they ate him," he said with a smirk.

"Ate?" Much said, aghast.

"Oh, don't worry," Corin said, cutting Bradok off before he could protest. "We don't have any Magma Tube Clansmen in these parts."

"Well, that's good," Bradok croaked.

"As far as I know," Corin added with a wink to Rose.

Their eyes had finally become accustomed to the light, and they lowered their hands. The ball of energy just hung there in the center of the passage, not moving. Its body, if the edge of its fuzzy round shape could be called that, seemed to expand and contract at regular intervals, as if it were slowly breathing in and out. Purple pulses of energy would occasionally leap from one side of its form to the other then back, skittering across its surface to form a constantly shifting spiderweb of arcs.

"So . . . what now?" Chisul asked.

"How should I know?" Bradok answered.

"You must have summoned it."

"No, I didn't. The fact that it appeared right when I said 'light' was just a coincidence."

"Quite a coincidence," Rose said under her breath.

"Major coincidence," Much added.

"I had a philosophy teacher once who said there were no such things as coincidences," Corin finished.

Bradok turned to the Daergar. "Meaning what?" he asked.

"Meaning that maybe our glowing friend here wants something," Chisul said.

All eyes turned back to Bradok. With a sigh, he rolled his eyes then turned to the orange energy ball.

"Ahem, uh, pardon me. What can I do for you?" Bradok asked, trying hard not to sound too awed or afraid.

The ball quivered at the sound of his voice, the distinct edges of its surface rippling like a still pond disturbed by a stone. Spiderwebs of energy erupted all over its body; then it zoomed around Bradok, circling him twice, before flying up the passageway. It stopped after a dozen yards, hanging motionless again. When no one moved, it pulsed twice, growing momentarily brighter.

"I think it wants us to follow it," Rose said after a long, tense silence.

Chisul pointed at Corin. "Didn't he just say they lead people to their doom?"

"He said *sometimes* they do," Rose said.

"That's often enough for me," Chisul said.

"Me too," Much agreed.

"I don't think it wants to hurt us," Rose insisted. "If it does, why didn't it lead us to our doom the first time?"

The orange ball pulsed again, almost impatiently.

"Well, it's going the same way we are," Bradok pointed out. "We may as well follow it. If we turn around, we'll lose the others."

"Where are the rest anyway?" Much asked Chisul.

"There's a big cave up ahead," the cooper's son said. "No mushrooms, but a lot of crystals. They're waiting there."

"All right," Bradok said, slowly moving up the passage. "Let's play along for a while. See where Blinky is taking us."

As Bradok moved forward, the light retreated, always staying ahead of them, just within sight. When it reached the cave, it darted over the heads of the startled dwarves who sat, waiting for Chisul's return. The chamber itself was large, with thousands of milky-white crystals growing from the walls, floor, and ceiling.

As the energy ball entered, the crystals seemed to leap to life, their glasslike edges reflecting the light brilliantly. It looked as if the single orb of pale orange light had been suddenly boosted by hundreds.

The edgy, sleep-deprived dwarves reacted as one, seizing their weapons and their loved ones and huddling together fearfully. Kellik lashed out with his warhammer, shattering a freestanding crystal into a thousand glittering shards.

"Wait!" Rose cried as others stood, ready to begin swinging at anything that glittered or gleamed. "It isn't hurting us."

"Says you," Chisul muttered, his hand on his short sword.

Meanwhile the orange light zoomed around the room, ignoring Bradok and the dwarves completely. Gradually it slowed and began orbiting an enormous crystal at the far end of the cave, revolving around the trunklike structure with changing light pulses.

"It's beautiful," Rose decided.

Bradok would have felt a lot better about the beauty of the pulsing ball of light if he knew whether it promised doom or salvation.

Suddenly the ball of light began to accelerate, spinning around the crystal so quickly that it seemed to create a solid band of light. The reflections around the room seemed to jump and flicker across the smaller crystals with incredible speed, a shimmering movement accompanied by a deep, bell-like tone.

"What is that?" Bradok said.

"The crystals are singing," Much ventured.

The sound grew and Bradok could swear he heard different notes joining in, slowly changing the cacophony into a harmonious chord.

"Look," Chisul said, pointing.

All the dwarves were staring already. All around the chamber, individual crystals were changing color. Before, they had all reflected the orange light of the energy creature, but as they watched, they burned from within, reds, greens, blues, and yellows.

New balls of light began to slide out of the crystals, adding their brightness to the room. At least a dozen new balls of light emerged and floated over to the giant crystal.

The orange light stopped spinning as its companions crowded around it. One by one, they flew through the crystal, penetrating its smooth surface the same way the orange one had flown through Bradok the first night he'd witnessed them. With each pass, the crystal began to glow pale blue from within. After a few moments, the glow became a blinding light encompassing the entire cavern and the dwarves had to cover their eyes again.

When the lights finally stopped moving, the giant crystal pulsed with inner light. Each pulse seemed to push the light outward, and the surrounding crystals began to glow again as well. Soon the entire room sparkled with twinkling lights. Bradok noticed that even the shards of the crystal Kellik had shattered were renewed and glowed.

"I tell you, it's beautiful," Rose repeated.

"I've never seen anything like it," Kellik said in his gravelly voice.

"What's happening now?" Much said, grabbing Bradok's attention by the urgency in his voice then grabbing his shirt as well.

The old dwarf was pointing at the first orange ball of light, which hung in the air in front of the giant crystal. Its surface rippled and bulged, as if something inside of it were trying to escape. The other lights hovered around the first one, but not too close. Each time its surface rippled, the orange light seemed to dim and the ball of light fell a bit, drifting toward the floor.

"I think it's sick or something," Bradok said. "Maybe dying."

"Why did it bring us here, then?" Corin asked. "To witness this?"

"That's exactly right," Rose decided, her face splitting into a smile. "But I don't think it's dying. Look!"

The energy creature pulsed and bulged again, and it seemed to expel a small burst of light from its body that hung motionless in the air like a miniature star. After a moment, the light seemed to collapse in on itself, forming a perfect, orange sphere.

"See," Rose said. "It's more like it's—she's—pregnant."

Rose had no more than said those words when a second small ball of light was expelled from the mother-light. Four more followed before the orange ball began to brighten again. She was just above the floor, hovering there with her babies zipping around her like playful puppies. Whenever they drew close enough, purple tethers of energy would jump between mother and offspring.

"She's bonding with them," Tal said, agreeing with his sister.

"How do you know so much?" Chisul asked suspiciously.

"It's what most species do," Tal said with a shrug.

"It's beautiful," Rose said for the third time, dabbing tears from her eyes.

"I hate to be the practical one," Chisul said, "but unless she's offering to let us borrow a couple of her babies to use as light buddies, I think we've wasted enough time here."

Rose shot Chisul a hard look and elbowed him in the ribs.

"What?" he protested. "As interesting as this is, it isn't getting us anywhere. I think we should move on."

"He's got a point," Kellik said grudgingly.

"What do you think?" Rose asked Bradok.

Back to him again, Bradok thought with a sinking feeling. Before he could respond, however, the baby lights zoomed away from their mother. They darted over to where Bradok stood with the others, zipping around them all, hovering, then moving off.

One let Rose touch it glancingly with her outstretched fingers before shooting away.

After a few minutes of that, the mother pulsed with light, and the babies returned to her, circling around her as she hung just below the massive crystal. Purple energy tethers jumped from the babies to the mother then from the mother to the side of the giant crystal. All of them glowed brighter and brighter until, with a thunderous crack, a fragment of the crystal popped out of the side, like a cork from a keg. A torrent of glowing water issued forth from the hole, splashing across the base of the crystal and filling a small depression in the stone floor.

In less than a minute, a small pool had formed at the base of the radiating crystal. Then the torrent of water dwindled to a trickle. The water or fluid or whatever it was glowed. It almost seemed as though the crystal were bleeding from a wound.

The light creatures pulsed in unison, and all but the mother rose up and disappeared into the ceiling as if it were nothing more than smoke. The mother light hung in the air a moment longer, pulsing gently; then she, too, disappeared into the stone.

"So there it is. Some fireworks and a disappearing act. And what's left behind? Do you think your friend the orange ball of light is inviting us to drink from her glowing pool?" Chisul asked sarcastically.

Bradok shook his head. It didn't make sense to him either.

"Are you two daft?" Much exclaimed, laughter in his voice. "It's a moonwell."

They all stared, Rose beginning to laugh too. Bradok had heard of such deep pools where the water had absorbed so many minerals that it actually glowed with weird energy, but he'd never seen one before. Most dwarves thought they were legend.

"Reorx has blessed us," Kellik said happily. He dropped to one knee and bowed his head, offering a prayer of thanks. On either side of the big smith, his boys did the same.

"Aye," everyone intoned when the prayer was finished.

Bradok felt like the odd man out. He'd never been the kind of dwarf who prayed and he wasn't much for attending temple, yet there he was, leading a ragtag group of believers in Reorx's name.

He felt like more of hypocrite than anything else as he knelt and pretended to pray along with the rest.

Standing up, he reminded himself that he had actually met Reorx and knew he was as real as Much or Chisul or Rose. He'd seen Reorx with his own eyes, or at the very least, a messenger of the god's. He must be blessed, somehow, even if he wasn't a believer.

"Moonwells are reputed to possess the power of the gods,"

Much whispered into Bradok's ear. "Maybe it can restore our glowstones."

"Thanks," he whispered back then proclaimed Much's idea as if it were his own.

The dead glowstones were brought out and passed to Bradok, who took them over to the glowing pool. He had no idea what he was doing really, but he determined to make a show of it. Slowly, he dipped the stones into the water, setting them gently on the bottom.

The water itself felt like any other water to the touch, but it seemed to cling thickly to his fingers as he withdrew them, soaking into his skin rather than running off.

"What about the compass?" Chisul said. "Why not try that?"

Why not, indeed? Bradok took out the compass and stared at it. What if it got a little wet? It had no inner works to spoil. He flipped it open, expecting to be greeted by the Seer in a swimming dress, but instead she did not appear. That was odd but sometimes happened. Perhaps she dreaded the coming immersion, or maybe her power had faded too much. His course of action was decided. With only the barest of hesitation, he snapped the compass's lid closed and lowered it reverently into the pool.

"How long till we know if it works?" Tal asked.

Bradok shrugged dumbly.

"Let's leave it in for the night," he said, looking around at the glowing crystals filling the cave. "This looks like a nice, warm, bright place for everyone to get some rest."

CHAPTER 17
Starlight Hall

For the first time in many weeks, Bradok woke up peaceably. No one had roused him. No sound had penetrated his weary mind to raise any alarms. No sense of impending danger compelled him to consciousness. He just felt a weightless, euphoric feeling as he floated up from the depths of dreaming to full consciousness.

It felt wondrous.

Bradok opened his eyes and looked at the cave ceiling above. The glowing crystals had dimmed considerably since the night before, but there was still plenty of light shining. A few people were up and about, but most still slept. He gave a thought to just rolling over and going back to sleep, but he knew if he rested too much, it would just make him more tired later.

With a sigh, he rose, brushing the dust from his pants and shaking the dirt from his cloak. He changed his shirt and went to the moonwell to splash some water on his face. As he approached the shallow pool, it seemed to have grown brighter rather than dimmer, as the crystals had. The water shimmered only faintly, retaining very little of the luminescent silver light that it displayed the previous night. However, two bright points of light burned coldly from the bottom of the little pool.

Bradok's face broke into a wide smile as he rolled up his sleeve. He thrust his hand in the freezing water and withdrew the two glowstones, revived and returned to a brightly glowing state.

"It worked," Corin said, materializing beside him.

Bradok tossed the Daergar one of the stones with a grin then retrieved the compass. Flipping open its lid, the Seer appeared immediately, hovering in the air. She extended her spear, but instead of pointing at the only exit from the crystal chamber, she gestured toward a spot to one side, against one of the walls.

"Maybe she's confused," Corin said, scratching his beard.

The image of the Seer screwed up her face in a look of disdain.

"All right, all right," Corin said. "Don't get testy. I'll go check it out." He winked at Bradok then rose and bowed to the Seer before moving off toward the wall she had indicated.

"What was that all about?" Rose's voice greeted Bradok as he put the compass away.

"Corin and the compass were having a difference of opinion," he said wryly.

Rose knelt down beside the pool and splashed a handful of water on her face, doing her best to wipe away the dirt of the road with a little towel.

"Oh, I see the pool recharged the glowstones," she said with a note of her old cheerfulness.

Bradok nodded, polishing the compass with the hem of his cloak before putting it away.

"Do you think this water's safe to drink?" Rose asked, eyeing the still-glowing liquid.

"I usually don't make a point of drinking things that glow," he said.

Rose smiled and nodded. "Good point," she said.

As Bradok dried the glowstones, a long silence began to

stretch between them. Rose seemed to be absently combing her hair, and Bradok wanted to broach a delicate subject.

"How are you feeling? How's your arm?" he asked finally.

She involuntarily put her left hand over the bandage. "It's healing," she said. "It's fine," she added but in a brisk, uncertain manner that seemed to cut off further inquiry.

"Let's see," Bradok said, pulling a strip of cloth from his bag. "I'm sure it could do with a fresh bandage."

"I tell you, it's better," Rose said, putting her hand over the bandage again.

Her face was defiant with anger. Bradok had expected trepidation, maybe even fear, but anger seemed out of place.

"Come on," he said, reaching for her arm. "We need to see how you're doing."

"Don't touch me," she growled, pulling her arm back out of reach.

"I was just—" Bradok started to say, but Rose cut him off.

"You're not my husband, you're not my mother, and you're not my doctor."

"No, your brother is your doctor," Tal cut in. "Isn't that confusing enough?" he added good-humoredly, trying to allay the tension.

Bradok turned to find Rose's brother standing with his arms folded across his barrel chest. "Bradok is right," he said with more sternness than Bradok had ever heard from him. "Let's see that arm."

Rose glared back at him. Bradok felt out of place. It was nothing short of a contest of wills between sister and brother, more than patient and doctor. Eventually, Rose looked away apologetically and held her arm out for Tal to examine.

"Let's see what we have here," Tal said, his genial manner returning instantly.

Tal unwrapped the bandage and peeled away the bloody

cheesecloth. They all stared. Bradok had seen wounds where part of the underlying muscle had been damaged. Usually such wounds closed up but left a hole where the missing tissue had been removed. When Tal pulled the bandage off Rose's arm, they saw that the depression made by the surgery had partially filled in.

"Hmmm. This is unusual. I can't see that it's good," Tal said in a low voice, nodding for Bradok to take a closer look.

The entire area that Tal had cut away pulsated with a strange, yellow light, and Bradok could see tracks running out from the area that shot out into Rose's arm, like weird veins.

"Yes," Bradok said. "Definitely not good."

"Cutting it seems to make it angry," Rose said, sounding composed.

"Why didn't you tell me about this sooner?" Tal demanded.

"What would you have done?" Rose asked angrily. "Amputate?" She looked from Bradok to Tal. "What if it's already gone deeper? You just going to keep cutting till there's nothing left of me?"

Tal sighed. "We can try again," he said, clearly discouraged.

Rose shook her head. "No," she said. "If I'm going to die, I prefer to do it whole."

"I can respect that," Tal said. "From now on, I want you to keep me apprised of any changes. Agreed?"

Rose nodded somberly and allowed Tal to wrap up her arm again.

"Now I want you two to promise me something," she said when Tal finished. "I don't want to become one of those . . . things. I want you to swear," she said, "swear by Reorx's Forge that you'll let Thurl . . . do what he does best. Swear you'll kill me first."

Tal and Bradok exchanged dark looks, neither wanting to look the other dwarf in the eyes. Sensing their hesitation,

Rose grabbed them each by their shirtfronts and yanked them closer.

"Swear it," she whispered.

"I swear," Bradok said solemnly. He meant it, too. He'd let Thurl kill her before he saw her become a shambling horror, but before it came to that, he would do anything possible, move mountains, to change her fate.

"Me too," Tal said sadly.

Rose released them and tightened the bandage back around her arm. Then she stood up and walked away.

"Wow," Bradok said, sorely chastened. "She's really something."

Tal chuckled.

Bradok shot him a questioning look.

"She's not the easiest person to get close to," her brother said. "Your timing is bad too. Are you sure you want to try?"

Bradok laughed. It seemed like such a strange question in light of all that was happening. He looked Tal in the eye and nodded.

"Don't get me wrong," Tal said. "Rose is a real beauty who's been chased by many a dwarf. It's just that she's a hard person to love. And I have no idea what this disease is going to do to her."

Bradok lowered his eyes at the reminder.

"Rose never got the message that she's a girl," Tal continued with more spirit. "She wants to be the best at everything, do everything for herself. Most men want to feel like their woman needs them, and Rose doesn't want to need anyone. In the end, she drives everyone away."

Bradok nodded.

"Hey, there's a passage back there if anyone cares," Corin's voice rang out, interrupting his thoughts.

He'd forgotten that the compass had pointed to one of the walls and that Corin had gone to investigate.

"The crystals have grown over it, but there's definitely something back there," Corin said. "I'm going to get Kellik, and together we'll smash it open."

"Good job," Bradok said.

"What's he doing?" Corin asked, pointing at Tal.

Tal was filling several canteens with the water from the moonwell.

"I figured I'd maybe soak Rose's bandages in this," he said, holding up the canteen. "If this glow-water really is blessed, it might help. I don't see how it could hurt."

Bradok rose and trailed after Corin. The Daergar had found Kellik, and the pair were making their way to the side of the chamber. As Bradok approached, the smith swung his hammer and shattered one of the smaller crystals that bulged out of the wall. A few minutes of heavy work, and Bradok could see that there was indeed a small opening behind the transparent wall.

Over the next half hour, the three of them took turns swinging the massive hammer and clearing a wide enough passage to admit the survivors. Bradok broke the last crystal away, sending it clattering across the stone floor in glittering fragments.

Panting and wiping the sweat from his face, he handed the hammer back to Kellik.

"That's really something," Kellik said, staring down the dark hole. "Everywhere we go there are secret passages. I wonder how long this one's been hidden here, how many dwarves have gone right by it?"

"No telling," Corin said with a weary shrug. Then he turned to Bradok. "It'll take a few minutes to get everyone ready to move on. Why don't we send someone ahead to scout the territory?"

Bradok took a long pull from his waterskin before he nodded. "I'll go," Thurl said, close behind them, startling Bradok.

Bradok hadn't been aware of the dwarf's presence. Coughing and spluttering, he spat water all over Corin and Kellik.

"Don't ever do that again," Bradok gasped. "Sneak up on me like that."

"I shall wear a cowbell from now on," Thurl said, a devious smile on his face.

Bradok pulled one of the resuscitated glowstones from his pocket and handed it to Thurl.

The thin assassin smiled more normally. "I prefer the dark," the Daergar explained. With an unexpected swiftness, he stepped into the tunnel and darted into the blackness.

"He gives me the creeps," Kellik said, passing Bradok back his waterskin.

"He wouldn't be much of an assassin if he didn't," Corin said with a chuckle. Bradok laughed too.

As he took a drink from his waterskin, however, Bradok heard the sound of running feet. He swallowed quickly as Rose appeared.

"You'd better get over here," she said then turned and hustled back to the center of the chamber.

Everyone seemed to be gathered around Tal, who was kneeling over someone Bradok could not see.

"It's Lyra," Urlish Hearthhome said as Bradok and the others arrived. "Xurces thinks it's time. She's going to have her baby."

"Baby?" Bradok asked dumbly.

"Xurces?" Much echoed from Bradok's left. "What's that strange man doing anywhere near that sweet girl?"

"Xurces is all right," Corin said.

"Easy for you to say," Much growled, clearly dissatisfied.

"One side," Bradok said, pushing his way through the crowd.

He came up to where Tal was kneeling and immediately wished he were anywhere else. Lyra lay on the ground, breathing in great gasps. Xurces knelt by her, holding her hand and whispering comforting words in her ear. Tal had Lyra stripped below the waist with her legs splayed apart. Worse, he seemed to be doing something that Bradok was sure would get him slapped if he ever had tried it with a girl.

"She's not ready," Xurces said after a minute, withdrawing his hand. He pulled his cloak off and threw it over Lyra's legs for modesty's sake.

"What's the timetable?" Bradok asked, trying to sound knowledgeable and sophisticated.

Tal rose, wiping his hands with a towel, and led Bradok a few paces off.

"She's exhausted herself," he said. "Her body is trying to expel the baby so it can use all of its resources to keep her alive."

"She's had a full night's rest," Bradok said, not understanding.

"That's not going to be enough, I'm afraid," Tal said worriedly. "She's seriously overextended herself in the last week. She needs several days of rest at least, to have a chance."

"We can't wait here that long," Bradok said, not even bothering to consult the compass. "Our food supply is running low."

"We could carry her," Much suggested.

"She's not one of the children," Bradok said. "How can we carry her?"

"That's easy enough," Much explained. "We take the lantern poles and a cloak and make a stretcher."

"How do we attach the poles to the cloak?" Tal asked.

"Come on," Much said irritably. "Just wrap it around the poles then fold it over on itself twice. Her body weight will keep it from slipping. The least we can do is try."

Bradok stared openmouthed at Much. His old friend had many hidden gifts and talents.

"I picked up the idea from some humans during my travels," he continued. "Once you make the stretcher and get Lyra in it, we just need four dwarves to carry it. Have them roll up their cloaks for padding and carry the poles on their shoulders."

Bradok and Tal exchanged looks that said plainly that they had no better ideas.

"Get to it, then," Bradok said, patting Much on the arm.

Much flashed a wide smile and hurried off to get the lantern poles. Bradok started to turn away when Tal caught his arm.

"Speaking of humans," he said. "I'm worried about Perin."

Bradok looked around and spotted the big human sitting with his back against the wall, apparently taking deep breaths as though meditating.

"What about him?" Bradok asked. Perin was one of the few survivors that Bradok never heard any complaints from. He was always around when they needed him, always polite and helpful.

"I don't think the air down here is good for him," Tal said.

Bradok gulped a few breaths but didn't notice anything unusual about the air. Like most dwarves, Bradok could smell mine gas or detect foul air from almost a mile away.

"Maybe the air is a bit stale, but—" he began.

"That's just it," Tal interrupted. "Dwarves are denizens of the underground. Our lungs can handle all kinds of thin or tainted air, even gas for a while. Humans aren't that robust."

Bradok gave Perin another probing look.

"All right, keep an eye on him," he said, not really sure what they could do about Perin's problem if Tal's theory were correct.

"I have been keeping an eye on him," Tal said, leaning over to pack up his doctor kit. "Something else I thought I should mention. Did you know he's keeping a journal about our journey?"

"No," Bradok said, only half listening.

"Well, it's some kind of journal," Tal said. "A very strange one, if you ask me. I tried reading it over his shoulder once, but he's writing in some language I've never seen."

"I didn't realize you knew that much about languages," Bradok replied, distracted.

"Well, I really don't . . ."

Bradok's attention wandered to where Much seemed to be having an animated discussion with Xurces. "Excuse me a minute."

He stepped away from Tal and quickly headed over to Much and Xurces.

"Lyra is a sweet girl," Much was saying, not entirely pleasantly. "She doesn't need the likes of you around."

"You misunderstand my motives," Xurces said in his soft voice.

"I don't know anything about motives, but I heard why they locked you up," Much returned. "For you, a woman's heart is some kind of plaything."

"I won't deny that I misused many women in my day," Xurces said. "At my trial, the prosecutor insisted that he had proof that I had fathered over one hundred children."

"My point exactly," Much said.

"But I must assure you," Xurces pleaded. "The desires that drove those actions are long gone. I have the scars to prove it."

"What makes you so darn interested in Lyra all of a sudden, then?" Much demanded.

"I am merely exercising compassion," Xurces said sincerely. "Lyra worked as a barmaid and fell prey to someone like me, several someones, if truth be told. Now she has a daughter and another child on the way and no one to take care of her."

"And you think that's your job?" Much said. "As some kind of penance?"

"Yes, maybe penance," Xurces said. "But it goes deeper than that. They say I fathered one hundred children, but I've never seen even one of them, much less been there when they were born.

"Now," he went on, "I have the chance to do good and help Lyra and experience what I was too selfish to participate in before."

Much seemed to mull that over, the frown on his face stubborn. "All right, but I'm watching you," he said after a long pause. "If I get even the hint of something going wrong with you, you'll wish those prison guards had killed you instead."

Xurces looked more relieved than offended. He simply smiled mildly and bowed his head.

Much turned and walked away muttering. Bradok started to follow, but Corin stopped him.

"He really is harmless, you know," he said of Xurces.

"How do you know?"

"With a face like his, every woman in the penal caves wanted him for their man," Corin said. "He could have had any of them, or all of them, but he never touched even one."

"Is it because of . . ." Bradok started, not knowing exactly how to finish.

Corin shrugged. "I don't know if he can't or if he just won't," he said. "But either way, it means that Lyra is safer with him than with just about anyone."

"I hope you're right," Bradok said.

"Bradok?" Thurl's voice echoed across the space.

"Here," Bradok said.

Thurl waved at him from the hole in the crystal wall then disappeared inside. Bradok pushed back through the crowd and followed slowly, waiting for his eyes to adjust. When at last he could see, he found Thurl waiting for him just up the passage. The scarred dwarf stood before what looked like a wall. As Bradok got closer, he could see that it was, in fact, a wall made of expertly baked bricks. A large hole opened in the middle of the wall, and several bricks were strewn on the floor in front of it, as if they'd been pushed through from the other side.

Bradok stuck his head through the hole and gasped. Inside was different. The path had been finished with flagstones on the ground and carved, shaped walls cut smooth. A bracket for a torch had been mounted on the wall, but there was no torch.

"What do you think?" Bradok asked Thurl. "Is this Daergar?"

"Daergar don't build like this," Thurl said. "Besides, the floor is covered in dirt. No one's used this tunnel in a very long time."

"That doesn't mean no one lives in here."

"I'd guess not," Thurl said. "We should tread softly, just in case."

Bradok pulled out his compass. Sure enough, the Seer's spear pointed straight down the disused tunnel. Their luck was changing.

"Go get the others," he said. "Tell them we have to be extra quiet."

Thurl nodded and left. Bradok pulled a few more bricks from the semicollapsed wall, making the opening big enough for the others to pass through, then climbed over to the other side. In the darkness, he couldn't make out any decoration or design to the stonework. It seemed plain and functional but well made.

When the lanterns arrived, they didn't reveal anything new.

"What if these are Daergar tunnels?" Chisul hissed as he climbed through the wall.

"What if they're Theiwar?" Bradok shot back.

"Either one would be a problem," Corin said as he followed Chisul.

"I doubt there'll be trouble," Much said, coming next.

"Why do you say that?" Corin asked.

Much pointed at the dirt-covered ground. "I don't know about your people," he said, "but no self-respecting dwarf would let his tunnels get into this state. I'd say these were abandoned long ago."

"You have a point," Corin admitted.

"Abandoned or not, I want four armed dwarves leading the way, weapons in hand," Bradok said. He drew his sword, and Chisul, Corin, and Much drew theirs as well. Corin had borrowed Tal's sword since the doctor was always excused from guard duty.

They moved slowly down the passageway with their band of survivors trailing behind. The way ran straight and slightly down, turning only once, to the right. Finally, it ended in a set of carved double doors. Each heavy stone door had an intricate arch carved on its surface. Under the arch, a field of stars blazed around a single larger star that had been painted red. The impression was of eyes peering out from behind the doors, watching them.

"What do you think?" Bradok asked Kellik, running his hands over the carved arches. Each arch seemed to be made up of four separate vinelike strands that wound together into a single, unified strand at the top.

"If they used graphite on the hinges, they should still open fine," Kellik said. "Grease would have dried up over time."

"I don't see a latch," Bradok said, bracing himself and placing his hand against the wall.

"Wait!" Corin said, quickly stepping forward. Bradok edged aside as the Daergar got so close to the door his nose almost grazed the stone.

"I don't believe it," he said, running his hand reverently over the arches.

"Don't believe what?" Kellik said. "It's just a door, isn't it?"

217

"Not the door," Corin said, pointing at the red star. "It's Starlight Hall."

Jeni and Thurl had come up behind Corin, and they gasped at his words.

"It can't be," Thurl said. "Starlight Hall is just a fairy story, something to tell children when they go to bed."

"What is he talking about?" Bradok asked Corin.

"It's a myth," Corin explained. "One of the oldest stories in Daergar legend.

"Nine hundred years ago, a dwarf named Galoka Starlight tried to convert the Daergar back to the worship of Reorx. He taught that the family of dwarves could never be reunited until we are all unified under one god."

"I bet that went over well," Kellik harrumphed.

Corin shrugged. "According to the legend, Galoka had great success in several Daergar cities, before the Underking took notice of him."

"What happened then?" Bradok asked.

"The Underking put a price on Galoka's head and ordered his followers killed." Corin continued. "According to the legend, a dwarf named Ekin ran ahead to Galoka's stronghold, before the Underking's army got there. Ekin died from the exertion, but he did manage to warn Galoka of the approaching army. Galoka took his followers and fled into unexplored caverns, vowing to build a city where all dwarves would live together in peace."

Bradok frowned. "It's an interesting story," he conceded. "So what makes you think this door has anything to do with Galoka?"

"There's more to the legend, love," Jeni said in her airy voice. She was listening intently even though she seemed to know the story.

Corin nodded. "Over the years there have been many dwarves who became lost in the deep caves, sometimes for years. When they finally returned, some told tales of a fantastic city called Starlight Hall. A city deep under the earth where live trees grew and fantastical machines did all manner of work."

"When was the last time someone came back and told such a thing?" Bradok asked skeptically.

"Well, not for a long time," Corin admitted. "Though there was a dwarf who found a strange sword back in my grandfather's time. The sword wasn't really magical, but it wouldn't rust."

"That's true," Thurl said excitedly. "I saw that sword once. It looked as bright as the day it was forged."

"So you think this city is close?" Bradok said. "That this is the symbol of Starlight Hall?"

Corin nodded. "My mother sang me the rhyme when I was just a child," he said. "I never forgot the words: 'Seek the eye of red, under branches twined. If the city of Starlight ye would find.' "

Kellik and Bradok exchanged glances.

"If he's right, then the end of our journey could be no farther away than right behind this door," Bradok said soberly.

"Well, what are we waiting for, then?" Kellik said. He put his shoulder against the stone door and pushed. It shuddered for a moment, then swung inward with a soft grinding noise.

A blast of stale air rushed into the hallway, stirring the dust on the floor and making some of them cough. A vast, dark space lay beyond. High above them, tiny lights flickered on the ceiling, like a field of stars in the black abyss.

As Bradok and the others moved out of the hall and into the cavern, their lanterns illuminated massive stone columns, carved with meticulous detail. A stone bench stood near them, richly detailed but lying on its side.

"The stars," Rose gasped as she moved out of the tunnel. "The lights on the ceiling are laid out like the stars in the heavens."

Bradok looked up. He hadn't spent enough time on the surface to know much about the heavens above Krynn. But a single red star glowed off to one side of the display, and he knew instinctively that it represented Reorx's Forge.

He took a lantern from Marl Anvil and moved deeper into the chamber. More columns rose up, like massive trees, reaching up to the hidden ceiling. Huge halls branched off to either side. Finally, the lantern lit up a massive building carved out of the living rock. In the center of the building stood an enormous clock, its hands stopped at 2:36. Above the clock, metal cables poked out of the building and stretched up into the darkness.

Bradok lowered the lantern and studied the base of the building. Enormous carved doors like the ones they'd just come through were lying broken and shattered on the ground.

"It looks like Starlight Hall is still a legend," Bradok said to Corin. "A ruined legend. Nobody has been here for a long time."

CHAPTER 18

Remnants

Bradok made his way toward the big building with the enormous clock. He hadn't noticed at first, but the floor of the cavern was littered with all kinds of debris: everything from scraps of clothing and bits of metal to fragments of wood and bone.

He climbed over the broken door and stepped into the clock building. Inside there was once-ornate furniture that had been smashed to bits and murals on the walls that evinced aging and deep gouges. Each painting seemed to depict one of the dwarf clans making their way to a shining city in the distance.

A spiral staircase of metal ran up to a second level, and another shattered set of doors led deeper into the building. Bradok wanted to see the workings of the giant clock. He tested the stairs with his foot and, finding them sound, began to climb.

The room above stretched up well over two stories. It housed the massive gears, chains, and cams that kept the time and moved the hands. To Bradok, there seemed to be more machinery than was necessary for a clock. He traced several of the gears and shafts and found they led to other mechanisms unrelated to the clock. Each of them had a set of metal cables running from a giant spindle that ran out through a hole in

221

the wall. Despate the thick layer of dust and debris, all the apparatus seemed to be intact.

"I wonder how long this place has been here," Corin said, coming up the stairs gingerly, followed by Much.

"Judging by the dust, I'd say a long, long time," Bradok said, wiping encrusted grime from a large metal pulley.

The pulley had been painted black, no doubt to resist corrosion, but as Bradok looked at the stripe he had wiped clean with his finger, he realized there was no rust or corrosion anywhere.

"I'd guess it's all still in working order," he pronounced.

"Why not try it, then?" Corin said, taking hold of one of the massive gears and putting his shoulder into it. Nothing happened.

"Stuck somehow, I'd say," Corin said with a grunt. "Pretty big machinery. What were they using it for, power?"

"Water is my guess," Much said.

Bradok turned to find the old dwarf examining a long horizontal bar with what looked like flat metal gears protruding from its center. Below the bar, a metal trap door covered a hole in the floor that was cut just large enough to allow the bar to be lowered through it, using a winch assembly mounted to the wall.

"Give me a hand," he said, pulling on the trap door. After it scraped across the stone with a noisy screech, Bradok and the others could clearly hear the sound of running water below.

"Hey, not so fast. Fooling with this stuff might not be a good idea," Corin said. "We don't know what any of it does. Some of it might be simply broken; some of it might be dangerous. It wouldn't do for a frozen gear to bring the whole works down on our heads."

"He's got a point," Bradok agreed. He leaned close to one of the giant mechanisms and wiped it with his sleeve. Tiny letters had been etched into a plate, to which was attached a movable arm.

"Some of the mechanisms are labeled," he pointed out. "This one's got a lever to account for something between summer and winter."

"This one has levers for five irrigation zones and two different fountains," Much said. "Maybe it's the master control for the city's water."

Corin whistled. "It's hard to imagine something like this existing here underground."

"I helped design air shafts for some of Ironroot's newer caverns," Much said, stroking the machinery reverently with his calloused hands. "But I've never seen anything like this craftsmanship; it's incredible."

Bradok opened his mouth to say much the same thing when he heard Rose calling his name. Her voice sounded urgent and frightened.

"Here," he called, running to the stairs and starting down.

Rose rushed into the room over the broken door. "There's trouble," she said then led him back out into the square.

The second lantern hung suspended from a statue in the middle of an elaborate fountain that Bradok had missed on his way in. Dwarves were gathered around the slumped figure of one of their group.

"Is it Lyra?" Bradok asked worriedly.

Before Rose could answer, however, the crowd parted to reveal Tal standing over Perin. The human seemed paler than usual, and he breathed in great gasps. In a flash, Bradok remembered the blast of stale air he'd tasted when they'd entered the cavern.

"We need to find a vent or something," Tal said as Bradok arrived. "He's dizzy and incoherent. For some reason he can't breathe right. If this lasts much longer, he is in danger of dying."

"What is it?" Much asked, coming up behind Bradok.

"We've got to take a chance," Bradok said after a long moment.

"What do you mean?" Rose asked.

"This city is too big not to have proper ventilation, and it's too deep to rely on just an open shaft," Bradok said. "They must have had some way to move the air around down here, and I'm betting it's controlled by the machine in the clock tower."

"Get going, then. Give it a try," Tal said. "I don't know how much longer Perin can survive breathing like this."

Bradok turned and raced back to the tower. Corin had stayed behind, using a glowsac to investigate the machinery. He looked up excitedly when Bradok and Much came pounding up the steps.

"You won't believe what this machine does," he said.

"Control the city's ventilation system?" Bradok asked as he and Much moved to inspect the open slot in the floor.

"How did you know that?" Corin asked with wide eyes.

"Lucky guess."

Bradok took hold of the chain that ran through a gear and controlled the height of the horizontal water wheel. He pulled hard, feeling the resistance, until finally it broke free. As Bradok hauled on the chain, the bar was lowered slowly into the water. When the flow hit the metal blades, the shaft began to turn. A moment later it shuddered and stopped as the gears on its end meshed with gears hidden below the turbulent surface of the water.

Slowly the shaft began to turn again, driven by the water. A second shaft, running vertically up to the ceiling of the chamber began turning as another gear transferred the water horizontally. A groan came from the machinery as it shook off the years of disuse. Amid creaks, clangs, and rattling, the gears began turning and the enormous clock started to tick.

Dust rained down with chunks of debris and cobwebs as the operation shuddered to life. Bradok coughed and covered his face with his cloak. In the midst of the din, he heard Much shouting something. He looked over just in time to duck a metal lever swinging straight at his head. As it passed over him, Bradok suddenly became very aware of all the dangerously moving gears and undulating cogs. One wrong step in that place could crush a limb or catch at the edge of a cloak, yanking or strangling a dwarf to death.

"We've got to watch ourselves," he shouted at Corin, not entirely sure the Daergar leader could even hear him.

Much pointed. Bradok nodded, and the pair made their way carefully over to the ventilation controls. Above the moving gears and cogs, a brass plate read *Main Ventilation*. Below were six levers in a row, all of them frozen in the up position.

Bradok shrugged and reached for the closest one.

"Wait a minute," Much yelled over the din. "Why that one?"

"We have to start somewhere," he said.

"Everything else is marked," Much said. "These probably are too."

He wiped off one of the levers with his cloak, revealing more engraving, but with all the dust in the air, it was impossible to read.

"We need more light," he said.

"Over here," Corin called.

He stood by the mechanism that operated the clock. Bradok could see a miniature version of the hands outside the wall, mounted into a gearbox on the clock machine. A giant lever thrust out of the machine nearby and rose up above Kellik's head.

"Help me with this," he said, using all his weight to attempt to pull the lever down.

"What are you doing?" Bradok demanded, rushing over so quickly he nearly got hit by a spinning gear.

"It's a twenty-four-hour clock," Kellik explained, hanging off the lever. "To change the setting, you just move the hands on the little clock and then pull this lever to synchronize."

"How do you know that?" Much shouted over machine noise.

"It's written on the plate behind the clock," Corin said.

Bradok and Much leaned in and examined the little clock sticking out of a brass plate. Unlike a normal clock, it started at one and counted up to twenty-four. Kellik had moved the hands so they pointed down at the noon position.

"Why should we bother setting the clock?" Bradok said. "What we have to concentrate on is helping Perin."

"It says there's a Daylight System attached to the clock," Much said, squinting at the engraved plate. "If this clock still works—and it's a good bet that it does—the clock will think it's midday, noontime. So it might light up this place."

Bradok nodded excitedly. He had to jump to reach the end of the giant lever. He caught hold and hung, suspended, his entire weight on the metal beam. Corin joined him and slowly they felt it begin to shift and break free.

With a screech and a clang, the lever snapped down, dumping the dwarves on the ground in a heap. The mechanism sped up, whirling and clanking, and Bradok imagined he could see the giant hands sweeping across its face on the tower outside. As they neared the midday hour, the lever began to rise up again, and the machinery slowed to its normal pace.

"So much for light," Corin said when nothing happened.

The words were barely out of his mouth when a loud grinding sound filled the tower. A metal cable high above the clock mechanism began to turn, and Bradok followed it over to another assembly of gears and wheels. The cable pulled a giant wheel, spinning it almost halfway around until it stopped. Then a gear somewhere engaged, and the entire machine whirred to life.

Gears began turning spools of metal cable, playing some out and reeling others in. Some of them moved easily, while others clearly resisted the effort after so many years of immobility. One of the cables screeched and stopped, the cam pulling relentlessly against it, stretching it. Somewhere above, whatever it had been attached to had refused to wake and go to work.

"Get back," Kellik yelled. "There's too much tension on the thing. If it snaps, the loose end will slice up anything it hits."

The cable kept stretching and stretching, while the pitch of the machine changed as it pulled relentlessly. A metallic clang suddenly echoed through the tower, and the cable went slack. With the machine no longer restrained by the cable, the other spindles sped up, and suddenly an explosion of light flooded the tower.

Bradok swore, covering his eyes. When he could see again, a rosy light that could only have been sunlight illuminated the tower.

"Reorx's beard," he swore again.

The light shone in through a small hole in the high ceiling and struck a curved reflector that diverted it down into the room.

"They've got some kind of mirror system that reflects in light from outside," Much said, awe in his voice.

"Look at this," Corin said, bending down by the ventilation controls.

Bradok and Kellik joined him. With the bright light flooding the room, they easily read *Main Hall* on the first lever.

"Try it," Much said as Corin took hold of it.

Unlike the lever to reset the clock, the Main Hall lever was short and thin with a bulbous end. Corin grasped the bulb and, without any seeming effort, pulled it down.

A gear somewhere in the bowels of the machine engaged, and one of the six shafts that emerged from the machine began to spin. It spun slowly at first but picked up speed until it whirled. From somewhere outside, a clanking, screeching noise erupted then seemed to grow in pitch, higher and higher until it disappeared.

"Did it work?" Bradok asked.

They all looked at each other then raced down the spiral stair and out over the broken door. The cavern outside was blazing with light that descended into the cavern from three shafts in the ceiling. Below each shaft, giant crystals caught the light and sent it out in targeted beams. Some struck reflectors, like the one in the tower, shedding gentle light down into the cavern. Other beams vanished into holes in the walls and ceilings, no doubt heading off to illuminate other parts of the city.

In the bright light, Bradok could see that the main cavern had been carved in the shape of a cross, with four arms radiating out from the central square. Elegant buildings had been cut into the walls on either side and, although it was abundantly clear from the trash in the streets that they had been looted, neither time nor defilement diminished their true beauty.

Along the lanes were planters with long-dead trees, twisted and skeletal, attesting to the decay of Starlight Hall. At the far end of one of the cross arms, there stood a round void, as if something had stood there and had simply vanished. From his vantage point, Bradok could see that the hollow hole left behind appeared perfectly smooth. For some reason, the sight disturbed him.

A strange coughing noise caught his attention, and Bradok glanced up at the ceiling. Great gouts of dust and debris were being vomited out from behind metal grates in the ceiling.

"Cover your faces," he yelled to the group still gathered around the central fountain.

"What's happening?" Corin asked, covering his face with his cloak.

"It's the vents," Much said, laughter in his voice. "Who knows how long they've been out of use? And now they're busy pushing all the years of muck out of them."

Even through his cloak, Bradok could tell that Much was right. The dust and debris rained down for a full ten minutes.

As the dust finally began to drift out of the air, Bradok rejoined Tal and Perin at the fountain. As the minutes passed, the human seemed to be breathing easier, his color returning.

"That was the right thing to do," Tal said.

"Lucky guess on my part," Bradok said. "I don't know who this Galoka guy was, but this city of his is amazing. I've never dreamed anything like it."

"I want to know how they're moving so much air," Much said. He took a deep breath and let it out slowly. "In another hour or so, the air should be completely replaced. It's incredible."

Perin stood up slowly, gripping Bradok's shoulder for support. "Thank you," he said, breathing deeply. "I feel like myself again."

He wobbled a bit, and Tal put out a hand to steady him. "Take it easy for a while," Tal said. "We can rest here, can't we?" he asked Bradok.

Bradok checked the compass. The Seer held her spear at her side, which usually meant it was all right to stop. He nodded to Tal. "We can stop here," he said.

"Good," Much said, rubbing his hands together eagerly. "I'm going to inspect those machines, see what I can learn."

"Maybe there are some books or murals that tell the story of Galoka and his followers," Corin said with equal zest.

"It looks pretty picked over," Bradok said, plopping down by the fountain. Then he looked at them and smiled. "Explore all you want," he said. "Just take someone with you."

Corin looked for Omer and motioned to the other. Omer grinned and ran after him, still clutching the rag doll Much had made for Teal. Bradok had noticed that the dwarf never went anywhere without the doll. He seemed happy enough as long as he had the doll close by.

Bradok leaned against the base of the fountain and watched the hands on the clock turn, counting off the minutes. It felt so good just to sit and rest, he didn't notice as several hours passed. Only the diminishing light in the cavern eventually alerted him. Clearly the daylight above was fading into night.

He rose just as Corin returned with Omer, Kellik, and Rijul in tow.

"Have you just been sitting here all this time?" he asked, chuckling.

Bradok nodded.

"Boy have you missed it!" Rijul said, full of youthful enthusiasm. "This city is enormous. All sorts of things to explore. There's at least three more caverns off this one."

Kellik nodded. "They've all been looted, like this one, but it's like the looters didn't know or care what they were looking for," he said.

"What do you mean?" Bradok asked.

"The inside of the buildings have been trampled," Corin said. "The furniture is smashed, the tapestries ripped, but we've found weapons and tools and valuables just lying around in the mess."

"Who tears a building apart but doesn't take weapons or valuables?" Bradok wondered.

"Someone who is stupid," Kellik said, shrugging.

"Or someone looking for something specific," Rose said, joining the group. She held what appeared to be a book with a metal cover.

"I found this inside a burned-out library," she continuing, holding out the book, made entirely of polished steel, so they could all see.

Bradok knew instinctively that it had been made of the same, corrosion-proof steel as everything else. At the edges, along the spine of the book, ran an intricate metal hinge so the book could lie flat for easy reading. The front had been painstakingly engraved with the title: *Galoka, His Travels and Teachings*. Below that was a subtitle: *The Chronicles of Starlight Hall*.

Something in Bradok yearned to touch the strange metal book. He reached out and opened the cover, revealing fifteen metal pages bound into the spine with small metal rings. Each page was perfectly flat, and each was the same size. Tiny rows of engravings marched down the pages like columns of ants, and Bradok had to lean in close and squint to read the words.

"I'm sure it's all very fascinating," Chisul's voice interrupted them as he came striding up with a small group, all carrying the fruits of their scavenging. "But what makes you think the people who wrecked this place were looking for that?"

"I didn't say they were," Rose said, still cradling the book reverently. "But whoever burned the library wanted these people's knowledge destroyed. I bet they didn't count on a metal book that was able to survive the fire."

"Yeah, I can agree with that," Chisul said, a grin on his face. Then he looked around at the magnificent hall. "This whole place feels good, feels right."

"What are you talking about?" Much asked, joining the crowd.

"Just that this place is perfect," Chisul said. "It's got light, air, clean water. We've even found some seeds for trees and vegetables and a garden cavern where they used to grow food.

"In fact, this place has got everything we need. Best of all, there's no one to protest us just moving in," he added.

"I don't know," Corin said worriedly, running his hand through his beard. "Something bad happened to the people here, and someone sure tried to destroy this place."

"Maybe a long time ago in some fairy tale," Chisul mocked him. "But no one's been here for decades, maybe even centuries."

Bradok had to admit Chisul made good points.

"There's no telling if these caverns are truly secure," Much argued. "We've barely begun to investigate all of them."

"We can secure them one at a time," Rose said eagerly. "Check each one out, make sure they're safe, and then move on."

"I don't think that will work," disagreed Jeni in her dreamy voice, which drifted above the crowd.

All eyes turned to where the peculiar Daergar girl stood, rocking from one foot to the other, undulating her hips as she moved.

"I bet the compass won't let us stay here very long at all," she said.

Bradok reflexively put a hand to his pocket then hesitated. He liked the idea of staying in the fantastic city, and he wasn't sure he wanted the opinion of Reorx's compass. Before he could extract it from his pocket, however, Corin spoke up.

"Why do you say that?" he asked Jeni, narrowing his eyes. "What do you know? Have you discovered something you haven't told us about?"

Jeni shook her head, pointing to a pile of rubble at the base of the clock tower. Bradok had been staring at the tower for hours and hadn't noticed anything odd, but as one the group followed Jeni's pointing finger and approached the rock pile.

"What are you getting at, girl?" Kellik demanded.

He opened his mouth to say something else, but the words died in his throat. There, in the center of the pile, everyone saw the same thing: covered in dust and looking for all the world like a rock was a skull. Once Bradok could see it, he also saw what looked like an armored chest and arm, ending in a long, curved spike.

"What is that?" Rose said fearfully.

Bradok pushed his way to the front and picked up the skull. What had made it so hard to see before was that it didn't look like a skull, at least not like any he'd ever seen. There weren't any holes for eyes, just a smooth, curved surface all the way across the front of the face where the eyes should be. Two vertical nostril slits sat high in the center of the forehead, and the upper jaw held a double row of backward-facing, needlelike teeth.

Much bent down and picked up two long, curved bones from the floor, holding them up close to the skull. They were long enough to be arm bones, but everyone could see they were wicked, curving teeth.

"This jaw bone is two separate pieces," Much said, holding the huge teeth in place against the skull in Bradok's hands. "The bottom part must be missing."

It was the largest jaw anyone had ever seen or imagined. The sight sent shivers up Bradok's back.

"What was it?" Bradok asked Corin.

The Daergar reached out and took the skull, pouring water from his bag over it. As the dust disappeared, the skull took on a green hue, like bottle glass. Even more disturbing, Bradok could see Corin's hand through the side of the skull.

"It's not bone," Corin said, holding the skull up for everyone to see. "It's chitin."

"What does that mean?" Lyra asked in a small voice.

"Chitin is what insect skeletons are made of," Urlish Hearthhome said.

"That's no insect skull," Chisul said. "It looks human or maybe elf."

"Only if humans had no eyes," Perin said.

While the others argued, Bradok studied Corin. The dwarf's normally easygoing manner had hardened, and his left eye was twitching.

"Tell me more. What do you know about these chitin creatures?" Bradok asked.

"He doesn't know anything for certain, I'm afraid," Xurces cut in. "There are old legends, nothing more than bard's tales really, of a race of humanoid insects who burrow deep in the earth."

"This is no legend, Xurces," Corin said, holding up the skull. "This is real."

"Well, what do the legends say about these insects?" Chisul asked.

Xurces sighed as if he didn't believe he was having such a preposterous conversation. "They're called the Disir, or at least that's what I've heard them called. They're supposed to be deep-dwelling insects with armored bodies, swordlike arms, and ravenous appetites. They'll eat just about anything, even some rocks."

"That's it?" Kellik said.

Xurces shrugged. "Until five minutes ago, it was just a story to frighten disobedient children," he said. "I never really paid attention to the details."

Kellik brought out his hammer and a crowbar and began clearing debris. Bradok, Chisul, and Corin helped until half an hour later they had uncovered all the rest of the skeleton.

Kellik whistled, glancing at Xurces. "The next time someone tells that story, you can tell them it ain't a story," he said.

The skeleton had four legs attached to an oblong, tail-like piece that Urlish called the abdomen. Above that, a massive chest sprouted two arms that ended in serrated, swordlike blades. They assembled it partly on the ground, but even so, its size was enormous.

"I would not want to meet that monster in a dark alley," Much said once they had all the pieces laid out.

"Dark," Xurces said, snapping his fingers. "I just remembered something else about the legend. The Disir are blind. They prefer the dark. They hunt with sound, like bats."

Much and Bradok looked at each other then turned slowly, looking up at the clock tower above them where the cogs, shafts, and gears were churning merrily away. It suddenly seemed like an awful lot of noise.

Watching them, Chisul also looked up and felt terror. "Turn that thing off," he yelled. "Turn it off now!"

CHAPTER 19

The Hive

It took ten full minutes to get the water drive out and stowed. In the silence that followed, the only thing that could be heard was the ragged breathing of the survivors. Every ear strained to hear something, anything. No one knew what, exactly they were listening for, but everyone knew they would recognize it once they heard it.

"I don't hear anything," Xurces said after what must have been a full half hour of silence.

"Maybe they didn't hear us," Lyra said in a frightened voice.

"If there's anyone left to hear anything," Kellik said.

"I don't want to stay and find out," Bradok said, pulling out the compass and staring down through its crystal top.

As the light-gathering machine shut down, the stream of twilight from outside ceased. The only light that remained were the giant crystals that had bounced the beam around the cavern. They seemed to have the ability to store some of the light that passed through them and they glowed, pleasantly dim, shedding enough light to see by but still giving the impression of night.

"What's down there?" Bradok asked, pointing down the lane of dead trees.

"A couple of big doors that lead to a rough tunnel," Rose said.

"All right," Bradok said, rechecking the compass and shouldering his pack. "Let's head in that direction."

The doors at the end of the tree-lined hall were large and ornate. They looked almost decorative, but Kellik pointed out the massive iron bars that could be dropped from a hidden slot in the ceiling. Once in place, the bars would keep the doors closed against just about any menace. The fact that they were still slotted in their holes in the ceiling made Bradok wonder again: Just what had happened to Galoka and his followers?

The passage beyond appeared to be a natural tunnel, like the ones they'd followed all the way from that first beach where the skeleton of Silas's boat lay decaying. With a sigh, Bradok pressed forward. Kellik was closest to him, trailed by Much, Perin, and old Marl Anvil. The rest of the survivors followed at a short distance.

"Well, this is interesting," Rose said, coming up beside Bradok. "Evil mushroom people behind us and killer insect creatures ahead. Never a dull day here in the underground."

"What makes you think the killer insects're ahead of us?" Bradok asked.

Rose offered a thin smile. "No reason," she said. "That just seems to be the way our luck's been running."

Bradok nodded with a humorless smile.

"What do you want to do when we get out of here?" Rose asked as they walked along with the others.

"What do you mean, get out of here?" Bradok asked, surprised.

Rose smiled genuinely. "When we get out of here," she repeated. "When we finally reach the surface again. Then what?"

Bradok hadn't given it any thought and he said so.

"What if Much is right?" she prodded. "What if we're the only dwarves left alive? What if all the towns are gone?"

"I suppose we'll have to start over ourselves, then," he said, wishing she would switch to a more pleasant topic.

"All right, so let's say you're starting all over fresh," Rose said. "What would you want to do?"

Bradok laughed. He realized that she was doing a good job of distracting him and the others from their fears as they continued to explore the area for any signs of the dread killer insects.

"Hmm, I see what you mean," he said. "There won't be much use for a jeweler anymore. But I'm good with delicate metalwork. I suppose I could be a tinker; you know, make pans, hinges, locks, and such. You?"

Rose shrugged. "My family have been merchants for six generations," she said. "I think I'd like to be a rancher and raise cows and pigs and goats. Assuming we can find some left alive."

Bradok chuckled.

"Your friend here wants to be a builder," Rose said, nodding in Much's direction.

"A builder of what?" Bradok asked skeptically.

"Everything," Rose said. "He said he helped rebuild Ironroot's ventilation and water systems when he was young. I bet he could build a mill and set up irrigation for farming."

Bradok had trouble picturing Much working on millwheels and aqueducts. What his friend really liked to do was drink and talk.

"I want to be a brewer," Corin's voice came from behind them.

They turned to find the Daergar a few paces behind them.

"All those years in the penal caves made me quite a connoisseur of rotgut. I'd like to try my hand. It would be nice to drink something that wasn't made of boiled mushrooms."

Rose chortled. "It sounds like what you really want to be is an innkeeper," she said.

Bradok was only half listening. Up ahead, the passageway forked. Automatically he pulled out the compass and flipped open the lid. Glowing smoke rose up out of it and coalesced into the form of the Seer. When Bradok reached the fork, she extended her spear, pointing left.

"This way," Bradok said.

He'd scarcely put the compass away when they came to a second fork. The spear pointed right. Then another fork, and another, and another, each time the spear telling them which way to go.

"It's like a maze," Corin said an hour later.

"It reminds me of something I saw once," Rose said. "Some humans put two pieces of glass together with dirt between them. Then they put ants inside and watched them dig. They called it an ant farm."

"What are ants?" Omer asked, curious. He was walking up front with the lead dwarves, clutching his rag doll.

"Insects," Rose said.

Bradok shivered involuntarily at the word, thinking of the dead Disir.

Corin stopped abruptly. "You mean these tunnels remind you of ones dug by insects?"

Rose shook her head. "I just meant that they twist and turn a lot," she said. "Then again . . ."

Bradok had slowed and Rose bumped into him.

"What are you doing?" she asked.

The faint light of the open compass illuminated the passage for several yards ahead. Just at the edge of its light lay a glossy black body. Bradok froze. Willing his limbs to move, he lurched forward, holding the compass high.

The light washed over the body on the ground. It had a hard, outer shell with a segmented body and four walking legs. The torso and head, however, were different from the Disir skeleton in Starlight Hall. It was decidedly female, with a line of eight breasts running down its front. The head had a much smaller mouth, and its arms ended in hands with three long fingers. The body was smaller than the other, perhaps a little shorter than the average height of a human. All over the creature's outer shell were thousands of little cracks, as though it had come under tremendous pressure and tried to shatter but couldn't.

Bradok felt his arm going numb then realized that Rose had it in a death grip.

"Is it dead?" she whispered.

"Yes, thanks be to Reorx," Bradok said, seeing the stain left by the vital fluids that had leaked out from the many cracks.

"What happened to it?" Corin said, edging closer.

Bradok kicked the dead Disir with his toe, but it didn't budge. "I don't care," he said, checking the direction of the Seer's spear. "Let's just keep moving."

"Quietly," Rose said.

"Right," Bradok said, turning to Corin. "Pass the word: less talking, everyone."

The sandy passage grew wider and wider until it became a broad avenue. On either side, Bradok could see the bulbous protrusions of eggs buried in the sandy dirt. Each looked about the size of a man's head. Several of the eggs had broken open, but there were no signs of any young. Two more shattered insect bodies lay at a juncture to a side passage, but there was nothing else.

Bradok could feel his skin crawl as he walked on in silence. Everyone carried weapons but nothing came rushing out of the darkness to meet them. Still, with every step they took, Bradok could feel the tension growing inside of him. He began to think it would be better if they were attacked. As formidable as he imagined the Disir to be, he was afraid of the tricks his terrified mind might play on him.

At that precise moment, a horrible nightmare appeared out of the darkness. In his overwrought state, Bradok cried out in alarm and fumbled for his sword.

"Stop," Corin commanded, putting a restraining hand on his shoulder. "That one's dead too."

The body of a Disir warrior stood there, leaning against the wall of the tunnel, giving it the illusion of life. Its massive jaws dangled open as though it were ready to eat the next thing foolish enough to come near it. The long, wicked blades that made up its arms hung loosely at its sides, dragging in the sand.

Like the others, the Disir warrior appeared to have been shattered by some strange pressurized force.

"What could have done this?" Bradok asked, running his finger along one of the long fissures in the creature's body.

"Could whatever destroyed Ironroot have struck here as well?" Rose asked.

"I'm grateful for it, whatever it was that killed these nightmares," Corin said. "We're among the nests of these creatures, can you imagine what they'd do if they caught us here?"

"I prefer not to think about that, if you don't mind," Bradok said. "Let's go."

Several hours later, just when Bradok was ready to call a halt, he detected the faint smell of fresh air drifting down from somewhere up ahead. Twenty minutes later, the cavern opened up into a massive, empty hole. The roof of the new cavern extended well beyond their meager light, hiding above in impenetrable shadow.

Without any encouragement, the dwarves staggered out of the tunnel and dropped down on the rocky floor. They hadn't had much of a rest for the better part of a day. The stretcher with Lyra arrived, and the dwarves carrying her set her down gently before collapsing nearby.

Xurces followed the stretcher, carrying the sleeping form of Lyra's daughter, Jade. He reverently deposited the girl beside her mother then staggered off to find a place of his own to rest.

"We can't stay here," Urlish Hearthhome said in a hoarse whisper.

"Why not?" Corin asked, sitting with his head on his knees.

"Haven't you fools ever seen an anthill or a beehive?" she demanded.

Bradok and Corin exchanged blank looks, but Rose went pale.

"She's right. I've been thinking the same thing. This must be the core." She gasped. "The center of the hive."

The men leaped to their feet, their weapons in hand, and stood there, sweating, straining their ears for a sound, any sound.

They heard nothing. "Whatever killed those others must have destroyed the whole hive," Corin said with obvious relief.

"Maybe," Bradok said.

"We shouldn't stay here," Urlish hissed.

"Everyone's exhausted," Rose said in a whisper. "We can't go much further right now. Better to rest, at least for a short while."

"She's right," Thurl said, coming out of the darkness on silent feet. "We may have to fight these things eventually, but I'd rather be rested and fresh."

Bradok quickly checked the compass. The Seer had her cloak wrapped about her, and her spear lay hidden beneath.

"All right," Bradok said, though the idea of sleeping there made his flesh crawl. "If the compass says it's safe, then it's safe."

"Wouldn't hurt to make sure," Rose said.

Thurl smiled, showing his pointed teeth. "I'll check out the rest of the cavern," he said. "I can move quietly." Without hesitation, the ex-assassin melted back into the darkness.

"Let's make camp here tonight," Bradok said to the others. "Pass the word for everyone to keep as quiet as possible, though."

That command wasn't needed; within minutes, most of the dwarves were fast asleep. Only Bradok, Rose, Corin, Tal, and Much stayed awake to talk things over and divide the watch.

"There are a whole bunch of Disir bodies over there," Thurl said, materializing close to them so suddenly that he gave them all a start. "But other than that, the cavern's empty."

"Have someone wake me for the third watch," Corin said, heading for his gear.

Bradok reached out and caught the Daergar by his cloak. "Sleep on your sword," he said. "Pass the word to anyone you trust."

Corin nodded then disappeared into the semidarkness. Bradok made his way back to where the large passage emptied out into the enormous cave. The rear guard had been set up there, and he smiled to see Rose, Tal, and Thurl waiting for him.

They engaged in small talk for an hour while everyone quieted down. Then, bone weary, Bradok returned to where he'd spread out his cloak and lay down. He thought he had too much on his mind to sleep, but before he knew it, the blackness encompassed him.

He woke what felt like an instant later with Thurl poking him in the ribs with the tip of his boot. Bradok knew that a lot of time had passed. The roof of the cavern, far above, could be clearly seen as sunlight streamed through its wide cracks.

"What's going on?" he asked groggily.

"Trouble," Thurl said.

He put out his hand, and Bradok took it, allowing the Daergar assassin to help him to his feet. Bradok brushed the dirt from his cloak and whipped it over his shoulders.

"Over here," Thurl said, moving off toward the side of the cavern.

A large group had gathered in the dim circle of the diffuse light filtering down from the ceiling so impossibly high above.

Much, Corin, Kellik, and Rose were among the assembled dwarves.

"How far up do you think that is?" Kellik said as Bradok drew closer.

"It's at least a mile," Much said.

"I don't care how far it is," Chisul said. "It's a way out."

Bradok looked up at the glowing slits high above. They were indeed some kind of conduits to the surface world, but Much was right, they were far away—very, very far away.

"I say we try to send a few of us up there to check it out," Chisul said. "Let them check if the path is safe."

"What path?" Bradok asked.

Chisul smiled and pointed over his shoulder to the wall of the cavern. It took Bradok a moment to penetrate the darkness since his eyes had adjusted to the light. As his vision cleared, he could see that a narrow footpath had been cut into the wall. It ran up and around the cavern, spiraling upward toward the openings in the ceiling. He couldn't see where it ended.

"What do you think?" Chisul said, grinning widely. "It's worth a look, right?"

Bradok grinned back. It looked promising. He stepped closer for a better look. The path was narrow and had no safety rail, and Bradok shuddered as he imagined what a single misstep would mean. Still, if they moved slowly and carefully, they might reach the surface.

Instinctively, Bradok's hand sought Reorx's compass in his vest pocket. He moved back into the light and held the little brass device out into the glow. As he reached for the catch to open the lid, his eyes caught the intricate engraving on the lid. Once he'd seen words there, urging him to have faith. To his astonishment, there appeared new words, revealed in the etching:

It is the Dwarf who perseveres in the correct road who receives the reward.

His heart sank. Without even opening the compass, he knew what it would show him. Sure enough, he saw after flipping its lid, the Seer extended her spear straight away into the darkness. The thought of following the Seer made him groan. He hadn't realized how much the light had cheered him in just a short time.

The other dwarves were just as dismayed when they crowded in to see the Seer, suspended in the air above Bradok's palm.

"Oh, come on!" Chisul exploded. "What are we trying to do here?"

"We're trying to survive," Much said mildly.

"Survive?" he said. "Is that it?"

A nervous silence followed; then Chisul continued. "We all know we can't stay underground forever if we want to survive," he said. "We've been lucky up to now, finding just enough mushrooms to feed us for a few days here, a few days there. If we want to stop anywhere, we're going to need a cavern this size full of mushrooms and we're going to have to start farming them.

"I haven't seen anything as promising as that so far," he said, daring anyone to meet his gaze. "Have any of you?"

"Reorx has a plan for us," Bradok said quietly. "If we follow the compass—"

"Damn the compass," Chisul retorted, pointing up at the light far above their heads. "There's the surface world. It's just a short climb away. Once we're there, our chances of survival go up dramatically."

"You don't have any idea what's up there," Kellik said, loyally supporting Bradok, though he had his doubts. "Don't forget what happened the last time we disregarded the compass."

Chisul opened his mouth to reply, but before he could speak, a violent tremor shook the cavern, sending several dwarves tumbling to the sandy floor. Someone screamed and dwarves scattered.

A sinkhole had opened in the floor, the sand dropping down and falling away. A second later, to everyone's horror, a living, breathing Disir emerged from the depths. It was an awful sight that Bradok would recall in his nightmares to his dying day.

Its dark head rose up, shiny, glistening, and eyeless. Its mouth opened, revealing an expandable lower jaw and rows of curved teeth. The greenish outer shell was transparent, so Bradok could see its vitals right through its armored chest. A pale, blue light shone out from a glowing organ, right behind where the eyes would have been. It looked as if the killer insect had only one large eye in the center of its face.

The creature pulled itself out of the hole with two long, swordlike arms, bristling with serrated spines.

Bradok was frozen in fear. Much grabbed his arm and shook him, pointing over to the far side of the cavern. At least a dozen more holes were opening in the floor all over the chamber.

"To arms," Bradok yelled. "Here they come!"

CHAPTER 20

Bloodshed

Attack before they get out of their holes," Thurl yelled, charging the first creature that had emerged.

Bradok scooped up his sword and raced after the assassin. Thurl reached the creature first and drove his dagger right into its head, punching through its chitinous armor and plunging straight into the glowing organ. The Disir went berserk, lashing out with its blade arms and squealing in pain.

Close behind, Bradok chopped downward, slicing right at the joint of one of its legs, severing its limb, and sending the creature collapsing face-first into the sand. Before it had a chance to recover, Much and Corin were hacking it to bits.

Pain exploded in his leg, and Bradok turned to find another killer insect crawling up out of the sand toward him. It had lashed out with its arm and sliced across Bradok's calf muscle. The cut didn't look deep, so he decided then wasn't the time to worry about it. He hurled himself into the fray, chopping down on the Disir's arm. Unlike the blades from Starlight Hall, Bradok's sword had been imbued with a certain magic by the elves who had crafted it. It sliced through the creature's arm easily, sending bits of it and the black ichor inside the Disir flying.

The killer insect reared back, flailing with its remaining arm and screeching a shrill, high-pitched sound. Bradok stepped in and drove his sword straight through the creature's chest. The enchanted blade pierced the armored hide easily, and Bradok jerked it free as the Disir fell back, dead.

As Bradok stumbled past the dead creature, Kellik slammed another one in the chest with his warhammer. With a sound like shattering stone, the insect's body cracked, shattering like the other dead ones they'd found. The Disir shrieked in agony, its arms and legs lashing out in all directions as it writhed on the ground.

All around him dwarves battled the swarming Disir. Hot blood spattered Bradok's face, and a scream, filled with pain and despair, tore the air. Bradok turned as a body fell at his feet. He recognized his fallen comrade as one of the hill dwarves but didn't have time to stop and see if he could ease his suffering.

A blood-spattered Disir bore down on him, its double-hinged jaw gaping wide. It slashed at Bradok with both arms at once, forcing him to fall back. When the killer insect raised its arms again for another strike, Bradok dashed in, running under the blades and striking at the knee joint on the creature's right foreleg. His sword cut cleanly through the bulbous joint, and the insect staggered.

With the Disir off balance, Bradok brought his sword down onto its back with both hands. The blade bit into the armor, and black ichor spewed out from the wound. The Disir kicked out, catching Bradok in the gut and sending him flying into a column of rock.

Bradok gasped for air as he struggled to his feet. The Disir turned, lurching under the burden of its wounds. Bradok brought his sword up just as the monster collapsed, its limbs pawing the sand. There it lay, bleeding to death from its wounds.

"No time for that," Much said as Bradok paused to catch his breath. "There's still more of—look out!"

Much shoved Bradok hard, causing him to stumble away. In the sand, right where he'd been, a Disir blade arm had gouged a trench in the sand. The creature whirled to focus on Much, who was backing away. The old dwarf gripped a short sword, but Bradok doubted Much or his weapon was any match for the hulking monster.

"Here," Bradok yelled, clanging his sword down on the stone of a nearby column. "Over here, you big dumb bug!"

The Disir turned and, with a speed Bradok didn't fully expect, lashed out with its swordlike arms. Though its arms pointed downward, they were longer than one would expect. Bradok barely had time to duck behind the column of rock before the chitinous arm slammed into it, gouging a deep cut out of the stone.

Bradok hacked at the arm, chopping off the tip. The creature retaliated, reaching around the column and slashing Bradok's left arm, driving the tip of its remaining good arm into the dwarf's side. Bradok cried out with pain and fell backward with the force of the blow. His sword went spinning out of his grasp as the Disir rose above him, ready to impale him.

Bradok rolled as the creature's gleaming arm came down. Pain whipped across the side of his face as the arm slammed into the sand, grazing him. Blood ran into his eyes, blinding him.

The Disir pulled its arm back for another strike. Frantically wiping the blood from his eyes, Bradok scrambled back. A shadow swept past him; then Thurl was there, wielding Bradok's sword. The Daergar assassin easily parried the Disir's arm, knocking it aside and running the enchanted blade straight through the creature's torso.

The Disir reared back, and Thurl jerked the blade out of its chest. The dying creature lunged at Thurl, its massive maw spread wide. Thurl sidestepped the creature with a grace that seemed impossible. As the Disir fell, Thurl brought Bradok's sword around and struck off its head.

Bradok tried to rise, but a piercing pain in his side sent him crumpling to the ground. His shirt and cloak were soaked in blood. Bradok unclipped his cloak and wadded it up, pressing it against the wound in his side to contain the bleeding.

"Stay down," Thurl said as two more Disir emerged from the hole in the ground. "I'm starting to enjoy this."

Thurl advanced on the creatures easily. When the blind monsters lashed out at him, he methodically cut off their limbs, literally disarming them with repeated slashes until he could step in and deliver a fatal blow. He moved with the smoothness of a dancer performing an intricate ballet of death. Occasionally a Disir would strike him a glancing blow, leaving a trail of red over his scarred flesh, but his wounds were superficial.

"Lay down," Tal said to Bradok, suddenly at his side. Without waiting for cooperation, he pushed Bradok down hard and tore open his shirt.

"Hold this to his head," Tal said to someone Bradok couldn't see. "He'll lose that ear but it can't be helped. I have to tend this other wound first."

"What about the Disir?" Bradok croaked, wincing at the pain as Tal cleaned his wound.

"They're all dead," Rose's voice answered.

"It looks like it was a small scouting party," Thurl added, coming into Bradok's vision. "Only a dozen or so."

"They'll be missed, then," Bradok said. "They'll send more to find out what happened to the scouts."

"Not for hours, if we're lucky," Thurl said.

Tal pressed his silver flask up to Bradok's mouth. "That means we have to hurry and get you patched up and ready to travel," he said. "Drink this."

Bradok tried to protest, but Tal forced the flask into his mouth. Whatever was in there had a sweet, sticky flavor and burned all the way down into the soles of Bradok's feet. Almost immediately his vision blurred and a heavy, contented feeling swept over him.

"Hold him down," Tal said, his voice seeming to come from a great distance away.

Pain shot through Bradok's side, but he didn't seem to have the willpower to care. He could hear Tal and Rose talking as Tal labored on Bradok's wound. He seemed to be stitching it together like a tailor would close a rip in a shirt. That didn't make any sense to Bradok, but his foggy mind couldn't make sense of anything.

"Just wrap up his head," Tal said after an indeterminate amount of time had gone by. "Hurry," he added as Rose lifted Bradok's head. "There are others we must save."

Eventually, the stinging sensation in Bradok's side and head began to fade. At the same time, he began to feel the world gradually coming back into focus. When at last his vision cleared, he found Rose sitting beside him. Her hands and arms were stained with blood, and she was scrubbing them with sand.

"I . . . we . . ." he said, struggling to form words.

"Lie still," Rose said firmly. "You need to rest now. We're going to need to travel in a few hours, and you have some healing to do before that. And then it's still not going to be pleasant."

Bradok opened his mouth to speak, but something caught his eye. He reached out and grabbed Rose's arm. She tried to yank her arm away, causing Bradok to cry out as pain shot through his side.

"Stop that," Rose said, letting him see her arm.

The gray patch of skin had grown considerably and glowed a sickly yellow color. A tiny mushroom protruded from the center, and Bradok could see several more forming just below the surface.

Bradok swore.

"I didn't want to bother you with what's happening to me," she said, withdrawing her arm after Bradok released it. "I've been putting the moonwell water on it, but it's still growing. I'm going to have to leave soon, or I'll become a danger to everyone."

"Book," Bradok croaked.

"What?" Rose asked, wrapping a fresh bandage around her arm.

"Metal book, from Starlight Hall," Bradok said. "Maybe the metal book has a cure."

"Bradok," Rose said hesitantly. "I don't need false hope." But her face showed that it was something she hadn't thought of.

"What's he doing awake?" said Tal, coming up to them. "He needs to sleep at least four hours before he can travel."

Something was pressed to Bradok's lips, and more of the burning liquid ran down his throat. He preferred to stay awake, to reassure Rose, but the strength of the liquid was not to be resisted. The world faded to black, and Bradok knew no more.

CHAPTER 21

Dance of the Mushrooms

The pain woke Bradok—a dull, throbbing ache that seemed to run from the top of his head to the tips of his toes. He didn't mind the pain so much; after all, it meant he was alive.

He lay in that half-waking dream state for what felt like hours. Just beyond the reach of his senses, full consciousness waited, but there seemed to be no hurry to rush there. Bradok knew when he finally woke, the pain would be more real and more bothersome.

As his mind drifted, he gradually became aware of sounds. Confused at first, the sounds resolved themselves into snatches of garbled conversation and the weeping of children.

Bradok tried to force his mind awake, but whatever Tal had given him to sleep made it impossible to focus. He needed something to hold on to, something to use as an anchor to pull himself into wakefulness. The conversations were too vague, and he couldn't ever seem to understand the words. Finally, he became aware of an odor—not the smell of blood nor the smell of the caves, but something far more pungent.

With a jolt, his drifting mind caught hold of the name he'd been seeking to put to the smell—rot. The odor was the stench of death and decay.

"Rhizomorphs," he gasped, remembering, his eyes popping open.

He lay on the sandy floor of the great cavern, looking up at the fading light shining through the hole in the ceiling. Gritting his teeth, he tried to sit up but flopped back onto the sand immediately as white-hot pain tore through his side. Involuntarily he gripped the wound, only to have his hand pulled away.

"Don't do that," Rose said. "You'll start bleeding again."

"But we've got to go," he insisted, trying to sit again. Thurl's bandaged hand pushed him down. "Don't you smell that?" he asked, pushing at Thurl's unmovable hand. "The Rhizomorphs are coming. We've got to get out of here."

"We smell it," Rose said, gently. "Tal is still tending some of the wounded. As soon as he's done, we'll all move on, together."

Bradok tried to push Thurl's hand away again. He noticed the scarred ex-assassin was missing the ring finger on his left hand.

"I got cocky," he said in response to the questioning look Bradok gave him. "That fancy sword of yours makes a dwarf feel invincible."

"All right," said Tal from somewhere nearby. "You all know your jobs. Let's go."

"This is it," Rose said, reaching under Bradok's shoulders. "Give your right hand to Thurl."

Bradok did as he was told, and Thurl slowly pulled him up, with Rose lifting from behind. Exquisite pain tore through Bradok's body, and he bit his lip to keep from crying out. When he finally reached his feet, he wanted nothing more than to lie down again. Thurl slipped Bradok's arm over his shoulder for support.

After a moment, the dizziness passed and Bradok found he could stand on his own, albeit a bit wobbly.

"You lost a lot of blood," Rose explained. "If you feel dizzy, lean on Thurl."

He nodded and gently ran his hand over his side and shoulder. Both wounds were on his left side, so someone had tied his left arm into a sling. He reached up to his right ear and felt a thick bandage there as well, wrapped around his head.

"Tal couldn't save your ear," Thurl said.

Bradok shrugged, glad simply to be alive. "A man can live with only one ear," he said.

He looked around for the first time. A line of dwarves were moving to the side of the cavern, toward the exit passage. Some wore bandages; others bore simple scrapes and cuts. Even before he thought to count, however, Bradok could tell there were fewer dwarves ready to move on than there were before.

"How many?" he gasped, taking an unsteady step after the group.

"Fifteen," Rose answered, not meeting his eyes.

"Who?" Bradok said, not really wanting an answer but knowing he must be told.

Rose recited the names. Some Bradok didn't recognize, and some were losses he took personally. Old Marl Anvil had fallen while defending his grandchildren, leaving the eldest, Starlight, to lead the family.

Along with the dead, many were wounded. Corin and Kellik had both been slashed badly, Chisul had been stabbed like Bradok, and Perin had lost two toes on his left foot.

Bradok walked on in glum silence. The price for survival was getting higher all the time.

As they passed a side passage, the air currents shifted, and suddenly Bradok absorbed a whiff of fresh air. He'd gotten too used to the stench of decay, but the fleeting fresh air reminded him.

"How far are they behind us?" he asked, trying to control his stomach.

The assassin shrugged. "No one really wanted to go back and look," he explained dryly.

"We're hoping the hive confuses them," Rose added. "It is pretty much a mess."

"Omer, Much, and Tal stayed behind to brush away our tracks as much as possible," Thurl said.

Bradok staggered, and Rose moved to steady him. He grunted in pain as her hand touched his wounded side, and the light-headedness he felt struck him like a wave. His feet dragged on the ground behind him as he used all his will to force them to work.

"Have him drink as much water as possible," Tal said from somewhere not far behind him.

A waterskin was pressed against his lips, and he drank. Gradually the world around him came back into focus, and his errant feet began to obey him again. Bradok didn't know how long he'd been delirious, but it must have been quite some time. When he came to himself fully, however, the stink of decay was gone. Apparently they had moved far enough away from the Rhizomorphs. He breathed deeply, relishing the good air and the respite from danger.

Over the next few hours, Bradok fell into the rhythm of slow but steady walking. After a few miles, his body seemed to cooperate better and he didn't need Thurl's support as much. No one said much about the catastrophe they'd experienced, and Bradok was grateful for that. Sooner or later, they'd have to deal with their losses. Someone would have to say something about the dead ones, and he knew it should be him. Still, such things weren't easy for Bradok. He didn't know how he would face Starlight Anvil and her siblings. The compass had led them to that cavern; he had to take that responsibility and offer what comfort he could.

When they finally stopped for the night, no one seemed to feel like talking. Bradok's whole body ached, and he felt bone-weary as he eased himself down onto the stone floor. He wanted to go straight to sleep, but Thurl pressed a large hunk of mushroom into his hands.

"Eat," Thurl said.

"You don't have to be my nursemaid, you know," Bradok said grouchily, taking a bite out of the stale mushroom.

"Yes I do," Thurl said good-naturedly, cutting off a hunk of mushroom for himself.

Bradok shook his head. "I saved your life; now you saved mine," Bradok said. "I'd say we are even. Any debt you once had to me is canceled."

Thurl smiled, and the scratch on his cheek began to bleed a little as the facial movement dislodged the fresh scab.

"You risked your life to save me," Thurl returned. "You didn't have to, but you did." He took a bite of mushroom and shrugged. "I would have fought the Disir anyway," Thurl added with his mouth full. "You were in trouble, so I helped. I am still in your debt."

Bradok wanted to argue, but he just didn't have the energy. Corin had told him that assassins like Thurl had to be attached to a wealthy house or government body to ensure their skills were used wisely. While Bradok had no use for an assassin, he wondered if maybe having Thurl around close to him wasn't such a bad idea. At least that way, Bradok could keep an eye on the Daergar.

He finished chewing his mushroom and slumped back on the stone floor of the passage. He wanted to ask about the others, about the dead, the wounded, about Rose, but before he could even form those desires into coherent thoughts, sleep overcame him.

Weeks earlier, Bradok had finally gotten used to sleeping on the hard ground. He could bear it with ease. Unfortunately, his wounds made it nearly impossible for him to be comfortable. He slept fitfully, wanting to toss and turn and regretting the impulse when searing pain accompanied any attempt to roll off his back. Worse, his dreams kept his mind busy with terrifying images of black, chitinous heads with glowing blue bands shining through their eyeless faces. The killer insects seemed to burst out of the darkness, to fall upon the dwarves in their sleep, yet every time Bradok started awake, fully expecting to see the living nightmares swarming over him, it was only a dream.

When Much announced that the time had come to get moving again, Bradok felt as if he had barely slept at all. Rose helped him to his feet, and they started walking again.

"Nobody died last night," she said after a mile or so. "Everyone seems to be on the mend. That's good news at least."

Bradok had been dreading that report, and he breathed a sigh of relief. "I never asked," Bradok said, thinking out loud. "How many of us are left?"

"Twenty-four," Rose said.

Bradok's heart sank. They'd started with fifty or so, and they'd lost more than half. His face fell.

"None of it's your fault," Rose said softly with a sweet look.

A sickly smell suddenly washed over Bradok, strong and pungent. Rose noticed the smell too.

"The Rhizomorphs," she said, her nose wrinkling up.

"Go spread the word," Bradok told her. "Send every available fighting man to the rear, and tell the others to double their pace."

He took out the compass and pressed it into her hands. "Take this just in case," he said.

"In case of what?" Rose demanded. "You're too sick to fight. You have to go to the front with the other sick and wounded."

"Go," Bradok said in a voice that made it plain there was to be no argument or debate.

Rose gave him a dark stare but turned and went.

Bradok reached for his sword then wished he hadn't. The mere motion of reaching across his body ripped at the wound in his side. Gritting his teeth, he grabbed the hilt with the tips of his fingers and gingerly slid his blade free of the scabbard.

"What do you think you're doing?" Kellik asked, coming up quickly from the rear guard.

"Don't turn down any help cheerfully offered," Chisul's friend Vulnar said. Maybe Bradok imagined it, but he thought he saw Vulnar wink; whether the wink was intended for him or Kellik, he wasn't sure.

"What's the situation?" Bradok asked determinedly.

"The situation is you are in no shape to fight," Corin said, materializing close by.

"They definitely know we're here," Kellik added. "But I think we're still pretty far ahead of the main group."

"Then where is this stench coming from?" Thurl said, tying a handkerchief around his face. "It feels awful close."

A wet, squishing noise answered. Down the path where they had come, a dozen forms shambled into the light. They moved faster than Bradok remembered, pressing up the path toward their quarry.

"I was afraid of that," Corin said, gesturing. "They sent some of the less affected ones ahead to try to slow us down."

Bradok raised his sword, a bit more slowly than he would have liked. Thurl and Much stepped in front of him with their swords.

"You take any that get through," Much said.

"Aim for their legs," Chisul said.

The Rhizomorphs shambled closer, heedless of the wall of dwarf flesh and steel that blocked their path. They slammed into the defenders without even slowing down, attempting to bowl them over.

One tall dwarf with mushrooms growing where his eyebrows should have been leered at Bradok over Much's head. His skin was pale and gelatinous with glowing fungi sprouting out at odd angles. He opened his mouth, as if about to yell. Instead an enormous red tongue lashed out, striking Bradok on his arm over the heads of the others. The blow didn't strike hard, but where it touched his skin, it burned. With a cry of surprise and disgust, Bradok chopped the tongue in half and shook it from his arm. It landed on the tunnel floor, still twisting and thrashing.

Much ran the tall Rhizomorph through, but it had no apparent effect on the creature. The Rhizomorph slashed Much across the chest, knocking him backward. The monstrosity attempted to step over him, then, and go after Bradok. As it moved, however, Thurl chopped one of its legs off at mid thigh. With a cry of anger, it toppled sideways. Turning to Thurl, the thing bit his left arm and hung on. Thurl reversed his stroke and decapitated the Rhizomorph, sending its head rolling back down the tunnel.

Kellik was busy meanwhile. Never one to be subtle, he raised his warhammer and brought it down on the head of the nearest Rhizomorph. The thing's head exploded like an overripe melon, sending bits of gray goo flying in all directions.

Chisul and Vulnar had cut two of them down and were trying to prevent the ones in the rear from rushing them all at once. Just as it seemed they would be overwhelmed, Perin and Tal arrived, rushing into the creatures with flailing swords.

Bradok watched as his friends began to push the Rhizomorphs back, slowly but surely. Bits of gray flesh spattered the walls and ceiling as the dwarves hacked the mushroom men to pieces.

A flicker of movement down the tunnel beyond the fight caught Bradok's eye, and he looked up in time to see three more Rhizomorphs advancing on them. Two of the creatures carried a third between them. The one in the middle seemed to be having some kind of fit, thrashing and convulsing. As Bradok watched, it began to swell and grow.

"They're trying to release a spore cloud," he yelled.

Bradok recalled how quickly and how far the previous spore cloud had spread. They were already within the radius of the impending explosion.

"Run for it," Corin shouted, grabbing the fallen Vulnar and yanking him to his feet.

As everyone turned and fled, Thurl swept his hand out from beneath his cloak in a long, fluid movement.

"Everyone, hold your breath!" he shouted as he loosed his dagger, which sped from his hand.

It struck the writhing Rhizomorph right in the gut, and the hapless creature erupted.

CHAPTER 22

The Trail of Blood

A golden cloud of spores rushed up the tunnel and surrounded the fleeing dwarves. Bradok could feel the spores burning his arm where the Rhizomorph's tongue had touched him. His eyes teared up, making it hard for him to see as he ran, holding his breath.

An uneven spot in the floor caused him to stumble, and he fell flat on his face, the air rushing from his lungs upon impact. Pain shot through his body like lightning. His side felt as if it were on fire, and his shoulder as though someone were trying to twist his arm from his body. It took all his willpower not to take a breath and suck in a lungful of spores. He leaped back to his feet and ran. He could feel himself getting dizzy from the lack of air; then the cave before him began to shimmer on its own. Staggering, he put out his hand to guide himself along the wall of the tunnel.

Rough hands grabbed him and dragged him forward. He stumbled on as best he could, until the pain in his arm seemed to subside.

"You can breathe now," Kellik's voice came out of the fog.

Gasping and coughing, Bradok sank to his knees and shook his head to clear the dizziness.

"Here they come again," Thurl said behind him.

Bradok heard the hiss of steel blades whistling through the air and the wet sound as they struck diseased flesh. He pushed himself to his feet, ignoring the searing pain in his side, and raised his sword.

Behind him the dwarves and Perin were hacking and slashing at the Rhizomorphs crowding the hallway. A pile of severed limbs and unidentifiable chunks of flesh were strewn on the ground. The Rhizomorphs fought with their hands, rending flesh whenever they could with their long, clawlike nails. Occasionally one of their pink tongues would lash out at an opponent's exposed flesh.

As Bradok moved up behind Thurl and Much, one of the ghastly creatures spat a wad of yellow goo directly at them. Much ducked, and Thurl dodged, but the wad hit Bradok on his shirt. The yellow substance appeared to contain some of the spores from the yellow cloud.

While being careful not to cut himself, Bradok scraped off the spores with his sword and flung them to the ground.

Just then someone cried out in pain. "My eyes," bellowed an older dwarf named Serl, falling over onto his back and clawing at his face.

The Rhizomorph in front of him stepped into the gap and leaned down, trying to take a bite out of Serl's leg. Bradok stepped forward and chopped the creature's head from its body.

He moved to the fallen hill dwarf and saw that the yellow goo covered his face.

"Tal!" he yelled, dropping his sword and reaching painfully for his waterskin.

Tal was there in an instant. The doctor bore many cuts and scratches on his arms, a testament to his intense combat. "Hold him," he said, pulling out his own waterskin, for Bradok was still struggling to produce his.

Bradok tried to keep Serl still as Tal washed the muck from

his eyes. With only one good arm, it wasn't an easy task.

"Duck," he heard Thurl yell, and instinctively Bradok hurled himself sideways.

A long pink Rhizomorph tongue sailed over his head and struck the cave wall. Someone severed it, and the next instant it fell, writhing, on the floor. Bradok kicked it away in disgust.

Bradok picked up his sword and got painfully to his feet. The remaining defenders had killed and dismembered enough of the Rhizomorphs that now only a handful remained. Little by little, the dwarves and Perin were driving the monsters back.

Bradok moved among the still-flailing limbs and bodies, striking the heads of any that appeared still capable of causing trouble.

A few moments more, and it was over. Bradok stood on weak legs. He slowly moved his sword across his body, trying to catch the tip of it where it belonged, in the top of his scabbard.

"Are you all right, lad?" Much asked, taking Bradok's sword for him and slipping it into the empty scabbard.

He nodded, feeling tremendous exhaustion.

"You're bleeding again," Thurl said in a disapproving voice.

Bradok looked down to see a red stain soaking through the bandage on his side. "There's no time," he said, pushing Much's hand away. "I'll be fine. We need to get back to the main group and spur them to keep going. There's no telling how long it will take the rest of these walking mushrooms to catch up with us."

"Yeah," Chisul agreed. "Stay ahead of them." The big dwarf was cradling his left arm, which appeared to have been burned by acid.

Bradok held up his own arm, looking at the wound, and realized that it was burned like Chisul's, though not so badly.

"I counted about twenty in this group," Perin said. "How many more can there be . . .?" He let the question trail off glumly.

"Can he walk?" Bradok asked about Serl.

Tal waved his hands in front of Serl's eyes. The big dwarf's eyes appeared white and watery and didn't follow Tal's hand.

"He's been blinded," Tal explained. "It might just be temporary; I can't tell yet."

"Well, I might be blind, but I'm not deaf," Serl said, sitting up. "And I can still walk. One of you lead me along and I'll do fine."

Corin and Vulnar each took one of Serl's hands, guiding him quickly up the passage. Bradok started after them, more slowly, hampered by his wound.

"Keep going until you find the others," Bradok called. "I'll catch up."

"I'll stay with him," Thurl said.

"Tell Rose to use the compass," Bradok called as the other dwarves began to outpace him. "She'll know what to do."

Bradok and Thurl walked along in silence and darkness, their eyes adjusting to the lack of light. Finally, when Bradok could no longer hear the tread of the dwarves in front of them, Thurl paused. He stretched his arm out from his cloak. He'd wrapped a handkerchief around his forearm. A large, dark stain covered it.

"This may be a problem," he said, showing his wound to Bradok.

"What happened?" Bradok said, panting with the effort of walking.

"One of them bit me," Thurl said.

"Before or after the spore cloud?" Bradok asked.

"After," Thurl said. "I'm worried about it." Such a declaration seemed out of character for the normally stoical Daergar.

"Corin said no one knows how the Zhome is spread," Bradok said. "I think that if it was spread in such a mundane way as bites, Corin would know about it."

"Still," Thurl said. "Rose has the Zhome on her arm, right where she was scratched in our first encounter with the Rhizomorphs."

"True," Bradok agreed worriedly.

"Almost everyone was wounded this time," Thurl said. "We may all be infected."

Bradok sighed heavily. "Well, we'll just have to deal with that somehow," he said.

"How?" Thurl asked. "If we're infected, sooner or later, we become Rhizomorphs. If that happens, we become a danger to everyone, so it stands to reason that before anything like that happens . . ." He let the sentence trail off.

"I see what you mean," Bradok said grimly. "We either have to abandon those who carry the Zhome germ at some point, or we have to kill them."

"Such decisions are difficult," Thurl said. "But perhaps they are made more easily and rationally in advance, when we are discussing the problem in the abstract and no one particular person's life is on the line."

Bradok wondered at Thurl's resoluteness. "What do you suggest?"

Thurl reached into his belt and pulled out a small crystal phial. "A few drops of this in someone's waterskin before bed, and they'll never wake again," he said. "Quick and painless."

Bradok thought about it, not answering for a long time. Perhaps Thurl's idea was the most humane option, but as the group's leader, the decision would fall to him. He would have to decide when to abandon or kill those who suffered from the Zhome. He would have to decide whether to abandon or kill Rose. But as leader, wasn't it his responsibility to act on behalf of the group?

"Thank you, Thurl," Bradok said, quietly. "If the time comes that we have to let one of our own go, I will keep your idea in mind."

"I live to serve," he said in response.

"Where did you get that potion, may I ask?" Bradok asked.

"I've had this for the last thirteen years," came the reply. "I keep it secret. Keeping things secret is my trade."

They walked together for more than an hour before they caught up to the other survivors. The main group had stopped in a cavern sparsely dotted with Reorx's torch mushrooms, giving off light that reflected off the damp ground. A pool of water fed by a waterfall was off to one side, filling the cavern with cool spray and a damp smell. A shallow, fast-moving stream ran away from the pool, across the floor, and into a deep fissure against the opposite wall.

A small knot of dwarves had gathered around Tal. Rose saw Bradok approaching and immediately hurried over.

"You'd better come quick," she said, her face pale.

In his wounded condition, Bradok had expended most of his energy just putting one foot in front of the other. Hurrying was no longer possible for him, but he lurched after her.

Rose shooed away some of the crowd so he could get through them. Serl lay on the ground with Tal kneeling over him. When Bradok got a look at the dwarf's face, he felt like retching. Mushrooms were already growing out of Serl's eyes and nose. He lay on the ground as though dead; the only sign he gave of life were the ragged breaths that came at infrequent intervals.

Bradok glanced at Tal, but the doctor could only shrug and shake his head.

Suddenly Bradok's arm was jerked up in the air so hard and fast that he gasped at the lancing pain. It was Corin who had done it, and the Daergar was staring at his arm. Bradok saw it too: A tiny mushroom had embedded itself in the wound left by the tongue.

"It's a spore," Corin said.

Bradok squinted and saw that, at the base of the mushroom there was a small, opaque seed, about the size of an orange seed.

"We've got to get it out before it takes hold," Corin warned.

Bradok nodded. Tal approached with a pair of long metal tongs and, taking hold of the seed, yanked it out. Bradok grunted as it trailed a small root that had already begun burrowing in his flesh.

"Check everyone who fought," he said, rubbing his arm ruefully. "Strip down and look everywhere."

The thought of Zhome spores growing in their flesh had the usually modest dwarves stripped bare in moments. There was a gasp as Chisul took off his shirt; a row of tiny mushrooms were growing in his back, right where Bradok had seen the gray patches before.

"There's nothing to be done," Tal said quietly once he'd examined Chisul. "It's as bad as Rose's arm."

Chisul nodded with dismay; he and the others had suspected that Rose was infected, but after the fight, so many of them were.

Everyone was checked over and over, and twelve spore growths were found. Those were removed as best as they could, but it was possible they were all doomed. Bradok was just too spent and sore to care. When they were finished, he pulled Rose aside.

"I'm not sure I can go on," he told her, "and there's no one fit enough to carry me. I want you to take everyone ahead without me. I'll catch up if I can."

Rose just shook her head. "Everyone's spent," she said. "It's only terror that drove them this far. We need to rest."

"If the Rhizomorphs are close—" Bradok began, but Rose silenced him.

"Yes, we may die if we rest here," she said. "But if we push

on, you and the children and the other wounded may collapse from exhaustion. I'd rather make a stand and fight the
Rhizomorphs when we're fresh, not when we're too done-in
from running."

Bradok thought about that for a moment then shrugged.
"We should find a defensible spot," he said then added, "just
in case."

A surprised look crossed Rose's face, and she drew out
the compass from a pouch on her belt. "It's like it heard your
words. It jumped," she said, holding it out to Bradok.

Bradok took the compass and opened it. The glowing
mist swirled inside, but the Seer did not appear. Confused,
he closed the lid and examined it. The engraving around the
purple stone had changed again. Bradok took the compass
over by one of the glowing mushrooms and squinted down to
peer at the tiny letters.

"In the damp hollow ye can hide, so long as no sound comes
from inside," Bradok read.

"Maybe it means that crack where the little river disap-
pears," Rose said, pointing.

"But what does this mean, about no sound?" he
wondered.

"Stay here," Rose said. "I'll check it out."

Bradok gratefully eased himself down onto the damp floor
while Rose took one of the lanterns over to where the stream
of water disappeared. He'd closed his eyes for only a minute
when someone materialized beside him, sitting down.

"Have you had a chance to look at that metal book?" Tal
asked.

Bradok knew what the dwarf wasn't saying. The metal
book might be their only hope against the Zhome and the
Rhizomorphs.

"No," he said. "How's Serl doing?"

"There's nothing else I can do for him," Tal said, discouraged. "I fear he hasn't got much time left."

"What about Chisul and Rose?" Bradok asked as evenly as he could.

"I don't know," Tal replied. "All we can do is watch."

He looked as if he wanted to say more, but Rose picked that moment to return.

"That crack looks to go all the way to the center of Krynn," she said. "I don't think there's anything down there."

Bradok shrugged. "Try the waterfall," he said.

Rose left again, and Bradok explained about the inscription on the compass to the confused Tal.

"Even if we find a place to hide," Tal said, "we still have to do something about Serl."

Bradok nodded. He intended to ignore that problem as long as he could.

"Found it," Rose said, returning, her hair dripping wet. "There's a small cave behind the waterfall. You can't even spot it from outside, and you have to wade through the water to get inside. It should be big enough for everyone."

"All right," Bradok said, getting up very slowly. "Let's get everyone inside and settled. No time to waste."

The cave was exactly as Rose described. A little sandbar ran along the cave wall where the waterfall poured down. When Bradok ducked through the flow, he found himself in a surprisingly wide cave with a damp, musty smell. The walls and floor were stone, and Bradok had to steady himself, for his weak feet wanted to go sliding out from under him on the slick surface.

One by one, the dwarves entered. Bradok sent the women and children to the back, leaving the ground by the water's edge for the warriors. He almost laughed at the thought. Thurl was the only one of them who had anything close to warrior training. They were just simple, ordinary folk, doing whatever they could to survive.

Tal and Kellik brought Serl in on the stretcher and laid him down near the water. Corin stayed out long enough to brush away any sign of their flight into the cave.

"You've got to exert yourself less," Tal said, coming up beside Bradok. "You started bleeding again." He opened his bag and pulled out the strips of cloth that he used for bandages. He repacked the wound and wound a bandage tightly around Bradok's stomach, making it a little difficult for him to breathe normally.

The shoulder wound wasn't as deep and seemed to be mending well, though Tal recommended Bradok still keep it in the sling.

"Let's take a look at that ear," Tal said finally. He unwound the wrapping and peeled away a bloody wad of something.

"Can you hear all right?" he asked, snapping his fingers in front of Bradok's face.

"It's a bit faint on the right side," he said.

"That's to be expected when you lose an ear," Tal said. "It doesn't look too bad. We'll need to change the packing every few days, and it should be scabbed over well enough in a week or so."

"Serl's awake," Corin said, coming over with Kellik and Rose. "He wants you."

Bradok made his way over to where Serl lay. The old dwarf was trembling as if he were freezing, and his skin had a gray pallor.

"Bradok," he gasped, reaching out to take the proffered hand. "I can hear them."

"Hear who?" Bradok asked.

"The Rhizomorphs," he said. "I can hear them talking, in my mind. They're looking for us. They're trying to use me to find us."

Bradok didn't know what to say.

"I won't let them," Serl croaked. "I need your help, though." He gripped Bradok's hand tightly. "I wish you to end my life. I'm no use to you alive. I'm no use to them dead."

Bradok wanted to protest, but he didn't know what to say. Serl's bravery and selflessness moved him.

"Thurl," he said. His voice wasn't loud, but as he suspected, the assassin seemed to appear out of nowhere.

"You called," he said.

Bradok handed the Daergar Serl's water bag.

"Thurl is putting something in your water," he told Serl.

Serl nodded, understanding.

"Thank you," Serl said to Bradok, tears leaking from the corners of his milky white eyes. "You've done a splendid job, my boy," he added softly. "Get the rest of these people to safety."

"I'm sorry," Bradok said.

"Don't be," Serl said, a smile creeping across his face. "I've lived a long time, and I've had a good life. I have no regrets, except that I won't be around to celebrate when you reach safety."

Thurl pressed the bag into Serl's hands.

"Now if you don't mind," he said, releasing Bradok's hand. "I think I'd like to be alone."

Bradok put his hand under his leg and painfully forced himself to his feet.

"Don't bother about burying me," Serl added stoically. "As soon as you can, get yourself out of here and to safety."

"I will," Bradok promised; then he and Thurl turned and walked away.

Rose had laid out Bradok's cloak with his pack for a pillow. Knowing what had just transpired, they all watched Bradok, waiting for him to say something. Rose wondered what he was feeling.

"We'll set a watch tonight," Corin said as Rose helped Bradok lie back on the makeshift bed.

"What do we tell everyone in the morning?" she asked finally when Bradok quietly announced that Serl had wished to die.

"The truth," Bradok said gruffly. "That Serl died peacefully in his sleep. Now, everyone, get some rest."

Rose and Tal stood and left. Corin remained, considering Bradok for what seemed like a long time.

"Something on your mind?" Bradok asked.

"I didn't think you had it in you," Corin said. "We Daergar are taught that you higher-ups are all soft and spineless. I see some of that is wrong. You did what you had to do."

"Thanks," Bradok said, not sure if he was flattered or offended by such remarks.

"I had a mind to stay with you only until we got somewhere where I could get my bearing, then go my own way," Corin added. "But now I think I'd like to stick by you for a while."

"Why?" Bradok asked.

"I figure we've got a better chance at survival with you than with anyone else," Corin said. "You've grown as a leader. You don't want to make the hard decisions, but you do anyway."

Corin pulled up his hood, making his face disappear into shadow. "Get some rest," he said, looking out over the sleeping band of dwarves. "I have a feeling tomorrow will be a very long day."

He strode away without a backward glance. Bradok turned to where Serl lay, a still figure draped with a cloak. He knew he couldn't sleep; there were too many things weighing on his mind.

Within three minutes he had fallen into a deep, dreamless sleep born of exhaustion.

CHAPTER 23

Don't Make a Sound

Something touched Bradok's face, and he started awake to find a hand pressed down over his mouth.

"Don't make a sound," Rose whispered in his ear.

When he nodded his understanding, she gently removed her hand. He sat up more quickly than he should have, confused by being awakened in such a manner. Pain lanced through his side, and he crumpled back to the ground, biting his tongue to stifle a groan.

Rose's hands grabbed him gently under his shoulders, and she helped him up slowly. Behind Rose, Bradok could see Much waking Kellik in a similar manner. Bradok looked at Rose questioningly.

Putting her finger to her lips, she pointed past Bradok, out toward the curtain of water that separated them from the cavern outside. Through the waterfall, Bradok could see the glow given off by the Reorx's torch mushrooms. Suddenly, a dark, humanoid shape passed in front of one of the lights. As Bradok watched, he saw other forms moving around the cavern, drifting in and out of the pools of light.

Then a figure loomed out of the darkness, passing by the pool just beyond the waterfall.

There was no mistaking its form. Four segmented back legs

held up a humanoid torso with long, backward-facing sword-like arms; transparent body armor; and a glowing blue organ where its eyes should be. Apparently it hadn't taken the Disir long to realize their scouting party had gone missing.

"How many?" Bradok mouthed at Rose.

Rose shook her head and shrugged, then held up ten fingers twice.

Even if it was just a guess, twenty Disir were far too many for Bradok's battered and wounded band. He reached for his sword belt and gingerly began to strap it around his waist.

"What now?" Bradok asked Rose, leaning close so she could hear his barely audible whisper.

"We're waking everyone," she explained. "Much thinks the waterfall is confusing the Disir with all its noise and echoes, so as long as we're quiet, they won't know we're here."

"They'll find this cave eventually," Bradok said.

Rose shrugged. "Maybe not. There aren't any obvious cracks or openings. Remember, we had to walk through the water to get in."

Corin approached, treading slowly and quietly. "I need your help," he whispered, leaning down so Bradok could hear him. "I need to wake Omer up, and someone has to help me keep him calm. The last time we fought these things, he cowered in the tunnel. They terrify him."

"Why me?" Bradok asked.

"Remember Teal?" Corin said. "You're the only one he'd give her body to. He trusts you for some reason."

Bradok nodded and stood. He picked his way slowly among the dwarves to where Omer lay. Much and Kellik had managed to wake most of the others, and all eyes were turned toward the waterfall and the certain death that lay just beyond its fragile curtain.

Corin shook Omer gently. The lad opened his pale blue eyes. Bradok was amazed at how innocent he looked. His body showed the first signs of manhood, and his beard was beginning to come in, yet his eyes and face reflected a childlike mind.

"Hi, Corin," Omer said before Bradok could shush him.

"You have to whisper, Omer," Corin said. "It's very important."

"Why?" he asked.

Omer's voice couldn't have been very loud, but it seemed to Bradok as if the boy were shouting. Reflexively, he turned his head and stared at the Disir pacing just beyond the waterfall. He thought he saw the creature pause for a moment, then go back to its searching, but at that distance, he couldn't be sure.

"The bad creatures are looking for us," Bradok explained. "If they hear us, they'll try to hurt Teal. You don't want that, do you?"

Omer clutched the rag doll to his chest protectively and shook his head anxiously. He cast his eyes toward the waterfall and shut them tight against the horror he'd glimpsed.

"Don't worry," Bradok said, patting Omer on the shoulder. "They won't bother us if they don't hear us, so just be as quiet as a mouse."

Omer didn't open his eyes again; he only nodded.

Corin motioned Jeni over and told her to keep an eye on him. Jeni sat and held Omer's head in her lap, stroking his hair gently. Her kindly manner almost made Bradok forget that she was the woman who had been imprisoned for murdering her own children.

Corin gave Bradok a nod to indicate Omer would be all right then stood. Bradok got up and followed Corin back to where Rose waited anxiously.

"Look," Rose said as they arrived, pointing.

The Disir that had been patrolling the bank by the waterfall had been joined by a second, and the two seemed to be conversing in a strange language made up of clicks and groans. After a short talk, they both began to probe the depths of the waterfall with their long arms.

"Can those things swim?" Rose asked.

"I hope not," Bradok said. "Their bodies are pretty heavy, and they really don't have anything to paddle with."

"No, look, they can't. Thank Reorx for small favors," Corin said.

The Disir had finished their probing of the water, apparently finding it too deep for their liking. They had another short discussion; then the second one went away.

"What do you suppose that means?" Rose hissed.

"No idea," Corin said. "One thing's for sure, we're not going anywhere soon with that thing hanging around out there." He nodded at the Disir who had resumed his patrol along the water's edge.

"Maybe we could kill it real quiet like," Thurl said.

Everyone jumped. Bradok stifled a curse. The Daergar assassin had crept up on them so silently.

"That won't help. There's more of them out there," Rose said.

"But if I could kill that one," Thurl said, "and then maybe we could sneak out of here somehow."

Rose shook her head.

The crunch of gravel announced another arrival. Bradok turned to see Xurces kneeling down beside them.

"We've got trouble," he said in a ragged whisper.

"We know that, Xur," Corin said, nodding at the patrolling Disir.

"No," Xurces said, "another kind of trouble." He pointed over his shoulder toward the back of the cave. "That kind."

Behind Xurces, Bradok could see Lyra, lying back on her blanket. Her daughter, Jade, was holding her hand. Lyra's breathing seemed to be coming in great gasps.

"You've got to be kidding," Corin said, glancing nervously back at the Disir. "Couldn't be worse timing."

Bradok stifled another curse. "Rose, go find Tal," he said quickly. "Then get over there and help. For Reorx's sake, keep her quiet."

"If it's all right, I'd like to go too," Xurces said. "I promised her I'd hold her hand through the delivery."

Bradok exchanged glances with Corin before jerking his thumb in Lyra's direction. "Go," he said.

As Rose and Xurces made their way back to Lyra, Much, Chisul, and Kellik joined the other dwarves warily watching the Disir poking around on the other side of the waterfall.

"Lyra's tough," Bradok whispered to the newcomers. "She'll stay quiet."

"I hate to burst your bubble, lad," Much said in a low voice, "but I've seen babies birthed before, and they don't come quiet."

"He's right," Kellik said.

"And when that baby cries," Chisul said, "the Disir will know right where we are."

"I guess we'd better do something fast, then," Tal said, joining the group, "because that baby will be crying soon."

"Shouldn't you be helping Lyra?" Kellik demanded.

"I'm more needed here," he said. "I'm a doctor, not a midwife. Rose can handle what's happening with Lyra."

"There's too many to fight," Chisul hissed. "It's hard to count them all, but I figure there are at least fifteen, maybe more."

"We can't just sit here debating," Thurl said impatiently. "Somebody's got to do something."

"Look," Chisul gasped, pointing through the waterfall.

The rippling water made it difficult to distinguish anything clearly, but Bradok could see a line of shadows moving past one of the pools of mushroom light—moving past and away.

"They're leaving?" Chisul said, feeling a surge of hope.

"It sure looks that way," Much said, nodding enthusiastically.

"Then why is that one still standing around out there?" Corin said, pointing at the Disir who stubbornly stayed outside the waterfall.

"They must be leaving him behind, like a guard or something," Kellik whispered.

"One guard shouldn't be too hard to deal with," Tal said.

"That's what I've been saying," Thurl said.

"There may be others, out there beyond the light. We need to get out there and take a look," Much said irritably.

Bradok silenced them with a gesture. After checking to make sure the Disir hadn't heard them, he spoke quietly. "We need to give the others time to get far away from here," he said. "Then we'll kill this guard nice and quiet and dump his body in the pool."

"And if there are others?" Corin said.

"We'll have to deal with them too," Bradok said.

"What about Lyra?" Tal said.

"We can carry her as far away from here as we can. We will stop long enough for her to give birth, then pick her and the baby up and keep going. With any luck, she'll have the baby quietly," Bradok said, adding, "and fast."

"That's a lot of luck you're counting on," Corin said, his whispered voice still managing some sarcasm. "We haven't been very lucky so far."

"At least it's a plan," Thurl said. "I can see us doing it."

"Yes, it's a plan that gives some hope," Chisul admitted.

"So how long before we act?" Corin asked.

Bradok turned to Tal. "Go ask your sister how long Lyra's going to be," he said.

"You can never tell with these things," Tal cautioned. "But I'll ask."

"But how in the world can we kill the Disir silently?" Chisul asked. "Last time they took a fair amount of effort."

Thurl held out his scarred hand to Bradok. "Give me that fancy sword of yours," he said.

Not wanting to go through the pain of drawing his sword, Bradok turned so Thurl himself could pull it from his scabbard.

Thurl nodded at the heft of it. "One of you needs to attract his attention," Thurl said. "Throw some rocks through the waterfall and into the pool. While he's distracted," Thurl said. "I'll rush in and cut off his head with this." He held up Bradok's sword, his eyes gleaming. "Quick and silent."

"Bad news," Tal said, hurrying back. "Urlish says the baby's coming right now. It'll be here in minutes."

"Then I go now," Thurl declared.

"Wait," Bradok said, putting out a hand to stop him. "It's too soon. If there are other guards, they will call the warriors back."

"If that baby cries, all hell is going to break loose," Much said, nodding at Thurl.

"We have to try it now," Corin said. "We have no choice."

Still, Bradok hesitated. "All right," he said finally, praying it was the right decision. "Chisul," he said, "you and Kellik gather some small rocks then meet me at the water's edge." He turned to Thurl, clapping him on the shoulder. "Get yourself in position then give me a sign. We'll do our part. Good luck to you."

Thurl grinned, showing his pointed teeth, as he stole over to the edge of the water. He moved so stealthily, Bradok could have sworn the scarred dwarf was gliding above the ground.

Thurl waited until the Disir had turned back toward the far end of the pool before slipping slowly through the curtain of water. He raised his hand then dropped it, giving the signal. Simultaneously, Chisul and Corin hurled fist-sized rocks through the waterfall and into the pool near where the monster stood.

The Disir snapped to attention, raising its bladed arms and looking around the pond for the source of the splash. At that very instant, Thurl darted forward from a different angle. The Disir was significantly taller than Thurl, so the assassin had to swing Bradok's enchanted blade high over his head, then down in a glittering arc, landing right on the joint where the upper and lower body joined.

With a crack that echoed through the chamber outside, the Disir snapped in half. Its lower body staggered for a moment then seemed to just plop down on its four stubby legs. The upper body hit the ground with a loud thud. The Disir opened its mouth, perhaps attempting to cry for aid with its last breath. Thurl didn't give it the chance; he stepped forward and kicked the upper body into the pool, where the stricken creature sank like a stone.

"Chisul, Kellik, Corin," Bradok commanded. "Get out there and see if there are any others about." As they went, Bradok heard a slap and the sound of a baby crying. He turned to the survivors.

"All right, everyone," he announced loudly. "We're leaving right now. Pick up your gear and our new mother and move fast."

The cave erupted with activity, everyone bustling at once, gathering their gear or helping to move Lyra, who was nursing her newborn, onto the stretcher. The fresh sounds of combat pulled Bradok back around. Corin and the others had left the cave and joined Thurl, who was attempting to fend off two more Disir. One of the enormous creatures was slashing down at the assassin with its bladelike arms. Thurl screamed and fell back to the edge of the pool.

"We're ready," Rose said, coming up beside him.

Reluctantly, Bradok tore his eyes away from the fight as Corin, Kellik and Chisul stepped between Thurl and the Disir. The survivors stood silently. Their gear had been packed and stowed, and four volunteers carried the stretcher on their shoulders.

Bradok reached into his pocket and pulled out the compass. The Seer pointed to an opening in the near side of the outer cavern. He handed the compass to Rose, closing her hand over it.

"Get going," he said. "Don't stop. Don't stop for anything."

"What if there are turns or side passages?" she asked. "How will you find us?"

Bradok unslung his pack and dug around in it hurriedly, coming up with a stick of chalk.

"Mark your path," he told her.

"But the Disir—" she started to say.

"They are blind," Bradok reminded her. "Now go and make sure someone holds a cloak over Lyra so she doesn't get wet and sick."

Bradok turned, scooping up his battered pack. A ragged cry came from outside. His comrades needed help.

"Tal, you're with me," he said and walked as quickly as he could through the curtain of water, Tal at his side.

Outside, Chisul, Kellik, and Corin were busily chopping the last Disir into bits. Each had bloody wounds, though none seemed too serious. Strewn on the ground around them were the bodies of two more Disir. Thurl lay, pressing his cloak to a wound on his leg, and Much knelt by the lake, apparently clutching his stomach.

"You all right?" Bradok said, putting his hand on Much's shoulder.

The dwarf straightened up and opened his cloak, revealing a bloody stump where his right hand should have been. "Not so good," he said.

"Tal, get over here," Bradok yelled.

"I'm sorry, lad," Much said as pain crossed his face. "I tried to do my best." He grimaced again. "I guess I'm just too old."

"Don't kid yourself," Corin said, panting heavily. "If you hadn't distracted that Disir when you did, it would have been my head he took off. I owe you."

Tal knelt by Much, examining his wound.

"There isn't much I can do right now about an injury like this," he said, pressing a bundle of rags into Bradok's hands.

"Make sure the wound is clean and wrap it tightly while I help Thurl."

Bradok did as he was told, peeling Much's shirt away from the bloody stump and packing the wound with rags. He wound a long strip around the wound and up the arm, keeping it tight. Last, Bradok tied the remaining strips of cloth into a sling. All the while, Much grimaced and quietly groaned with pain.

Thurl's wound was also serious. The Disir had made a deep slash in his calf muscle, and Tal had to stitch it up before he wrapped it.

"He'll be all right to walk a little," Tal explained. "Though it'd be better if he had a walking stick or cane."

Corin picked up Bradok's sword and used it to chop one of the Disir's swordlike arms free. He cut a piece off the bottom of his cloak and tied it around the severed end to serve as a pad.

"How's this?" he asked, carefully passing the makeshift cane to Thurl.

"Practical," the ex-assassin said as Tal helped him to his feet. He gripped the wrapped top of the cane and stabbed the point against the ground, testing his weight. He took a step then whipped the cane over his head. "Very practical."

"We ought to get going," Chisul said. "They're going to send someone back to check on these guys sooner or later."

"All right, but let's push their bodies into the water," Bradok said. "Maybe they won't find the bodies right away and that'll buy us some extra time."

As Corin, Chisul, and Kellik shoved the pieces of the dead Disir into the pool, Bradok realized the black ichor that made up the Disir's blood was all over the floor of the cavern. There was no way to hide that, but Bradok hoped the absence of bodies would confuse any returning Disir. They couldn't see the blood, of course, but no doubt they could smell it.

"All right," he told everyone once the bodies were gone. "Let's go. We need to move as fast as possible, but don't push it." That last was directed at Thurl.

At a brisk walk, they followed after the main group, leaving the lit cavern and passing into a dark passageway that angled slightly upward. Bradok told them about Rose and the chalk, which sent Corin scrambling back down the path. The Daergar returned with a glowing mushroom. "It'll be hard to see the chalk marks in the dark," he said with a grin, holding up the light.

Bradok hadn't thought of that. Their darkvision worked well enough, but dwarves saw things in the dark mainly in a fuzzy black-and-white. A chalk mark would elude them.

They pressed on, following Rose's occasional marks. There seemed to be many more side passages than before, and Bradok was glad she had Reorx's compass showing her the way.

"I think we should pick up our pace," said Thurl. "I hear noises behind us."

Everyone stopped, each straining to hear. There, so faint as to be on the edge of hearing, they could hear echoes of the clicking and chirping language of the Disir.

"There's no way we can outrun them," Chisul said.

"They don't know which passage we took," Corin said. "They'll have to send scouts down all of them. That'll delay them."

"Leave me behind," Thurl volunteered. "I'll go down one of the other side passages. Once they find me, they'll think I'm just a straggler from the main group. I'll fight them, and no matter what happens to me, they'll follow the wrong path a while."

"No one's leaving anyone," Bradok said, suddenly remembering that wasn't true; they had left Serl, his body wrapped in his cloak, still lying behind the waterfall.

"We can carry you, Thurl," Kellik said, motioning for Chisul to join him. Each of them grabbed one of Thurl's legs and carefully lifted him into a sitting position. Thurl put his arm around each of them, linking them together as one.

"You up for this, old man?" Chisul asked Kellik.

"No barrelmaker's son will best a blacksmith, you young puppy," Kellik replied good-humoredly.

They started up the passage at a quick walk, sharing Thurl's weight.

Bradok, Corin, Tal, and Much followed.

"Will they ever stop following us?" Tal wondered.

"No," Corin said. "We have to keep going. If we stop, we die."

CHAPTER 24
Teal's Legacy

A glowing light up ahead indicated the main group. At last Bradok and his bloodied warriors had caught up. Twenty minutes later, they could see Jeni and Omer bringing up the rear.

Bradok could hear Chisul and Kellik coming behind him with Thurl. They were panting, but neither dwarf would admit their exhaustion. Behind them came Much, cradling his maimed arm and leaning on Tal. Corin was walking a ways behind and listening for any sign of Disir pursuit.

Corin had lost track of the Disir about an hour past, but he still strained to hear something, anything. The caves in that part of the world were made of sandstone, and sound didn't carry as it did with granite or some other hard stone. Bradok had to keep urging Corin to keep up, for the Daergar kept dropping back to "take a better listen."

By the time they reached Jeni and Omer, Corin was nowhere to be seen.

"He'll be along," Much said, noting Bradok's distress. "He's not stupid."

"I can walk from here, gentlemen," Thurl said as his bearers came up to where Bradok stood, breathing heavily.

Neither dwarf spoke; they simply set Thurl down gently

and collapsed against the walls of the narrow passage.

"No rest," Bradok said, handing Kellik his waterskin. "Take a drink; get your strength back. We have to get going again as soon as possible. You know we can't stop."

Both dwarves shot Bradok a dirty look, but they drank and pushed themselves to their feet, trudging after the limping form of Thurl.

"Corin'll catch up," Much said, pulling at Bradok's cloak with his remaining good hand. "Come on, Rose needs you up front."

Reluctantly Bradok nodded. He dropped the still-glowing Reorx's torch mushroom on the path for Corin as he turned and hurried up through the midst of the marching dwarves as fast as his wounds would allow. He ached everywhere and felt as though he hadn't slept in weeks.

The other survivors also looked exhausted. They were at the end of their strength and their hope. Bradok passed Perin and gave the human a nod. Though he, too, was bone weary, Perin seemed to be breathing better.

"Tal," he said, tapping the doctor on the shoulder.

The doctor grunted something.

"Go walk with Perin," Bradok said. "It looks like he's breathing all right, but I wouldn't mind your professional opinion."

Tal grunted something else that might have been a curse aimed at Bradok, but he dropped back to walk with Perin.

A sudden draft of air roused Bradok's attention. Up ahead, the tunnel opened into another cavern. Instead of halting to let a few men check it out, Rose had led the whole group right into the cavern.

"We'd better get up there," Much said, noticing Bradok's sudden concern.

They pushed their way through the group up to the front. The cavern was as tall as the one with the opening to the sky, but it was longer and wider by far. A sandy island of earth ran out from the entrance to their tunnel like a bubble, vanishing into the biggest chasm Bradok had ever seen. Reorx's torch mushrooms by the hundreds grew along the left wall, illuminating a small ledge that ran to several tunnel openings and eventually to the spot of bare floor where Bradok and his friends stood.

Much whistled, walking close to the edge and looking down into inky blackness below.

A cool breeze blew up from the depths, bearing with it the smell of rock tinged with the stink of decay. The smell reminded Bradok, uncomfortably, of the Zhome. He pushed his way to where Rose stood and looked down at the compass in her hand.

"Which way?" he asked. "We can't stop yet."

Rose gazed toward the edge of the jutting ledge. Not believing her, Bradok looked into the compass and found the Seer pointing in the direction Rose was looking.

"That's impossible," he said. "There's nowhere for us to—"

But there was somewhere. Nearly hidden in the darkness, a long, narrow pathway of rock jutted out from the edge, like the prow of some rocky ship. Bradok couldn't see all the way to its end, but he knew it connected to the far side of the chasm, otherwise the compass wouldn't be directing them there.

"There's no way we can get Lyra across that narrow space," Rose said nervously. "It couldn't be more than a yard wide."

"We'll have two men carry her," Bradok said with a confidence he did not feel. He took a step forward, but Rose caught his shirt.

"Where are you going?" she demanded.

"Someone's got to try going over to the other side and make sure it's safe," he said.

Rose shook her head. "Not you," she said. "One way or another we're going to have to convince everyone to cross.

Nobody in their right mind is going to want to try if you slip over and die."

"I'll go," Much said, taking Rose's lantern. "I'm a much lighter fellow anyway," he said, winking at Bradok and displaying his bandaged arm stump. "Especially now. Once I'm across, I'll plant the lantern at the other end so you can see better."

He took the lantern and started out, making his way carefully across the bridge of stone. Bradok watched with an equal measure of wonder at his friend's bravery and fear for his fate. One misstep, and Much would plunge into the unknown depths. Finally, after what seemed like hours, Much turned around and waved the lantern over his head.

"He's across," Rose said in a gasp. Clearly she'd been holding her breath too.

"All right," Bradok said. "You get everyone moving across while I make arrangements for Lyra."

Rose raised her voice and gave instructions to the group while Bradok made his way to where Lyra and her new baby were situated. It suddenly occurred to Bradok that he didn't know if Jade, Lyra's daughter, had a brother or a sister.

"Thank you," Lyra said when Bradok knelt beside her.

"I didn't do anything," he said, blushing slightly.

She pulled open her cloak and revealed the sleeping baby, which was almost red in color with a mass of dark, curly hair on top of its head.

"You kept us alive," Lyra said, beaming. "You made sure we were safe." She turned back to the sleeping infant. "I'm going to call him Bradok."

Bradok was stunned. So it was a boy and named after him. He didn't know what to say, only that he didn't deserve so much praise.

"Bradok!"

Kellik's cry was heard above the crowd. Bradok stood and spotted the big smith on the far side of the group by the chasm, pointing at the left wall. With a bad feeling in his gut, Bradok saw that the empty tunnels that led to the narrow ledge were no longer empty. A dozen Disir had emerged there and were making their way gingerly along the ledge toward the spot where Kellik stood.

Bradok looked down at Lyra then at Xurces and Vulnar, who had been part of the group carrying her stretcher.

"Pick her up and get across that bridge," he said. "Now!"

They looked momentarily skeptical until Bradok barked, "Now! Do your best!"

The two dwarves sprang into action, lifting the stretcher and pushing through the crowd toward the narrow walkway. Thurl, Perin, and Tal joined Bradok as he approached Kellik.

"That ledge is pretty narrow over there," Kellik said, pointing to a spot nearby. "If we bunch up here, they'll only be able to come at us one at a time. Our chances will improve."

"Their reach is twice ours," Thurl said, holding up his short sword. "We need longer weapons to keep them at bay and maybe knock them off the ledge."

"There go our only poles," Bradok said, pointing to where Xurces and Vulnar were carrying the stretcher. Even moving slowly, the two were halfway across the bridge with their burden.

"Use your hammer," Tal said to Kellik. "Maybe you can break away a piece of the ledge, make it even more narrow for them."

"That's a good—"

"Bradok!"

Bradok turned to see Corin come racing out of the tunnel. "There you are!" he said with some relief.

"Here I am, but they're right behind me," he gasped.

Bradok swore. "Fall back," he said. "We have to buy some time to give the others a chance to get across the bridge."

Rose was hurrying the dwarves on the near side of the bridge, but there were still a dozen or so who hadn't crossed.

Just as Bradok and his men pulled back to protect them, Disir came pouring out of the tunnel.

Omer screamed and jumped away, but Jeni pulled him back toward the bridge. Rose shouted for everyone to speed up, and Bradok swore in frustration and pain as he jerked his sword from its scabbard.

At that moment, Bradok knew he would die. There were at least thirty Disir bearing down on them. His handful of tradesmen and merchants and one trained assassin stood beside him, as resolute and unmoving as any professional troop of soldiers.

But they weren't soldiers.

They had no armor, no training, and only scanty weapons at hand. The Disir were relentless killing machines. It would be a slaughter.

The worst part, Bradok thought, is that there won't be anyone left to make a song of it. In his heart, he knew the hardy band of survivors deserved a song.

The Disir seemed to hesitate a moment as their sightless eyes swept the group, the blue organs in their heads pulsating. One of them lashed out suddenly, slamming its blade-arm into the ground.

Bradok and the others raised their weapons, ready for the onrush. Instead, the first creature lifted its arm, so they could see that it bore a scrap of colorful cloth. With a sadness that quickly turned to a fire in his belly, Bradok recognized the rag doll Much had made for Teal. Omer had been carrying it ever since the girl's death and must have unknowingly dropped it when he fled.

The sight of the monstrous Disir with the doll impaled on its ugly arm made Bradok angrier than he'd ever been. It seemed like more than a simple insult to Teal's memory; it felt like a blow against everything that Bradok held as good and decent.

He could hear his heart pound in his chest as he tightened

his grip on his sword. Whatever else happened next, he would do his best to chop that despicable Disir to bits.

"Teal!"

It surprised Bradok that the voice was not his own.

"No!" Omer yelled.

The young dwarf with the child's mind ran by Bradok, knocking Thurl down in the process. He rushed up to the Disir, reaching in vain for the doll that the monster held just out of reach.

"Omer, stop!" Corin shouted, horrified.

The Disir jerked back its arm, dislodging the doll, then lashed forward, slicing it neatly in two. Bradok didn't know if the thing knew it was just a doll and not a living child, but it clearly didn't care.

Omer screamed, though he himself had not been struck. But it was as though he had gone berserk. A flash of orange light erupted in the space before the Disir, and Bradok had to cover his eyes. When it subsided, he saw Omer standing before the Disir, shaking with rage. His skin seemed translucent, and Bradok could see orange fire outlining the veins below his skin.

"You hurt Teal!" the man-child roared. His voice seemed to shake the very ground with its power, and several of the Disir shrieked in pain as the sound overwhelmed their senses.

With the casual gesture one might use to pick a mushroom off a cave wall, Omer reached out and tore the sword arm off the Disir that had so offended him. The creature squealed in pain and lashed out with its other arm. Bradok watched in horror as the tip of the blade punched through Omer's shoulder and out his back.

Yet miraculously, Omer gave no sign that the wound bothered him. Swinging the arm like a scythe, he lopped off the creature's head, sending it spinning over the edge and down into the chasm.

Time, which had seemed to move in slow motion before, leaped forward and everything seemed to happen at once. The

Disir rushed forward, and Omer charged into them, taking them on all alone, yet cutting a swath of death through their ranks and roaring in anger as he killed. Black Disir blood splashed over Bradok, but he couldn't take his eyes off the amazing scene. A splash of red blood was spattered on the wall by some Disir as they surrounded the boy, lashing at him with their razor-sharp arms. All the while, bits of chitin and ichor flew in all directions.

In a minute it was over. Broken and shattered Disir lay everywhere, their black blood seeping from their body armor and oozing in a dark river over the edge of the chasm. And somehow, there was Omer, alive, standing in the middle of the carnage, slumped and leaning on the Disir arm he'd used as a weapon. The orange fire behind his eyes faded, eventually back to his normal piercing blue. His body shuddered and he fell, finally succumbing to wounds that seemed to have flayed the skin right off his body.

"Omer!" Corin shouted, rushing forward. He lifted the young dwarf in his arms and carried him out of the mess of dead Disir, laying him reverently on the clean ground by the bridge.

"Tal!" Corin yelled, tears streaming down his face. "Do something."

Bradok looked at Tal, but the hill dwarf only shook his head. What had just happened was beyond his ken. Omer's wounds were too deep and too many. Bradok wondered that he still lived at all.

"I couldn't save Teal," Omer said, his childlike voice strangely gentle. "I sorry. Tell Teal, I sorry."

"I will," Corin said, holding Omer's hand in a death grip. "You did good, kid," he said, brushing away tears.

"I did?" Omer asked, seeming surprised. "I never did good be . . . before."

Corin cupped the bruised and bloody face. "Sure you did," he said. "You were always my good boy."

Bradok knew that Corin had taken Omer in when they were in prison, but he hadn't known just how much Corin thought of the boy as his own son.

"Corinthar," Omer murmured, using Corin's full name. "I scared."

Corin lifted the boy and hugged him fiercely. "Don't be scared," he said. "I have a special job just for you. Would you like that?"

Omer nodded weakly. "I a good boy," he said, pride in his faint voice.

"You go on to Reorx's Forge now," Corin said, choking back sobs. "You find a good spot for the rest of us and guide us there. Save the good spot for when we come. Can you do that?"

Omer nodded. "Teal be there?" he asked.

"Yes," Corin said.

"I tell her not to burn her feet on the sparks," Omer said, a smile flitting across his face. "Love Teal," he whispered. "Always love Teal."

His head lolled back, and Bradok knew Omer was dead.

Corin kept holding him for a long time, his shoulders trembling as he sobbed. No one spoke; there wasn't anything to say. Finally, Corin laid the young dwarf down gently on the stone floor. His hand trembled as he smoothed the unkempt blond hair down and wiped the blood from Omer's face with the hem of his cloak.

"He didn't deserve his fate," Corin said in a quiet voice. "He was just a boy when that thrice-damned Theiwar took him and tortured him, made him a rat in one of his experiments. He had the strength of a dozen men—you have witnessed that with your own eyes—but the mind of a little boy. My people put him in prison for it."

He smoothed the boy's cheek. "He didn't deserve this."

"Yes, he did," Bradok said, eliciting a gasp from Kellik and Tal. "This is a death worthy of any dwarf," Bradok continued, his voice rising with pride. "None of us will ever be worthy of his sacrifice. Only someone as pure as Omer could have this death."

Corin looked up at Bradok with a mixture of pain and pleasure on his face.

"Look at him," Bradok said as all eyes turned to the fallen boy. "Teal was a mountain dwarf, but Omer didn't care what clan she came from; he loved her for who she was. He loved her so much, he was willing to face creatures that terrified him—for her."

Bradok stared around at the somber faces of his makeshift soldiers, taking the time to look each of them in the face.

"Someday, Reorx willing, we'll escape this underground prison," he vowed. "When that happens, we need to remember the lesson of Omer's life and his death. If we take that lesson with us wherever we go, then we'll survive, no matter where we end up."

"Pick him up," Thurl said sternly. "Such a hero should not lie in the dirt."

Bradok took off his cloak and handed it to Kellik, who helped Corin wrap the body. When they were finished, Corin lifted the corpse of Omer and, without so much as a hesitating step, strode manfully across the bridge to where the others waited.

Bradok slipped his sword back in its scabbard and followed.

CHAPTER 25

The End of the Road

Corin carried Omer's body to the far side of the crevasse and laid it on a shelf of stone that protruded from the wall. He sat next to the wrapped body for a long time with his hand resting on the still form, as if hoping for some sign of life. Bradok didn't know what it felt like to lose a child, but he could see it in Corin's eyes.

"This ground is too hard to dig a grave," Much said in a soft voice. "Let's gather some stones for a cairn."

As one, everyone moved, gathering loose stones, even ranging up the nearby tunnel. Kellik stood watching over the scene, his warhammer on his shoulder. After a long moment, he turned and walked back out onto the narrow bridge. With an almost casual swing of his hammer, he hefted it off his shoulder and brought it down in the center of the narrow causeway.

The heavy sound of the hammer on stone drew everyone's attention.

"What are you doing?" Rose cried, rushing to the edge of the narrow bridge.

"The Rhizomorphs and the Disir are still over there on that side," Kellik said, swinging the hammer again with a resounding crack. "This is the only way across, so I'm going to close the door on 'em."

Again he swung his hammer hard.

"Do something!" Rose shouted to Bradok as Kellik struck the bridge again. "He's going to kill himself."

"Tie a rope to yourself, you moron," Bradok yelled.

Kellik stopped, hammer in midair, then turned and walked back, looking rather sheepish.

"Sorry," he mumbled as Rose and Much cinched a rope around his chest and tied it off to a column of rock.

"Think next time," Bradok said with a wry grin. The grin vanished, and he added, "We've already lost too many friends."

Kellik nodded and went back to work, swinging his hammer. Bradok turned and joined those who were piling rocks around Omer's body. In a few minutes, the boy was completely covered.

Corin had moved aside as the other survivors paid their final respects. "Thank you all," the Daergar said once the cairn was finished. Then he sat down again by the mound of rocks.

Much took a step toward the Daergar, but Bradok put a restraining hand on the old dwarf's shoulder.

"Let him be alone for a while," he said.

"Bradok," said Rose at his shoulder, her voice urgent.

He didn't have to ask what caused that urgency as the stench of death washed over him. The Rhizomorphs were coming again.

"Hurry up, Kellik," he yelled, turning back to the bridge.

On the far side, he saw them come shambling out of the tunnel. If the Rhizomorphs noticed or cared about the bodies of the Disir littering the floor, they showed no sign. Instead they locked their gaze on Kellik and the narrow bridge he was trying to destroy.

Kellik swung his hammer again and again, gouging great chunks out of the bridge. The Rhizomorphs howled and staggered forward, determined to take the bridge before he could bring it down.

"Run, Kellik!" Rose screamed.

Bradok swore and grappled with his sword, trying to draw

it despate the hobbling pain of his wound. Before he could free the weapon, Chisul charged by him, sword in hand. He leaped over Kellik, heedless of the yawning chasm below, and charged into the advancing Rhizomorphs.

The first of the mushroom men had already reached the bridge as Chisul met them, bowling them over, sending some screaming into the blackness below. He chopped at arms and legs, keeping the stunned Rhizomorphs at bay as Kellik continued to hammer.

A thunderous crack echoed through the cavern followed by the creaking and groaning of stone.

"There she goes," Kellik yelled, racing along the bridge.

Beneath him the narrow causeway of stone began to crack away, broken in the center by the smith's strong blows. Kellik dashed along the collapsing stone, leaping to safety as the last of it dropped away. Across the wide crevasse, the other side of the bridge still stood, reaching out over the expanse like the prow of a ship.

Chisul had heard the bridge falling, pushed the nearest Rhizomorphs away, turned, and ran. The gap was far too wide, yet Chisul didn't hesitate, vaulting toward it with a look of grim determination. The Rhizomorphs shot globs of yellow spit at him, which clung to his cloak, but none hit his exposed face.

He was only two paces away from the gap when one of the fallen creatures behind him darted out its long tongue and caught him fast by the ankle. Chisul's eyes went wide, and he cursed and screamed as his feet were pulled out from under him.

The Rhizomorphs were on him in a second, dragging him back, pinning him down, swarming him. One of them, who might have been young and beautiful before the Zhome made a perverse mockery of her body, bent down and pressed her lips to Chisul's. He thrashed and kicked as she breathed her killing spores into his lungs.

His body spasmed, his head beating down on the ground and his feet flailing. In just a few moments, his body lay still.

A gob of yellow Rhizomorph spit sailed across the gap and past Bradok, falling with a heavy, wet slap onto the stone of the ledge. He and the others edged back. Chisul and Kellik had effectively cut off the mushroom men, but they were still trying to figure out how to get at their foes on the opposite side.

"Get back," Bradok ordered, stepping back.

The survivors filed out of the cavern, making sure to keep well away from the edge. The Rhizomorphs on the far side of the gap hooted and called, yelling threats and obscenities that everyone ignored. The last to let them out of their sight were Bradok and Corin. Bradok kept his eyes on Chisul's still form until the receding passage obscured it. Poor Chisul— Silas's son wasn't such a bad sort after all, Bradok thought. He didn't deserve to be condemned to an eternal death as an abomination of nature.

The loss of Omer and Chisul affected everyone. As the group moved through the shapeless tunnels following the pointing image of the Seer in the brass compass, the only real sounds to be heard were the intermittent demands for food from little Bradok.

The tunnel ended after another day's travel. Beyond it a small cavern promised comfortable sleep for the first time in days. They all needed sleep desperately.

* * * * * *

Four days after Omer's death, however, Bradok was still haunted by nightmares. Every night he saw images of the boy's pure blue eyes as the life drained out of them, and of Chisul, kicking his heels on the stone as the spores consumed him.

Rose told him the nightmares would pass and so would the bad memories.

Much told him it wasn't his fault, that Omer and Chisul had saved them all.

All that was true, of course, but it didn't assuage Bradok's guilt. Somehow Omer's death came to symbolize all the dwarves he'd lost on their journey. He felt himself to be a terrible leader.

As bad as the dreams were, they didn't compare to the dread of waking. Every mile they walked, Bradok couldn't help but wonder what new terror would emerge from the dark to steal away more of his friends. The number of the survivors kept dwindling. Every time anyone asked him to make a decision about something, he had to force himself to appear calm and rational. Inside, he felt worthless.

"You're taking too much on yourself," Rose said as they started out one morning after he had slept so badly.

"I'm the leader," he said. "If we find food, I get the glory. If someone dies, I take the responsibility."

"That would be true if you'd recklessly sent people to their deaths," Rose said. "Chisul and Omer gave all they could to protect us. They were willing to fight and to die if necessary." She put her hand gently on his arm. "Your leadership has kept us from losing more."

She was right. Worse, he knew she was right, but he still felt guilty. But if he didn't feel bad, he told himself, then he wouldn't be worthy to lead. The kind of leader who didn't feel the deaths of those he led would be a depraved leader.

Bradok wanted to answer Rose, but nothing he thought of seemed appropriate to say. He did notice that she hadn't removed her hand from his arm. As his mind took hold on that, his senses suddenly became aware of something—something changed, different.

"Wait," he whispered, holding up his hand.

Not all the others had heard him, but most stopped in response to the raised hand. Throughout the group, both men and women placed their hands on their weapons.

At first, Bradok couldn't say what it was that had caught his attention. Nothing in the dim lantern-light seemed out of place, and no sound reached his waiting ear. Still, something had shifted.

A puff of air as gentle as a baby's breath touched his whiskers, carrying with it a strange yet familiar scent. Bradok had to reach back into the archives of his mind to identify it. When, at last he remembered, he shouted.

More explosive laugh than shout, the sound echoed down the passageway as Bradok kept on laughing and laughing.

"Wha—?" Rose said, her grip on his arm tightening.

"Follow me," Bradok said, turning to face his friends. "Quickly now."

He turned back to the tunnel and dashed forward at a slow jog so even the stragglers could keep up. It had taken him some time to identify the odor that seemed to fill up the tunnel.

It was the distinctive smell of mountain trees, of pine.

The others smelled it too, and Bradok could hear their cries of joy and their ringing laughter joining his. The tunnel ended right before him, emptying out into a wide cavern virtually overflowing with peppertops and honey mushrooms, wall root, and blackroot. There was enough food to feed them for a year, longer if they were careful to cultivate new growth.

A dazzling burst of light burned at the far end of the cave. Bradok had to squint just to see the ground before him, but he did not stop running. Laughing like a schoolboy on holiday, he raced out through the opening and into a humid blanket of warm air.

The light overwhelmed him, however, and he dropped to his knees after a few strides, feeling the prickle of grass beneath him. Rose fell beside him, laughing as heartily as he had and rolling over him and into the grass. Before he knew what he was doing, he'd pulled her up and kissed her. She kissed him back and for a long moment, the two just lay there in the grass, joined together in a circle of blinding light.

Bradok let her go as his vision began to return to normal. They'd been in the darkness so long, it took a full ten minutes before he could see anything farther than a few feet away. When his vision did clear, it felt like coming out of a dream.

"What happened?" Rose gasped as her vision also returned.

Above them, the sky was burning red with great, undulating clouds that appeared black against the sky. They found themselves sitting above a little mountain valley lined with trees and green meadows. A coursing stream cut its way through the valley and continued on down the mountain into the far side.

Beyond the valley, however, smoke arose along every horizon, great black gouts that reached up and stained the sky.

"It's as if someone burned the world," Rose said in awe, clinging fearfully to Bradok's sleeve.

Bradok thought back to Ironroot and Silas and the believers and all the signs and warnings there he had ignored. "I wonder if there are any other survivors besides us?" he said.

"Surely there will be," Jeni said, coming up near them.

"There have to be," Kellik said, close behind.

"It doesn't matter," Bradok said, turning to face his little group of friends. "Reorx has led us here, to this place. There's food and shelter in the cave and timber aplenty here."

"And ore," Kellik said, pointing up to a red-stained rock on the mountain.

"Right," Bradok said. "We'll build a forge, and we'll make the tools we need, and we'll build a new home right here."

"Can we really do all that?" Kellik's son Rijul piped up.

"We don't exactly have enough people for a city," Lyra cautioned.

"We'll do it," Bradok said. "It'll just take time."

Rose hugged him close while all the survivors cheered. He knew it would take work, but Reorx had prepared that land for them.

* * * * * *

Six weeks later, Rose shook Bradok out of a sound sleep. Outside the cave, the sun was peeking through the clouds. Since he'd had guard duty the night before, Bradok had slept late.

"Look," Rose said, sticking her arm under his nose.

"What am I looking at?" he asked, groggily rubbing his eyes.

"Me! It's gotten smaller," she said boastfully.

Bradok studied her arm, staring at the gray patch of skin where the Zhome had first manifested itself. He hadn't dared to look at Rose's arm in quite a while, but the affected skin did seem to be smaller than he remembered it, much smaller.

"How?" he asked, looking intently at her arm.

"I thought the Zhome was getting smaller, but today I did something and it actually shrunk before my eyes."

"What did you do?" he asked.

"I got hot," she said. "So I took off the bandage to let my arm breathe."

Bradok stared blankly.

"It's the sunlight!" she told him. "As soon as the sunlight hit my arm, I felt it tingling and I saw the Zhome actually shrink."

Bradok jumped to his feet and pulled his boots on.

"Corin!" he yelled, dragging Rose out of the cave into the light.

A moment later, the skinny Daergar came trudging up the path, shouldering the axe he'd been using to cut fuel for the forge. He had a cloth bound round his eyes to protect them from the sun. None of the Daergar seemed to be able to stand the full daylight without a bandage.

"I don't believe it," he said when Rose showed him her arm.

"Take off your shirt," Bradok said. "Lie in the sun and try it yourself."

Hesitantly, Corin stripped off his shirt, exposing the gray streaks on his chest with tiny mushrooms growing in them. Within twenty minutes, three of the mushrooms had dried up and fallen off.

"I wouldn't believe it if I didn't see it with my own eyes," he said, standing up and showing the results to Rose and Bradok.

"My people thought there was no cure," Corin added ruefully. "Most Daergar live their whole lives without ever seeing the surface world. How could they possibly guess that the dreaded Zhome could be cured by something as simple as sunlight?"

"So take your shirt off for a brief time every day when the sun is out," Rose said. "Not too much. The Zhome will heal, but you don't want to get sunburned on top of everything else."

Corin smiled, slipping his shirt back on.

"So sunlight isn't all bad, eh? Live and learn! I'm going to go tell Urlish about this," he said, excusing himself.

Bradok raised an eyebrow as Corin hurried off. Urlish was the quiet farmer Rose had brought with her in the trade delegation. She didn't seem Corin's type, but they all had been through a lot together, and here and there dwarves were pairing off.

Speaking of that, Rose sidled up to him. "You know what this means?" she said, her hip touching his and her shoulder pressing into his chest.

"What?" Bradok asked, looking down into her beaming face.

She elbowed him hard in the ribs, which only made him gasp a little. "It means we don't have to worry anymore. We can have children," she said. "Just as soon as I'm cleansed."

Bradok put his arm around her and kissed her.

Whatever else their new life brought him, he doubted he could be happier than at that moment.

* * * * * *

Bradok opened his eyes in the predawn darkness. Something had roused him from sleep, and he lay awake, listening. After several minutes, he'd resolved to go back to sleep but knew that he had to get up in an hour anyway.

With a sigh, he swung his feet out of bed and stood, pulling on his robe. Moving as quietly as possible, he crossed the wood floor and stepped out on the balcony outside his room. In the distance the first light of the sun could be seen painting the lowlands a pale gold.

He'd watched the sun come up almost every day for six years, rising on the little community they had named Kresthorn, which meant "Journey's End" in the Elder Tongue. Below him, he could see the wheel of Much's mill turning relentlessly in the little stream.

Smoke rose from the chimneys above Kellik's forge, and Bradok knew Hemmish and Rijul were up already, getting the forge prepared for the coming day's work.

Below them, in the bowl of the valley, Corin and Urlish were tending a neat little farm with orderly fields of vegetables and grains standing all in rows.

Tal had married Starlight Anvil, the eldest of the Anvil grandchildren. Despate the difference in their ages, they seemed perfect for each other. Tal tended his gardens and the small apple orchard they had planted, serving as doctor whenever the need arose.

Next to the orchard, Xurces and Corin had put up a small brewery that wouldn't go into full-scale production until the apple trees matured.

Xurces married Lyra, and they seemed happy just to be together and brew ale and raise Jade and little Bradok.

Even Thurl found a place, putting his knowledge of foul chemicals to better use as the town tanner.

The only person who had not stayed in the new dwarf

community was the human Perin. They all had grown fond of him and missed him.

He had disappeared in the middle of the night one week after they arrived there, taking the metal book from Starlight Hall with him. Nobody minded, but Bradok couldn't understand why the human would want a book of stories about Galoka and his people. It didn't seem like the kind of thing that would interest a human.

A hand touched Bradok's leg, and he looked back to see a little red-haired girl looking up at him.

"Teal," he said, picking her up and setting her on the railing in front of him. "What are you doing up?"

"She heard you and insisted I know about it," Rose's sleepy voice answered as she joined him on the balcony.

She wore a simple robe, like the one Bradok had, though hers barely concealed her bulging middle.

"It's all right," she said as Teal snuggled into Bradok's shirt. "Your son was kicking me anyway." She put her hand on her belly and smiled. "I think he wants out."

"You're sure it's a boy?" Bradok asked.

Rose smiled. "Of course," she said. "He's way too jumpy to be a girl."

"Then I've decided," Bradok said. "I don't care if Corin likes it or not; if it's a boy, we're calling him Omer."

Rose put her arm around Bradok, and little Teal let go of her daddy in favor of nuzzling her mom.

"I think that's a wonderful idea," Rose said.

Chapter 26
Official Reports

The Journeyman stood on a stone parapet overlooking the courtyard in front of the anvil chamber. He wore a light woven robe and sandals bound with a simple belt. The wind chilled him, cutting through the plain garment as a slushy rain fell over the City of Lost Names. He didn't know when the Aesthetic would arrive, but he watched a few minutes anyway, staring out into the gray pallor of the stormy sky.

It didn't matter, he told himself. He wasn't likely to see that particular Aesthetic coming.

Shivering as the wind blew the rain over him, he turned and made his way back inside. The wet leather of his sandals slapped the stone staircase as he passed down a level to the snug chamber he had made his residence.

As he opened the heavy door, a wave of heat rolled out of the room, enveloping him. He stood there in the door for a moment, allowing the feeling of warmth to swell within him before he entered. He'd been cold for so long that he relished the warmth, savoring it like lingering over a fine meal.

He stepped inside, closing the door behind himself, and crossed the carpeted floor to a high-backed, overstuffed leather chair. Though the Journeyman liked his pleasures, the room itself was simple. A plain bed stood in one corner with a wardrobe and a night table nearby. A washbasin and cloak rack were farther along the wall, just past the space where the door opened.

Along the opposite wall, the Journeyman had an immense writing desk with many drawers for pens, ink, paper, and other sundries. And in the far corner stood an iron stove with a coal scuttle in front of it and a black pipe on top that carried the smoke out through a hole in the stone.

The chair sat next to the stove with a cushy footstool resting before it. A small book table stood by the chair, and a magical lantern hung over it, suspended by a curved piece of wood that attached to the back of the chair.

The Journeyman sat, kicking off his sandals and crossing his feet on the stool. On his left foot, the two little toes were missing, and the wound hadn't quite healed, causing the Journeyman to ease one foot gently over the other when he crossed them.

Not by coincidence, the stool stood a mere foot from the stove. On the table, beside the chair, a brandy snifter lay on an angle, cradled in a wood frame that suspended the glass over a lit candle. Below the brandy warmer, there were a number of books, all with bookmarks hanging out of them, attesting to the Journeyman's usual habit of reading several books at once.

He picked up the glass, careful not to touch the hot spot. Swirling the brandy absently in his left hand, he reached out and took the topmost book off the pile. That book was unlike its fellows in almost every way. The book had been made entirely of metal: cover, spine, pages, and all.

Because of its weight, the Journeyman slipped it into his lap before he opened the cover and leafed through the few metal pages to the final one.

"Comfy?" a mocking voice echoed through the chamber.

The Journeyman turned to confront a spectral visitor regarding him from just inside the door. He stood only about five feet tall and wore the flowing robe of an Aesthetic, though both body and robe were transparent, allowing the Journeyman to see the planks of the door behind him.

"I'm sorry I didn't knock," he said, clearly intending the comment as a joke. "May I come in?"

The Journeyman chuckled, perhaps not very mirthfully. "And if I say no?" he asked.

"Then I will leave until it is convenient," the Aesthetic said.

The Journeyman put his glass back on the warmer and shut the metal book. "My, my," he said. "I see you have developed some manners over all those years."

The specter smiled, taking no offense. "I see you brought what I asked for," he said.

The Journeyman looked down at the book in his lap then back at the Aesthetic. "Why do you want it?" the Journeyman asked. "You were there when it was found. What's so special about this book, Chisul?"

The ghost chuckled. "There's a name I haven't heard in quite a while," the specter said, a wistful smile crossing his face. "Where did you come up with Perin, by the way?"

"It's ancient Elvish," the Journeyman said. "It means 'Traveler.' "

Chisul's ghost laughed. "I see you're as imaginative as ever," he said.

"Don't change the subject," the Journeyman said, holding up the metal book. "What's so special about this?"

"It isn't the book that's dangerous," Chisul said. "It's what's in the book."

"That can be said of all books," the Journeyman said.

"This is rather a special book," Chisul said. "You see, Galoka and his people were being taught things by Reorx himself. Things they shouldn't know."

The Journeyman shrugged. "So Reorx was cheating to help his people," he said. "So what? They all do it."

"Not like this," Chisul said. "Starlight Hall was just a foothold. Reorx meant it as a beacon to unite the dwarf clans and bring them back under one rule."

"That would never work," the Journeyman said. "Most of the clans hate each other."

"The other gods didn't think so," Chisul said. "They feared a united dwarf nation. They feared the power Reorx would wield if that ever happened. It was a chance they were not prepared to take, so they created the Disir specifically to destroy Starlight Hall and to keep its existence secret."

"How could that be?" the Journeyman asked. "The gods never agree on anything."

Chisul shrugged. "Fear is a great motivator," he explained.

"How did you find out about all this?" the Journeyman asked. "You didn't seem to know anything about it when Rose found the book."

"That was the past," Chisul said. "I've learned many things since that time. Being an Aesthetic helps, too."

"So why is this book so important?" the Journeyman asked. "Starlight Hall is gone; no one even remembers it."

"That's right," Chisul said. "The only evidence that Starlight Hall ever existed is *that* book."

The Journeyman stared down at the gleaming book in his hands. He'd read it twice. It was very interesting, containing everything about the founding and building of Starlight Hall. Their fantastic machines and their alchemical metals were all detailed, as was their faith and their unification goals.

"So this book is dangerous," he said.

"If the gods knew it existed, they'd kill anyone who had touched it," Chisul said.

"So you sent me on that little walk to keep this from getting out into the world," the Journeyman said.

Chisul nodded. "That, and of course to witness and help."

"Just so," Chisul continued. "If Bradok and those who survived had kept this book, word of its existence would have spread, little by little. By the time the gods learned of it, thousands could have been contaminated, maybe tens of thousands."

"It could have triggered another Cataclysm," the Journeyman gasped.

"So you see why it's better off being lost," Chisul said, putting out his hand.

The Journeyman looked down at the book, running his hand over the smooth steel of the cover, then he handed it to Chisul. The specter grabbed the book, supporting the metal with his transparent hand. The Journeyman decided he would never get used to that.

"I've got a very safe place picked out for this one," he said, slipping it inside his robe.

"Is there something else?" the Journeyman asked when the specter didn't leave immediately.

"I did wonder," Chisul said. "What happened to Bradok and the others?"

"They made it out," the Journeyman said. "You can read all about it," he added, gesturing around the room at his table and writing supplies, "eventually."

"I always felt sorry for him," Chisul said, nodding. "Because he was in love with Rose but she had the Zhome."

"She got better," the Journeyman said with a smile.

Chisul cocked his head to the side. "What do you mean?" he asked.

"Sunlight," the Journeyman said. "It kills the Zhome. Didn't you know that?"

Chisul laughed, shaking his head. "Something as simple as that," he said.

"I've got a question for you," the Journeyman said. "Why did your spirit linger? You told me you didn't learn about the dangers of this book until after you died."

"I lingered for quite a different reason," he said with a mischievous grin. "I'm not dead."

"What do you mean, you're not dead?"

"My body never died," Chisul said. "It's still alive somewhere, shambling around in the bowels of Krynn. So long as I'm alive, my spirit is bound here, even though it has taken leave of my body."

"That's monstrous," the Journeyman said, shuddering.

"Just so. But I've made the best of it," Chisul said good-humoredly. "I've spent quite a lot of time figuring out how to get my hands on this." He held up the book, chuckling.

"Do you remember the first time we met?" the ghost asked.

The Journeyman nodded. "After the first time I used the Anvil," he said. "You were with the group of Aesthetics who came to see me."

"That's not the first time we met," Chisul said, shaking his head. "The first time we met was in my father's shop, after you convinced him to let you be his apprentice."

The Journeyman opened his mouth but stopped. "But that can't be. I hadn't gone back in time yet then," he said finally.

"Time doesn't work like that," Chisul said. "When I saw you here, at the Anvil, I recognized you. I knew then that I had a job for you and that it was you I would send to get the book."

"Time is complicated," the Journeyman murmured, musing on his words.

Chisul just nodded.

"What will you do now?"

Chisul shrugged. "I'm sure I can find something to occupy my time." He turned and drifted toward the door. "Perhaps I'll look in on you again," he said, pausing at the door. "We're old friends now. And I've come to find your exploits most amusing."

"How did you manage to become an Aesthetic, if you don't mind my asking?" the Journeyman queried as Chisul turned to leave.

"You'd be amazed what you can get away with when you have all the time in the world," he said.

"That's not an answer," the Journeyman said.

"No," the ghost said, "it's not." He nodded toward the tall writing desk. "I like your souvenir," he said. "It's very . . . appropriate."

With that he drifted right through the door and disappeared, his words still ringing against the room's stone walls.

The Journeyman sat for a long time, considering the door, absently sipping his brandy. At length, he set the glass aside and added another shovelful of coal to the fire. As the stove began to heat up again, he picked up the next book on the pile and leafed through to the page where his ornate bookmark lay.

Before he began reading, however, he cast a glance up to the top of his desk where a little rag doll sat, lovingly cleaned and repaired.

RICHARD A. KNAAK

THE OGRE TITANS

The Grand Lord Golgren has been savagely crushing
all opposition to his control of the harsh ogre lands of
Kern and Blöde, first sweeping away rival chieftains, then
rebuilding the capital in his image. For this he has had to
deal with the ogre titans, dark, sorcerous giants who have
contempt for his leadership.

VOLUME ONE
THE BLACK TALON

Among the ogres, where every ritual demands blood and every ally can
become a deadly foe, Golgren seeks whatever advantage he can obtain,
even if it means a possible alliance with the Knights of Solamnia, a
questionable pact with a mysterious wizard, and trusting an elven slave
who might wish him dead.

VOLUME TWO
THE FIRE ROSE

Attacked by enemies on all sides, Golgren must abandon his throne
to undertake the quest for the Fire Rose before Safrag, master
of the Ogre Titans can locate it and claim supremacy
over all ogres—and perhaps all of Krynn.

December 2008

VOLUME THREE
THE GARGOYLE KING

Forced from the throne he has so long coveted, Golgren makes a final
stand for control of the ogre lands against the Titans . . . against an
enemy as ancient and powerful as a god.

December 2009

JEAN RABE

THE STONETELLERS

"Jean Rabe is adept at weaving a web of deceit and lies, mixed with adventure, magic, and mystery."
—sffworld.com on *Betrayal*

Jean Rabe returns to the DRAGONLANCE® world with a tale of slavery, rebellion, and the struggle for freedom.

VOLUME ONE
THE REBELLION

After decades of service, nature has dealt the goblins a stroke of luck. Earthquakes strike the Dark Knights' camp and mines, crippling the Knights and giving the goblins their best chance to escape. But their freedom will not be easy to win.

VOLUME TWO
DEATH MARCH

The reluctant general, Direfang, leads the goblin nation on a death march to the forests of Qualinesti, there to create a homeland in defiance of the forces that seek to destroy them.

August 2008

VOLUME THREE
GOBLIN NATION

A goblin nation rises in the old forest, building fortresses and fighting to hold onto their new homeland, while the sorcerers among them search for powerful magic cradled far beneath the trees.

August 2009